Juniata Valley

Juniata Valley

Virginia C. Cassel

THE VIKING PRESS

NEW YORK

First published in 1981 by The Viking Press
625 Madison Avenue, New York, N.Y. 10022

Published simultaneously in Canada by
Penguin Books Canada Limited

Library of Congress Cataloging in Publication Data
Cassel, Virginia C. Juniata Valley.
1. Pennsylvania—History—French and Indian War, 1755–1763—Fiction.
2. Juniata Valley, Pa.—History—Fiction. I. Title.
PS3553.A7954J8 813'.54 80-25173
ISBN 0-670-41085-3

Printed in the United States of America

Set in CRT Caslon

To my maternal grandfather,
James Franklin Enyeart,
whose generosity of spirit inspired
the character of Silas Enyard

AUTHOR'S NOTE

So many persons helped me in one way or another while I was writing this book that it is impossible to list all of them. My friend Penelope Katson deserves special thanks for typing the manuscript and for her unflagging interest and encouragement. In Washington, D.C., Sallie Grimes typed several of the early chapters. My cousin Harry Enyeart was most generous in suggesting source materials. Dr. William Dabney of the History Department, University of New Mexico, lent me books on colonial history. The librarian of the Army War College in Carlisle, Pennsylvania, sent me a bibliography on the early wars in that state. The personnel of the Library of Congress and the University of New Mexico library deserve thanks for their courteous assistance. Floyd G. Hoenstine suggested source materials.

John McCall, a good friend, reviewed several chapters for me. I was also helped by the Georgetown writers' group to which I used to belong and, more recently, by the group of writers that I organized in Albuquerque.

My editor, Abigail Luttinger, deserves a very special word of appreciation for her unfailing enthusiasm, humor, and sound critical judgment. Cork Smith, a senior editor at Viking, and Rhoda Gamson, manager of the contracts department, were extremely helpful in interpreting publishing rights. Saul Cohen, of Santa Fe, New Mexico, gave me legal assistance.

July 30, 1980
Albuquerque, New Mexico

THE GRAVESES

John Graves (1731-57)
m. Susannah Norris (1736-)

Rachel (1753-)

THE ELDRIDGES

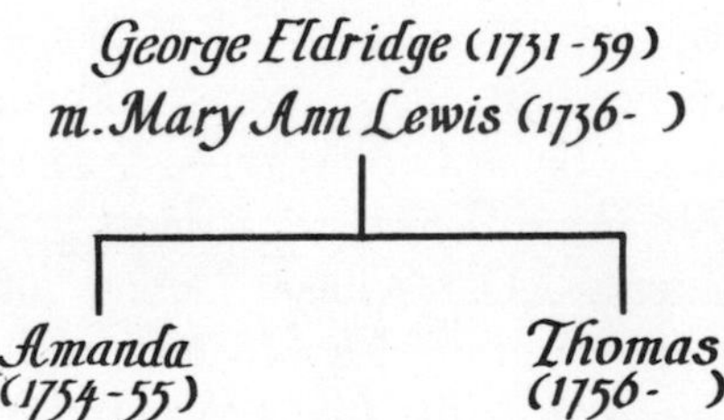

THE McCULLOUGHS

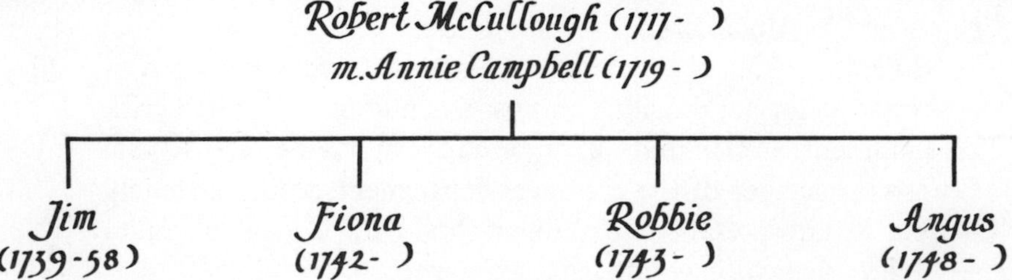

THE ENYARDS

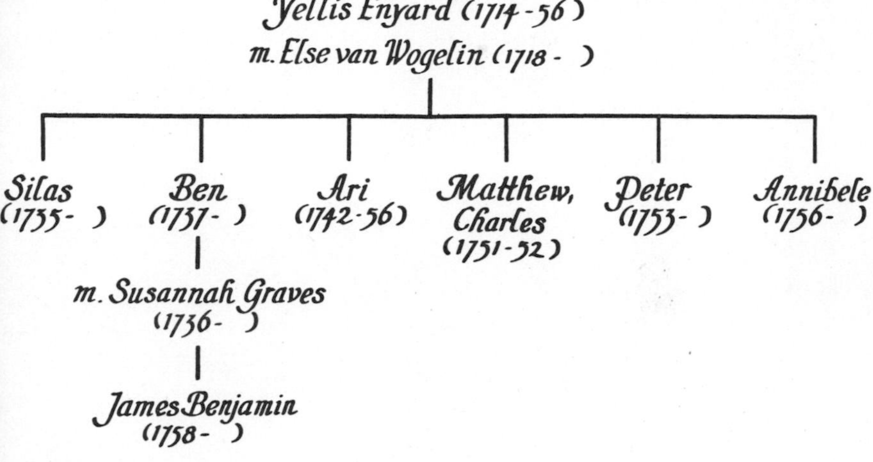

THE ABBOTS

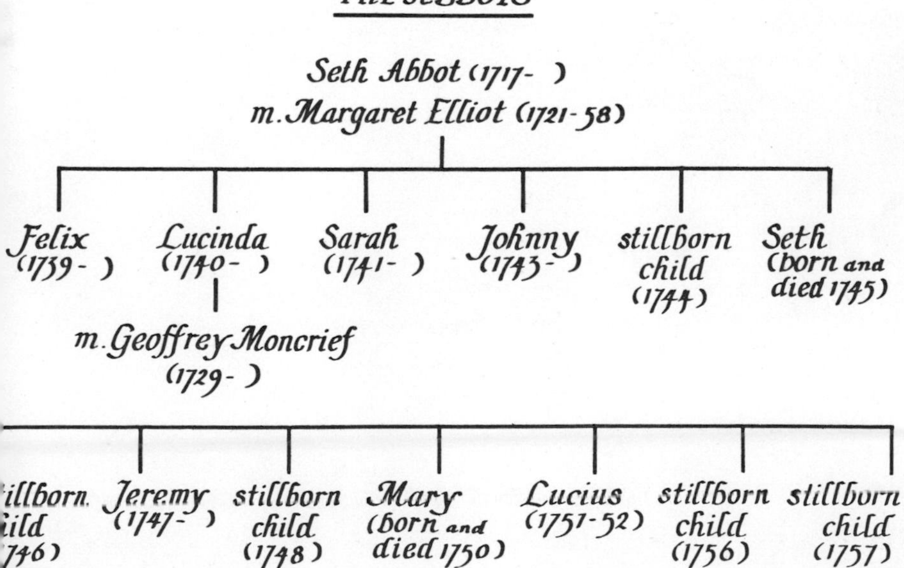

Juniata Valley

CHAPTER I

The Homecoming

It was very early in the morning and the fields and woods were veiled in mist when John Graves and Francis Wilson set out in June of 1756 for the salt lick on the western side of Tuscarora Mountain. They left their families with their neighbors, the Bighams, as Pennsylvania's Juniata Valley had been alarmed since spring by reports of Indian raids on the other side of the mountain, and traders en route to Philadelphia to replenish their packs had told them of massacres, cabins burned, and horses stolen to the west of the valley.

John Graves, a cautious man, had been of two minds about the expedition, but Francis Wilson had been quick to point out the advantages. Salt was in short supply since rumors of the Indian troubles had kept most people from making the two-day journey. If they each took a pack horse in addition to their mounts, Wilson argued, they could bring back enough salt for their own needs and still have plenty to sell to the families at Fort Shirley, which was their nearest fort.

Samuel Bigham's place was well fortified with guns and powder, and there were several other families living there for protection. John's wife, Susannah, and their little girl, Rachel, would enjoy the company, Francis insisted, for the settlers seldom had occasion to visit each other. Francis's wife, Maria, had been pleased at the prospect, and his two boys looked upon it as an adventure.

John admitted there was truth in Francis's arguments, but he was still uneasy. He remembered Susannah's reaction when he had mentioned the subject.

"Stay at the Bighams'! Oh, John, they aren't our kind! They mean well, I suppose, but they're so—so crude. They haven't any manners."

"It's only for two days."

"It will seem an eternity if we stay with them."

"They're good folks," he had told her. "They haven't had the advantages you had for schooling, but they are decent and hard-working and honest."

"I'd rather stay alone with Rachel."

Usually he did not cross her, but this time he was firm. "I won't hear of that, Susannah. Things are too uncertain now. If we go, you must stay at Bigham's."

Finally Francis had brought up the oxen, a subject dear to John's heart. They had often spoken of someday buying a team in common, since their holdings adjoined. "John," he said in his most persuasive manner, "you and I been talkin' of wantin' a team of oxen. We could get them west meadows cleared in half the time if we had a strong team. With the crops doin' so well this year and the money from that salt, we'd have near enough to buy them. It ain't often a man gets an opportunity like this."

So they went. It was hard traveling up the mountainside; heavy rains had dislodged rocks, which obstructed the trail, and the ground was slippery with pine needles. Here and there a large tree, felled by lightning, barred their way, and vines and creepers hung in long ropes, so that they had to duck their heads. Both men had seen an occasional mountain lion or a bear in these woods and were constantly alert. There were also rattlers in the forest, and other settlers had told them to listen for strange bird-calls, which the Indians frequently used as signals.

About four in the afternoon of the first day, they arrived at the salt lick and, after careful reconnoitering, filled their hempen bags with salt, tied them securely on their pack animals, and started for home without stopping to eat. They traveled single file, pushing their horses harder than John had ever done before in order to reach the top of the mountain before dark. As they rode, with their Pennsylvania rifles slung across their saddles, they drank from their leather water canteens and ate some corn bread and wild plums they had brought along.

When they came to a stream, they dismounted to refresh and feed their horses. John rubbed his animals down with handfuls of moss, and ten minutes later they were on their way. Shortly before night descended, they reached the summit and found shelter under an overhanging rock, and some dry leaves to bed down on. Francis was to sleep first, while John kept watch; then he would guard while John slept.

As Francis made himself comfortable on the rough ground, John thought how good it would be to let go of all one's cares and fall asleep like his little Rachel. He could see her small plain face framed in straight brown hair, her wide-set, light blue eyes that were full of laughter one minute and wise and solemn the next, her smile that never failed to bring a responsive smile from him. She was tall for three and mature for her age. She resembled the Graves side of the family, but she had Susannah's quick mind, although she was by nature milder—sweet-tempered, people said.

He reminded himself that this was no place for woolgathering; he'd best keep a sharp lookout. It was almost two years since he had made the trip for salt, and then there had been a group of men, not just the two of them. There were no Indian troubles then, for it was before the great Battle in the Wilderness near the French fort of Duquesne, where the English general Braddock had been defeated.

Just outside the rock overhang, John peered into the darkness and listened attentively for any strange sound, but he could see nothing and heard only the faint rustlings of small woodland creatures.

After several hours, he reached over and shook Francis lightly by the shoulder to rouse him. Francis stretched and sat up to take his turn as sentry. John lay down and tried to adjust his tall, angular frame for sleep, turning from one side to the other, tense from long hours in the saddle and the strain of constant vigilance. He had never known he had so many muscles before.

He heard the mournful hooting of an owl and listened to hear if it would be followed by an answering call, which could mean savages in the area. But all was silent. As soon as he closed his eyes and tried to find a more comfortable position, he smelled the overpowering odor of a mountain lion. He sat up, grabbed his gun, and looked about, fancying he saw two golden eyes staring out from the shadows, but it was only his imagination.

John wished he were braver. He was ill at ease in the forest. He loved farming, turning the rich limestone soil of the valley, seeing the work of his hands bear grain. He had increased his yield over that of his neighbors by putting a fish head in each corn hill, as the settlers in New England had been taught by the Narragansets. And he was skilled with animals; neighbors rode miles to get his help for a sick cow or a horse gone lame.

He closed his eyes and thought of Susannah, wondering what he should do if the situation in the valley became worse. He had been aware since the raids started of Susannah's strained look, although she said nothing. He had no right to make her miserable just to hold on to his rich acres. On the other hand, it wouldn't be easy to sell their lands now that word of the Indian troubles had spread throughout the province of Pennsylvania.

The Juniata Valley was a paradise when he had brought Susannah here from Philadelphia: the lush valley surrounded by the foothills of the Alleghenies with the river running swift and clear, teeming with fish; the plentiful game—elk, deer, bear, possum, raccoons, wild turkeys, woodcock, and in fall the migratory birds from Canada. A man didn't have to be an expert shot to provide his family with an abundance of the best provender. It saddened him to think of leaving.

He thought of the first time he had met Susannah. He had loved her from the moment he saw her, over four years ago. He remembered her white lawn mob cap with its ruffle framing her heart-shaped face, the dark curls just touching her shoulder, her pert little nose and big gray eyes with long lashes, the proud lift of her chin. She had worn a cherry-and-white striped short gown with a white fichu outlining her throat, and a petticoat of palest green. Her shoes, he recalled, had silver buckles. He had thought her the prettiest girl he had ever seen.

John had gone to her uncle's house in Philadelphia to claim a modest inheritance; her uncle—whose ward she was—was a lawyer. When their business was concluded, Josiah Norris sent for his niece to fetch sherry and biscuits to celebrate the occasion.

Seeing John as a likely prospect for a young woman of no means, he began to push the match. She was sixteen, John twenty-three.

John needed no urging. He would have walked from Philadelphia to the farthest reaches of the wilderness to win her. To this day, after four years of marriage, he still did not know if she loved him. He consoled himself with the thought that she was a woman who had few passionate feelings, who hid her deepest emotions.

With his inheritance he purchased a fine team and outfitted their Conestoga wagon not only with the necessities but with such items as a bedstead, feather pillows, a warming pan, and—of all things—a mirror, just to please her.

On their long journey westward Susannah began to tell him about her life.

When both of her parents died in a carriage accident in southern Maryland, she was an only child, eleven years old, with no inheritance and no one to protect her, until her father's brother arrived by coach from Philadelphia. Josiah Norris had never married and had no understanding of children. He lived well, read a great deal, and was a devout Presbyterian, convinced that he was of the elect, chosen from the beginning to be saved.

"Susannah," she said, mimicking her uncle's pompous manner of speaking, "I hope you are mindful of your good fortune in finding a Christian home such as mine. I trust you appreciate your good fortune and never forget to thank Divine Providence for His mercy."

"Uncle Josiah was so sanctimonious, but I didn't dare to speak up to him. I was afraid he would abandon me, and then where would I go? So I learned to pretend. I would clasp my hands and look down and tell him that I was very grateful for his charity."

Remembering her words four years later, John still felt his heart contract in pity for her.

"I'm not really submissive, John. But I had to seem so in order to get Uncle Josiah to send me to a dame school in Philadelphia. He used to ask me all sorts of questions about what I had learned. He spoke of my becoming a governess. 'You know, Susannah, you cannot expect to marry into a well-connected family. Those of wealth and prominence frown upon one of their sons marrying a penniless orphan. In spite of the standing I enjoy, I cannot be of assistance in that.' "

It had disturbed John to learn that she put so much importance on possessions. She urged him to go to a slave auction in Maryland and bring back three Negroes to do the heavy work. She dreamed of creating a plantation in the Juniata Valley similar to her parents' home, but John was opposed to the buying and selling of slaves. Susannah called him obstinate; what she failed to understand was his need to clear his own fields, to plant and harvest with his own hands.

Francis Wilson shook him to announce that it was time to be on their way.

John fed the horses and gave them lumps of maple sugar to quiet them. Then, mounted on his mare with the pack horse's long halter tied to his saddle, he carefully guided them through the dense underbrush until they reached the narrow trail. It was still dark in the woods, but occasional shafts of early dawn light pierced the shadows and illuminated here and there thick masses of mountain laurel, which still had a few late blooms of delicate pink and white.

After an hour and a half they came to a brook purling over small white pebbles. Francis did not stop but pushed on toward Bigham's eager to see his family. Realizing how thirsty his animals must be, John dismounted. Squatting, he cupped his hands for water and drank deeply, then filled his canteen, and started after Francis, who was so far ahead that the tall trees shut him from view.

Suddenly his mount neighed in terror and reared on his hind legs, throwing John to the ground. The pack horse uttered a high, piercing sound, and before he could catch them, both animals disappeared into the forest as a huge brown bear lumbered across the trail. John was so frightened that at first he was unable to move. He lay on the ground, certain he would be killed. The giant animal paused briefly, swinging its great head from side to side as its little red eyes sought the horses. John looked frantically for his gun. Terror seized him then, and he jumped up and dashed off in the direction of the horses. The bear did not follow.

John went deeper and deeper into the woods, stopping occasionally to listen for sounds that might indicate where his animals were. He realized in a moment of panic that he had left the trail some time ago and might never find it again. It was then that he stopped, hands clutched at his sides. "Help me to find them," he prayed.

If I were an animal, where would I head for? he asked himself. The brook! That was where he'd find them.

After hours of searching, his legs bruised by rocks, his face and hands cut and scratched, he saw the horses standing quietly by the brook where they had stopped in the morning.

He approached them slowly, carefully, calling them by name. They whinnied and let him stroke them. The bags of salt were still securely lashed to the back of the pack horse, but the mare's bag was gone. It did not matter. The important thing was that he had found them.

After a short time he recovered the trail. When they neared the spot where they had smelled the bear, he was afraid they would panic, but both animals continued on. At the place where the mare had thrown him, John spied his gun lying beneath an elder bush. Since his powder horn had been strapped to his shoulder, he felt complete now, and unbelievably lucky as he started down the mountainside.

The sun was high overhead, so he knew Francis must have reached home long ago. Some of the tiredness seemed to leave him; it had been a hard journey, but it was almost over.

By midafternoon he came to a place that overlooked the valley where Bigham's blockhouse was situated. John reined in his mare and stared in disbelief. The blockhouse was a charred ruin, smoke curling upward from its smoldering logs. There was no sign of life; here and there in the fields, inert objects that looked like dolls were flung down among the sprouting wheat and young cornstalks. John felt the bile rising in his throat, and leaning over the mare's back, he vomited. He forced the mare down the mountain trail, with the pack animal following. As they neared the scene of carnage, the animals, smelling blood, became restless and frightened. John had to use the butt of his gun on the mare's rump to make her move forward. He was so afraid of what he would find that he could scarcely breathe.

The first figure he recognized was Samuel Bigham, lying in a pool of blood with a tomahawk in his forehead. He had been shot and scalped and his face bore a look of intense surprise. He had evidently been hoeing wheat, for his hoe lay a few feet away.

A few yards from Bigham, John came upon one of the men who had been staying at the blockhouse, his face and torso mutilated almost beyond recognition.

Everywhere he looked he saw bones and bits of hair, dismembered bodies lying in blood. The stench was overwhelming and flies and gnats swarmed over the remains. Again and again John retched, finally bringing up bile. He forced himself to continue his search for some sign of Susannah and of Rachel, walking slowly across the field in the direction of the Kittaning Trail, looking for some shred of evidence that they might have been taken captive.

Suddenly he stopped and picked up a corncob doll. His heart raced painfully. It was Rachel's, yes, he would recognize it anywhere; she had tied a scrap from one of her outgrown dresses around it. Some clear part of his mind told him it could belong to another little girl, as the families in the valley all bought cloth from the same traders. Slowly, laboriously, he forced himself to go over all the girl children who had been staying at Bigham's: Mrs. Duffield's child was too young for a doll, Sarah McCahan was already churning and spinning, Elizabeth Entriken was all of twelve or thirteen, beginning to look like a woman. No, Rachel was the only little girl who would have had a doll.

In a state of shock, John Graves mounted his horse and, with the pack animal following, started on the thirty-mile journey southwest to Aughwick. He never could recall how he got there. He thought at times he was in a nightmare, that he would waken shortly to find everything all right. At other times he knew that what he had seen was only too true, that he must tell the militia at the fort so they could find his family and the Wilsons.

Finally the mare foundered and refused to get up. The pack animal had withstood the rigors of their journey better, and had John had sense enough to remove the salt bags from her back, she might have carried him that last mile to Aughwick. But John was too deranged to think of that. Instead he started off on foot, leaving the horses beside the trail.

People at the fort spoke of his appearance there early in the evening as something they would never forget. He staggered through the stockade gate like one drunk, his eyes bloodshot and haunted.

"Colonel Armstrong! Must see!" he cried.

"What is it? What happened?" asked the commander of Fort Shirley.

"Massacre Bigham's! No sign of Rachel and Susannah, Wilsons. Gone! All gone!" he managed to say before he lost consciousness.

CHAPTER II

Fort Shirley

When John Graves regained consciousness at Fort Shirley, he was unable to respond to questions. He sat on a bench in the small room designated as the headquarters of Lieutenant Colonel John Armstrong, his big hands lying slack between his knees, his lips moving soundlessly. The odor of his sweat was rank in the room since he had not washed for several days.

"I think he needs a bath and some clean clothes," observed Armstrong. "He'll be more comfortable then. Perhaps if we get him some victuals, he'll be able to tell us what happened. Can you find something that might fit him, Mr. Lewis? Pity most of the folk here have only what they came in."

When Ensign Lewis left the room, he had to push his way through the crowd outside the door. People tried to detain him for information about the destruction of Bigham's blockhouse. "Please, I can't tell you nothin'. He's not told us nothin' more—just what you heard him say," he protested.

The door opened and Colonel Armstrong stood in the fading light, his smooth florid face showing strain. He spoke softly so that those on the fringes of the crowd had to strain to hear him. It was a simple trick he'd learned to command attention. "I know you are all anxious for details of what happened at Bigham's. But the man is unable to tell us anything at present. If you will all go about your business, I promise to report to you just as soon as he is able to talk."

Armstrong watched as the crowd began to disperse. As commander of the Second Battalion of Pennsylvania's Provincial Militia, he was responsible for all the forts of the western side of the Susquehanna: Fort Shirley, known to the settlers as Aughwick, Fort Lyttleton, and Fort Granville. They had been built by Governor Morris in the fall and winter of 1755–56 and were situated about twenty miles apart. Each was supposed to maintain a garrison of seventy-five men. However, the dilatory response of the Provincial Assembly to requests for funds to provide men and supplies had left most of the forts in a precarious position, so that the men who had been recruited for the militia resigned in disgust when their pay was not forthcoming. Colonel Armstrong wondered how long Fort Shirley could hold out should a large force attack them.

The problem, he thought, was that the Provincial Assembly, which had the right to determine how funds were to be appropriated, was dominated by the Quakers, who refused to vote money for the militia or for ammunition. They were convinced that goodwill and honesty were all that was needed to maintain peaceful relations with the Indians. They felt no responsibility for the frontier families' safety and were far enough removed from the wilderness so that they felt secure.

Damn the Assembly, Armstrong said to himself. There they sit in their grand houses with their families safe and secure, with plenty of provender, fine clothes, servants to do their bidding, while these poor folk are trying desperately to eke out a living with only their courage and strength and will to help them. Damn the Assembly for its selfishness. I wonder just how long those fine gentlemen could stand this life. . . . I shall have to write another letter to beg for funds to pay these poor devils and to provide ammunition and physicians—and sign it: "Your most obedient and humble servant, John Armstrong."

A sudden sound from the man in the room interrupted his thoughts. He turned, closed the door, and crossed to where John Graves sat. He was saying something about a salt lick and a doll. Colonel Armstrong bent over and put his hand on John's shoulder, but could make no sense of the disjointed muttering.

Armstrong paced the floor, pushing out his lower lip as he always did when thinking deeply. Finally he stopped and turned to the ensign, who had brought fresh clothes for John.

"Mr. Lewis, I believe we shall need to use something stronger than tea or stew to unleash his tongue. Rum, Mr. Lewis, rum might do it." At the look of surprise on the young officer's face, he added, "You know my views on drinking when on duty. Well, they haven't altered. This man is not on duty and he has information we must have. Send one of the traders to me, please."

Mr. Lewis gave a startled "Yes, sir" and disappeared.

The colonel knew the traders who had taken refuge at the fort had brought rum originally intended for the Indian trade, a practice he deplored but could do little to stop. Traders were for the most part a disreputable lot, delighting in cheating the Indians and making sport of the women. Lewis returned with Jeb Hawkins, whose tightfistedness was the subject of much banter.

"Let's have some of your rum, Jeb. Quickly," Armstrong told him.

As Ensign Lewis took the tankard from the trader and held it out to John, the colonel spoke. "I'm Colonel Armstrong, sir. If you will just drink some of this, perhaps we can help you."

Jeb, watching John clutch the colonel with both hands, wondered if the rum would unloosen his tongue or knock him out. The man was so exhausted he couldn't stand on his feet, and he appeared to be in shock. The trader took the tankard from Lewis and held it to John's mouth.

"Now just take a good swaller. You'll feel like talkin' then, and the colonel and his men can help ya."

A shudder ran through John's body, but he seemed calmer.

"Now then, sir," said the colonel, "what is your name?"

John leaned toward him, peering into his face. "Graves. John Graves. You Colonel Armstrong? You the commander?"

Armstrong smiled. "Yes, Mr. Graves. This is one of my orderlies, Ensign Lewis, and this is Jeb Hawkins, who is taking refuge here."

"Where—where am I?" John asked then, looking from one to the other.

"You're at Fort Shirley. You came in on foot an hour ago. Can you remember what made you come on foot?"

Graves wrinkled his forehead in the effort to remember. "Fort Shirley? Then—then you must send the—militia—after them! Now! There's—no time to lose."

"Send them after who? What happened, Mr. Graves?"

"The Injuns! They—they burnt the blockhouse. Mass—massa—killed most of them. But not Susannah and—and my little girl, Rachel—"

"Susannah is your wife, sir?"

John roused himself. "She—didn't—she didn't want to stay at Bigham's. Susannah—got—got a mind of her own, she does."

"Why was she at Bigham's with your daughter?"

John's face reflected the struggle to remember. "It was Francis that talked—talked. He can talk you into going—going what—what's against—your best—judgment."

"Francis? Francis who?" Colonel Armstrong asked.

John shook his head. "Just Francis. Neighbor. We were going—" He stopped, befuddled.

Jeb Hawkins stepped into the breach. "Would that be Mr. Wilson, Francis Wilson that lives over near Bigham's?"

John caught the trader's arm. "You know Francis? Why didn't he wait for me at—at the spring? Where—where is Francis? I searched and searched. Samuel Bigham scalped—and bodies lying all over the fields."

The silence in the room was alive with shock and horror as each of the listeners imagined the scene.

"Did you find Francis Wilson there?"

"No—no Mrs. Wilson—no boys. I couldn't—find Susannah and Rachel. Found doll. Rachel's doll—corncob."

"Where was the doll, Mr. Graves?"

He made a supreme effort to collect his thoughts. "I found my little Rachel's doll—made of corncobs—found in—the fields—Kittaning way. Find Susannah and Rachel." Wearily he closed his eyes and slumped in the chair.

Early the following morning, a company of militia from Fort Shirley set out to search for the missing captives while John slept.

They had not gone more than a mile when they found the mare, near death from lack of water and the hard journey. They watered and fed her and sent one of the rangers back to the fort for a wagon to bring her in.

Shortly after sunset the search party returned with news. They had followed the path toward Kittaning from the ruins of Bigham's blockhouse northwestward for many miles. At one spot they had come upon the remains of an Indian campfire and, just beyond, had found near the trail a small gold locket containing a lock of dark hair. To John Graves it was a message from the Lord: it was Susannah's locket with its snippet of Rachel's hair. So they were alive! John was certain of it now, and begged to accompany the rangers the following day.

The third day, full of hope, John joined the search party. Before long he saw a tiny bit of red calico clinging to a thorn bush growing near the trail. It was from one of Rachel's little dresses. As he called to the men, he disengaged the torn bit of cloth from the thorn. "It's hers, all right—Rachel's. She must have caught it on this bush and torn it!" He sounded jubilant.

Several of the men, wiser in the ways of the Indians, said nothing. Though they continued to press forward till darkness descended, they found no further evidence to suggest that Susannah and Rachel and the other captives were alive.

At the end of five days they returned to Fort Shirley on Aughwick Creek, exhausted and discouraged.

After their return John joined the militia. It was the only hope he had of finding his family, and he could not think of returning to his farm without them. He made an excellent soldier, enduring without complaint the hardships of bivouacking where chance found them, sleeping on the ground, sometimes in a drenching rain, riding thirty or more miles without a rest, wearing the same sweaty clothes for days on end, living on stale biscuits and such small animals as they were able to find.

As the summer wore on, John's body hardened with the rigors of military life and he grew thin and gaunt. His fair skin darkened, after first turning red and peeling, and the luminous eyes, his most striking feature, were shadowed with dark smudges. He had a full beard now, and long, dark hair that fell below his collar. Susannah had always trimmed his hair for him, but Susannah was gone now.

Never a talkative man, John withdrew more and more into himself, listening to the conversations of the men but saying little. At times the discussions became heated as they complained about the callousness and indifference of the Provincial Assembly. The piety of the Quakers who dominated it was a special subject of derision. John learned that in January some of the frontiersmen, outraged by the Assembly's lack of response to their repeated requests for help, had taken the bodies of massacred settlers to Philadelphia and hauled them through the streets. A mob surrounded the Pennsylvania Provincial Assembly House and placed the bodies at the entrance to the hall, demanding immediate assistance. After meeting for hours, the Assembly had offered a reward for the heads of the instigators of the depredations: Shingask, and the infamous Captain Jacobs, a powerful chief known for his cruelty and the ingenuity of his methods of torture. But this did nothing to relieve the severe distress of the frontier families.

As he listened to their passionate denunciations, John Graves wondered why he had not been more aware of the dangers of this part of the frontier in the past year. Was it because he was too engrossed in his family to bother to find out what was happening? He had been content within his own paradise and had refused to look at what lay beyond. . . . And now he was paying for his neglect. Not only that, but Susannah and Rachel were suffering as well.

One morning in July Corporal John Graves was scouting with some rangers in the vicinity of Bigham's blockhouse. He had not been to visit his own home since the tragedy, but others had reported it was still intact as recently as the previous week.

"Better take a look around, John," one of the older men suggested. "Might be some things you'd want to take to Aughwick." John nodded, although he dreaded going back.

As their horses neared the farm, he was amazed how peaceful and inviting it looked. He saw with fresh eyes the stoutness of the cabin walls, the sturdy door and shutters, the well-made roof. The mare gave a low whinny as they reached the cabin door. John dismounted while the others kept watch. He noticed the dust covering everything as he entered the cabin; by the fireplace was a nest of field mice. A garter snake slithered across the floor.

The bitterness rose in John's throat and he thought he was going to be sick. He wanted to cry out his grief and rage at the injustice of it all. All their work and planning—it had come to this. He caught himself just in time to avoid facing the possibility that they might be dead; the thought coiled just below the level of consciousness like a rattler about to strike.

John crossed to the shelf that held their few books and the candleholders. To his surprise and relief, he found the *Iliad* intact and the Shakespeare with only one corner chewed. He slipped them into his knapsack and went to the bed, where he saw mice droppings among the dust that lay over the coverlet. He pulled open the heavy lid of the chest that held their clothes and the quilt Susannah had made after their marriage. A faint delicate fragrance arose as he lifted Susannah's two winter dresses and her long red wool cloak, and the wool stockings she had knitted. Lavender. There were Rachel's little garments, too, all fresh and clean as if waiting for her.

At the doorway one of the rangers called to him, "Can't take all day, John. We'd best be movin' out."

John nodded. Resolutely he folded the quilt, then on second thought returned for the red cloak and fastened both inside his blanket roll at the back of his saddle. He did not answer when one of the rangers asked, "Got what you wanted, John?"

His face was bleak as they turned their mounts and headed west.

Later in July, Conrad Weiser, the interpreter for the Provincial Assembly, arrived at the fort to confer with Colonel Armstrong about providing greater protection for the settlers in the valley. He had lived among the Mohawks in the province of New York for many years. He spoke their tongue perfectly and was trusted and liked by both Indians and whites. He was old now, but still vigorous.

The day after Weiser's arrival at Fort Shirley a courier from Philadelphia brought the news that the Assembly had at last voted a grant of several thousand pounds "for the Crown's use" in the colonies without stipulating how it was to be used. Governor Morris assured Colonel Armstrong this was done to ease the conscience of the Quaker members; however, the funds could be employed as the colonel saw fit. This was what Armstrong had been waiting for. For some time he had been convinced that the Indian raids were planned at the Delaware village of Kittaning, the headquarters of the two chiefs of that tribe whose names spread terror among the settlers—Shingask, whom they called "Shingas," and Captain Jacobs. Kittaning must be destroyed. Armstrong needed to recruit several hundred men for the expedition, both from those now staying in the forts and from Carlisle, the nearest town. The object of the expedition must be kept secret until they were actually on their way, lest someone, if captured and tortured, should betray it to the Indians and the French.

Colonel Armstrong spoke to John Graves about Conrad Weiser, suggesting he might want to ask him about the Indians' treatment of captives. He saw the quick gleam of interest in John's clear blue eyes, the sudden gathering of energy in the man.

"That's a good idea, Colonel. I'll do that." The next morning John sought out the interpreter.

"Graves? John Graves?" said the old man. "You're the man whose wife and child were captured over at Bigham's blockhouse with the Wilson family. What do you want of me?"

"Mr. Weiser, folks say you know more about the Injuns than any man on the western frontier. Can you tell me what they do to their captives?" he asked, leaning toward the older man and gazing at him intently.

Weiser took in the tightness about the mouth, the deep furrow between the brows; here was a man in mortal trouble. Colonel Armstrong had said he was young, but he did not appear so. Weiser wished he could reassure him, but he knew John Graves would not be satisfied with half-truths or empty suppositions.

"Can't rightly tell," he answered. "Customs differ among the tribes and no one knows which tribe it was that burned Bigham's.

We believe it was Delawares but we can't be certain. I'm better acquainted with the Mohawks and the New York tribes than with the Delawares. When a clan loses a warrior by death or by capture, it is customary for the woman who is head of that clan to ask for an enemy to be captured to take his place. If she wants to, she can adopt the captive instead of having him tortured and killed. If it was the Senecas or Mohawks, now, they generally adopt them. And once they do, that captive is a blood relative. They are very good to those they adopt."

"But they have to take to Indian ways," John protested, feeling repelled. He could not imagine Susannah, who was so particular and so private, living as an Indian.

"There's lots of things worse, Mr. Graves. I know of several villages where most of the people are white captives and most of 'em wouldn't leave if they had a chance."

John was shocked. He had heard stories that this was so, but had never really believed them to be true unless the captives were escaping from the law. But for white women who were brought up in God-fearing homes to accept the ways of savages was something he could not understand. "How can that be?" he asked, his voice trembling with emotion. "The red men are savages! You heard what they did at Bigham's—I saw it. Babies murdered, women and children shot and scalped, some of the bodies so cut up you couldn't tell who they was! I never saw such butchery!"

"Yes," said Conrad Weiser, pausing to light his clay pipe. "They're cruel in war. And they never forget or forgive a wrong. But they gave us fair warning at Carlisle two years ago that the squatters had to give back the land they took without a by-your-leave or they'd take to the warpath. You know what happened. Not more than forty families paid for their spreads. The others, who were too poor to pay, just stayed on. Same thing in fifty—Secretary Peters sent soldiers out to warn the people the tribes would take up the hatchet if they stayed. So they threw themselves on the mercy of the magistrates over to Carlisle and the militia burnt their cabins. But did that keep them out? Inside a few weeks those people returned and built new cabins on the site of their old ones. When a man's poor and hasn't had much chance to provide a living, he's going to go after land." He puffed slowly on his pipe, his expression thoughtful.

John leaned toward him. "If these lands belonged to the Delaware, why did the Penns urge settlers to come here?" he asked.

Weiser blew a cloud of fragrant smoke before replying. "Avarice is one of the oldest of human faults, Mr. Graves, and every nation has some who are flawed with it. Most whites don't think of Indians as having any rights—they think of them as animals. So if they want to take over territory that belongs to a tribe, those people don't scruple about it. It doesn't hurt their conscience to cheat Indians or to go back on their word.

"From what I've learned, old William Penn was different. But I opine his sons have strayed far from their Quaker upbringing. They're interested in making profits from their land-settlement company so they maneuvered up at Albany in fifty-four to buy a great piece of land from the tribes of the Iroquois League—the Six Nations—for the sum of four hundred pounds. Took in the valley of the Juniata and much more than the Indians realized. I was there as an interpreter so I know. It shamed me to belong to the same race as those money-grabbers. They planned to sell that land to new settlers for a tidy profit.

"Wasn't long before the chiefs that hadn't been present at the treaty-making heard about it. They were outraged, as they had a right to be. They claimed the Indians who agreed to the treaty hadn't understood the points of the compass, so they didn't realize how much territory they were selling.

"It is acts like this that are causing the Indian troubles. It may lose us the friendship of the Six Nations. For years the French have been trying to win them over but so far only a few tribes in southern Canada have gone over to the French side. And the Delawares and their friends the Shawnees and Mingoes. Maybe a few of the Maumees. I'm not sure about the last.

"The fur trade is the pivot in all this—the French are determined to control it. The Iroquois have always preferred to deal with the English traders, who give them better value for their peltries. The French are the most parsimonious people the Lord ever made, Mr. Graves. Why, I've seen them give a few bolts of poor cloth, some beads, a few trinkets, and bit of rum for the finest ermine, beaver, otter you ever saw. And all the while they're trying to plant the idea in the heads of the chiefs that we are taking over their land and driving off the game, forcing the tribes to move west. Since the Indians depend on the game for just about everything, this threatens their whole livelihood. Trouble is, what the French say is true."

John, listening to the old man, was aware once again of how little attention he had given to this situation. "But the ones who are stirring up the troubles aren't those who are having to pay for their avarice," he said with bitterness.

"That's true. The Good Book says we get our just deserts in the hereafter, but sometimes it seems like it would be more just if they were to get their punishment in this life," Weiser observed.

John leaned toward Weiser. "The woman captives . . . how do they treat them?"

The older man spoke without hesitation. "I lived among them for many years and I never heard of any Indian forcing a woman against her will. That's a mighty serious crime to them. In some ways they're more civilized than the whites. I could mention a few white men I know of who don't scruple to have their way with women."

"And the children they capture?" John asked.

"They're very fond of children. They're not as strict as white folks. The children have a good life. I have a lot of respect for the Indians, Mr. Graves, though I don't like some of the things they do."

As Weiser saw the pain on John Graves's face, he put aside his pipe, knocking the bowl lightly against his stool to remove the dottle. "I wish I could help you find your wife and child. Guess you'll have to leave it in the hands of the Almighty," he said quietly.

John murmured his thanks; then, turning his head so that Weiser would not see his eyes, he walked away.

It was shortly after this that they heard of the destruction of Fort Granville, which was thought to be impregnable. Rangers from Fort Shirley found a lone survivor in the forest one morning in August, his ears amputated and his face and chest covered with deep knife wounds. They carried him to Aughwick and feelings ran so high that men readily volunteered to set out on an expedition to find and kill the perpetrators.

Since the Delawares were the tribe involved in the destruction of Granville, Colonel Armstrong decided he could wait no longer to attack their stronghold. In the middle of August he went to Carlisle to procure men and horses for the expedition, taking John with him. On the twentieth he wrote to Governor Morris:

Carlisle, 20th of August 1756

May it please Your Honor—

Tomorrow, God willing, we march to Fort Shirley to begin our expedition against Kittaning.

I did not have details of the destruction of Fort Granville at the time I sent you by express rider the melancholy news of the massacre of the garrison there. Since then I have been able to question the lone survivor, Peter Walker, whom our rangers found in the forest four days ago, more dead than alive.

According to Walker, there was a Scotsman named McDowell stationed at Fort Granville who could speak Delaware. He spoke with the Delaware chief, Captain Jacobs, who told him that they are planning to attack Fort Shirley with four hundred men soon.

This is a grave concern; our water supply lies outside the walls of the fort, so that the enemy can easily take possession of it, and there is no well. If we are attacked, I doubt we could hold out unless strongly garrisoned. But I cannot evacuate the fort without Your Honor's permission.

Lyttleton, Shippensburg, and Carlisle (the last two not finished) are the only forts that will, in my opinion, be able to provide protection to the settlers.

According to Walker, Captain Jacobs claimed his braves could take any fort that would catch fire, and that he will make peace with the British when we have taught him to make gunpowder.

We are so short of ammunition that I shall have to use the powder stored here for emergencies. Before the fall of Fort Granville we could have held a fort with half the amount of gunpowder and half the number of men. Now it will require double the number to maintain any fort.

I am, honored sir,
Your most obedient and
humble servant,
John Armstrong.

Colonel Armstrong laid down his quill pen and sealed the letter with his special stamp on the hot wax. At that moment there was a discreet knock.

"It's Corporal John Graves, sir."

"Send him in. And then find the courier for Philadelphia, please."

John Graves entered, hat in hand. He was carrying a letter and looked ill at ease.

The colonel rose with a smile. "Well, Mr. Graves, are you finding it difficult to get good horses for our purpose? Do the people think our offer of one shilling sixpence a day too little?"

"No, sir, it's not that. I've got twenty-seven animals and with what we have Aughwick and those from Fort Lyttleton, we'll have the fifty you need."

"Good. Is it the letter you're concerned about? The courier leaves shortly with the dispatches for the governor and the Assembly."

"I don't know if it's proper to send a letter to Philadelphia in the military dispatches when it's not of military concern. It's personal."

"Well, for a man who has been giving outstanding service to the Second Battalion, I think we might make an exception."

"It's very important, sir. My wife's uncle is a lawyer, Josiah Norris, and I'm sending him my will and asking him to post a reward for information about my wife and child. I haven't told him before about their capture and I think I owe it to him to let him know what happened."

The colonel stroked his chin. "I suppose it will come as a shock to your wife's uncle to hear the sad news."

"I suppose so, sir."

"The courier will be leaving shortly. With conditions as they are, there's no way of telling how long it will take to reach Philadelphia."

"I'm much obliged, colonel. I—I wonder if I can ask something else?"

"Certainly."

"Last week when we were out ranging the woods near Bigham's, we found my cabin still standing. Well, I brought back a quilt Susannah made and her red cloak. I'd like to be certain those things are in good hands in case something happens to me. Also I've been saving my pay so that I'd have a little money put aside for her. Do you know where I could leave it while we're on the expedition?"

Armstrong pushed out his lower lip and clasped his hands behind his back, turning away from John toward the window. "I suppose it should be someone here in Carlisle?"

"Why, I don't rightly know, sir."

"Carlisle is rapidly becoming the last outpost," the colonel said dryly with a suggestion of sadness. "I expect she'd come here first to find you instead of Philadelphia. There is an elderly lady—a Mrs. Graffius over on Elm Street—who is as reliable a person as I've ever met. I think she'd be glad to keep things until such time as Mrs. Graves returns."

"I'm much obliged, sir."

"Not at all. I'm glad if we can help. . . . What did you say the uncle's name is?"

"Josiah Norris."

"I have heard of him," the colonel said slowly, trying to recall where he had heard the name. "I think Josiah Norris occasionally writes barbed letters to *The Pennsylvania Gazette* under the pseudonym 'Friend of Plato.' His pen wields a certain influence among the powerful, who dislike to see their manipulations brought to light."

John was amazed. Susannah had never spoken of such a thing. "Are you sure it's the same man?"

"Yes, I'm certain. His pen name allows him the freedom to say things that a private citizen cannot utter. Few know the identity of Plato's friend. This may turn out to be fortuitous. If Norris is outraged enough by what happened to his niece and her—your—child, he will write a denunciation of the Assembly for its indifference to the needs of the people on the frontier, and that may tip the balance enough for them to vote us some appropriations."

"Well, sir, what do you know. I hope so!" John said fervently.

"At times their callousness makes me so angry I am tempted to resign my commission." Armstrong, seeing John's startled look, continued, "I speak in jest, Mr. Graves. I could not betray the people's trust in me by resigning." He took John's letter and inserted it with the others in the leather pouch. "I will write you a message for Mrs. Graffius. Let us hope Providence will look kindly on our venture and bring us good news."

CHAPTER III

The Encounter

Thirty miles southwest of Fort Shirley, in an area known as the Great Cove, lived a number of families who had settled there during the early 1750s, attracted by the rich soil and plentiful game. In some instances their holdings adjoined, so that they did not feel as isolated as many of the other people living west of the Susquehanna.

When word of the destruction of Bigham's blockhouse reached them that summer of 1756, only the German family, the Stotts, were frightened enough to leave. The others told themselves Bigham's was over sixty miles to the northeast, and besides, Fort Lyttleton and Fort Shirley were between them and the scene of the massacre.

One hot day in early August Mary Ann Eldridge took her son from his cradle and unbuttoned her dress. She sighed deeply as she put the child to her breast. The baby had been fretful all morning because of the heat and the flies, so she had soaked a clean rag in barley water and given him that to suck, but it had not satisfied him. She put aside her work then and took him in her arms, seating herself by the cabin door, which was shaded by a huge chestnut tree. A thin breeze waved the grain in the far field where her husband, George, was harvesting. It played hide-and-seek in the leaves of the chestnut and caressed her bare skin.

Sitting there in the lazy August noon with the child's soft weight in her arms and his mouth drinking deeply, she should have been content. Nursing Thomas was a joy to her. The child was exceptionally beautiful, with his father's smooth olive complexion faintly stained with rose on cheekbones and chin, his head well shaped and covered with a cap of silky dark brown hair, his body perfectly proportioned.

Ordinarily, she liked to watch his small face as she counted her blessings, but today she was too preoccupied for such things.

She had begun to worry when George told her at breakfast that their nearest neighbor, Mr. Abbot, was planning a trip to Fort Lyttleton, ten miles north, to deliver some corn to the hungry settlers who had fled there for safety from their isolated farms on the other side of the mountain. "He said folks is talkin' about the Delawares crossin' the mountain and burnin' and killin' on this side now," George had told her.

"Mercy sakes, why should they be doin' that?" she had said. "You and Mr. Abbot and Mr. Enyard went over to Carlisle a year ago to pay the magistrates for our land. We ain't squatters like the McCulloughs, though poverty is no disgrace."

"You heard about Burnt Cabins," he answered. "The savages has long memories. They're determined to drive the settlers out. They're too danged ornery and ignorant to pay any mind to them that paid the magistrates for their acres—"

She interrupted him, her cheeks a brighter pink than usual, her blue eyes dark with excitement. "You know as well as I do that most folks ain't paid. They just moved in and stayed. I guess the Injuns has a right to be upset about it. But killin' people don't solve nothin'."

His face darkened with scorn and bitterness. "If that land belonged to the Delawares, why didn't they stay there? This is just wilderness, it don't belong to nobody; them squatters come here and worked to build cabins and clear the ground and now them thievin' savages claims it's theirs! They ain't got no cause to start massacrin' the whites. The governor ought to send in troops and blow them all to kingdom come!"

"But they ain't all on the warpath," she reminded him.

He snorted in derision. "They're all cut from the same cloth—animals, all of them. Filthy, lying, deceitful! Unless the government wipes them out, they'll always be givin' us trouble."

"You mean to kill them in cold blood—even them that is peaceable?"

He nodded.

"But there's women and children and old folks," she protested.

"They're still Injuns, ain't they? Those brats'll be raised in the same way as their fathers, them that's old has done their share of mischief, their squaws is willin' to lie with any man that'll have them. Only way is to exterminate them."

When George spoke with such hatred, Mary Ann trembled, for he did not seem to be the man she loved. Even his face changed.

Finally Thomas, having drunk his fill, went to sleep. Carefully she laid him in his cradle and then went inside the cabin. Its walls were stout and properly notched, its chinks filled with wattle to keep out the rain and the cold. The roof was slightly pitched so that the snow would slide down its split shakes. Above the mantel of the huge stone chimney hung one of their Pennsylvania rifles, and the other hung above the door, both with their powder horns within reach. From the rafters Mary Ann had hung branches of dried herbs to use in flavoring their stews or to prepare as medicines, using remedies handed down from her grandmother.

She regretted that there was no glass for their two windows, remembering the delicate wavy light from the handblown panes in her parents' home. She and George had made do with paper smeared with bear's grease and had hung the heavy wooden shutters with their oiled leather hinges on the inside for safety.

Two objects brightened the dim interior and gave the cabin a touch of home: the crazy quilt folded over their bunk bed and the glowing red Pennsylvania dower chest, with its traditional Rose of Sharon design painted in green and gold, flanked by blue turtle doves. This was her special pride. Her father, a prosperous farmer in the Gwynedd Valley near Philadelphia, had bartered four valuable peach trees for it from a German family. Now, whenever she saw it, she thought of home: the sprawling white farmhouse with its many chimneys nestled into the rolling countryside, the big red barn filled with hay and oats, the neat chicken house and pigpen; the wide lawns fringed with flowers and tall trees, the beehives behind the springhouse, the dovecote with its sound of doves murmuring amid the flutter of wings.

Today, for some reason, she wondered if she would ever see

her beloved home again. Usually cheerful and practical, she felt troubled and sad this morning. Was it because of her conversation with George about the Indian troubles to the north of the valley?

Mary Ann rolled up her sleeves, picked up the leather bucket of water, and poured the water into the iron kettle on its crane. After the water had heated, she carried the heavy kettle to the cleared space beyond the cabin and began to wash their clothes, but her thoughts kept reverting to the past.

Shortly after their marriage, they had started out in a Conestoga wagon from the Gwynedd Valley with all their earthly goods fastened under the wagon's frame or beneath its billowing canvas top. George had always felt the need to settle in some solitary place away from the towns. He was looking for good rich bottomland with a spring of clear sparkling water. They had gone deeper and deeper into uncharted territory, always on the alert for Indians, but the Tuscaroras in this part of the wilderness were few and had not bothered them.

When they came to the Great Cove, a broad, peaceful valley set in the foothills of the Allegheny Mountains, and saw the river flowing quietly between banks of wild flowers and ferns, they knew they had found their place.

The Abbots, Enyards, and Stotts had all helped them build their cabin and barn near the spring. Beyond the cabin Mary Ann had planted sunflower seeds and sweet williams brought from her mother's flower garden. On one side she planted herbs to cure colics and fevers. She and George had worked hard to make a home.

They had had their griefs, like most couples, she reflected, her eyes lighting on the small grave beyond the cabin door where they had buried their firstborn, Amanda. The little girl had caught the croup before she was a year old and died in her mother's arms while George watched helplessly. But the Lord had been good. Five months ago Mary Ann had given birth to the fine healthy boy, named Thomas for her father. His coming had brought them great happiness and helped to ease the pain of losing Amanda. They looked forward to more children, for she was just twenty and in excellent health.

Her thoughts reverted to the Indians. She wondered if they would come this far south, and her heart seemed to stop beating at the thought that Thomas might be killed.

After wringing out the hot water from the freshly washed clothes, Mary Ann carried them to the stream to rinse. Resolutely she dismissed her concern about the Indian raids and began to think how fortunate she was . . . a husband she loved who cared deeply for her, a fine healthy son, a snug cabin in the beautiful Juniata Valley—what more could she want, or need?

In enumerating her blessings, she remembered the neighbors—the Abbots and the Enyards. Mrs. Abbot had taught her to make red dye and saffron yellow from certain berries and roots, and often sent over cheese she had made, for the Eldridges had no cow and the Abbots were fortunate enough to have two.

The Enyards' large holdings were completely surrounded by woods. Although she didn't see the family often, Mary Ann liked them, especially Silas, the oldest son, who was a big, good-natured fellow. George had teased her about Silas Enyard, claiming he was sweet on her. She had noticed Silas's eyes lingering on her in a way that was flattering but a bit upsetting as well, although she had done nothing to provoke it.

A short time later George came to the cabin and sat down on the flat-topped log that served as a step. He had been cutting the standing grain, because he was concerned that a thunderstorm might blow up and ruin his fine crop. He was a handsome man, but hard work in the sun had etched deep lines in his forehead and about his eyes. His face and forearms were burned brown, and he appeared older than his twenty-five years, in spite of his sinewy body and hard muscles.

"Why don't you rest for today?" Mary Ann asked him.

"Might just do that, though I'd like to get the rest of the wheat cut in case it rains. But I'm plumb tuckered." George wiped his sleeve across his dusty face and put his head on his folded arms. His shoulders ached from swinging the scythe all morning.

Mary Ann went to him and began to knead his shoulders, massaging deeply to relieve the strained muscles. Then she went to the spring and filled a gourd with water. "This will perk you up," she said.

She had not buttoned her dress after nursing the baby, for the day was exceptionally hot and the breeze felt so good on her bare skin; she wondered what her mother would say to that. Well, things were different in the settlements and the farms surrounding them. People lived close to each other there and most went to church on the Sabbath and some even tried to find someone to teach their children to read and cipher.

"I hope," she said wistfully, "someday they'll be enough folks in this valley so's we can have a school. I'd like for Thomas to know his letters and do sums. It must be fine to know how to read."

George raised his head and looked at her briefly, then gazed at the distant mountains. "If we were to get a school in this here valley, things wouldn't be like they are now. There ain't no room to grow when you get lots of people livin' close by. When there's enough so's there's a school, there's always somebody tellin' the rest what they can't do." She did not answer. "That's a good spring," he remarked, to end the conversation.

Realizing she could not get him to agree, she changed topics. "Did they ever find out where the Injuns took them people they captured when they burnt Bigham's blockhouse and massacred so many?"

"Still no trace of them. I reckon they took them over the mountains to Kittaning."

"That was in June," she mused. "Almost two months gone. I wonder . . ." She stopped, the worry shadowing her eyes.

"Ain't no use in worryin', Mary Ann. That was miles from here. Besides, they won't attack us when we paid for our acres and got a land warrant to prove it."

"But if they can't read, how're they going to know which families just come and took the land? When that treaty was signed up at Albany, the Injuns claimed they didn't know how much land they was sellin' to the Quakers. If they'd been able to read, they couldn't have been cheated like that!"

"Read!" George's voice was scornful. "Injuns read! They're just savages little better than dumb animals."

"The Lord made them same as you and me. Just because their ways is different and they speak different don't make them animals!" Her eyes flashed now. "I don't hold with white folk tryin' to take advantage, like the Penns. They calls theirselves Quakers, but they don't think twice about cheatin' the Injuns."

George was too tired to argue.

"Besides," she continued, "when have they ever given us trouble? The Tuscaroras here in the valley ain't bothered us. It was some of them showed Mr. Abbot which roots and berries is good for dyein' cloth."

"I don't want to talk about it," he said.

Mary Ann felt contrite over making such a fuss when he was so tired. She linked her hands behind his neck. "I don't like to differ with you, George. I always feel bad after we differ."

"Well, I knew you was a spirited woman when I married you."

"But I do love you, George Eldridge, with all my heart!"

"I know you do."

"I don't want to displease you." Her eyes were troubled.

"Every couple is bound to differ sometimes," he said. "You don't hear me complainin', do you?" He looked up at her with a gleam of humor lighting his fine eyes, then he pulled her onto his lap and kissed her, pulling the horn pins from her hair.

When he looked at her in a certain way and called her his lass, she still felt her heart beat faster. He liked to undo the thick braids of her hair so that its heavy gold fell across her shoulders and hung below her waist. He would bury his hands in the shining mass, his mouth against hers, then slowly kiss her forehead, chin, ears, throat. She took such pleasure from his love-making that she sometimes wondered if it was sinful. Now he put his hand inside her dress and began to fondle her breast.

"Oh—George!" she cried, the Indians forgotten.

His eyes twinkling, he stopped kissing her long enough to ask, "Like it?"

"You know better than to ask," she said, one hand about his neck, the other caught in his hair. With that he lifted her in his arms and carried her into the cabin.

* *

It was midafternoon when Mary Ann decided to visit her friend Mrs. Abbot, who lived a short distance away.

"You do that," George told her, stretching and glancing up at the sky. Not a sign of a rain cloud in that expanse of blue. He could rest, keep an eye on the baby, and have time for his whittling. He was making his wife some fine spoons from a branch of walnut that had broken off in a storm.

Mary Ann wrapped a hoecake she had baked that morning in a clean cloth and picked some mint to take to Mrs. Abbot. She threw him a kiss as she left.

George called after, "Mind you, don't stay too late, girl!"

She laughed. "I won't be long."

The way to the Abbots crossed several open meadows dotted with daisies, then a short stretch of woodland where there was a semblance of a rough path. About half a mile beyond, screened by tall trees, she could see the tops of the Abbots' chimneys.

Mary Ann thought of Maggie Abbot, who had not been well. She had developed milk leg, so it was very painful for her to get about.

Mary Ann saw the Abbots' cows munching clover while Jeremy kept an eye on them. George had promised her a cow when Amanda was born, but a year ago there had been a terrible battle in the wilderness near the French fort of Duquesne, in which the Indians and the French had ambushed a great army of British soldiers. After that there was no more talk of a cow. George didn't think it wise to leave home. The only trips he made were to the mill about six miles away, where the settlers took their wheat to be ground into flour.

Felix, the oldest of the Abbot boys, was mending a harness. He was a sturdy lad of seventeen with broad shoulders and powerful muscles. "Pa took a wagon of corn to the fort this mornin' and Johnny went with him," he said by way of greeting. "They're payin' an awful lot for food since so many folk has gone to stay there 'cause of all the rumors about Injuns crossin' the mountains and killin' settlers. People is so scared they didn't take any provender with them. Just run for their lives."

Mary Ann fanned herself with her sunbonnet. "Ever since the

massacre at Bigham's people's been frightened. But that wasn't hereabouts."

"'Bout fifty or sixty mile from here," Felix said.

"George and your pa don't seem to be worried much. They think a lot of it is rumors that keeps people stirred up."

"Well," Felix replied, "we ain't never had no trouble with the Tuscaroras."

Mary Ann found Maggie Abbot propped up in their large bunk bed, her swollen leg on a folded quilt. She was stitching scraps of cloth together for a coverlet. Lucinda, their sixteen-year-old, was trying to ease her mother's pain with a poultice of herbs. She was very blond, with yellow braids and thick, pale lashes. She had a fine rosy complexion, a broad nose, and full lips, but her expression was resentful.

Mary Ann, noticing the girl's full figure, guessed that Lucinda had reached the time when she needed a husband, and that this might account for her sulky manner. But she remembered Lucinda always had been a strange one, secretive and withdrawn, never really revealing how she felt, never looking at you directly. Mary Ann had always felt uncomfortable with her and found it impossible to draw her out.

Sarah, the younger daughter, was spinning. Mary Ann had always liked her, for with Sarah she knew how things stood; there was no holding back as there was with Lucinda.

The large room was stiflingly hot. At one side a ladder led aloft; it was there that the children slept. Near the rafters overhead flies hung motionless in the heat. Through the window Mary Ann saw the vivid wings of yellow-and-black butterflies flashing and the sun shining so bright on the wheat that the air appeared to shimmer. From the vegetable garden came the sharp, shrill sound of cicadas. Everything seemed suspended, as if time were standing still.

Maggie Abbot was pleased to see her. "You're a brave girl, Mary Ann, to come over here by yourself."

"We don't reckon they'll come this far south," Mary Ann answered, referring to the Delaware. "George says a lot of the talk about them comin' over the mountain is just rumors. He don't take much stock in it."

"Pa says the same. He says we won't be bothered, since we paid them for our holdin's," Maggie replied. Mary Ann decided not to voice her fears regarding the warrants. Maggie had enough to worry her. She untied the napkin and held out the hoecake and the mint.

"Now that's real kind of you, Mary Ann. I keep askin' Lucinda to dig up some of that mint from the woods and plant it in the garden but she ain't done it," Maggie Abbot said.

"I got my hands full as it is," said Lucinda.

"It wouldn't take that long," said her mother.

Mary Ann, aware of the tension between the two, interrupted. "You feelin' any better?"

"My legs has been givin' me pain ever since my last child was born. Guess I'm gettin' too old for havin' babies."

"You expectin'?"

Maggie nodded. She spoke of the plans she had made for when her time came, and Mary Ann offered to help.

Now their conversation reverted to the rumors of Indian raids on this side of the mountain. Sarah's busy fingers stopped their spinning and Lucinda paused in making salt-rising bread.

"It sounds like the French is stirrin' up the Injuns and makin' them believe it's to help them get back their land," observed Mary Ann.

Maggie lowered her voice so that her daughters would not hear. "We hear the French is offerin' a bounty to the Injuns for every scalp they take from a white settler!"

Mary Ann stared in disbelief. "Dear Lord!" she said.

Maggie's face clouded. "I'm afraid we're in for trouble, and I ain't in no condition to travel."

"Well, maybe things will settle. Let's hope so. Remember to send for me when you start your pains. I'll just bring Thomas and stay till the baby's birthed. George can manage for a few days."

Maggie's face softened. "I don't know what I'd do without you, Mary Ann. You're a real comfort."

Mary Ann laughed. "Take care of yourself. And now I'd best be gettin' home. It's about time for Thomas's feedin'." She rose and kissed Maggie's cheek.

"Now you have Felix walk you home. You shouldn't ought to go through the woods alone," Maggie called after her.

Felix was pleased to be asked to accompany Mary Ann. She made him feel manly, never teasing him the way his sisters did. Besides, he thought her very beautiful. He had heard his parents say George Eldridge was a very fortunate man to have won such a strong and comely wife. As he walked beside her in the cornfield, he noted her straight back, trim waist, and the swelling curves of her breast. He wondered what she looked like naked, then blushed at the thought.

Once he had gone over to help Mr. Eldridge with something and he had walked in when she was nursing the baby. He remembered how white her skin was below the neck in contrast to the golden tan of her face and hands, for she always wore the high-necked dress of the frontier. The color of her face matched her hair, and her smooth, high cheekbones were the color of wild roses, her long-lashed eyes as blue as the sky.

Mary Ann thought about her worrisome conversation with Maggie. Suddenly, she saw a slight movement in the wheatfield that adjoined the corn. Her eyes widened in astonishment as she caught a glimpse of a naked copper-colored shoulder through the waving grain and then in mounting fear saw a scalplock of long black hair trimmed in red feathers. She caught Felix's arm and whispered, "Injuns, Felix! Run, run!"

But there was no possibility of running. At that moment six braves in war paint arose from the wheat and surrounded them, the foremost grasping Mary Ann by the hair, for her sunbonnet had fallen off and was now hanging by its ties on the back of her neck. She gazed at the brave in terror, unable to move or utter a sound. She had a blurred impression of a grinning face painted grotesquely in red and black.

He said something to the other braves and they piled onto Felix all sorts of plundered articles: an iron hoe, two large brass kettles, some bullet molds, a featherbed mattress. Felix was pale beneath his tan and was breathing so rapidly that she could hear him.

Mary Ann's captor thrust into her hands a long-handled iron frying pan such as those the nonresisters brought from Germany.

Then he uttered one word, "Come!" In her panic she failed to realize that he had spoken in English.

Two of the Indians led the way, followed by Felix, staggering with the plunder, then two more braves, Mary Ann and her captor, and, in the rear, a very young warrior, who looked to be not more than fourteen. They went single file, moving swiftly and silently through the wheat. The captives struggled to keep up with the pace.

Although her heart was still racing, Mary Ann noticed that their route led them away from the Eldridge and Abbot cabins. She felt weak with relief, remembering that George would be inside the cabin with the baby. Usually he was in the fields this time of day, for in summer he often worked until sundown. Oh, Lord Jesus, she thought, don't let any harm come to George and Thomas.

They continued in this manner for several miles, entering the dense forest, where one of the old Indian trails led over the mountains. It was difficult walking now, for the path was very narrow, and brambles and sharp branches caught at her skirt and at Felix's load. Just when Mary Ann thought she could not continue but must drop there in the woods and be scalped, her captor said something and the leader turned off the trail, leading them to a small clearing near a brook.

The Indian who had seized Mary Ann motioned for them to rest, squatted on his heels, and brought out a small deerskin pouch tied with a thong. He extracted some moldy biscuits and green corn, giving each of them an equal portion. Mary Ann had heard that it was considered bad manners by the Indians to refuse any food they offered, so she steeled herself to eat. Felix, a healthy young man with a prodigious appetite, ate his share with relish, for it was long past time for his evening meal.

Mary Ann's captor then knelt beside the brook and cupped his hands to drink deeply, motioning for the captives to do the same. The icy-cold water was pure and refreshing and they felt somewhat better after this brief pause.

When they resumed their march, Mary Ann watched two of the warriors disappear in the thick woods that surrounded the clearing. Were they going ahead to prepare for their torture?

She thought with anguish of her infant son and her husband, wondering if they would ever know what had happened to her. At this her captor pulled her around to face him. He gazed at her, then said in strongly accented English, "No hurt, no kill."

She looked at him in disbelief.

He smiled and made a motion of scalping, then shook his head, repeating, "No hurt!" He pointed to himself and said several times, "Tawaugoa, Tawaugoa."

Some clear part of her brain told her he was trying to reassure her, that he would not have told her his name otherwise. "T-Tawaugoa?" she repeated weakly.

He nodded, looking pleased, then pointed to her. At first she did not understand, but since his glance betrayed no hostility, she finally realized he wanted to know her name. "Mary Ann," she said tremulously.

"Maully Ann?" He tested the name several times to get the sound of it; then he smiled. The next words he spoke were incomprehensible to her.

She had no idea what he had said, but she nodded to keep his goodwill. She must survive! She thought repeatedly of her child, for the pressure in her breasts was beginning to hurt now and she wondered what George would do to feed him. Please let him take the baby to the Abbots, Lord! she prayed.

It was nearly sunset; neither Mary Ann nor Felix would ever have been able to keep to the trail, but the braves never hesitated. They moved swiftly and silently as the ground began to slope upward. At times Mary Ann found it difficult to continue the steep ascent, burdened as she was by the heavy frying pan and her long skirt. If she paused, Tawaugoa would give her a push. At first this had frightened her, but after it happened several times she understood that this was his way of helping her where the trail was very rough.

Before the light died completely they had ascended the mountain and started down the other side. Here the path was easier, less overgrown. When they emerged onto a flat wooded plain the captives had lost all sense of time. As they drew nearer to the Indian village, small bark huts surrounded by cornfields, they saw fires burning and women stirring something in large iron pots.

Dogs and children were running about, the children's voices shrill in the summer night. Fireflies briefly lighted tiny lanterns and a pungent aroma rose from the cook pots.

At their approach a thin old woman darted out of the shadows and put her hand first on Mary Ann and then on Felix. Immediately, four other old women, their lips daubed with red clay, surrounded them, glaring malevolently at the two prisoners.

Tawaugoa spoke to the first woman. "How are you, Peace Woman? You have outrun the War Women again. I have brought only two captives this time."

"I am very well, nephew. There is too much bloodshed. We can use them if they are strong and willing to work. We shall know soon."

Mary Ann and Felix, understanding nothing of this exchange, saw Tawaugoa's face harden at the old woman's last words.

They watched as two rows of warriors were drawn up facing each other, standing about six feet apart. They were naked except for breechclouts and wide silver bands about their upper arms. Their faces and chests were painted with black war paint, their eyes encircled with red, and their heads plucked, except for four-inch patches on top, from which hung long scalplocks adorned with beads, silver brooches, and small feathers. Each carried a stout club, and in the rear half-grown boys held lighted flambeaus of wood, which gave the scene a mysterious quality.

Felix looked at Tawaugoa for explanation. Tawaugoa motioned for him to drop his burden, saying, "Must run!" The young man understood, for he had heard traders tell of this Indian custom. If one could dodge the blows, they would not be repeated, for the Indians respected courage and skill.

Deliberately Felix put down his load. Summoning all his courage, he walked unhurriedly to the line of waiting braves as the women left their cook fires to watch. Like a sprinter preparing for a race, he tensed his muscles and bent forward slightly; then with an enormous burst of energy he darted between his assailants with such speed that only two were able to touch him, and those were just glancing blows. When it was over, his heart raced and his legs felt weak and there was a sharp pain in his side. But he was unhurt.

Now several of the men motioned to Mary Ann. Tawaugoa appeared to be arguing against it, but they insisted. She did not put down the heavy frying pan but gripped its handle with both hands as she stepped to the line of warriors. As the first brave raised his club to strike her, a stray wind lifted his breechclout, and she swung the iron pan with all her force, hitting him in the groin so that he bent double in pain and dropped his club.

At this the older men laughed immoderately and the others in the line began to change their opinion of this paleface. Several did not attempt to strike her, having acquired a healthy respect for the way she swung the heavy pan, but the last brave determined to prove his superiority. As he swung his club, she brought the pan down on his head, sending him reeling and finally knocking him to the ground.

At this, the women surrounded her, tearing at her dress and pelting her with clumps of soil and sand until she swung at them with such force that they, too, moved away from her.

Mary Ann stood alone, her skirt ripped and dragging in the dust, one sleeve torn, her hair falling down her back, her face flushed and streaked with dust. She still held on to the frying pan. Never had she felt so alone. A wave of homesickness swept over her and she thought with anguish of her infant son and her husband. She sank down on the ground and covered her face with her hands, but her despair was beyond tears. Tawaugoa gazed at her intently. He had captured a rare woman; she was his prize. "Maully Ann strong! Very strong. Good! Come, we go to women."

She got up then and followed him to a part of the camp where several women were gathered. The old woman who had touched them as they were led into the village now approached, regarding the girl with curiosity. Tawaugoa spoke to her for several minutes while she nodded and continued to stare at the captive. Pointing to the old woman, he said several times, "Melakome."

Mary Ann nodded, too exhausted to speak. The old woman took her by the hand leading her to a quiet place away from the huts, where a deerskin was stretched over evergreen boughs and pegged to keep it taut. She motioned for the girl to lie down, then seated herself beside the improvised mattress.

The yapping of the village dogs and chatter of the inhabitants were muted there. A little breeze had sprung up, so that the evening was pleasantly cool.

The old woman stared and then pointed at Mary Ann. "Maully Ann?" The girl nodded.

Pointing to herself the old woman said, "Melakome."

Mary Ann shifted her position on the deerskin, trying to find some way to ease the pain in her arms and legs and back. She wondered if she would awake to find George sleeping peacefully with one arm flung across her shoulder, and her baby lying asleep in his cradle. Then, seeing her guardian sitting immobile not three feet away, she knew it was no dream.

The night sky above the trees was filled with stars, remote and mysterious. Fireflies stabbed the dark and a vagrant wind scattered the embers of the cooking fires and tossed the branches. She thought her heart must break with grief and fear and the loss of all she knew and loved. It was late, very late, when at last she slept.

As dawn light filled the sky, Felix Abbot was taken away to a distant Indian village, from which he would be taken to a Shawnee camp in the Ohio wilderness.

CHAPTER IV

Tawaugoa's Prize

Mary Ann's exhaustion was so great that she fell immediately into a deep troubled sleep. She dreamed that six braves in full war paint pursued her as she ran through a dense forest, stumbling over hidden roots and rocks. Her hair came unbound and caught on the branches of a tree. She twisted this way and that, struggling to free herself as the Indians approached. Now they were almost upon her. The foremost was Tawaugoa, who gazed at her intently, then lifted a long scalping knife and reached for her hair. "No hurt, Maully! No kill! Friend!" he cried as he lifted up her hair.

At that she screamed and wrenched herself from the dream, sitting up on the pallet and gazing about wildly.

In the clearing before the bark huts the late morning sun beat down, touching the trampled grass with brilliant light. Leaves on the trees nearby shone with the sun's radiance, fluttering delicately in the breeze, which was scented with pines and bruised herbs.

There were no men about, except for a number of aged sitting outside the huts, smoking long clay pipes, their expressions remote. A short distance away, women stirred the contents of iron pots. Small children darted among the women, at times coming dangerously close to the fires. One of the women drove them away with a large wooden ladle, laughing as they scuttled off like beetles. Dogs chased each other, snapping at one another's tails, until several women grabbed burning brands and struck them.

There were yelps of pain as the mongrels slunk off with their tails between their legs.

Melakome came to Mary Ann's pallet and looked down at her silently. Her wrinkled face showed no emotion as she studied the captive. Then she motioned for her to follow, and led her away from the village to the bank of the stream. There four young Indian girls stood knee-deep in the water. The dappled light threw into relief their firm thighs and breasts as they stooped to let the water ripple over their shoulders.

Mary Ann saw them smile as they pointed to her bodice. She was aware for the first time that her milk had stained the front of her dress. She was conscious again of the pressure in her breasts and realized she had not nursed her child in twenty-four hours. She wondered with mounting anxiety who was caring for Thomas.

Melakome motioned that she should bathe. She was dirty and disheveled from her long forced march over the mountain. Her dark red calico was ripped at the shoulder and clumps of soil still clung to the skirt. She pulled off her drawers and threw them onto the bank; then, looking about to make certain there were no men near, she lifted her dress above her head and tossed it aside. Kneeling in the stream, she relaxed in the water, rubbing her body to wash away the dirt.

The pressure in her swollen breasts was intolerable, so she began to expel the milk while the girls watched curiously.

"How strange that she has milk to spare," one said.

"You forget she came a long way over the mountain after our braves captured her," said another girl.

"Her body is very white, yet her face and hands are a golden color," observed the tallest girl.

"Will you adopt her, Melakome, to take the place of your nephew?"

"I have not decided," the old woman said. "I shall see how well she works with the women."

"She looks strong. Remember how she hit Nakomee with the frying pan?" The speaker began to laugh and the others joined in.

"She has courage," Melakome said thoughtfully.

The prettiest of the girls now spoke. "I think Tawaugoa favors her. He did not want her to be hurt."

Melakome gave her a reproving look. "I do not believe he is so foolish as to want a white woman. He promised to bring me a captive. He is a man of his word. There is no way he can take Maully to wife. If I decide not to adopt her, she will be killed."

"Of course, Melakome. You are the Peace Woman of our village and you sit in the councils of our tribe. We meant no disrespect."

The old woman's face relaxed into a slight smile. "Then go, Wa-we-tah, bring her some proper clothes."

"Yes, grandmother."

Sitting on the mossy bank, Wa-we-tah pulled on leggings of blue trade cloth trimmed with beadwork and scarlet ribbons. Then she arranged about her trim waist a yard and a half of blue cloth, wrapping it with a beaded girdle. Over that she put a red calico smock and fastened it at the neck with several large silver brooches. She put silver bracelets on her wrists and slipped on moccasins trimmed with porcupine quills, small pieces of tin, and tufts of deer's hair dyed red. Mary Ann thought her very lovely. With her smoothly braided black hair and graceful figure, she was like a bright bird momentarily alighting on the shadowed bank.

The girl turned and ran through the trees; in a few minutes she returned with an armful of clothing, which she gave to the old woman.

Now Mary Ann began to wash her hair, and the girls drew closer, talking together excitedly. Finally one put out a hand and touched the thick mane. At this the others began to finger it. Mary Ann cringed in fear, wondering if they intended to hurt her. At the expression in her eyes, they began to laugh and she realized they were merely curious.

"It would make a fine ornament," one observed. "All that gold hair hanging from Tawaugoa's belt. It's longer than most."

"Maybe she bewitched him. Our grandmother sent him for a captive and he brings her back. But now he doesn't want her to be adopted. For then she will be his cousin." They giggled.

"Perhaps she is a white witch sent to destroy Tawaugoa. Even though she is only a paleface he was moved by her."

Melakome looked at them in disapproval. "That is enough! Let there be no more talk of white witches! She is only a paleface from the Delawares' hunting grounds. If she fits into the Shawnee way of life, I shall make her a daughter of the Deer clan. There is nothing more to say."

The girls lowered their heads and emerged from the stream.

Melakome motioned for Mary Ann to come, too. As the captive reached the bank, she picked up her torn dress and the drawers, indicating that she wished to wash them. The old woman nodded.

As soon as the clothes were spread on bushes to dry, the girls began to help Mary Ann dress in the clothing Wa-we-tah brought. They arranged a piece of faded trade cloth about her waist, fastening it with a girdle less skillfully beaded than the Indian girl's. They slipped a smock faded to a rose-red over her head and pinned the neck with a brooch made from several sixpence.

Melakome, watching closely, nodded in approval.

Mary Ann felt restored by the bath and the clean clothes, which were both comfortable and practical. As they returned to camp, much of her fear left her. She told herself they would not be so particular about her if they were planning to kill her.

She looked about with intense curiosity. Escape would depend upon her powers of observation, and she must learn their habits before she could make any attempt.

Children ran about naked, their sturdy brown bodies fleet and graceful. Babies, securely fastened to cradleboards, were watched over by small girls while the women worked in the cornfields. The sight of the babies with their bright black eyes and straight black hair reminded her of Thomas. A wave of desolation swept over her.

Melakome, aware of the captive's emotions, led her to a large iron pot, where a stew bubbled. She dipped a bowl into the pot, then held it out, dripping, to Mary Ann.

The girl had not eaten in twenty-four hours and was ravenously hungry. "A spoon?" she asked. "Can I have a spoon?"

The old woman looked at her without comprehension. Mary Ann noticed several women eating from such bowls, using their fingers to retrieve the larger morsels and tipping the bowl to drink the liquid. This done, they wiped their fingers on the grass. She followed their example, disliking to use her fingers but being careful to show no disdain, for she knew she must win their approval before she could earn their trust.

When Mary Ann had eaten, Melakome showed her how to clean the bowl with moss, then led her to another part of the camp, where a group of women were grinding corn. The women looked up, their eyes full of hostility, their shoulders tense. When Melakome spoke to them, they shifted their position so that the captive could take her place among them. Mary Ann knelt and tried to concentrate on the task. She felt completely at the mercy of these women.

The corn was poured into a hollow in a large flat stone and crushed by rubbing a smaller stone over the kernels. It was wearisome work, but she was determined to do it well and shortly established a rhythm in her grinding that produced results.

The women ignored her at first, until she asked, "What do you call this here?" pointing to the stone. They exchanged looks and after she had repeated the question several times, one woman understood. She told Mary Ann the Shawnee word for "stone" and corrected her until she said it properly. There was a slight release of tension then.

The day passed quickly. Mary Ann was surprised to find the women working happily in groups, all sharing the care of the younger children. She noticed several women nursing the same baby at various times and wondered at this. The older children were allowed more freedom than in a settler's family. They were noisy, happy, and full of high spirits. The whole village was their playground. There was no set time for meals, for the fires under the iron cook pots burned all day. When one was hungry, one helped oneself.

When the shadows lengthened, Mary Ann felt again the poignant tug of memories of home. Help me, Lord! Keep George and Thomas safe and help me return to them soon, she prayed silently.

Surely, she reasoned, they must be searching for her. George and the Abbots would have told the soldiers at Fort Lyttleton of their capture, and the militia were probably out looking for her and Felix at this very hour. She felt a surge of hope at the thought and told herself she must never think of the possibility that her husband and child might be dead. Again she wondered how to escape, but she did not know her way over the mountain and had no weapon to protect herself. She would have to stay until the militia found her.

Had she known her captors were the dreaded Shawnees, her fear would have increased tenfold. All the settlers had heard tales of their savagery.

She thought over the events of the day. She had learned their words for "water," "stone," and "eat." She must try to please them, and she saw that trying to learn their language had brought a measure of acceptance.

Beside her Melakome dipped her fingers into cornmeal mush cooked with beans and squash and flavored with wild honey. She made loud sucking noises as she ate, then wiped her hands in the long grass.

The sky was luminous and clear, with the trees etched black against its deepening blue. Along the lower reaches of the heavens the dying embers of the sunset glowed apricot and rose. Everything was hushed and filled with peace. It made Mary Ann think of the eternity her mother had spoken of.

As the first star of evening appeared, Melakome began to sing in a cracked monotone:

"Eye of the Great Spirit,
Creator of sky and earth
And of thy children,
The Shawnees,
Look on us with thy favor.
Make our young men fearless
and strong,
Give our young women many
children,
O maker of the universe."

The old woman's words meant nothing to the captive, but something in her manner gave Mary Ann the feeling that this was a prayer. She began to feel reassured. They were not going to kill her or torture her. She sensed that Melakome's attitude toward her had changed, as if she had become her friend and protector.

The second night Mary Ann slept inside Melakome's hut with two of the young girls.

She was awakened early by the shouts and cries of the children. When she emerged from the hut, she saw that the stream was filled with them, all splashing about. Young women sitting on the bank unfastened their babies from their cradleboards and plunged them into the cold, clear water. Some of the infants cried out but most seemed to be taking it stoically. Mary Ann decided the Indians must put great importance on cleanliness. She did not know Shawnee mothers subjected their children to this cold-water plunge the year round in order to make them strong.

The second day passed much as the first, with no sign of Felix or the braves. Mary Ann began to lose some of her fear, but her longing for her child was with her constantly. When she passed the Indian babies with their stolid little faces and shining black eyes, the pain of separation was particularly sharp.

Melakome found new tasks for her to do. She showed Mary Ann how to skin small animals so that the fur was removed in one piece. This required patience and skill. She started to teach her how to do the intricate beadwork that adorned their clothing. Mary Ann was also learning more Shawnee words. As she tried out her new vocabulary, the women exchanged glances, their faces shut tight, only their eyes revealing that they were pleased.

One morning Mary Ann saw two braves in war paint enter the village, and she knew they had come to prepare the Indians for the arrival of captives.

Outwardly all was calm. People resumed their work, children played quietly without their usual laughter and shouting, the ancients continued to sit in the shade, smoking their long clay pipes. But the silence filled Mary Ann with a powerful foreboding, and she wondered if she was about to witness the atrocities she had heard about. Some of the men began beating drums of rawhide, others shook gourd rattles. The din grew.

Suddenly a war party led by Tawaugoa appeared through the trees. They had with them five captives: a German couple and their two teenage sons, and an English-speaking woman about thirty years old, who kept calling on the Lord to deliver her. The German woman and the two boys made no sound, but their eyes were terrified. The man seemed to be pleading, but since he spoke in German, Mary Ann had no idea what he said. The captives' anguish was so apparent that she could not bear to stand by without trying to help them. She began to run toward them, crying, "Please, oh please, don't hurt them!"

She felt someone grip her arm and heard a voice that she recognized as Melakome's. The old woman was very angry. She placed her hands on Mary Ann's shoulders and shook her. In spite of her age, her grip hurt. Then she nodded to Wa-we-tah. "Take her away. She's only a paleface. She has no knowledge of our customs."

Inside the small bark hut the cries and screams of the captives were muted, but Mary Ann's vivid imagination conjured up pictures that revolted her. She felt ill and weak when at last Wa-we-tah appeared and took her back to the crowd. She saw the captives being led away: the English-speaking woman was being dragged by one arm, the other arm obviously broken, her head bleeding profusely from a deep gash; the German woman hugged her chest, her lips set in a tight line, her eyes blazing with a murderous hatred; the husband limped and moaned, his face streaming with tears. There was no sign of the teenage boys.

Melakome looked at Mary Ann with scorn; she felt contempt for a paleface who tried to interrupt a time-honored ceremony and impose the white man's foolish ideas on the proud Shawnees.

Mary Ann crept back to the hut, too shocked to partake of food. Sometime later Wa-we-tah looked in, but seeing her despondency, she slipped away.

Finally Melakome sought her out. She said nothing but her face was disdainful as she indicated Mary Ann was to resume her work. Mary Ann had never been more miserable. She realized then just how precarious her situation was; she must never again try to stop them if she wished to survive.

The following day Tawaugoa sent for her. She had not seen him since the evening of her capture and now she was afraid as she stood before him. She looked at him in astonishment, for she had never seen him without the disfiguring war paint. He was strikingly handsome and had great dignity and self-possession. His tall muscular body was clothed in an open-necked calico shirt belted at the waist with a series of large silver coins, and tight leggings of blue trade cloth trimmed with porcupine quills and tufts of deer's hair. On his chest was an ornate silver medal. Heavy silver pieces hung from his ears, and his hair had been plucked except for a strip running from forehead to nape, adorned with small shells, red feathers, and silver beads.

But it was his face that held her attention. His eyes were deep-set, slightly slanted, alive with humor and intelligence. The planes of his face were perfectly symmetrical, the cheekbones high and sloping, the nose strong, the mouth well shaped. He studied her for several minutes. Finally he asked, "Maully happy?"

She did not answer. How could she be happy after being deprived of her freedom and separated from those she loved?

"Melakome says Maully speak Shawanee," he said.

Her blood raced at the sound of the word. The Shawnees! Everyone on the frontier had heard about their cruelty and savagery. She paled and he saw that something he said had frightened her badly.

"No hurt Maully. Speak Shawanee, be happy. Maully teach Tawaugoa speak with paleface tongue?" he asked.

She nodded. Some of her fear left her.

He grinned. "Tawaugoa speak with French," he said. "No can trick Shawanees now. When Tawaugoa speak with English, no can trick Shawanees." With that he strode away, leaving her wondering about a savage who spoke French and wanted her to teach him English.

Sometime later he spoke with Melakome. "It is good for me to learn the tongue of the English. The day may come when the

French are no longer our friends. Then we must work with the English." The old woman looked at him shrewdly.

"It is well that you remember you could one day be the chief of the Shawanees," she said. "Too close contact with a paleface is not wise."

He frowned, knowing her fear that he would take Mary Ann to wife.

"You do not need to be concerned," he told her. "When the Green Corn Ceremony comes again, I shall marry my brother's widow, as is our custom. Then the year of mourning will be over."

Melakome smiled slightly to show she was pleased. "I did not believe you would forget your obligation, nephew."

Mary Ann noticed the women exchanging glances whenever Tawaugoa sent for her, and she realized they believed he was attracted to her. She wondered if he hoped to make her his wife. She was beginning to like him, but she had no intention of granting him her favors. She loved her husband, and however long it took to return to him, she would be true. She wondered why this handsome man, who was greatly esteemed, should be without a wife. She did not know enough Shawnee to ask Melakome or Wa-we-tah about it. Besides, it seemed too bold a question.

Mary Ann was awakened early one morning by the outraged cries of a newborn child. She thought at first it was Thomas, but when she looked about in the pale gray light of predawn, she realized she was still in the Indian village, lying in the old woman's hut. The baby's crying continued. Struggling to her feet, Mary Ann started off in the direction of the sound. She found Melakome bent over the figure of a woman. On a blanket nearby lay a newborn male child, its tiny fists waving helplessly, its wrinkled red face emitting shrill howls at the enormity of having to leave its safe nest.

Mary Ann acted instinctively. She bent down and picked up the child. Opening her dress, she began to nurse him. The child, secure in her arms, reacted at once. He drank his fill and then fell asleep as Melakome watched beside the dying mother. When

Mary Ann put the child down to rest on the blanket, she saw in the old woman's eyes an acceptance that she had not seen there before.

There was a sudden rattling sound from the mother, and Melakome straightened the woman's limbs and closed her eyes. Picking up a cradleboard she had propped against a tree, Melakome wrapped the child tightly in clean cloth, after putting moss between his legs to serve as a diaper, and bound him to the board. This she fastened on her back with a tumpline across her forehead. She motioned for Mary Ann to precede her back to camp.

As soon as they had reached thc cluster of huts, Melakome wakened several women and sent them off to care for the dead woman. Then, when the dawn was far advanced, she took Mary Ann and the infant to Tawaugoa, speaking to him at length. As they talked, they glanced at her from time to time.

"She meant no harm, nephew," said Melakome. "The child was hungry and she acted as any Indian mother would. She misses her own infant and has so much milk that she must get rid of it. It is very painful to have so much milk."

He was silent a moment. "It is well," he said finally, "but it will not do for her to become too attached to this child. That is the way of the palefaces. She must learn new ways."

She looked at him shrewdly. "If I decide to adopt her, she must do as the Shawanee people do, but she will be happier if we let her care for Ahotah's son until he returns from his war party."

"He will be pleased to find another son," Tawaugoa said.

Her sharp old eyes studied him. "Your brother's widow is still young enough to give you sons," she said quietly.

"When all she gave him was three daughters?" His voice was bitter.

She saw him look at Mary Ann, who was working some distance away, the cradleboard bearing Ahotah's infant propped against the wall of the hut.

"What Shawanee would want sons in whose veins flowed the blood of the enemy?" she continued. "Such children would be neither Shawanee nor paleface. They would belong nowhere."

She knew by the expression on his face that she had touched him. "Our blood is weakened every time an Indian takes a paleface wife. In time this would destroy our people as surely as famine and war destroy them." She had finished now. She had given him something to think about. She knew how much he respected her judgment.

"Then you are planning to adopt her?"

Caught off guard, Melakome hesitated. "I have not decided," she said stiffly, turning away.

She was angry with him for showing that he desired this young woman with the golden hair. It was not the custom for a Shawnee brave to show his preference. Marriages were arranged by the mother's brother. But Tawaugoa's uncles were all dead now. She did not believe he would be foolish enough to go against tradition and take a paleface to wife. She decided she would adopt Mary Ann, for then Tawaugoa could not marry her. She would be kin—his aunt's daughter. Still, Melakome did not blame him for his reluctance to wed his brother's widow. The woman was a shrew, known for her bad temper and meddling. Well, Tawaugoa would put a stop to that. He would not let her dominate his hut, that much was certain.

In the month that followed, Mary Ann found life more tolerable with the infant to care for. She would prop the cradleboard near a tree while she worked and feed the child when he cried. Looking down at his small, dark face so unlike that of her son, she marveled that caring for this hapless little creature could bring her comfort.

When the warriors were in the village, Tawaugoa would send for her and she would speak English with him; in return he taught her Shawnee. She was amazed at the speed with which he learned. He had an alert mind and a will to master the language such as she had never encountered before. As she tried to explain a certain idea, his eyes would flash with a sudden gleam of understanding as he grasped the meaning even before she had finished the explanation. She had never met anyone as smart.

When she caught him looking at her with frank admiration, she grew silent and embarrassed. Aware that this distressed her, he would immediately assume an impersonal expression, paying strict attention to the lesson. She began to find her moments with him the high point of her days. With the others she must always be on guard. She knew he looked forward to these times as eagerly as she did.

Tawaugoa told Mary Ann that the Shawnees had taken to the warpath because their friends, the Delawares, owned the lands where the palefaces had built cabins. In vain she tried to explain about the land warrant they bought; the idea was too complex for him to grasp with his marginal understanding of English. So they spoke mostly of the Shawnee customs. She learned that Melakome was not his mother but rather his mother's sister, and that the old woman, as clan matriarch, had great authority and the right to vote on matters involving the Deer people.

Of the probability of his becoming chief he did not speak, for it would have sounded boastful and vain.

Mary Ann discovered that their winter campsite was many days' journey away, in the vast wilderness known as the Ohio country. Before the deep snows of winter, he said, they would return there. She shuddered at his words.

CHAPTER V

The Harvest

It was stifling weather this August day as Yellis Enyard and his sons Silas and Ben swung their long scythes in the fields of wheat. They had been harvesting since just after sunrise and now their clothes were soaked with sweat and their throats were parched.

Silas Enyard, the older of the sons, paused to wipe a forearm across his face. He wished Pa would cut down the trees that separated their holdings from those of their neighbors, the German Stotts, whose farm lay on the far side of the east woods. It would be good to be able to see plowed fields instead of nothing but endless trees.

To his surprise, he saw his father coming toward him. It was not like Pa to stop working until the task was finished. He wondered what made him interrupt his harvesting.

As Yellis drew near, Silas saw that he looked determined. It always irked him when folks said he took after his father, for although he loved him, he did not want to be like him. Yellis was set in his ways, insisting on doing things as they had always been done, suspicious of anything new.

"I been meanin' to talk to ya alone, son," Yellis said. The resemblance between the two men was striking: both were large-boned, of medium height, sturdy in build, and had broad faces, wide-set blue eyes, and dimples in their chins. But Yellis's hair was now touched with gray and his mouth looked stubborn, whereas Silas was very fair and his lips had an engaging humorous twist.

"I reckoned it must be somethin' important to make ya stop mowin'," Silas said, smiling.

"It is important," his father said brusquely. "It's about time ya was gettin' married. You're almost twenty-two and ya should be startin' a family. Your ma and me was wed when I was nineteen. By the time I was your age, ya was born and Ben was on the way." Pa looked off at the distant woods and paused, remembering the twin boys who had died on the journey to the Pennsylvania frontier; he never spoke of them, but Silas knew he had never really gotten over their deaths.

"Well, speak up!" Pa said.

"I ain't found a girl to take my fancy," Silas said, feeling the blood mount to his face, for he never lied to his father.

"Well, now, don't know that it's so important to find one that gets ya all riled up. That passes after a while. A man needs a good, steady woman that he can count on, someone to give him sons."

Silas knew Ma had been just fifteen when Pa married her, and that her family had not wanted her to marry so young, especially when the man in question proposed to take her off to New Jersey to homestead. But the two of them had been determined, and he believed neither had regretted their decision.

"Frontierin' is hard work," Pa went on. "A man needs a strong woman to help him. It's time ya was doin' somethin' about it. The Abbot girls is good workers and they come from a respectable family. That's important, son. That Lucinda looks like a good breeder."

Silas was dismayed. It sounded like the breeding of farm stock, to hear Pa talk, and he did not agree at all that the feeling he knew to be love would pass. Further, he did not find Lucinda Abbot appealing with her sly ways. Yet if he didn't speak up, it would be just like Pa to say something to Mr. Abbot and he'd be tied for the rest of his life to a girl he did not love—or even like.

"Lucinda ain't the one for me," he said stiffly.

"Well, now, Sarah's a good worker, not as strong as Lucinda but she's got a better nature."

That was Pa, always wanting to arrange things. Silas did not often oppose him, but this was different. "When I'm ready to wed, I'll do my own choosin'!"

Pa opened his mouth to say something, then closed it. Silas

knew he didn't know what to make of his son's reaction, but he couldn't tell Pa he had fallen in love with George Eldridge's wife, Mary Ann, three years ago. She was seventeen then, a bride. She'd paid no more attention to Silas than to the Enyard's old hound dog, but he had gone on loving her just the same.

Whenever he thought about her he felt a surge of emotion. She lifted his spirit like the sight of a wheatfield in full head with the sun shining on it and a breeze waving the stalks, or like a slender white birch tree in early spring. There was no hope for it, no hope at all. But once he had committed himself, his devotion would remain.

He wondered how long he could hold out against his father. When Pa set his mind on something he wouldn't let it go. About the time you'd think he had forgotten, he would quietly bring it up again, only then he'd have a plan in mind.

It was funny that Pa should mention Lucinda, for ever since the cabin raising at McCulloughs' last year, Silas had a suspicion that his brother Ben was sweet on her. He had noticed the two of them go off to the big rock beyond the trees, and later he had seen stains on Ben's pants. Well, if anything happened between Ben and Lucinda, it was she who started it. Ben wasn't the sort to take advantage. If Pa had known, he'd have given Ben a real thrashing, for he had strict ideas about dallying with girls.

Ben, carrying a jug of cold spring water to the others, was daydreaming about Lucinda Abbot. She was never far from his thoughts since that bright June Sunday when the neighbors had gathered to raise the McCullough cabin. Robert and Annie McCullough and their five children, carrying everything they possessed on their backs, had walked all the way from the settlements. Ben was ashamed that his awkward fumbling had resulted only in a premature staining of his pants just when things seemed to be progressing, so he had improved upon fact: night after night, lying beside Silas in the loft, he explored Lucinda Abbot's provocative body in imagination. In his fantasies he was the aggressor, Lucinda his admiring victim.

When he awoke one morning, hollow-eyed, his mother had

dosed him with an herbal remedy that kept him running for two days. Loudly he protested he did not need a purge. She looked at him suspiciously but did not comment.

Now, as he approached Silas, he put his fantasies about Lucinda aside.

"Brought ya some water," he said.

Silas lifted the jug and let the cold water pour down his throat. "Pa's tryin' to persuade me to marry."

"Who'd he have in mind?"

"Lucinda."

Ben felt his face grow hot.

"Ya gettin' too much sun, Ben? Best to wear a hat like Pa does."

Ben, feeling his blush deepen, saw the laughter in Silas's eyes. "No, I ain't," he said, irritated.

"Ya kind of fancy her yourself, don't ya?" Silas asked.

Ben did not meet his eyes. "That was—that was last summer," he said, with what he hoped was dignity.

"Well, I ain't interested in her."

"What's wrong with her?" Ben asked, the ravishing creature of his fantasies beginning to obliterate the image of the girl who had tried unsuccessfully to seduce him.

"Ya know as well as I do she's kind of bold. I fancy a woman that's more modest. I want to do the choosin'—and the courtin'."

Ben's face flushed a deeper red as he remembered his excitement when Lucinda took his hand and put it inside her dress. "I'd not want to marry her," he said. He had thought about marriage. It meant babies and being tied to one woman for the rest of your life and working from sunup to sundown to provide for them. He wasn't looking forward to it.

"I'm glad ya feel that way, Ben. I was afraid she was windin' ya around her little finger."

"What did ya tell Pa?" Ben asked, to change the subject.

"I told him I'd do my own choosin' when I was ready to get married."

"Ya told Pa that?"

"Yup. I don't mean no disrespect, Ben, but a man's got to do his own choosin' about somethin' as important as marriage."

Ben had always envied his older brother, Silas. Everyone liked him. And he was independent. Ben took after Ma's side of the family, the van Wogelins of Staten Island; he had reddish hair, fair skin that freckled, and a lean, wiry body. He was a good worker—Pa always said so—and he kept his thoughts to himself. Ma said he took after Pa in his ways—once he had made up his mind, he never changed it. And he could never say he was sorry. She said this came from pride and warned, "Pride goeth before a fall."

"Ya got somebody ya fancy?" he asked.

Silas ran his fingers over a stalk of wheat, crumbling the kernels in his hands. "It's hopeless," he said quietly.

"Why's it hopeless?"

"She's—married."

Ben's mind reeled at the thought of his brother having a secret love for a married woman. That was as bad as seducing a girl who was a virgin.

"Oh, she don't know how I feel. And I don't want Pa to hear about it. He wouldn't understand."

"What will ya do about it?"

"Nothin'. There's nothin' to do. She's as fine as the Lord ever made. I—don't count on marryin'. It wouldn't be seemly to pledge myself to someone else when I love her."

"Ya mean to stay single?"

Silas nodded.

"Pa'll have somethin' to say about that," Ben said.

Yellis, in the far field, was beckoning Ben to bring the water jug now.

"I'm my own man." Silas spoke quietly, looking older than his twenty-one years.

"I wish I could stand up to him like ya do," Ben said.

Silas put a hand on his shoulder. "You're nineteen, Ben. Ya got to think for yourself. Pa means well, but he ain't always right."

* *

That night Ben realized that the woman his brother loved must be Mary Ann Eldridge. He wondered if Silas had the same lustful feelings for her as he felt for Lucinda.

"Does she—does she get you all riled up?" he asked.

"Who?" Silas rolled over.

"Ma—the woman ya were talkin' about in the fields today."

Silas was silent for so long that Ben thought he was refusing to answer. Finally he said, "It's hard to explain, Ben. I have to keep a tight hold on my feelin's and sometimes it's mighty hard. The first time I saw Mary Ann I couldn't take my eyes off her."

Ben marveled at his brother's honesty. Never would he be able to admit to feelings as Silas did.

"If I let myself think about her and George, I . . ." Silas stopped.

"I don't mean to pry," Ben said.

"I try to be thankful that she's so happy," Silas continued. "The last thing I think of before I go to sleep is her. Just seein' her in memory kind of fills me with peace."

"I ain't ever felt like that," Ben said. "Is that what bein' in love is?"

"I don't know. I suppose it's different for each of us, accordin' to our nature."

Ben was silent, wondering what it must be like to find a woman who drew forth your deepest devotion.

Silas, feeling the old ache that began whenever he thought of Mary Ann, was lost in memories. He saw her flushed face, the lovely line of cheek and chin, the shining mass of golden hair caught up in a knot, the smooth tan of her skin. He was a lucky man to have met such a woman, he told himself, for there weren't many like Mary Ann; it was wonderful to find someone he could love so completely. A feeling of peace filled him. Mary Ann's sweetness was like a promise of God's grace.

That morning the mother of the family, Else Enyard, stood in the doorway searching the deep blue sky for signs of rain. This was going to be another hot day. Early mornings in August were usually refreshing, with a breeze bearing all the mingled scents of late summer: freshly cut hay, the long grasses in the fields, sassafras, thyme, honeysuckle, and the rich, pungent odor of the earth itself. But this morning no breeze stirred the tasseled corn or waved the wheat. In the distance the heat appeared to shimmer, and cicadas made a fretful buzzing.

In spite of her thirty-eight years Else Enyard was an appealing figure, trim and fine-boned, although she had borne seven children in the twenty-three years of her marriage. Her fine white skin was lightly freckled, her face delicately lined. The hair combed smoothly back and fastened into a knot had once been red-gold but now was streaked with gray. But her expressive hazel eyes were still lovely, her mouth warm and generous.

She was making salt-rising bread when her three-year-old son, Peter, ran into the cabin, his eyes dark with excitement, his small sturdy body tense.

"Ma, Ma! I seen them!" he cried, breathing fast from running across the fields from the woods.

"Seen what?"

"Brown men with no clothes on, and—and black faces!"

"What are ya talkin' about?" she asked sharply.

"I seen them runnin' over there." He pointed to the woods.

"What was they doin'?"

He looked confused and hesitated before answering. "I dunno."

"Where was you that you seen these brown men with black faces?" Else asked, lifting his chin to give him a searching look. Peter's wide, clear eyes never wavered. She had never heard of Indians using black paint on their faces. Besides, they had no trouble with the peaceful Tuscaroras who lived in the valley. What could the boy be talking about?

Peter hung his head.

"Ain't we told ya to stay out of the woods? There's rattlers in there and sometimes bobcats."

He rubbed one bare foot against his leg as if he had an itch. "Yes, Ma."

"Where was ya when you seen them?" she asked again.

"In my—my place." He didn't want to tell her about the secret place he had found: a little cave, all dry, and hidden by fallen tree trunks and vines.

"Didn't they see ya?" she asked, suspecting he was inventing again.

"N—no, Ma."

"How come?"

" 'Cause I was hidin' in my place."

Else sent Ari to fetch Pa, who put his big hands on Peter's shoulders. "What's this your Ma tells me about ya seein' Injuns in the woods, son? Are ya tellin' some more of your tales?"

The child hung his head.

"Speak up, Peter! I left my harvestin' to come up to the cabin. Where did ya see these brown men with black faces?" His father's face was very red from the sun and shiny with sweat.

But Peter wouldn't speak.

Exasperated, Yellis turned to go back to the fields, giving the child a light slap on the buttocks. "I don't reckon it's anythin' but one of his fancies, Else. If I hear any more of this, he's going to get a good whippin'."

Later in the day Else heard Ari scolding Peter. "Peter Enyard, what ya doin' takin' all your clothes off?" Ari's light voice came from the direction of the barn.

"I ain't Peter!" the child replied. "I'm a brown man. And— and I got a black face!"

"Who ever heard of such a thing!" Ari exclaimed.

"I can run without makin' no noise." Peter sprinted up and down on his toes.

Else, broom in hand, watched him from the cabin door. His naked little body was pale in comparison with the smooth tan of his face and hands and feet. Fear made it difficult for her to breathe. She knew Peter would never have thought of such a thing unless he had seen something.

She tried to speak normally. "That's enough, Peter! Ari, fetch the soap and washrag and scrub him good. He can't track all that mud into the cabin." She sat down and tried to control herself so that she could think clearly. A moment later she went down to the field where Yellis was working.

At the sight of her white face and frightened expression, her husband exploded. "What in tarnation's goin' on, Else? Ya look like ya seen a ghost."

"He's seen somethin', Yellis, I'm certain of it."

"Get hold of yourself, Else. The boy's got a powerful imagination, that's all." He patted her shoulder to reassure her, for he knew she was thoroughly frightened.

"I reckon Peter could have been tellin' the truth," she insisted.

"Then why ain't he spoke up? He wouldn't open his mouth when I asked him."

"Well, ya always think he's lyin' and whips him for it, so now he's afraid of ya. The Stotts believed them rumors about the western tribes comin' over the mountain. They went to Fort Lyttleton last week," she continued.

"I don't take no stock in rumors," he replied. "That Gottfried Stott's afraid of his own shadow."

"Well, there must be somethin' to it. The Abbots told ya just the other day they heard folks was goin' in."

"I'll believe it when I see the Injuns, not before." He turned and went back to his mowing.

All the rest of the day Else kept Peter and Ari within the cabin, finding one pretext or another to prevent their going outside. When Ari started for the spring to bring a bucket of water, she called to her, "Leave it, child. The boys can fetch it later."

Ari paused on the doorstep, "What's wrong, Ma?"

"Nothin'. I just want ya to stay inside now. Sun's so hot ya might get sunstroke, bein' you're so fair." It wasn't much of an excuse but she was too nervous and worried to think of a better one.

"Sunstroke?" Ari asked in astonishment.

"I want ya to do some spinnin'—and tell Peter a story whilst I mix up some johnnycake." Else tried to steady her voice.

"Aw, Ma, why can't I go out and play?" the little boy asked.

"Because I—I want ya to rock the cradle so's Annibele will sleep. No grumblin', mind, or I'll speak to Pa at supper."

When Silas came in for supper three hours later, Else threw

her arms around him, holding him close, her eyes brimming with tears.

Silas laughed and kissed her cheek, saying, "What'd I do to deserve such a grand welcome?" Then seeing her tears, he grew serious. "What is it, Ma?"

Before she could explain, she heard Yellis's heavy footstep. It was no use bringing up the subject of the Indians again, she knew, for Yellis did not take it seriously.

As Else braided her hair the next morning, she looked out the window at their peaceful acres framed with woods. She saw Silas milking in the shadow of the barn and Ben carrying a bucket of water from the spring. She heard Yellis sharpening their scythes. In the cradle Annibele began to whimper, and Peter sat up in his trundle bed and gave a great yawn. Ari was not in her bed but Else heard her call to the men, "Breakfast's almost ready."

The normality of the scene gave Else some measure of reassurance. She had not slept well, for the memory of Peter's experience in the woods could not be banished. Restless and worried, she had tossed and turned for several hours until finally Yellis had put his arm around her.

"It ain't like ya to take on so, Else. Do ya think I'd take a chance if there was any danger? Now tell me."

She bit her lip to stop its trembling. "No, I s'pose not."

"Then go to sleep. There's a lot of work to do tomorrow." He turned over after kissing her forehead and was soon asleep.

At breakfast Silas leaned toward his father. "Pa, I seen the Abbots' big wagon on the edge of the woods this mornin' when I was milkin'. They was headin' for Fort Lyttleton. George Eldridge was in his wagon behind them and Mr. Abbot was on the sorrel. Johnny was driving the team. They was too far away to hail."

"That's odd," Yellis said. "Just two days ago I saw Mr. Abbot and he told me he and George didn't take too much stock in them rumors. Wonder what made them change their mind."

"Maybe it's because Maggie Abbot ain't well," Else said. "Where was Mary Ann, Silas?"

He felt a stab of fear, for he realized he hadn't seen her or

Felix. "I didn't see her. I expect her and Thomas was inside George's wagon."

"How come Felix wasn't drivin' the team?" Ben asked.

"I dunno." It did seem strange, for Felix always drove the team.

"Yellis, do ya s'pose there's somethin' goin' on that we ain't heard?" Else asked, her eyes worried. "It don't sound right, somehow."

"Oh, I suspect if there was somethin' new we'd have heard about it," Yellis replied as he stood up. "Well, we'd best get started, Silas, Ben. I'd like to get the north meadows cut today before there's a thunderstorm to flatten that wheat."

"Hadn't we best take the guns, Pa?" Silas asked.

"Might as well," his father replied, though it was plain he didn't think it was necessary.

As he picked up his scythe, powder horn, and gun, Silas bent and kissed his mother's cheek. Usually she was cheerful and happy but today she looked anxious.

"Pa's tryin' to get me to marry," he told her, smiling to take her mind off the Indians.

"Don't ya let him push ya into marryin' before you're ready," she said.

"I ain't! I told him I'd do my own pickin' when the time comes."

"Good for you!" she said, patting his cheek.

Late in the morning the Enyards' two horses broke through the split-rail fence that enclosed their pasture and dashed across the fields in the direction of the east woods. Yellis stopped his mowing and shouted to his sons, who were reaping some distance away, "Silas, Ben! Get the horses!"

The young men threw down their scythes and dashed after the runaways, forgetting their guns lying in the field. Three paths diverged in the east woods: the northernmost one led to Fort Lyttleton; Ben took the middle one, which led into deep forests; and Silas followed the south trail, said to be haunted.

Ben, following the trace to the deep woods, panted from running across the fields in the burning sun. But it was cool in the forest, and the sweat dried on his body, so that his clothes no longer clung to him. His heart began to beat normally and he breathed deeply of the cool air, laced with the scent of pines and the sour aroma of leaf mold. Here there were trees felled by lightning years before, some of them giants of fifty feet or more. Now they were slowly disintegrating, and moss and red fungi grew on their undersides.

As he went deeper into the forests without seeing any sign of the runaways, Ben felt a little chill and began to think about their neighbors' departure for the fort. He heard a twig snap and his heart began to pound as he dropped down beside a tall stand of laurel. Cautiously he peered out, his scalp prickling and his palms sweating in fear. There was no sign of any Indians and he drew a breath of relief.

Where in tarnation were those horses? He stopped and listened carefully. There were only the usual sounds of the forest: small scurryings, bird calls, leaves rustling as a squirrel scampered up a tree, the faint ripple of water over stones. It should have been peaceful, but it wasn't. When he suddenly came upon a small clearing and saw the sorrel and the gray quietly nibbling bark off a tree, he felt safer. Swinging a leg over the sorrel's broad back, Benjamin started homeward, knowing the gray would follow.

Else had managed to keep Peter inside the cabin that morning, but Ari had begged to do the churning so finally her mother had consented.

Else seated herself by the window facing the back of the springhouse, took up her spinning, and rocked the cradle gently with her foot, hoping the motion would put Annibele to sleep. Peter sprawled on the floor, making a farm of horse chestnuts.

Suddenly Else heard Ari scream, a high-pitched cry of terror that went on and on. It came from the springhouse. She saw her husband running, and when he was within two hundred yards of the cabin, she heard a shot and saw him clutch his chest. Turning slowly, he pitched forward and lay face down on the grass.

At the same time she saw five Delaware braves, their faces painted with black stripes, emerge from the springhouse, carrying guns and tomahawks. Naked brown men, like Peter said.

Suddenly she realized that the thing the leader was holding aloft, which was dripping blood, was Ari's long red hair in two braids.

Grabbing the baby from the cradle, Else picked up Peter, climbed out the back window, and made a mad dash toward the woods, intuitively choosing the east woods, with the trail to Fort Lyttleton. Had not the Delawares been engaged in scalping her husband, they might have seen her flight. At any moment she expected to be brought down by a tomahawk or a shot and to have her children killed.

Her terror lent her energy and speed. On she ran, half sobbing as she gained the shelter of the woods and followed the course of the Crooked Run. When Peter's sobs became audible, she clutched him tighter, whispering, "Hush, child! Don't make a sound!" She covered several miles in this manner before her strength ebbed and she left the trail and sought cover, sinking down in the underbrush, where thick bushes would shield them from view. The children clung to her, Peter's face smudged with tears and dust, the infant, sensing her mother's fear, wailing with long shuddering breaths. To quiet the baby, Else put her to her breast, and stroked Peter's tow-colored hair. As soon as she could speak, she told him, "Ya must be brave, Peter. Don't be afraid! Silas and Ben will find us! I know they will."

After a few moments' rest she got up and, carrying the children, started off again. But her terror was so great that she could not remember where they had left the trail. She wandered back and forth, searching with mounting panic, trying to remember some particular tree or bush that she might have passed before. Everything looked the same. She went deeper and deeper into the woods, and the trees seemed to close in upon her. She had always been fearful in the forest; she had heard some folk tell of trappers, the first white men to come to the valley eight years before, who had gone mad from living in the wilderness.

She realized the sun must be setting, for the green gloom of the woods deepened. Night was coming and she knew she had to find somewhere to hide. In the waning light Else saw a stand of towering oaks whose heavily leafed branches formed a canopy that would offer some shelter; around the roots were deep drifts of last year's leaves. She dug a hole in the leaves and covered the children, leaving only a tiny place so they could breathe.

While they slept, Else's burning eyes searched the dark for signs of an enemy. She started at every rustle overhead, her body tensed for flight. There were moments when she again heard Ari's scream, saw Yellis die, saw the Indian carrying her daughter's bloody scalp. At such times she thought she would lose all reason. In her extremity she prayed, Help me, Lord Jesus. Help me to hold on for my children's sake.

Finally through the leafy cover Else saw a delicate lightening of the shadows. She had no idea how many hours had passed since she had lost her way back to the trail. Peter awoke and began to cry, "Where's Ari? I want Ari!"

"Hush, Peter, ya must be real quiet!"

"But where is she, Ma?" he persisted.

Oh, Lord in heaven, she couldn't tell him. She struggled to find a suitable answer that would be true and yet not add to his fear. "She's with Jesus now, child. Her and Pa. . . ."

This seemed to satisfy him, for he stopped crying, his eyes full of wonder. He wanted to ask more questions but his hunger pains drove them from his mind. "Ma, I'm hungry. It hurts!" he said, holding his stomach.

Else had forgotten that they hadn't eaten anything since breakfast the day before, nor had a drop of water. Resolutely she refused to remember the sequence of events that had led them here. If she thought about it, she'd be lost. "We'll find somethin'—effen—you don't cry."

"I'm awful hungry, Ma," the little boy pleaded.

"Be a good boy while I feed sister; then we'll look for somethin'," she promised, wondering what she could find in the woods. There were wild mushrooms but she did not know which ones were poisonous; the blackberries and elderberries were gone for this season. Then she remembered that beyond the woods were fields belonging to the Stotts. Maybe there she could find something.

As soon as she had nursed Annibele, they started off. After

half an hour they emerged from the woods and came to a large field of rye. The sun shone on the tall grain, and in the deep blue sky, larks were flying. "See, Peter, we found somethin', like I said," she said softly. She stepped into the field and set Peter down so she could break off the heads of grain for him.

"It's scratchy!" he said after the first mouthful.

Then Else remembered she had to use both hands to separate the kernels, so she put the baby in Peter's arms while she removed her drawers, and then, using them for a cushion, she laid Annibele on the ground. She broke off some heads of grain and rubbed them between her palms. "It will have to do, child. There ain't nothin' else."

Peter, seeing her outwardly calm, began to lose his fear. He ate the grain without complaint and felt better. As she stripped the stalks for him, they moved slowly across the big field, unmindful of the baby, who was now some distance away from them. Finally the boy was satisfied and Else looked around for the infant, but she was nowhere in sight. She tried to remember where they had entered the field, for it was just after that that she had laid her down. With Peter clinging to her skirt, and her heart constricted with fear, she started back in the direction she thought they had come from, her eyes searching the ground.

"Where did I put her, Peter?" she asked repeatedly but the little boy could only answer, "I dunno, Ma."

She must be losing her mind, she thought in despair, for she could not recall where they left the woods. The trees seemed to blur and run together like letters written in ink with a quill pen when water is spilled on them. If only the baby would cry so she would be able to find her. . . . But the only sounds were the soft whush of birds' wings and the murmur the breeze made in the rye.

The sun grew hotter as the morning wore on. The gaunt woman with the bedraggled towheaded boy wandered back and forth, crisscrossing the field a dozen times in their fruitless search. Now Else was calling, unmindful of any that could overhear her. "Annibele, Annibele! Where be ya, child? Cry so's I can hear ya!" Peter wailed, but she was too near the breaking point to hush him.

It was the boy who saw the militia coming on horseback from the woods, lean brown frontiersmen in fringed shirts and soiled buckskins. "Look, Ma, look—soldiers!" he cried, jerking her skirt.

Then he saw Ben. "Ma, Ma, it's Ben!"

When she saw Ben, Else seemed not to know what had happened. "Ben, I can't find Annibele. I—I don't rightly know where I put her! Help me to find her, Ben!"

"Oh, Ma, when I come home with the horses and seen what happened to Pa and Ari, I thought ya was all dead!" Ben cried, holding her to him with one arm as he put his other arm around Peter. His voice was breaking but she didn't notice.

The militia, summoned by Ben the day before, had been unable to start out immediately for the Enyard farm. They had not come upon the scene of carnage until this morning, and after burying the dead, had spent hours searching for the rest of the family. They were returning to the fort when someone heard Else's cries. Now they began to fan out over the rye field, Ben carrying his mother on the sorrel and one of the rangers carrying Peter on his mount. They went over the field carefully, realizing Else Enyard was too distraught to help them.

Someone heard a feeble cry near the dense woods. Dismounting and scanning the ground closely, he discovered the infant lying where her mother had put her. She was unhurt but her tiny face was puffed and reddened from fly bites.

As Else Enyard took the frightened baby in her arms, she cried out, "Annibele, oh Annibele! Thank the Lord you're found!" She hugged the child to her breast, tears running down her face.

It was not until they passed through the stout stockade gate at Fort Lyttleton that Else remembered something she needed to ask. "Ben," she said, her eyes still haunted but with a glimmer of awareness, "where be Silas?"

"I don't know, Ma. He didn't come back."

CHAPTER VI

Fort Lyttleton

Benjamin Enyard stretched out on the ground near the stockade fence and gazed up at the night sky. It was long past sunset and most of the inhabitants of the fort were asleep. He could hear their snores from the area of the blockhouse and occasionally he heard stirrings as someone got up to relieve himself.

On the platform that encircled the inner walls four sentries paced slowly, scanning the distant woods and the ridge for signs of the Indians.

Fort Lyttleton was favorably situated at the bend of Great Aughwick Creek, which flowed northward into the Juniata River some miles distant. A rough trail led north from the massive gate and followed the course of the stream some twenty miles to Fort Shirley. To the south, winding beside the creek, was a trace leading to the Great Cove, where most of the families in the region homesteaded. Several miles below the fort, where the stream was very shallow, the trail branched off eastward toward the settlements.

On either side of the creek, save for the trail, forests encroached. Only in the area immediately surrounding the fort had the big trees been cut and the brush cleared, in a semicircle that followed the bend of the stream. On the bank immediately to the east of the stockade was a flat-topped ridge where the trees had been blasted by lightning years before, leaving a swath of open land about ten yards wide. A sentry on lookout could readily detect any movement in that area, but a thick cover of young trees and bushes obscured the base of the ridge. Southward the bend of the stream and the surrounding wilderness hid the rough track from the view of those watching from the palisade bridge.

Within the stockade was the blockhouse with its overhanging upper story, its guardhouse and captain's quarters, a parade ground, and a grove of trees surrounding a spring of water. The grounds were extensive, covering several acres.

Ben heard a fish leaping in the water of the stream, frogs croaking, the hum of mosquitoes, and the shrill sound of crickets. Occasionally one of the sentries passing nearby would say something in a low voice to another guard, but Ben couldn't distinguish his words.

He was too distraught to sleep. He couldn't believe that only yesterday Pa and Ari were still alive. So much had happened in twenty-four hours. When he had finally recovered the horses and returned to the farm, he was so shocked and terrified by what he saw that his wits had completely deserted him. Although he saw no sign of Ma or the children, he assumed they too had been killed, and without searching for them, he had ridden to Fort Lyttleton as if he were pursued. Fortunately, the second horse had followed.

He had been taken immediately to the commander, Captain McWhirter, who questioned him closely. Had he searched for those who were missing after he had discovered the bodies? He had to admit he had not. He could not explain that his fear was so great that it was impossible for him to dismount and look for them. How long did he think his father and sister had been dead, McWhirter asked. He couldn't say. Did he have any idea how long it had taken to recover the horses? About two or more hours, he said. So he believed the Indians might still be in the vicinity of the Enyard farm? He did not know, he supposed so. The captain must have thought him a poor sort of man to have given in to his fears like a boy, but he couldn't very well bury Pa and Ari all by himself. And there was the possibility of an ambush, or the horses might have run off and left him.

"The militia are out searching for two of your neighbors who were captured yesterday—George Eldridge's wife and Felix Abbot," Captain McWhirter had told Ben. "So I won't be able to send out a search party until tomorrow morning."

Ben was too shocked to grasp the significance of McWhirter's words.

"Tomorrow, as soon as it's light, you will go with the militia to your farm to bury the dead and search for your mother and the children."

Now, as he moved his body to find a more comfortable position, Ben's thoughts were in turmoil.

He would never forget the sight of Ma and Peter wandering in the Stotts' rye, crying out for Annibele. He wondered what had happened to Silas, if the Indians had found him when they left the farm. This was what Captain McWhirter believed. The militia had searched the woods surrounding the farm but there was no sign of him. He wondered what they would do to Silas if they captured him.

He was tormented by shame that he had not been more manly, by uncertainty as to how he could cope with the change in his family, but especially by the loss of his illusions about his father, whom he had admired and loved. He realized now that it was Pa's stubbornness that had brought them to this. He had failed them when they needed him most!

Turning over on his belly, he buried his head in his arms and wept. Nothing would ever be the same again.

The next day Captain McWhirter announced that he was sending a group of experienced woodsmen to range the forests for traces of the captives; a second group would be sent with a military escort to harvest the fields nearest the fort and to recover any horses or cattle left behind; the third group was to remain within the stockade to secure the fort.

George Eldridge and Ben were ordered to remain within Fort Lyttleton.

"Them savages already have more than a day's start and they know all the old trails most of us ain't even heard of. Once they get into the deep woods headin' west, we ain't got a chance of findin' Mary Ann and Felix," George said in disgust.

"Why don't ya ask the captain about it?" Ben suggested. He felt he should be searching for Silas.

George rubbed his chin in thought. "Might just do that. Ya want to come with me?"

When George and Ben found the captain studying a map of the valley, he seemed preoccupied. He had just received word from Colonel Armstrong of Fort Shirley that he was to raise additional companies of militia to join with other forces for an assault on Kittaning. McWhirter had fifteen days in which to recruit and train men for the expedition. This presented a problem, since the men who had fled with their families to Fort Lyttleton were mostly farmers with little experience in ranging the woods, and none in fighting the Indians. And there was the additional problem of secrecy.

"Beggin' your pardon, Captain, but I was wonderin' if I can join the rangers. I'm concerned about my wife," George said.

"I can understand that, Mr. Eldridge," the captain answered. "But there are forests to the west of the fort where no white man except a trapper or trader has ever set foot. To scout this territory I need experienced woodsmen who can stay out a week to ten days and survive. That's a job for the rangers. Also, I'd be derelict in my duty if I left this fort protected by only young boys and old men. We have eleven women and eighteen children who are depending on us for protection."

He turned to Ben and it was as if he read his thoughts. "Mr. Enyard, I know you feel it your duty to search for your brother. A commendable sentiment. But you are the head of your family now. Your mother and your little brother and sister need you to take care of them."

"Yes, sir," Ben said, flushing.

McWhirter strode away.

"Gol durned bastard! If it was his wife been taken by savages, he wouldn't be sittin' inside the walls, lettin' somebody else do the searchin'." George spat as if to rid himself of something too bitter to swallow.

"I guess we got to do as he says."

"Takin' orders from that lily-livered jackass!"

"Come on, George. Ain't no use gettin' yourself all worked

up. He's in charge here, so we got to do as he says."

Captain McWhirter ordered all men who were guarding the fort to assemble on the parade ground for drill. He divided them into fours and lined them up in a column, had them march four abreast, stepping briskly to the rattle of a drum. The experienced militiamen on sentry duty on the bridge glanced down with amused smiles at the farmers practicing military drill.

McWhirter bellowed at them. "I told you sentries to watch the woods! You don't have eyes in the back of your heads. The next man I see neglecting his watch will get extra guard duty!"

After that, the men in the column felt less sheepish. But it was hard work, toting their heavy long guns while marching. They had trouble keeping in step, and some laggard was always running to keep up when they turned. After two hours they showed little progress. As they broke ranks, some grumbled about it.

"Where's he get the idea we was soldiers? We ain't come here ta join the militia!" complained the trapper, Brady.

"Mebbe it's ta keep us outta trouble," suggested one.

George Eldridge, hearing them, felt the tension mount in him. "What ya got to bellyache about? Your wives ain't missin'. Think ya can run to the fort for protection, do ya, but ain't willin' to learn what to do if we're attacked!"

"Don't see what this here marching is goin' to do to help us," someone said.

The others looked at George with resentment.

"He ain't the only one who's got some kin missin'."

Ben put his hand on George's arm. "Come on. Don't let them rile ya."

Ben found his mother sitting on a low stool with Annibele on her lap, while Peter stood watching some children at play. Maggie Abbot sat nearby, her swollen legs propped on a stool.

"How are ya, Ma?"

Else's eyes were sunken and lusterless, her face drawn, and her shoulders sagged with the weight of her misery. "It don't seem real, somehow," she said.

Ben didn't know what to say to her. He wondered if they would ever have peace in the valley again or if the Indians would continue their war until finally the settlers had to give up and move back east. If that happened, Pa would rise up from his bury hole to protest.

Maggie Abbot tried to comfort Else, but Ben knew there wasn't anything to say. The only thing to do was for him to let her know he'd take care of her if it was the last thing he ever did.

One afternoon when he had an hour free of duty Ben wandered along the western side of the stockade. He caught sight of Lucinda Abbot with the Eldridge baby and realized that since the morning of Pa's and Ari's deaths he had not thought of her at all. The notions he'd had about her before seemed childish and wild. A man who was head of his family had no time for such foolishness. In the course of time he'd find someone like Ma and get married, and it wouldn't be Lucinda Abbot! Near the stand of trees that hid the spring he saw Brady, relieving himself. Ben was surprised, for he had heard Captain McWhirter order Brady to sentry duty a short time before. Brady was an ugly fellow, hairy and barrel-chested, with a rough black beard and heavy eyebrows that met across his forehead. He lived alone in a poor cabin up the Crooked Run and no one seemed to know much about him. Last spring, Ben remembered, he had boasted of killing two Tuscaroras for sport, which had outraged Pa and Silas, for those Tuscaroras had never done any of the settlers harm.

The man did not see Ben's approach; he seemed to be waiting for someone. Then as twigs snapped and footsteps made a crisp rustling among the dead leaves that covered the path, Brady stepped behind some bushes to conceal himself.

Ben saw the McCullough girl, Fiona, come through the trees carrying a heavy wooden bucket of water.

She was a slight girl, about fourteen, with stubby brown braids and a pale thin face. She reminded Ben of a frightened young animal he'd caught in a trap once; he hadn't the heart to keep it so had let it go.

Brady stepped out of the bushes, arms folded across his massive chest, and barred her way. "Now where do ya think yer a-goin' with that pail, gal? Looks like it's a mite heavy fer ya."

Fiona put down the pail and Ben could see she was scared, for she started trembling and could hardly get her words out. "I'm takin' it to my ma," she said.

"No, ya ain't! Not till ya gives me a kiss." And with that Brady grabbed the girl and began tearing at her clothes while one broad, hairy hand covered her mouth. Fiona struggled and tried to kick him, but Brady was twice her size. Without waiting to see more, Ben went into action. He caught the trapper around the neck and held him, delivering a hard punch to his belly. Brady threw off Ben's hold and looked down at him with a leer. "Why, if it ain't the redhead whose pa and sister was scalped," he said, grinning.

Fiona McCullough watched, first in terror, then admiration. Though she had seen Ben at the cabin-raising the year before, she had paid him little attention. She was suddenly aware of the grace and power of his body, of his intense white face with its light freckling and regular features, now transformed with fury. She had heard folks say red hair was a sign of a terrible temper. Well, she could believe it now as he began pounding Brady with swift hard blows to jaw, belly, groin.

The trapper was taking a lot of punishment. One eyelid began to swell and sweat poured down his face as he panted and growled. His unwashed body emitted an overpowering stench, and his big spatulate fingers sought to grab Ben and toss him to the ground. But the younger man was too quick for him. Just as the trapper tried to close in, Ben sidestepped and slipped from his grasp.

Lowering his head, Brady determined to use his heavier weight to advantage. He rushed at Ben and gave him a mighty shove that sent him sprawling.

At this Fiona began to yell. "Help, help! They're killin' each other!" Several people, hearing her cries, ran to the scene.

Ben leaped up and again closed in on Brady, hammering him with punches that finally brought him to his knees. While the onlookers watched curiously, the trapper attempted to shake the blood from his face and get up, but he could not rise. He fell and lay clutching his side, moaning, his battered face twisting in pain.

The crowd parted as Captain McWhirter and an orderly arrived. "What's going on here?" McWhirter demanded.

Ben tried to control his anger as he straightened his torn shirt and wiped his cut lip. "This man was forcin' himself on Fiona McCullough, sir." He looked at the girl. Ari, she was like Ari. She stood shamefaced and blushing, holding her torn dress together, her bare feet showing below her faded blue calico skirt, her shoulders hunched as if to ward off a blow.

McWhirter observed her closely. She reminded him of someone, he didn't know who. "Is that true?" he asked her.

"Yes, sir," she said softly. "It was Ben that saved me."

The captain turned to Brady, his eyes blazing in his ruddy face. "Get up and stand at attention!"

The trapper struggled to his feet and stood swaying before him.

"Aren't you Patrick Brady? I thought I ordered you to stand sentry duty for four hours!"

Brady shifted from one foot to another, mumbling something.

"Speak up, man! And address me properly!"

"Yes, sir." Brady's good eye shifted so that he didn't have to look at him.

"When you address me, Mr. Brady," Captain McWhirter continued, "I expect you to look at me as you are questioned! This is a military fort, erected for the protection of the settlers. While you are in here, you are under my orders and, by gad, I intend to have those orders carried out! For leaving your sentry post without permission, you will receive twenty lashes. For attempted rape, ten more." McWhirter paused. "I warn you, if ever I hear of you raising your hand against any man, woman, or child in this fort, I shall have you thrown outside the stockade."

By now the crowd was excited. Their voices rose to an angry pitch as they hurled imprecations at the trapper.

Captain McWhirter raised his voice so all could hear. "I have taken care of this matter and there will be no further action or discussion about it! Is that clear? I am in command here. If anyone among you thinks to take justice in his own hands, he may leave this fort." He paused, waiting for dissent, but the crowd was quiet.

"At sunset," he continued, "all adults over sixteen are ordered to assembly on the parade ground to witness the punishment. That is all, ladies, gentlemen. You will now go about your tasks."

* *

When the harvesters had returned and had eaten their evening meal, the inhabitants of the fort gathered on the parade ground to witness Brady's punishment. To the somber ruffle of drums the prisoner was brought in, his hands tied behind his back, his hairy body stripped to the waist. He knelt as the colonel read the charges against him.

The scene was strange and frightening. As the sun sank and the sky beyond the big trees was suffused with an orange glow, the little knot of frontier folk in their homespuns and calico stood tight-lipped and grim, their faces haunted by the terror that had been part of their lives these past weeks. Some of the more sadistic had pushed their way to the front of the crowd to enjoy the spectacle. The soldiers, in long fringed hunting shirts and worn boots, stood at attention, their faces carefully blank, on either side of the prisoner, their muskets at their shoulders.

Fiona's mother stood as far back in the shadows of the palisades as possible. Her gaunt face worked painfully, for she was embarrassed and ashamed that they had to rely on someone outside the family for protection. Her husband had been gone with the rangers and Jim had been out with the harvesters when Fiona was attacked.

Jim stood beside her. Already poverty had left its stamp upon him: his shrewd brown eyes looked like those of a man in middle age although he was only seventeen. His long bony wrists stuck out of the sleeves of his old shirt and his pants were too short, for there was no cloth to add onto them.

Captain McWhirter was on the prisoner's right, far enough away that the long whip could not touch him. As he read the charges and the punishment, his ruddy face seemed more flushed than usual, the close-set eyes looked hard as flints.

The big whip hissed through the air and then struck the trapper's back; the flesh was laid open and blood began to flow. Some of the women closed their eyes, but they could not shut out the strange animal noises Brady made, nor could they block out the stench of his fear, for the man was unable to control his bowels.

Else Enyard stood near the back of the crowd, holding on to Ben's arm. Seth Abbot and his wife and George Eldridge were with them. Each time the whip descended, Else closed her eyes. She thought of Silas and prayed that if he had been captured, he would not be tortured. She made a promise to the Almighty that she would do all that she could to relieve others' pain if He would preserve and protect her oldest son.

Ben, feeling her distress through the pressure of her fingers on his arm, was also troubled. In most matters he trusted the captain's judgment, but he suspected this public humiliation would only make Brady more vengeful. And in spite of his loathing for the trapper, he could take no pleasure in seeing his suffering.

When it was over, the crowd was shaken and silent. Ben tried to put his arm around his mother's shoulders but she ran to the fence where the shadows were deepest and he heard her retching.

"Shall I fetch ya some water, Ma?" he asked when she came back.

She shook her head. "I guess sometimes ya got to be cruel, but I don't favor havin' to watch it!"

"Me neither," Ben said thoughtfully. "And I ain't certain it'll do him good. Maybe it'll just make him more vengeful, and he'll cause worse trouble."

"Lord have mercy!" Else said.

Brady's lacerated back did not heal. Infection set in and his wounds began to fester. There was no doctor at Fort Lyttleton and no medicines.

After the trapper's groans had kept many awake in the blockhouse, the captain had a small log lean-to built, and they moved the sick man to it. An orderly assigned to look in on him reported his wounds were beginning to smell and he was often delirious.

Only Else had the courage to enter the lean-to. She was appalled by what she saw—the big man, his body drenched in sweat, his matted beard covered with spittle, lay on a hempen bag stuffed with dry leaves, which had become fouled by his excretions. Steeling herself not to gag, she rolled him gently to one side until she saw the torn, suppurating flesh.

Else went at once to the captain, her chin firm in determination, her eyes hard. "Captain McWhirter, I don't mean no disrespect but somethin' has got to be done for Patrick Brady. He's layin' there in his own dirt and out of his head with fever. His back's festerin' somethin' dreadful!"

McWhirter felt reproved. "What do you suggest?"

"I'd like to wash him and tend those sores. That man's got one foot in the grave."

"That is very commendable of you, ma'am. A true Christian act of charity."

Else's determined expression did not change. "I ain't doin' it for that, Captain. He deserved what he got. But ya need every man ya can get and a sick one ready for the bury hole ain't much use to anyone."

The captain had to admit her argument was sound. He had been concerned about how he could get enough men for the expedition against Kittaning, which was to take place in just eight days, on August 30. He could not leave the fort unprotected. Brady could be useful. "You know there are no medicines here?" he asked. He had sent a request to the Provincial Assembly for a physician and medicines but had heard nothing.

"I know that, Captain. If ya can send somebody to our cabin, there's herbs to bring down the fever and salve to take the poison out. Ben knows where I keep them."

"How far is your cabin from here?"

"About ten miles." Seeing him hesitate, she added, "I heard there's talk of a big expedition settin' out shortly for Fort Aughwick. You'll be needin' remedies when the wounded return."

McWhirter wondered how she had heard about that. He was relieved that she did not know it was Kittaning they were aiming for.

"Very well, Mrs. Enyard, I shall send two militiamen with your son to fetch them within the hour."

"Thank you, Captain."

"Thank you, Mrs. Enyard. You have solved one of my problems and lightened my mind."

As she went to find Ben, she realized for the first time that it meant exposing him to danger. No one knew when they might encounter a war party, and the possibility filled her with such dread that she considered telling the captain she couldn't let Ben go.

Then she remembered the expedition. If Captain McWhirter sent Ben to Fort Aughwick, there would be nothing she could do about it. He was a man now—the only man left in her family. He would have to assume a man's responsibility.

It was amazing how Else organized the care of Brady. She had the children stuff a clean bag with fresh leaves for a pallet; then she bathed the patient, dressed his sores with her ointment, and brewed a potion to take down the fever. Ben was proud of her. Ma was the only person in the whole fort who cared a hoot about it. The captain thought about Mrs. Enyard, too, realizing she was just the person to be in charge of the wounded when they returned from the Kittaning raid. A remarkable woman. He wished there were more like her.

As Brady began to mend, Else felt less pressured. One afternoon after she'd washed him, Else sat down on a low stool to rest her back. She realized she'd been too busy to dwell on her recent loss. Not that she ever would forget Pa or her little Ari, but she could tolerate their deaths now. And Silas—sometimes she had the notion that he was still alive and that because she was helping Brady, someone far away might help her son.

At that moment the trapper opened his eyes. She could tell by the way he looked at her that he was clear in his mind.

"Ain't ya Miz Enyard?" he asked, regarding her curiously.

"That I be," she said. "How are ya feelin', Mr. Brady?"

"Like I jist come back from the bury hole."

"Ya was mighty sick. Some folks thought ya was a goner for sure."

"Ya been a-tendin' me?"

She nodded.

The man lay silent. Never had anyone lifted a finger to help him. He thought of the flogging on the parade ground and the grim-faced onlookers who wanted him thrown out of the fort. "What made ya do it?" he asked finally.

"Well," Else said slowly, "I didn't do it because I approved of what ya done. I just don't like to see sufferin'. And we needs every man we can get to protect the fort."

His eyes searched her face as if he wanted to remember every line, every wrinkle. He didn't know how to express himself. He hadn't had much experience with respectable folk.

Else rose to go. "Now just rest easy, Mr. Brady. I'll be back with your victuals later. I'll put some water by your pallet in case you're thirsty."

He watched her as she brought the water and put it where he could reach it; then he closed his eyes.

That night Else found it difficult to sleep. The rumors that a large expedition against the Indians would take place shortly had proved to be true. A Corporal John Graves had ridden over from Fort Aughwick to recruit horses for the expedition. He had a quality Else Enyard had never before encountered in a man—a certain sweetness of spirit that was not at all womanly. She would never forget him, she told herself, listening to his quiet voice, watching his expressive eyes with their deep melancholy.

"He looks like he ain't long for this world," Annie McCullough whispered.

"What do ya mean?" she asked.

"Looks too good for it, pure-like."

Corporal Graves had spoken to the inhabitants of the fort about renting the settlers' horses. "I reckon Captain McWhirter's told you about the expedition that Colonel Armstrong's planning. We're to join forces—the men from this fort and those from Fort Shirley—with militia from as far east as Carlisle. It'll be a big expedition and we're aiming to put a stop to the Injun massacres. We'll be gone for some time—maybe a week or more—and we'll need to rent horses to carry our powder and victuals and blankets. Colonel Armstrong is willing to pay a fair price for the use of your animals."

Many questions were flung at John Graves, and he had answered courteously, never losing his patience.

Else sat up and gently withdrew her arms from the sleeping children. It was close in the blockhouse, with all the people crowded together. She opened the top button of her high-necked dress and tried to fill her lungs with air but the fetid odors of unwashed bodies offended her, for even under these conditions she managed to keep herself and her two little ones clean. Quietly she got up and went outside, where the night was fresh.

What am I to do if somethin' happens to Ben? she asked herself. I could never manage the farm without him now that Silas is missin'. It's strange how I always thought Silas was my rock. . . . Yet Ben's managed every bit as good as Silas could. I never really appreciated him before. . . . She stopped in dismay. It was me and Pa held him back, me because I was so partial to Silas and Pa because he treated him like a boy, Lord forgive us!

She wondered how she could go back to the farm when the first hard frosts came and the danger of attack was over. The memory of what had happened there filled her with such horror that she did not know how she could endure to return, where every tree, every building, would be silent reminders of those she loved.

On the palisade bridge she noticed the sentries pacing quietly, stopping when their paths met to exchange a few remarks. She recognized one as Jim McCullough, whose family had just learned that their home had been found in ruins after a Delaware attack. The moon was visible now between torn drifts of clouds, and the soft ripple of the creek outside the stockade was soothing to her frayed nerves. She breathed deeply and tried to compose her thoughts, but her mind darted ahead to her eventual return home.

She'd get Ben to cut some of the trees that separated their place from the Stotts' so that they would no longer be hemmed in. The memory of her night in those woods with the two little ones was still vivid. But it would be an impossible task for Ben alone to cut enough trees over the winter and still manage the farm. Without Pa and Silas. And she'd miss Ari with her mild sweet ways. Without realizing it, she spoke aloud, "Oh Lord, if I could see her just once again and hold her."

On the bridge one of the sentries had heard her. Now he moved closer and spoke in a low tone. "Miz Enyard, ya all right, ma'am?" It was Jim McCullough. Else nodded, unable to speak. She thought how kind he was and wondered what his family would do, with no cabin to return to. Suddenly a thought occurred to her. Why should not she and Ben offer them a home until the Indian troubles were settled and the McCulloughs could rebuild their cabin? The men could build an extra room for Robert and Annie McCullough and their two youngest. Jim could bunk with Ben, and Fiona could share her bed. It would ease the loneliness. With Jim and Robert McCullough to help him, Ben might be able to clear that woods so they could see to the Stott farm after all. Her heart gave a leap of hope. Perhaps the return would not be so unendurable as she had thought.

Slowly she retraced her steps, lifting a hand in greeting to Jim McCullough as she went back to the blockhouse. Sighing, she lay down on the pallet and straightened Annibele's small soft body, moving Peter to one side so that she could lie between them. When Silas came home, she thought dreamily, they would have use for that extra room. Sooner or later both he and Ben would marry. It would be wonderful to have grandchildren. Her face lost its tension and a slight smile curved across her lips as she drifted off to sleep.

CHAPTER VII

Silas

Silas Enyard looked around curiously. Never before had he been so deep in these woods. He whistled softly for the missing horses but there was no answering whinny. He bent down to search for hoofprints but the trees grew so close together that they effectively shut off most of the daylight.

His thoughts swung to what he had seen early that morning—the Abbots' and Eldridges' Conestoga wagons heading for the fort. There had been no sign of Mary Ann. . . . At the thought of her he felt an unaccountable anxiety. He realized he and Pa had not gone to the mill in several weeks so they had not heard the latest rumors.

It was then that he thought of his gun. Why had he forgotten to bring it? He might find a bobcat in these woods.

Through the trees Silas saw the trapper's deserted cabin, but no horses. Rumor that a trapper named Turpin had disappeared there three years before under mysterious circumstances had given rise to the idea that it was haunted.

He was tense as he approached the cabin and noticed that the door was still intact and tightly closed. His curiosity now aroused, he leaned against it with all his weight to force it open. At last it gave way and he ducked his head to enter. At first the light was so dim that he could hardly see. He managed to find his way to a small window cut high on one wall; a hide had been stretched over the opening and fastened to the wall with pegs. Grasping the hide with both hands, he pulled, and it came away in a swirl of dust and cobwebs.

Silas stared. In the subdued blue-green light that filtered through the window he saw a human skull and vertebrae hanging from the rafters by a stout leather belt. On the floor beneath lay the remains of the man's clothing. He felt the hairs on the back of his neck tingle and was suddenly chilled. The revulsion he experienced was so powerful that his impulse was to run. He forced himself to walk, not run, from the cabin.

As he went deeper into the forest, he thought of the suicide. Perhaps the man had gone mad from loneliness, or maybe he had done some terrible thing that weighed down his spirit with guilt. He tried to imagine a set of circumstances so unendurable as to cause him to take his own life.

Abruptly he put aside such thoughts as he realized that he had been gone a long time, at least several hours. Pa and Ben would be wondering what had happened to him.

As he turned, he had a sudden sensation that he was being watched and was conscious of the overpowering odor of bear. His heart pounding, he looked around for a place to hide. Then he remembered hearing that Indians covered themselves with bear's grease before starting out on a war party. Indians! Good Lord, he wouldn't have a chance, alone and without a gun!

Silently five braves in black war paint glided through the trees and surrounded him. Before he could collect his senses, one of them grabbed him by the hair and another tied his hands behind him with a deerskin thong.

He was too frightened to make a sound, even when he saw two fresh scalps fastened to a pole. He felt faint, as if the air were being squeezed from his chest so that he could barely breathe; he recognized those scalps.

Ari . . . and Pa!

His shock was so great that he was not aware at first that they were going deeper into the woods, away from the farm. When they squatted in a clearing by a brook, the braves opened leather pouches and brought out moldy biscuit and roasted groundhog. His stomach turned. The leader of the party looked at him with disdain. "Eat! Make strong! Long walk," he said in English.

Reluctantly Silas accepted the proffered meat. Seeing that they were watching him closely, he steeled himself to swallow the morsel and was rewarded by their grunts of satisfaction. He must stay alive and try to escape. He tried to concentrate all his powers on living. If Ma and Ben and the other children were still alive, they would need his help. He must pay attention to the direction from which they had come, and do nothing to arouse their suspicions or anger.

That night they slept on the ground in the mountains, the braves taking turns guarding their prisoner.

Silas could not sleep, for it was impossible to relax with his hands bound behind him. As the hours passed he relived the agonizing events of the day, asking himself over and over what he could have done to prevent Ari's and Pa's deaths. Always he arrived at the same conclusion: nothing. His sorrow was the more profound for his inability to speak of it.

It seemed that Silas had just fallen asleep when he was awakened by kicks. Struggling to his feet with his hands still tied behind him, he saw that they would not partake of food at this time. The pain in his wrists had become almost unbearable, for the thong cut into his flesh and impeded the circulation. He was determined not to ask for relief; he would show them he could bear pain without flinching.

When their ascent became so steep that they needed to reach out for purchase, one of the braves came toward him with a hunting knife. Silas paled but the man merely cut the thongs to free his hands. The relief of having the blood flow freely to his hands was so great he felt like weeping, but he made no sound, only tried to keep pace with the two braves who preceded him.

That night they made a small fire and dried the scalps over it, scraping off the congealed blood. Silas, his hands bound again, turned his head aside, revolted.

After drying the scalps, they began to roast some chipmunks over the fire, and it was all Silas could do to keep the bile from rising in his throat. The leader offered him the meat, but Silas shook his head. "I ain't hungry." The man seemed to understand, for when one of the others began to insist that he should eat, he pushed the brave's hand away and said something that sounded like a rebuke. They let him alone then.

Silas's sufferings were so great that he began to lose his sense of time. The days flowed into each other, each taking him farther from those he loved, from everything that he knew. The determination to return to his family was all that kept him alive.

After several days they did not bind Silas's wrists, for the broken skin had begun to fester. His sores were very painful and the long forced march over the mountains was taking its toll of his strength.

Finally, one afternoon, the braves gave several piercing cries. Silas searched their faces for some indication as to what this meant. The leader spoke to him. "We go Delaware village. Loyalhannon."

The quiet was shattered by the firing of guns. When his captors showed no fear, Silas realized this was a welcome from the camp at Loyalhannon, and several minutes later they came to a clearing on the banks of a creek. Smoke rose from many cook fires and on the steep banks a large crowd awaited them. Beyond them Silas noticed a cluster of huts made of bark and hides stretched over poles.

There was a cleared place in the center of the encampment, where two rows of braves armed with heavy clubs faced each other, forming a kind of runway. He hesitated, but the leader pushed him forward and before he could gather his energy their blows fell upon him. He tried to dodge their clubs, to ward them off, but he was too exhausted. He stumbled and fell, unable to rise as the women pelted him with sand and the braves beat him into insensibility.

Silas did not know how long he had remained unconscious when he opened his eyes to find himself lying beneath a huge sycamore near one of the bark huts. His body ached so that he could scarcely move and his raw wounds smarted from the sand thrown at him. He tried to lift his hand to rub his burning eyes, but the effort was too much. He drifted off into a semiconscious state in which it seemed he was pursued by devils holding aloft Ari's red braids and Pa's gray hair.

After a time he felt a sensation of something cool and soothing on his wrists, and he opened his eyes to see a young Indian woman applying compresses of moss and herbs. He tried to ask where he was but was too weak to speak. She held out a gourd filled with a strange-smelling liquid and he took a few sips, wincing as the hot liquid touched his mouth. The girl sat on her heels, waiting patiently for him to continue. She was a slight creature, the bones of her cheeks forming deep hollows, her eyes enormous in a thin face.

Because of his sore lips, he took his time in drinking, and when he had finished, a great lassitude swept over him. His bruised body felt numb and curiously heavy, his eyes weighted, so that he could not keep them open. He made several attempts to ask her what was happening, but the girl put a finger on his lips.

The last thing he remembered clearly was seeing her standing in a ray of sunlight looking down at him. On her forehead was the tattoo of a small red turtle and her eyelids were stained with red. With her slight frame and small delicate bones, she looked frail, he thought, not at all the way he expected Indian women to look.

When Silas awoke again, his first thought was of escape. As soon as he felt strong, he must find some way to leave this camp called Loyalhannon and make his way back to the Juniata Valley to find his family. For that he would need a weapon.

Silas looked about with curiosity.

The interior of the hut into which they had carried him was circular, with a hard-packed dirt floor and platforms of tree limbs covered with skins of animals. Pottery bowls, blackened from many cook fires, and stone and wooden utensils were stored neatly under the platforms. In the center was a shallow pit with a smoke hole in the roof above it. A pole was stretched across the top of the domed roof, from which hung ears of dried corn, strips of dried pumpkin, clumps of roots used in cooking and in medicines, tobacco leaves, red cedar, and fragrant herbs. He wondered where they kept their knives and guns.

He was three days recuperating from his ordeal. When he finally got up, he found the sores on his wrists and his other wounds were nearly healed. Emerging from the wigwam into the bright August sunlight, he looked about him.

On either side of the banks of the little stream, arranged haphazardly, stood the Delawares' huts, some round, some oblong with arched roofs, others with pitched roofs. Skins of animals hung before the apertures that served as doors. In front of each wigwam was a fire pit for cooking, and to one side were silo-shaped holes dug out of the earth. He saw several women remove the bark lids from them and put in corn and nuts. An elderly woman was carefully skinning a rabbit and he watched to see where she put the knife, but before she laid it aside, the leader of the party that captured him came up to him.

Smiling, he thumped Silas on the chest and exclaimed in English. "No sick now. Paleface go sweat house. Make strong!" He began to propel him toward a small lodge on the bank of the creek, where a fire burned cheerily in a deep round pit. He motioned for Silas to remove his clothes, then left him alone.

A few minutes later the brave returned with several young men, carrying hot stones, which they piled around the interior. When they poured water on the stones the room filled with steam and sweat rolled down Silas's body until he felt weak and exhausted. This process was repeated several times before the leader pushed him out the door naked, pointing to the stream. Silas glanced about quickly, aware that there were women working nearby. But no one paid him any attention. As he slid down the mossy bank into the cold water he knew a moment of exquisite pleasure. He began to rub himself briskly and when he emerged some minutes later, he felt clean and wonderfully alive.

"Paleface like?"

Silas nodded, noticing the small tattoo of a wolf on the man's forehead and another on his chin. He was about Silas's height, large-muscled and trim. He wore a soft deerskin breechclout and a necklace of bear claws and small shells; on his arms were silver bands. Without the disfiguring war paint, his face was strong and good-natured, the eyes intelligent. He smiled. "Katoochquay." He thumped himself on the chest, repeating the name several times.

When Silas pointed to him and uttered "Katoochquay," he laughed. "Friends now. Delawares good to friends. Make paleface blood brother."

Never had it occurred to Silas that they might adopt him. He had heard from those who had traded with the Indians that this was a great honor, not lightly bestowed. He was not aware that the silence with which he had borne his sufferings was interpreted by his captors as courage of the highest sort.

The following day several braves led him to a spot where an ancient white oak and a black oak grew side by side. They plucked out his blond hair, leaving a scalplock, which they wrapped with a beaded garter and trimmed with small silver brooches. One of the older women bored small holes in his ear lobes and in the cartilage at the base of his nose, then inserted a small silver ring in his nose and large silver hoops in his ears. Now the men stripped him of the breechclout he had been given. The women and girls watched curiously, to his intense embarrassment, for never before had he been naked in the presence of the opposite sex. He blushed furiously as the men painted his body with red, brown, blue, and black designs, symbolizing that he was a member of the Wolf clan. The chief placed a belt of wampum about his neck and broad silver bracelets on his right arm. The braves began a song, dancing around him in widening circles as the spectators joined in. Silas, red-faced and grim, looked straight ahead as they led him to the council house, where he was clothed in a white ruffled shirt and blue fustian breeches; garters trimmed with porcupine quills, red hair, and beadwork; and a pair of fine moccasins. To his scalplock they tied red feathers. The humor of his appearance struck him and he wanted to laugh but knew it would be unseemly.

As the chief, Asallecoa, bestowed his Delaware name on him, he thumped Silas on the chest, repeating "Scoouwa" several times. Silas felt a moment of elation, followed by uncertainty about how he could adjust to this new life.

The chief's solemn expression did not alter but in his deep-set eyes there was a gleam of approval.

A feast followed to honor their new blood brother: deer meat with bear's oil and maple sugar, cakes made of cornmeal, baked in the ashes, and boiled beans, fresh fish, corn, squash. Silas was seated between Asallecoa and the leader of the party that captured him, Katoochquay. He ate heartily at first, for the strain and excitement had whetted his appetite. Then a memory surfaced: it was these braves who had killed his father and his sister. Abruptly his hunger left him. He sat among his blood brothers, helplessly confused and tormented, unable to reconcile the knowledge of their cruelty with their new kindness to him.

That night he slept alone in the bark hut next to Katoochquay's wigwam. He was tired from the excitement of the day and fell into a troubled sleep, dreaming that Mary Ann Eldridge stood before him, her long golden hair tumbled about her shoulders, her dress torn and stained with mud. She regarded him sadly, her eyes luminous and frightened. "Help me, Silas!" she cried.

"Where are you?" he asked in his dream.

"Far from home, among the Injuns." Before he could reassure her, she knelt beside his pallet and pushed aside his breechclout, touching him knowingly. He was amazed at her boldness. He heard a soft laugh and awoke from the dream to find the Delaware girl who had cared for him lying beside him. Her small breasts were bare as she pressed close. Her breath smelled of wild mint.

Thoroughly awake now and responding to overwhelming new sensations, he began to discover the excitement of knowing her intimately. She was no longer a Delaware girl whom he had recently encountered; she was a woman—warm, yielding, deeply stirring. When it was over, Silas felt a surge of power he had never before known.

When he awoke the next morning, she was gone. He saw the brave Katoochquay emerge from his wigwam, yawning and stretching. At the sight of Silas, his face wore a broad grin. "Scoouwa blood brother now. Need Delaware woman."

Silas flushed and looked away.

"Scoouwa like?" Katoochquay asked.

He nodded, embarrassed to be questioned about such a private matter.

"Scoouwa want other woman?"

"No." Silas said firmly. "I don't want no one else. She's just fine. . . . What's her name?"

Katoochquay laughed. "So Scoouwa like Ouana? Good! Ouana make good wife. Speak English, too."

Silas stared. He had only been here a short time and already he was married! First they had beaten him senseless and then had sent a gentle young woman to tend his hurts, and had adopted him into the tribe. And now, although there had been no ceremony, he was supposed to be this girl's husband!

Late in the evening when the cooking fires were only dying embers, Ouana led him to the little brook. Pulling him into the cold water, she bathed him carefully, her long graceful fingers lingering on his body. When he emerged from the water, tingling with the cold, he felt a powerful desire for her, for the sensuous pleasure of touching her small pointed breasts and slim hips, of exploring her fragile body.

He felt light, weightless, as he looked down at the girl sleeping so trustingly within the circle of his arms. He noted the rise and fall of her shallow breathing, the dark bronze skin stretched taut over cheekbones and high-bridged nose, the deep-set eyes closed now, the rich canopy of her hair. She was not beautiful by any standard known to him, and yet her very strangeness, coupled with her gentleness, tied him to her. She looked delicate, young, and defenseless. It was this vulnerability more than any other quality that attracted and held him.

As time went on, he wondered if they had given her to him to ensure that he would not try to escape, for he was growing more fond of her each day. It would be painful to give her up. And yet he knew he did not love her as he did Mary Ann.

In time Silas told her about his family, omitting only the part about the killing of Pa and Ari.

"What of the little sister, she of the red hair?" Ouana asked him.

"What about her?"

"Where is she now?"

He was silent for so long that she knew the question distressed him. "She's dead," he said softly. "Her and Pa died the day I was captured."

"Katoochquay and our braves?"

He nodded, the memory of it lying like a stone within him. She made no comment but began to prepare a food he especially liked. When she saw he could not eat, she put aside her own gourd and fasted also, sitting beside him in the twilight, her face thoughtful.

Silas did not want to be with her that night. He went outside and sat near one of the campfires to let her know he needed to be alone. No one questioned him or tried to draw him from his thoughts, for which he was grateful.

As one by one the fires died and the dogs slunk off to sleep, the camp grew quiet. Only the distant stars burned in the great arch of the heavens. Silas asked himself how he could live in friendship with those who had murdered his father and his sister, accepting the favors of one of their women. It was against nature.

And yet he could not view them the way most settlers did—as savages—for he had found the Delawares intelligent, practical, and honest. They had great courage and stoicism, qualities he admired. They shared the gifts of the earth freely with each other: all land that they claimed was tribally owned and respected as such. Each tree, each rock and stream had a spirit that was recognized. Because they saw the life-force that permeated all things and looked upon all animals as brothers, they took only what they needed to sustain life.

For those who broke their ancient taboos the punishment was swift and inexorable, but it was the same for all. There was no such thing as one going free or being given a lighter punishment because he was kin to a chief. Their justice, Silas decided, was like nature itself.

To those who earned their respect they were kind; to those who had cheated and deceived them, extremely cruel. And if their patience and goodwill were exploited long enough, they moved swiftly and with fierce vengeance to exterminate all who had wronged them. When this happened, even the innocent perished.

He thought of his people, the settlers whose hunger for land and independence had brought them to the wilderness. He saw with clear vision that they would never be driven out. As more and more journeyed west, they would outnumber the Indians. The changes brought by the settlers threatened the Indians' ancient customs, their respect for the graves of their ancestors. Silas began to look upon them as people lost in a dream of the past that could not endure. It filled him with sadness.

He rose and stretched, feeling stiff from the evening dews. No, he could not hate them. He could only grieve that such enmity should exist between Ouana's people and his.

Silas knew he must somehow leave there and find his way back to the farm. He would need a weapon, to protect himself from wild animals and to provide food on his long journey home. But not to kill his friends.

After Silas's adoption eight of the braves prepared to set out on a war party to bring back captives and plunder. These raids were always spontaneously initiated by the war captains in individual villages, for there was no concerted Delaware strategy. The tribe was too scattered for that. All night the braves fasted and stayed apart from the women lest they lose their courage.

A great bonfire roared, sending its smoke billowing upward, while the warriors stood in a circle about the fire, their faces and torsos painted with grotesque designs. Each man carried his tomahawk, war club, or spear. To the chant of "He-uh, he-uh" they moved in concert eastward, for it was in that direction they would go to make war.

Silas saw the face of his friend Katoochquay contorted with a fierce ecstasy, so changed as to be almost unrecognizable. Silas realized that to these people, making war on their tribe's enemies was a sacred obligation to protect and preserve the ways of their fathers. This was quite different from the attitude of the king's soldiers, who went into the army for pay or glory or adventure. Or to escape their debts.

After eight days, the warriors returned, giving the scalp halloo seven times as they approached the camp. Silas knew this meant they were bringing back seven scalps. Ouana saw that he was tense as the braves assembled for the gauntlet. As a Delaware, Scoouwa would be expected to watch.

The sun was declining, trailing long scarves of rose and apricot across the sky, when the warriors appeared, bringing three men, two young boys, and a little girl. The children were very frightened, their faces smudged with tears and dirt, their clothing showing marks of their hard journey. Several of the women began to lead them to the far end of the camp where they would not see the men prisoners run the gauntlet. But as they were hurried away, the little girl broke loose and ran toward one of the men captives. Before they could stop her, she grasped the man about the waist, sobbing, "I ain't gonna leave Pa! Please, please don't hurt him!"

Something in the child's gesture touched Silas. It was the sort of thing Ari would have done. Ouana went to her and pulled her hands away gently but firmly. "Come!" She spoke in English. Taking the child by the hand, she led her away. Several times the little girl looked back to see what was happening to her father.

In the excitement Silas managed to slip away unnoticed and follow the women and children. At his approach the children looked up, astonished to see a white man in such strange clothing, wearing a scalplock, nose ring, and ear hoops.

Silas stooped down and put his arms about the little girl. "Don't be afraid. They won't hurt ya. They likes children."

She stopped crying and regarded him with curiosity. One of the boys asked, "Ain't you a white man?"

He smiled, "I'm a captive, too."

"What will they do to Pa and the others?" asked the boy.

"It depends." Silas said. "It's their way of testin' a person's courage and strength. If they thinks you're a coward, they can be cruel. But if ya don't cry out and takes your punishment, they respects ya."

Their interest aroused now, the boys moved closer. "Did they torture ya?" one asked.

Silas hesitated. "I fainted before it was over so I don't rightly know what they done," he said. "Afterward they was real kind."

They heard a piercing scream and their faces paled. Instinctively all three clung to him, the little girl sobbing now.

"I think your pa will be real upset by your takin' on so. I

reckon he's a brave man, and he expects all of ya to be brave." He lifted the child in his arms. "What's your name?"

She didn't answer, burying her head on his shoulder and clasping her arms about his neck.

"This is my wife. Her name is Ouana." He had her attention now. The little girl lifted her tear-streaked face and stared.

Ouana put her hand on Silas's shoulder, her chin lifted in pride.

"How'd ya learn to speak Injun?" the smaller boy asked.

"Ouana taught me. . . . Now tell me what you're called."

"I'm John Southall and this here's my brother Ned and she's my sister Katy."

"And the rest of your family?"

"Ma and the baby was visitin' with a neighbor when the Injuns come. They didn't find her and Martha."

The second boy spoke up. "Paul Hollingsworth was just visitin' with Pa and Mr. Hoge—he's a blacksmith—was shoein' our horse when the Injuns come."

"I see. . . . Ya must have had a long journey over the mountains. Ouana can get ya somethin' to eat."

"I ain't hungry," said the taller boy.

"Me neither."

Katy looked up at Silas shyly. "What's your name?"

"Silas Enyard is my real name but the Delawares gave me a new one when they adopted me—Scoouwa."

"S—coo—u—wa?"

"That's right. You'd best call me that."

Ouana spoke. "Leave them with me. You must join the others or you will be missed." Silas did not want to leave the children, but he knew Ouana was right.

The children watched as he strode away. Ouana put her hand on Katy's head and smiled at them. Reassured, they followed her to a distant part of the camp.

Of the three men who had run the gauntlet, only one, Paul Hollingsworth, escaped with minor bruises. The blacksmith, Hoge, had received a head injury that left him with severe headaches and blurred vision. Southall suffered a broken leg. He was surprised when the medicine man set it neatly and bound it to splints carved from hardwood. After that he hobbled about, torn between his outrage at his capture and a reluctant admiration for the medicine man's skill.

Ouana told Silas the men were to be held for ransom; they were not worthy of adoption. She watched his face to discover the effect her words had. But he was learning to hide his emotions, as the Delawares were accustomed to do. He did not reply.

The men were given work to do and were allowed to move about the camp; they were not ill treated. Silas spoke to the one with the broken leg. "Morning to ya, Mr. Southall. I'm Silas Enyard from over to the Great Cove. I was captured at harvest-time. They made me a blood brother."

"I was wonderin' about ya."

"Ya got some fine children, Mr. Southall. I reckon you're concerned about them."

"Don't get to see much of them, they keep us apart." The man's eyes were hard, his mouth bitter.

"I want to tell ya they're bein' well treated. They won't come to harm."

"You mean, they're adoptin' them?"

Silas nodded.

The man's eyes narrowed in anger. "Why, them dirty thievin' savages! It ain't enough to capture us, they're tryin' to steal my children from me now!"

"But they won't hurt them! It's better than havin' them killed, ain't it?"

"I'd rather see them killed than bein' raised as Injuns."

Silas's jaw tightened. "I can feel for ya, Mr. Southall," he ventured.

"What'd ya know about it?"

"They killed my pa and my sister," Silas said, swallowing hard to ease the lump in his throat. His face was suddenly drawn tight in lines of grief.

The man's expression changed to curiosity. "Then how in Tophet can ya live with a squaw? And how could ya let them adopt ya? Ain't ya got no feelin's for your family?"

Silas looked troubled. "The blame's not all on their side, Mr.

Southall, whatever ya think. The Penns in Philadelphia tricked the Injuns into sellin' more land than they intended, and now they're losin' their huntin' because of the settlers movin' in and cuttin' down the trees. I ain't condonin' what they done to us, but the companies that sold us our land wasn't fair with them neither."

"Your talkin' like you're on their side."

"I'm just tryin' to be fair."

Southall turned away, muttering something about turncoats.

Ouana was teaching Katy Southall to weave reeds into a basket. The little girl was delighted and soon became attached to her. She begged to be allowed to skin squirrels, which required great care lest the knife slip and damage the pelt.

It was then Silas resolved to appropriate Katy's knife. He knew he would have to approach her cautiously, for already her loyalty was shifting to the Delawares. "Katy," he said to her, "can I borrow that huntin' knife ya use to skin squirrels? I got me a fat turkey yesterday and I want to cut it up for dryin' for winter."

"But that's Ouana's work, ain't it?"

"Well, she's plenty busy right now. Thought I'd give her a hand. . . ."

"Sure, Scoouwa." She handed him the knife.

He tucked the knife inside his shirt, looking about to see if he was observed, but no one was watching him.

Shortly after sundown it was discovered that Paul Hollingsworth was missing. A search party started out before the moon rose. Silas's fear grew as he thought of the knife he had hidden.

Ouana lay beside him, unable to sleep, aware of his anxiety.

"What'll they do to him if they find him?" he asked her.

"He'll get what he deserves."

He turned to look at her in a shaft of moonlight that fell through the smoke hole.

"You mean . . . ?"

"They'll kill him," she said matter-of-factly.

He felt sick, unable to assimilate the fact that this gentle girl could speak of such a thing without horror. "But it's natural for him to want to escape, to return to his kin."

"That is the paleface way. Our ways are different," she said, ending the conversation.

When the braves returned with Paul Hollingsworth he was more dead than alive. He was tied to a pole in the center of the camp and a fire was built around him. Silas, knowing he was expected to watch the torture, developed a running of the bowels so that he was unable to leave the hut. Ouana stayed with him.

As they listened to the screams of the dying man, she took Katy's knife from his leggings. "Did you think I would not find it, Scoouwa?"

He did not answer, too shocked by what was happening to Hollingsworth to think clearly.

"Would you have killed your blood brothers to escape?" Her voice held a vast contempt.

"I couldn't do that, Ouana! But I got a duty to my family. They need me."

"Our braves would not let you go willingly, you know."

He put his head in his hands. "They don't even know if I'm alive—or dead," he said, referring to his family.

"Tomorrow," she said without looking at him, "you will return the knife to Katy." She knew he would not attempt to escape now that he knew what was happening to Paul Hollingsworth.

CHAPTER VIII

Kittaning

As the early morning mists swirled around them, the long twisting column of men and horses, insubstantial as a dream, moved silently through the forest. At times only the men's heads were visible, floating disembodied above the fog, which was now dense, now thin enough to reveal shoulders in butternut brown or gray that blended with the browns and grays of the giant tree trunks. Occasionally a pale ray of dawn light filtered through the leafy ceiling, catching the brilliant red of a cardinal's wing or the rich dark sheen of a crow's feathers. Some of the men looked up, amazed to see such frail beauty in the menacing green gloom of the forest. Most of them did not raise their eyes from the trail. It was very rough in places and they had to keep a sharp watch.

They traveled single file, since the old Indian trace was only wide enough for one pack horse to pass. Dense underbrush and tall trees grew on either side, so that most of the area immediately beyond the path was almost impenetrable.

There were three hundred men under Colonel John Armstrong's command, representing seven companies: one from Fort Lyttleton, two from Fort George, two from McDowell's Mill, the colonel's own company, and one other from Fort Shirley. The older men and the weaklings had been left behind to garrison the forts.

A tall, gaunt man leading a lively and well-groomed mare was conspicuous among the militia from Fort Shirley. John Graves had changed in appearance since the capture of his wife and child: he had lost so much weight that his clothes hung on him, his eyes were underlined with dark shadows, his well-shaped mouth was grim.

Although the men in his company believed the settlers who had been captured after the burning of Bigham's blockhouse had been taken on to Fort Duquesne, John Graves clung to the forlorn hope that they might have been taken to Kittaning and could still be there. "If I find them, I'm taking them to the settlements," he told some of the militia.

"Ya mean you'd give up your *land* after all your work?"

"My land doesn't mean anything without my family. It's more important to me to have them safe."

To the rear of the long column of men was Patrick Brady. He was surprised that Captain McWhirter had selected him to accompany the militia, for only the strong and able were chosen. Brady did not suspect that it was McWhirter's lack of trust that made him decide to send him on the expedition. He was proud to be chosen, although his old fear of physical suffering surfaced. He could not face the immediate future with calmness as George Eldridge and Benjamin Enyard appeared to do. He was terrified of being tortured by the Indians and he wondered what he would do if the fighting was heavy and he was face to face with the Delawares.

Among the men leading horses in the forward companies was Ben Enyard, marching behind George Eldridge. He too was troubled by doubts as to how he would conduct himself under fire, but he tried to imitate the behavior of the experienced militia, whose boldness and courage he admired. He was resolved to conduct himself in a manner that would make Ma proud.

He thought often of Silas and wondered what had happened to him. Was he still alive? Would he ever return? Ben imagined his own death and Silas coming back to hear from Ma how he had died a hero in the raid on Kittaning. Just then Ben's horse stumbled over a large root and only his quick reaction prevented the animal from falling. He must stop his woolgathering. Time for that later. If there was a later time.

George Eldridge's thoughts were of his son, Thomas. He wondered what would happen to the child if he was killed and Mary Ann never returned. He wished he had made arrangements with the Abbots. They were fond of the baby and Lucinda was devoted to caring for him. Perhaps, if the Indians ever ceased their depredations, the Abbots would find a way to take Thomas to Mary Ann's family.

He thought of the other possibility—if he survived, how would he manage when he returned to the farm with an infant and no woman about the place? It was too bad Lucinda couldn't look after things until Mary Ann was found, but it wouldn't do for a young woman of marriageable age to share his cabin. Besides, he had noticed how she looked at him at times, as if she were inviting him to bed her. He had no desire to, for he loved his wife and always would. Without Mary Ann he had no future.

Jim McCullough and his father were marching with the men from Fort Lyttleton. They had made sure they were nowhere near Brady, for in spite of his apparent reform, both bore the trapper a deep resentment that bordered on hatred. Fiona had not been injured, but the memory of what Brady had tried to do could not be banished. Maybe now that there would be a big battle with the Delaware, he would get what he deserved.

Four days after the expedition had set out from Fort Shirley, a scouting party that Colonel Armstrong had sent on ahead reported finding the tracks of two Indians. From the freshness of the tracks and of the evidence that the braves had roasted a bear cub, they were not twenty-four hours ahead of the first companies of militia, the scouts said.

Armstrong decided to make camp then, for it was late in the day and the light was beginning to fade. He wanted his men to be fresh and unwearied for the assault on Kittaning, so he posted sentries and ordered the men to rest until dawn.

Early the next morning as the shadows paled, they broke camp and resumed their march to Kittaning. As the forward companies started out, the men tried to get their bearings in the dim light. The trace wound around large rocks and fallen trees, so that the men had to be careful not to lose sight of the column moving up ahead toward the west.

Colonel Armstrong sent an experienced officer, one of his best scouts, and two soldiers to observe the stronghold of Kittaning and bring him intelligence of the enemy's position. The men could see that he was troubled, for his answers that day were brief to the point of curtness. He was worried about the possibility of an ambush, which would be disastrous, with his men strung out single file, surrounded by dense forests where the Indians could pick them off one at a time. There would be no way the columns before or behind could come to the aid of those who were attacked. And he was deeply concerned about the inexperience of most of his troops. The settlers who had been pressed into service knew little about fighting, and many deeply resented having to participate in this expedition. He was certain some would slip away at the first sign of an attack.

That night as the troops stretched out on the ground, wrapping their blankets tightly about them to protect them from the woods' damp chill, Armstrong sensed their morale was low. They said little—a sure sign of dejection—and each man huddled into himself. Usually they swapped stories, bragged about their exploits. Was it because they were afraid? Yet he knew fear could be transformed into courage of the highest kind.

While they were chewing their dried corn and hardtack the following morning, a current of excitement passed down the long line. The scouting party had returned. The men waited in anxious silence for word to be passed to them of what the scouts had discovered.

"Well, gentlemen?"

The officer, a stolid Scotsman with a pockmarked face, saluted and assumed an air of self-confidence. "Nothing to fear, Colonel. The trail was clear all the way. We dinna meet no one."

Armstrong gave him a penetrating look. "Sergeant MacPherson, you've given me only part of the information I sent you for."

MacPherson's ruddy face darkened. "Sir?"

"What of the strength of the Delawares in the village? Have you no idea how many braves there are at Kittaning?"

The officer could not meet the colonel's eyes. "No, sir," he said stiffly.

"What of the village? Draw me a map, pray, of the disposition of the dwellings." Armstrong seized a long thin branch lying on the ground and gave it to MacPherson.

The sergeant cleared his throat and scraped away the forest debris to form a clear space on the ground. He began to draw a rough map. "Here is where we be now, sir, and this is the way the trail lies. We stopped here, just before this hill and then started back," he said in some embarrassment.

"But the purpose of your mission was to discover the lay of the village, its houses, and outlying cornfields so that my staff would know best how to plan our attack!"

MacPherson looked at his boots.

Armstrong bit his lower lip. Good Lord, they had no information on which to base a plan of attack! It would be sheer folly to continue when they had no idea of the number of Indians in the town and no knowledge of the layout of Kittaning. MacPherson's negligence could cost them dearly. "Well, there is nothing for it but to proceed," he said resignedly. "Let us be on our way!"

So they continued their march in order to reach the woods near Kittaning that night. They would attack at daybreak.

Ben Enyard and George Eldridge were startled when about nine o'clock that evening one of the advance scouts rushed up to Colonel Armstrong with new intelligence. "Colonel, I seen a fire beside the trace about one hundred perches* from out front."

"How many of the enemy were there, Meeks?"

"Three Injuns was all I seen."

"Order the scouts to retreat here at once as quietly as possible." Armstrong knew if his advance party was discovered, the Indians about the campfire would alert the village and his men would be ambushed or routed. There was no telling if green troops would make a stand and fight. He turned to Lieutenant Hogg. "Take twelve men and a scout and follow Meeks with all caution. I want you to observe the enemy by that campfire, but

* A perch is a linear measure equal to 5½ yards.

under no circumstances should you attack until dawn. Then try to cut them off. Leave the horses."

"Yes, sir."

As the lieutenant and his party followed Meeks into the woods, Armstrong conferred with his other officers on the best plan of attack.

Captain McWhirter spoke up. "It appears we'll have to leave the trail, sir, in order to avoid discovery by those savages by the campfire."

"It will mean a delay of several hours," Armstrong said.

"We can make a wide detour over the hills and across the valleys. It seems the only safe course," McWhirter answered.

"If we had accurate information about the lay of the village, we could plan in detail. . . . All we know is that Kittaning is spread out on both sides of the Allegheny, with huts strung out along the cornfields. We have no idea how many Indians are there now, nor even how many huts. We shall just have to take a chance."

When the advance troops reached the Allegheny River about five hundred yards from the village, they heard the beat of Indian drums, the whoops of warriors, and the pounding of many feet, stomping out the rhythm of a dance.

Ben felt his heart beating fast at the sound. This was what he came for, he told himself—to search out and punish the savages who had killed his father and his sister and stolen his brother.

Now that the moon was high above the trees, Armstrong could see the Delaware village clearly from the hill where his advance troops lay hidden. Immediately below them in the valley was a cornfield, and beyond, a scattering of bark huts. Opposite the hill on which he stood, a small eminence with more bark houses rose about forty feet above the valley. This was known as the upper town, Armstrong had been told. There a large, two-story building with loopholes stood, dominating the others. This was the home of the Delaware chief, Captain Jacobs. Beyond the low hill were more cornfields and then the Allegheny River, its smooth dark surface catching the moonlight. There were other cultivated areas on the west side of the river, and a few huts, which were still in deep shadow, so that it was impossible to determine their number. The colonel decided there were possibly thirty dwellings in all, although some of the buildings might be storage sheds.

Armstrong ordered the troops to lie quiet and wait until the last three companies arrived. Ben found it hard to keep absolutely still when every muscle was tensed for action. His left leg was becoming numb and he longed to get up and move about to keep his blood moving. Waiting was worse than fighting, because you had time to think. He wondered where George was. Then he noticed small fires in the cornfields below and wondered if the advance troops had been discovered. Colonel Armstrong had the same thought, for he questioned Baker and Ben heard Baker's low reply. "The Indians light them for keeping away the gnats, colonel. They'll be putting them out soon, since it's a warm night." Finally Ben dozed off. They had marched thirty miles since daybreak.

Colonel Armstrong had sent soldiers to the rear to guide the last three companies, which were now beginning to appear. Shortly before dawn he ordered one company to march along the top of the hill, where they would be opposite the cluster of huts in the upper part of the village. The other companies he deployed in the cornfield just below the hill, in order to surround the huts in the lower part of the town. Now that the rear columns were descending the last hill to join his men, he decided to postpone the attack for about twenty minutes, when it should be light enough to see more clearly.

Among the last three companies to arrive at Kittaning was the one to which Patrick Brady and the McCulloughs belonged. Since these men were not leading horses, they had been assigned to protect the rear of the column, in case any stray bands of Delawares followed.

As Robert McCullough started down the slope he found himself in company with Brady. The trapper did not see him, so intent was he on seeking a means of escape. Above his whiskers his face was ashen with fear. "Thinkin' of leavin' us, Brady?" McCullough asked in a conversational tone. "I'd think twice about it if I was ya. Because Jim and me, we're goin' to see that ya does your company proud. Ain't that so, Jim?"

"That's right. We'll be right alongside of ya."

"Now then, let's get goin'! Just remember, Brady, if we see ya headin' the wrong way, these rifles just might accidentally be aimed in your direction."

The trapper said nothing as he descended the hill in company with his enemies. He knew they were in deadly earnest. He wondered how they could be so calm.

As the pale rays of a watery sun filtered through the trees and spilled onto the valley, Colonel Armstrong signaled for the attack to begin. There was a sudden burst of rifle fire and small puffs of smoke hung suspended in the still air. Scores of Indians ran from the bark huts and the air was filled with shouts and cries. Armstrong looked about, trying to estimate the number of the enemy. There appeared to be at least a hundred engaged in the fighting and doubtless still more inside the huts.

The return fire was heaviest from the large, two-story house with loopholes. The colonel turned to McWhirter. "I want the huts on either side of the big house set afire, captain. We'll smoke them out." As McWhirter ran to carry out this order, Colonel Armstrong felt a sudden sharp pain in his left shoulder and realized he had been shot. He called to Captain Mercer to direct the firing while he climbed the hill to have his wound dressed. The militia appeared to be giving a good account of themselves, and there was no panic, thank the Lord.

The militia were amazed at the fire maintained by the Delawares. Several times they attempted to storm the town but were driven back. But apparently some of McWhirter's men got through, and soon the houses on either side of Captain Jacobs's home were blazing. The smoke grew so thick that it was difficult to see at times. In one of the burning buildings a brave began to sing a mournful death song. The men in the cornfield heard an Indian woman cry out, followed by a man's stern voice, saying something that sounded like a rebuke. Ben saw two braves and an Indian woman run from one of the burning buildings toward the cornfields. They were killed immediately.

A powerful-looking Indian jumped from an upper window of the big house, which was now burning, and a man named Baker took aim and shot him. (Later, when he examined the body, he discovered he had killed one of the perpetrators of the Indian wars, Captain Jacobs himself. He recognized him by the peculiar way he wore his hair: tied back and clubbed, fastened with a beaded ring.)

Two more figures jumped from the second story. Ben fired and saw that he had killed an Indian woman. This troubled him, but the men around him were jubilant. "That there's Cap'n Jacobs's squaw! Ya got her, Enyard!"

"How do ya know?" he asked, not knowing whether to be ashamed or proud.

"Did ya see her hair? It weren't in braids but cut short all around. I've seen her and there ain't no one else wears her hair like that!"

As house after house caught fire, there were tremendous explosions from the gunpowder stored in them, and some of the Indians and their white prisoners were escaping by dashing off through the fields to the riverbank.

When the roof blew off Captain Jacobs's headquarters, the men saw an arm and a leg blown so high by the force of the gunpowder that they landed in the cornfield. This was followed by the mangled body of a small child which fell not far from Ben. He hadn't expected it to be like this—killing women and children. They weren't to blame. It was the warriors they should be killing, not the innocent. Then he realized something he would always remember: in war it was not possible to punish only those responsible; all had to suffer.

John Graves, having searched the huts in the upper level of the village without finding a trace of his wife and child, made his way to the cornfield before the explosions began. He was in despair. But there was a chance he might encounter someone among the rescued captives who could give him news of his family, he told himself. He began to search the cornfield for the wounded.

The air was so full of smoke and the acrid fumes of gunpowder that the men in the cornfield were coughing and choking. John bent over a soldier lying on the ground, holding his belly. His entrails protruded from a huge hole in his side, sliding between his spread fingers. He looked at John with eyes glazed with pain, too near death to be aware of his surroundings.

"I'll get a litter for you," John told him, but the man gave no sign that he heard him. When John returned with the litter and another soldier, the man was dead.

"We can't take time to bury him," the soldier told John. "The colonel said we was to bring out the wounded before we do any buryin'."

Jim McCullough found himself in the middle of the lower cornfield, surrounded by broken stalks, spent and wounded militiamen, and the dead, sprawled in grotesque positions, their powder horns or guns still clutched in their hands. Billowing smoke obliterated the upper part of the village. Far off to the right, Indians—men, women, and children—and some white captives ran toward the distant forests, while on the ridge above the river, the physicians treated the wounded. As Jim picked his way carefully over the rubble, he caught a glimpse of Ben Enyard kneeling to reload his rifle. "Ben! Hey, Ben!" he called.

At first Ben did not hear him, as he took aim and fired at the fleeing braves running across the far fields.

"Ben! The colonel's ordered us to collect the wounded and bring them over to the ridge."

At that moment, Jim saw a white woman trying to run toward them. She limped painfully and clutched her belly, which was swollen with child. "Wait!" she cried. "Please! Please don't leave me!"

"Come on, Ben. Over here!" Jim shouted, beginning to run toward her. Her hair had come loose and fell about her shoulders.

"Thank the Lord!" she said, her voice breaking.

Jim put out a hand to steady her. "Ya hurt bad, ma'am?"

She shook her head. "It's my ankle." She began to sob hysterically. "My boys! They're gone!" She tried to break away.

"Ya can't go after them, ma'am," Jim told her.

"Let me go! Put me down! I got to find my boys." The woman's voice rose to a shriek. Ben seized her shoulders, shaking her to bring her to her senses. Then, as she continued to struggle, he slapped her sharply. Her eyes came slowly into focus. "Where are you takin' me?"

"To the physicians up on the ridge to get your ankle tended," Ben told her.

She touched her cheek, still stinging from his slap. "The Injuns took my little boys off to the woods. I had them on either side of me and when I fell over a stump, they were gone before I could get up."

"Were ya captured recently?"

"It was in June over to Bigham's blockhouse."

As they came to the top of the ridge with its knot of wounded, a tall militiaman strode through the press of people, carrying a wounded soldier. Carefully he lowered him to the ground and then stopped in astonishment before the woman.

"Mrs. Wilson! Maria Wilson!"

The woman stared at him.

"Don't you know me? John Graves, your neighbor."

"John Graves! You've changed so's I'd never knowed ya."

"Where's Susannah and Rachel? They are alive, ain't they?"

"Far as I know they're alive, John. They took them away from here after three days—them and some of the men they captured. We were told they was takin' them to Fort Duquesne."

"Duquesne?" That was deep in Indian country, forty or more miles to the south and west.

She nodded.

"Oh, Lord!"

She saw the hope die, the energy drain from him.

"Duquesne," he repeated, his eyes on the distant forests. "How were they when you last saw them?"

"Rachel held up wonderful for a little one. She did what she was told and never whimpered. And Susannah—she's a rare one,

John. Never showed she was afraid at all!"

"No," said John, "Susannah wouldn't let on." He squatted on the ground beside Maria Wilson.

"Tell me, how did they treat you?" John asked. "Were they cruel to you?"

Maria Wilson's face looked bleak. "Those first few days was—was like being in hell. We went on for hours without stoppin'. Then when they made a fire, they took out the scalps from Bigham's and—and dried them over the fire . . ." She stopped, covering her face with her hands. "They was the scalps of people we lived with," she said, recovering some calm. "The Duffield girl and Mrs. Entriken and Elizabeth and . . . After that"—she stopped, trying to control her trembling—"they gave us somethin' to eat, but not a one of us could get a mouthful down."

John Graves's voice seemed to come from a long way off.

"What's that?" she asked.

"I asked where the boys are now . . . and Francis."

She began to weep. John patted her shoulder awkwardly, trying to speak words of comfort, but in his desolation, he had none to give. He stayed with her until her ankle was bound tightly and she was put upon a horse for the return to Fort Lyttleton. Then he went to find the colonel.

"Beggin' your pardon, sir, but what of the captives that were dragged off to the woods?"

"We can't take the time to search for them, Corporal Graves. We'd be ambushed if we followed them into the woods. We've accomplished what we set out to do—destroy their stronghold and put them to rout."

"But we only rescued eleven, sir."

"I realize that, but it can't be helped."

Six hours after the battle began, it was over. All the captives had been brought together and the wounded put on litters. Colonel Armstrong gave the order and the long column began its return.

Presently those in the rear heard a man's voice calling from the edge of the woods, "Wait, wait! I'm comin'! Don't go and leave me to them savages!" They saw a white man, his clothes covered with forest debris, scrambling up the slope to join them. The weary marchers let him through when they heard he had been captured at Bigham's last June, for Colonel Armstrong would want to talk to him.

When the man caught up with the commander, he informed Armstrong that a bateau with a large party of Frenchmen and Delawares had planned to leave early the next day to take Fort Shirley at Aughwick, and twenty-four warriors newly come to Kittaning had set out the evening before, but he did not know the purpose of their expedition.

Alarmed by the man's news, the colonel had neglected to ask his name. He was surprised to learn it was Francis Wilson, whose wife was riding John Graves's mare in the forward column. "I'm much obliged to you, Mr. Wilson, for this intelligence. Now I have some good news. Your wife is with us in the forward column. She's not seriously hurt—no cause to worry."

Francis Wilson forgot to thank the colonel. With every ounce of energy that he had, he ran down the column to find his wife.

"Maria, Maria! Thank the Lord!" He threw his arms about her, tears running down his cheeks.

"Oh, Francis, I thought I'd never see ya again!" She searched his face. "Ya ain't hurt?"

He shook his head. "But they took the boys. I couldn't save them. . . ."

She stared at him, her mouth twisted. She began to moan. To those who heard her it sounded like a lament for the dead.

It was difficult for Colonel Armstrong and his officers to keep his men together. Some of them feared an ambush and slipped off into the forest by twos and threes. A few stray Delawares fired on the column, then disappeared among the trees.

Patrick Brady had managed to slip away when the McCulloughs were engaged in the fighting. He had fired his musket at the fleeing Delawares but without success, for he was not a good marksman. Now as he ran back the way they had come, he wished he could capture a squaw. He'd had a Mingo woman several years ago to warm his bed, but she had died, and since then he'd been alone. He looked about carefully, hoping to be able to take one of the pack horses and return to the fort, but they were kept on the ridge in order to carry the wounded. There was nothing to do but to walk. Slipping and sliding on the pine needles, he darted along, knowing that the Indians were either fighting in the cornfield or running off to the opposite woods.

Brady wondered what the McCulloughs and Ben Enyard would do to him if they found him. Just because he had gone to Fort Lyttleton to protect his scalp was no reason to try to make a soldier out of him. He wasn't going to stay around to be a target for savages and end up with a hatchet in his chest.

Half an hour later he heard twigs snapping and the low murmur of voices. He felt a sharp prickle of fear, then realized that savages didn't talk in the woods. Concealing himself behind trees, he drew near the sound of the voices, peering out cautiously.

In a small clearing three men from Captain Mercer's company were seated on a log, eating jerky and dried corn from their knapsacks. They could hardly turn him in for desertion when they had done the same thing. Assuming a confident air, he went toward them. "Howdy," he said, grinning. "Havin' yer dinner?"

The men gave him a curious stare. Finally one of them spoke. "Headin' back to the fort?"

Brady wasn't to be trapped by that one. "Headin' the same place ya are," he said affably.

"We're lookin' for Lieutenant Hogg and his men," one of them said nervously.

"Now ain't that somethin'!" Brady answered. "The colonel sent me on the very same errand. Guess he figgered it was important ta find him and he wasn't takin' no chances on ya bein' ambushed." He smiled in a friendly fashion, but his finger tightened on the handle of the knife hidden inside his pocket.

The men exchanged glances. Then one of them laughed. "Guess we all know where we stand," he remarked. "Ain't no use wastin' good powder on them varmints when they runs off to the woods. I got business to home waitin' fer me."

"Me too," said one of the men.

Brady nodded.

"Where ya from?"

"Over by Fort Lyttleton," Brady answered.

"Might as well join us," said the man. "Bein' alone in these woods ain't too pleasurable."

"That's what I figgered," said Brady.

Some time later they came upon Lieutenant Hogg, lying near the trail.

The first man stepped forward smartly. "Where be your men, Lieutenant?"

The young officer gave him a glazed look, for he was in great pain. "Dead or mortally wounded," he said. "Where's the colonel?"

"Back at Kittaning, collectin' the wounded and the captives."

"Did you succeed?" Hogg asked. He had lost so much blood that he was feeling light-headed.

"Blew up the village—set fire to the houses. Smoked them out. We killed most of them, except them that run off to the woods," the sergeant said, with some exaggeration.

"Tell Armstrong," said Hogg with great difficulty, "information was wrong—about the number of Indians at—at the campfire. Lots of Delawares—we killed three but the rest ran off. Fought them—in the woods—for an hour and a half. My men—all killed."

The men were silent.

"Tell Colonel Armstrong," repeated the lieutenant.

The sergeant nodded. Then his eyes widened. Just beyond the tree under which Hogg lay, something moved. The branches parted and three braves glided out of the trees, their faces contorted as they flashed their long knives.

"Defend yourselves!" the lieutenant cried. Brady and the three men from Mercer's company ran for their lives through the forest as two of the braves pursued them. The third was engaged in putting an end to Lieutenant Hogg's misery.

Several hours later the deserters caught up with Colonel Armstrong and the expedition on the Kittaning Trail. They told him of their encounter with Lieutenant Hogg and gave him Hogg's last message. In their version, the three braves who had surprised them became twenty; they had put the Indians to rout, they said.

Armstrong suspected their account was greatly exaggerated, but he was deeply alarmed by Hogg's message. Although the lieutenant had not said how many Indians were in the group about the campfire, they could be the twenty-four that Francis Wilson said had arrived at Kittaning the night before. Armstrong's fear of an ambush returned. They could not move rapidly because of the wounded. They had had to abandon their blankets in order to put the wounded on the horses and would be hard pressed without those blankets, for the woods were damp and cold at night.

He sent for Captain McWhirter.

"I remember seeing some horses in the woods near Kittaning, probably some they'd stolen from settlers," McWhirter said.

"If we could send some of the men back to get those horses, they could collect the blankets we had to leave behind," Armstrong said.

John Graves was the first to volunteer. "I'll go for them, Colonel, but we'll need more men."

Ben Enyard looked at Brady. "Me and Patrick Brady will go with him, sir." The trapper's face was a study in amazement, fear, resentment.

"That'll kind of make up for ya sneakin' off in the middle of the battle," said Robert McCullough.

As the ten men left the long column and started back toward the Indian village, Ben asked himself why he had been so foolish as to volunteer. But he had Brady just ahead of him, and since he had volunteered the trapper's services, he had to prove he was a man himself.

Brady was not able to contain his fear as well as Ben. As they neared Kittaning, he was beset with diarrhea. Ben felt a certain sympathy. They were within half a mile of the place where they'd abandoned the baggage, when a slight movement in the bushes caused John to call out, "Injuns!" Before they could fire their rifles, a blast tore out of the surrounding cover and grazed Brady's right forearm. He gave a yelp of pain and stood stock-still. Ben pushed him off the trail, and they ducked behind some elder bushes as three braves appeared. A burst of fire from several of the militia's guns hit two braves simultaneously. They pursued the third Indian but he soon outdistanced them.

As they approached the village, they saw no signs of life. Within an hour they had collected eight horses and fastened the baggage on them for the return trip. Brady's wound, though not serious, bled profusely and added to his fright. Ben applied pressure and used a powder-horn strap and a twig to form a tourniquet. As he stood up and picked up his rifle, his eyes met Brady's and he saw in them a faint glimmer of respect.

It was late in the afternoon when they caught up with the rest of the expedition. Brady carried his injured arm as a badge of courage.

There were times when Ben wondered if they would ever see Fort Shirley, and if they did reach it, would it be a smoking ruin. But on the seventh day the marchers caught sight of its stout palisades with smoke twisting upward from the blockhouse chimneys into a taut autumn sky. They gave a great cry. People within the fort heard it and rushed to climb the ladder to the catwalk within the fence, adding their voices to the cheer.

They had returned.

CHAPTER IX

A Man Divided

In the glow of the council fire the leaves on the oaks and maples gleamed gold and russet. Sparks flew upward into a twilight sky still warm with the vestiges of a spectacular sunset, and a little wind whispered around the edges of the clearing. That afternoon two messengers from the Delaware chief Shingask had arrived at Loyalhannon with wampum belts that told of the destruction of Kittaning.

Asallecoa summoned his people to hear the news. The faces of the braves seated about the fire were angry and outraged at this disaster that had befallen their kinsmen. "There were many pale-faces who attacked Kittaning," Asallecoa said, "too many to count. They killed twenty Delawares, among them Captain Jacobs, his wife and son, and the noted warrior Sunfish. Many were wounded. The village is destroyed."

Silas could not follow much of what Asallecoa said but he understood enough to know they were to remain at Loyalhannon. He wondered about his mother and Ben and the children; were they still alive? Often he thought of Mary Ann. Had she and George taken Thomas to her parents' farm near Philadelphia, where they would be safe from Indian attacks? He hoped so.

At times after he had lain with Ouana he would dream of Mary Ann; by some strange alchemy it was she that he took, her warm and yielding body that he explored passionately, only to awaken and find Ouana curled up beside him.

Ouana was aware of some barrier in their relationship. Although she had tried to forget the knife he had hidden, it had shaken her. She knew his first and deepest loyalty would always be to his own people. She wondered what she would do if he ever left her. Many mornings she awoke hollow-eyed and troubled.

Shortly after their marriage, Ouana had fashioned a handsome clay cooking vessel with designs of turtles and wolves painted on it, combining the symbols of her clan and his. It was a wedding bowl. Many of the women came by to admire it, for she was known for her skill in making pots.

One day late in the autumn he returned from a day's hunt to find her in tears.

"Why are you cryin', Ouana?" he asked gently.

"Something terrible has happened. Our wedding bowl is broken."

"But you can easily make another," he said to reassure her.

"You don't understand, Scoouwa. It is a bad omen."

He tried to make light of the situation, and that night their coming together reached an intensity that left him shaken. But long after he had fallen asleep, she lay awake, her body tense with apprehension.

The winter proved to be a hard one. The big trees were burdened with snow; the branches of the evergreens bent with its weight. The sky, gray as a squirrel's coat by day, red as sumac at sunset, was dull and opaque with no gleam of sunlight to brighten the landscape. As the weather grew colder, the game disappeared, and the hunters were forced to go farther each time they set out. Sometimes they would be gone several weeks. No one knew how long the winter would linger or when they could replenish their supply of gunpowder. Until they could make raids again, they were cut off from further supplies.

In January Katoochquay suggested that Silas accompany him on a bear hunt. As he took leave of Ouana, Silas was aware that her slim waist had thickened and that her breasts were fuller. She clung to him, reluctant to see him go, having a strange premonition of danger.

"Be careful, Scoouwa," she said earnestly.

He lifted her chin and saw that her large eyes were worried. "I will, Ouana. Is there somethin' ya ain't told me? Somethin' I ought to know?" He looked at her with concern, his voice gentle, careful to hide his conflicting emotions. When she did not answer, he continued, "Would ya let me go off without tellin' me if I'm to be a father?" He was ashamed now that he had not been able to love her more fully, when she had been so generous. He pulled her to him, assuming a light-hearted manner at variance with his true feelings. "There, there, child, it's nothin' to worry about. . . ."

Ouana lifted her head to study his face. In spite of the kindness and affection she saw reflected there, she was not reassured. She knew he would not desert her, that he would stay from a sense of obligation, but it was not duty she wanted from him.

"I am praying to Manitou for a son," she told him.

Silas kissed her tenderly. "Try not to worry, lass." He spoke with more assurance than he felt.

She did not answer but stood in the doorway, shivering in the bitter wind, as he followed Katoochquay into the woods.

The first night they slept in a cave against the side of a low hill. They gathered broken branches and chopped off tree limbs to build a large fire for warmth and protection. After they had eaten some of the pemmican and cakes of cornmeal mixed with bear's fat and wild honey that they had brought in pouches, they melted snow to drink. Katoochquay belched comfortably as they wrapped their fur mantles about them and settled down to sleep.

The second day they killed two raccoons and, later, a brace of wild turkeys. With hands numbed from the cold they removed the entrails and tied the game with rawhide thongs to the branches of trees so that they need not carry it as they went farther west.

When they came upon a stand of white birch trees, Silas thought of Mary Ann. For reasons he never understood, their tall, slim loveliness always evoked an image of her.

Katoochquay was speaking. "We peel bark off trees. Make hut." Silas thought it strange that Katoochquay always spoke in

English when they were alone. Although he considered the English his enemies, he was proud to have acquired a smattering of their language.

They set to work to make a birchbark shelter and before night fell were comfortably settled in their little hut. It was dry and warmer than the cave but the wind howled all night, rattling the dry branches, reminding Silas of wolves baying. Katoochquay quickly fell asleep, untroubled by the elements. Silas, usually calm and unworried, slept fitfully.

They found no game the third day. The cold grew more intense and it snowed again during the night. By morning there was a hard crust. As they searched for game, Silas wondered if they would be able to find shelter for the night. When they finally found their way back to the birchbark hut, he experienced a relief so profound that his eyes filled with tears.

The next day they stayed within their shelter, scooping up snow to melt for drinking water. It was difficult to find wood to feed the fire, and their fingers stuck to the handles of their tomahawks when they went out to lop off low branches. Silas began to doubt that they could survive. Katoochquay did not speak of his concern, but Silas sensed that he was worried.

The following day a bright sun splintered between the bare trees, glistening on the deep drifts, sparkling like gems on the evergreens' weighted branches. They felt a surge of confidence as they left the bark hut.

"We find deer today," Katoochquay said. By midafternoon they saw the tracks of a big buck in the snow and followed them for half a mile before cornering the animal and killing it. It was a prime specimen and its meat would stave off the hunger of the villagers for a time. They managed to remove the entrails and tied the dripping carcass to a stout limb.

Silas realized it would soon be dark. "We can't make it back to the hut today," he said, trying to keep the worry out of his voice.

"Now make big canoe. Tonight sleep in canoe. Next day put deer in canoe. Pull through snow."

"Canoe?"

Katoochquay nodded and began to lop off slender branches.

Silas had learned not to question him, for though Katoochquay could not explain some of his more ingenious ideas, they were unfailingly workable. Before dark, they had fashioned a crude sledge, which was Katoochquay's "canoe." It was strong enough to carry the game back to the camp and would serve now as a makeshift shelter against the wind. The following day they shot a doe and felt extremely fortunate. Again they spent the night under the sledge.

On the eighth day they found the opening of a cave partly hidden by snow. Katoochquay used a fallen branch to brush aside the snow and went inside, sniffing expectantly. He was grinning when he emerged. "Bear sleeps," he told Silas, pointing to the cavern. He began to search under the low spreading branches of evergreens for dry wood.

Silas worked with him. They piled armfuls of the wood just inside the opening and kindled a fire, fanning it to direct the smoke toward the cave's interior; then they crouched outside behind tall trees, guns primed.

There were faint rumblings and the sound of a large animal thrashing about, followed by a roar of rage. A huge brown bear lumbered out, its little reddened eyes darting about wildly, its hindquarters smoking. As Katoochquay fired, it saw him and ran awkwardly toward him. The report of the gun was loud in the stillness of the woods. Blood gushed from a hole just above the animal's left eye, but it continued toward Katoochquay, who was readying his rifle for a second shot.

"Run!" Silas yelled.

But the warning came too late. The bear's forepaw caught Katoochquay's left arm, ripping it open from shoulder to elbow. Katoochquay screamed and fell, his fur sleeve hanging in shreds. Silas aimed his gun. His heart was racing and he felt weak with terror.

When the air cleared, he saw the great animal backing away, swinging its head to shake the blood from its eyes. It was breathing heavily and growling in pain. On its underbelly a fresh spurt of blood showed where the second bullet had struck. Finally it fell clumsily and lay still.

Warily Silas approached and plunged his hunting knife deep into the body. Katoochquay lay under an oak, blood from his torn arm spreading over the snow. Silas knelt beside him and removed the thong from Katoochquay's powder horn to make a tourniquet. Katoochquay was silent, his eyes glazed, his face set in lines of suffering. His breathing was loud and irregular. As the blood was staunched, his eyes cleared and he looked at Silas. He muttered something in a voice so low that his words were lost.

"What's that?" Silas bent his head to catch the words.

"Brother . . . blood brother," Katoochquay murmured.

When they returned at last to the camp at Loyalhannon, their sledge was piled high with game. Silas was shocked to see how pinched were the faces of the people, and he was filled with pity. The storm had been so severe that they had given up hope of seeing Katoochquay and Scoouwa again.

Silas searched the crowd for Ouana, wondering why she was not there to greet him. When he saw the old woman known as Nawouna, he put his hands on her shoulders. "Where is Ouana, honored one?"

The woman looked at him in sorrow.

"What is it? What's wrong?"

"She is ill. Very ill." He did not wait to hear more. The crowd parted to make way for him, their faces full of concern.

Several women were gathered in the hut he shared with Ouana. They rose and left as he entered. Ouana lay on a pile of buffalo robes, wrapped in trade blankets with a deerskin coverlet. He knelt beside her, pushing back the hair that clung to her temples. As he looked at her, pity and guilt overwhelmed him. He had not welcomed their child and she had known. She had given him love and he had not been able to return it fully. The knowledge that he had failed her tore at him until he felt lost, swept away by a tide of emotion. "I wouldn't desert ya, lass, I would never leave ya, Ouana," he cried.

She opened her eyes and looked at him as from a great distance. Her hand touched his cheek. It was so delicate, that touch, as if a butterfly had brushed him. She tried to speak but could not. He propped her upright so she could breathe more easily and watched helplessly as her chest heaved, and her eyes dilated. Then she slumped against his arm and lay still.

How long he remained kneeling beside her he did not know. He was conscious only of something warm and loving having gone from him.

Outside the women began the lament for the dead.

CHAPTER X

Winter 1756-57

As Ben helped his mother into the wagon for their return to the farm in late October, he noted that her eyes were shadowed with anxiety and her mouth wore that determined set it showed at times when she was faced with an unpleasant duty. He suspected her offer to take in the homeless McCulloughs was not without self-interest, but he could not fault her for that. It would be a lonely thing to return to the farm with only the two small children. He remembered how it had disturbed him when he had to return there with the two soldiers to fetch the salves and herbs for Brady.

There had been a frost during the night and the ground was covered with a mantle as delicate as the white lace that fell from a gentleman's cuffs. Amid the creaking of harness leather and the excited voices of the children, they started on their way.

Captain McWhirter, watching them go, was briefly troubled by an incident that had occurred the day before. He had called the fort's inhabitants together to give them the news.

"Men! I have just received a dispatch from Colonel Armstrong saying that the Provincial Assembly has granted him permission to abandon Fort Shirley. Its position in case of a prolonged attack is indefensible," he had explained. Silence. They had looked at him in disbelief.

"Do you understand what this means?" It was hard to maintain his military bearing when he had a cold and had to blow his nose every few minutes. "It means that those forting at Aughwick"—he'd caught himself using their name for it—"at Fort Shirley will either come here or take their chances"—a low rumble followed, like a giant wave gathering force before it broke. He must be careful not to cause panic—"when the raids begin again." But they hadn't heard him; they were too caught up in their own exclamations.

"Damn them!"

"What right has the Assembly got . . ."

"Let them try frontierin' and see how they like it."

"Lily-livered . . ."

He tried to stem their anger. "You don't understand. The water supply at Fort Shirley—" Someone had thrown a small stone which grazed his shoulder.

"Sergeant, seize that man! I am in command here and there will be no disruption" —he'd dodged another stone, but stood his ground—"of order."

He was vaguely aware of voices raised to protest the stones.

"Fort Shirley cannot be defended in case of prolonged attack! Do you understand? Its water supply is outside the stockade!" His throat felt raw from the effort to be heard.

"First Fort Granville surrendered! Now Aughwick's closed! What do they expect us to do, give up our farms and go back—"

"Attention! Quiet! They are building a new fort at Carlisle," McWhirter had explained.

"Carlisle!" Disbelief showed on their bearded faces. It meant the Assembly was expecting the raids to continue and was abandoning the frontier; Carlisle was more than forty miles east of Fort Lyttleton.

"Listen to me! They will be needing recruits. The pay for militiamen is three shillings a day. If the raids continue you can go to Carlisle—or Chambersburg. . . ."

For a moment he shared their despair; then, reminding himself that he was employed by the Assembly on behalf of the Crown, he realigned his loyalties. "It is for your protection."

"What about our land?" Ben Enyard had asked.

McWhirter had hesitated before replying, caught off guard. "Some are trying to persuade the Assembly to promise that land warrants will be honored when peace comes." It was like throwing half a loaf of bread to a pack of hungry dogs, but they had to know there were some honorable men among the assemblymen.

"When peace comes! How many years will that be?" they snorted in derision.

Now, as the captain watched the Enyards and the McCulloughs starting home in George Eldridge's big wagon, he felt a certain sadness. Seeing the McCullough girl reminded him of Effie. He had not thought of her in a long time. He and Effie had had only two years together before the smallpox carried her off. He wanted to weep when he thought of her moldering in the churchyard on Locust Street, Philadelphia.

He straightened his shoulders, letting his thoughts slide to the McCullough girl. Although a mere child, she had a foreshadowing of womanliness to come. He wondered what it would be like to rescue her from the poverty that fate had assigned her, set her up in a pleasant home in Philadelphia. As his wife. He caught himself. "More fool am I. Why, I'm old enough to be her father!" Turning, he went into his office.

As the Enyards and the McCulloughs neared the farm, snow started to fall and the dry, whirling flakes gave an unreal beauty to the rough acres and encircling woods. The snow was beginning to fill the angles of the branches and cover the broken fences of the horses' corral, and the fields with their bent cornstalks. Ben slowed the team to take in the tranquil scene. The rough outlines of cabin and barn were softened by the falling snow. Here and there winter birds hopped about or swayed on bushes, pecking for berries or seeds.

Else caught her breath at the beauty that had once been so familiar she had not really seen it. When Yellis was alive there had been no time to note the living, changing loveliness of her family acres. Even the surrounding woods looked protective and eternal now, like the Lord's encircling arms. Her throat felt tight and she was close to tears.

It was surprising how quickly they settled in for the winter. The men built a new room onto the cabin, adding it to the fireplace wall so that the fire's warmth would heat the new addition; they cut a window in it, with an inside shutter to keep out the rain and snow.

Robbie McCullough set traps and supplied their table with squirrels and other small animals, and one night they had two wild turkeys for dinner.

Else, after organizing the renovation of the cabin so that all was clean and snug against the winter's cold, opened the chest that held their warm clothing and quilts. The McCulloughs had lost everything but the clothes they had brought to the fort. It wasn't right to keep the clothes of Pa and Ari, she told herself, so she and Annie McCullough picked at seams, saving the precious thread, cut and altered so that the newcomers had warm clothing.

Fiona fitted into Ari's two dresses as if they had been fashioned for her. She had begun to assume a delicate rounded femininity, and was a quiet gentle girl. Else noticed Fiona's shy glances and warm color whenever Ben was near. She supposed it was natural for Fiona to daydream about Ben.

One day after Fiona had swept the cabin clean and washed the plates and mugs, she went to the edge of the woods, unnoticed by the other women. She pulled Ari's cloak more tightly about her, for it was winter and the pallid sun could not warm the woods. She was looking for pinecones, which would be fine for starting the fire, and for acorns, now that their supply of cornmeal was almost exhausted. She had helped her mother make acorn bread when food was scarce at home.

Without thinking, Fiona went deeper into the woods than she intended. Suddenly she heard a slight rustle. She looked around wildly, realizing she had left the path and, in her panic, did not even know which way she had come. She dared not scream; she stooped down, covering her head with the brown cloak, hoping its color would blend with the surrounding bushes. Her sharp ears heard a gun click; it sounded as if just one person was approaching. Fiona heard the twigs crack as he drew nearer.

Then she remembered Indians made no noise in the woods. Could it be Brady? Just when she thought she would die of fright, Fiona saw between the tree trunks a man's shoulder in a fringed leather hunting shirt. Something of the set of that shoulder was familiar.

"Ben! Oh, Ben!" She was sobbing now, the tears running down her cheeks as she clung to him.

Ben looked down at her in dismay. He had thought there was a stray savage in the woods and had left the path on his return from the Abbots' to follow him. "Fiona, what were ya doin' here? I almost shot ya, girl!"

She was too distraught to answer.

He shook her in exasperation. "Who gave ya permission to go into the woods, Fiona McCullough? Ain't ya heard your pa and me tell all of ya to keep out of the woods unless we're with ya?"

With a great effort she tried to tell him, "I—only come to get some acorns."

"Acorns? Are ya a child to be playin' with acorns?"

"For bread."

"Bread? But Ma and your mother's grindin' corn this very mornin' for bread. What's got into ya, girl?"

She walked ahead of him, her head bent in embarrassment, as they went back to the cabin.

When Ben told her father what had happened, Robert McCullough was stern. "If I ever hear of ya settin' foot inside the woods without my leave, I'll whip ya with a birch rod, missy!" he told her.

That night, as Else was about to go to sleep, she heard muffled crying from the girl lying beside her.

"Fiona," she said, softly, so as not to awaken Peter, "ya all right, honey?"

There was no reply.

"Ya know," Else said carefully, "they wasn't tryin' to shame ya. They was tryin' to make ya understand how scared they was for ya. Could've been Injuns instead of Ben."

Fiona stuffed a corner of the coverlet into her mouth to stifle the sound of her crying.

"One thing I noticed about menfolk—when they really care about ya, they get right angry if they think ya put yourself in danger," Else continued.

Fiona shifted her position. Did that mean that Ben cared about her? she wondered. It couldn't be true; he looked upon her as a child. Sometimes she thought he must know how she felt, for she could feel the hot blood coloring her face and neck when he walked in.

Now she heard Else's voice come softly in the darkness. "Ya know, Fiona, we all care about ya. Ya been a real blessin' to Ben and me—it's almost as if the Lord sent ya to us to help us get over Ari. . . ."

Fiona felt Mrs. Enyard's arm encircle her shoulder and she moved closer.

None of them would ever forget that winter. Each day had a special luster.

Ben knew that his mother was proud of the way he had taken hold of his responsibility. It was gratifying to hear her praise when he organized the work efficiently, and even more satisfying to have Robert McCullough and Jim seek his advice.

When he remembered how stubborn Pa had been and how blind to their needs, a slow bitterness would rise in him.

Ma used to say he was like his father in his traits. She no longer said this, which pleased him greatly.

One evening Ben talked with his mother and the McCulloughs about what to do when the raids began again in the spring. "They're offerin' three shillin's a day for new recruits in the new fort at Carlisle. It ain't bad pay, that. I don't know how ya feel about it, Mr. McCullough, Jim, but I ain't goin' to take any chances by stayin' here when the raids start again."

There was silence in the big firelit cabin. Annie McCullough laid aside her knitting, her face bleak. The small children in the loft crept out of their beds and knelt on the rough boards to peer down at the adults. Robert McCullough cleared his throat. "What you got in mind to do, Ben?"

"It ain't such a good idea to go back to Fort Lyttleton. With Aughwick abandoned, folk will all be goin' there. It'd be smarter to go to Carlisle. If we go early in March, we can find a place for the women and children to live. It'd be a lot safer than Fort Lyttleton," Ben told them.

"But how'd we live with no place to grow our victuals and no huntin'? We'd need money, Ben!" Jim interposed.

"I'm comin' to that, Jim. I figure on joinin' the militia over there. On three shillin's a day there'd be enough to take care of Ma and Peter and the baby. If you and your pa was to join up, your pay would be enough to provide for a place for your family and for food, I opine."

Else thought how smart he was to have figured it all out before he brought it before them.

"The victuals is included when ya join?"

"So I heard. We'd get blankets and ammunition and rations as well as the three shillin's a day."

Robert McCullough looked at Jim. "What do ya say, son?"

"I guess there ain't nothin' better to do, Pa."

"I'm goin' over to see George tomorrow. He won't be needin' the wagon and might let ya borrow it and the horses—if ya want to go," Ben said.

George usually walked over to the Abbots' every other day to see his son, Thomas. He was very proud of the child. He thought ruefully what a pity it was that the child had been deprived of Mary Ann's love and care. Not that Lucinda neglected him; on the contrary, she was devoted to the boy.

Early in December when George failed to appear for his customary visit, Lucinda asked, "Pa, do you suppose somethin's happened to Mr. Eldridge?"

"I reckon not. He's probably just wore out with clearin' that west meadow."

"You don't suppose he's sick or somethin'?"

"I don't reckon so. Tomorrow Jeremy can go over to find out if somethin's wrong," said her father.

The following morning, Lucinda reached for her shawl and ran to the barn. She climbed upon the livelier of their two horses and set out.

Some time later Jeremy found the mare missing. Suspecting

what had happened, he went to his mother. A small worm of anxiety began to move within Maggie Abbot. "I suppose in case George's sick or had an accident, it's better Lucinda went. But if she ain't home within an hour, I want ya to go over there, Jeremy, and see what's happened," she told him.

Jeremy was familiar with Lucinda's tricks so he was not surprised to find the mare inside the Eldridge barn. Whistling tunelessly, he started for the cabin, determined to have it out with her for going to see George when Pa had told him to go. When he knocked on the door, Lucinda opened it. Her greeting surprised him.

"Jeremy! I'm that glad to see ya! He's sick, real sick. I found him lyin' on the floor with a fever."

George Eldridge was lying on the bunk bed with his clothes on, his eyes bright with fever, his body shaking with intermittent chills. "What do ya want me to do, Cinda?" Jeremy was shocked by George's appearance.

"Ya can chop some wood and fetch me some water. I'm goin' to boil some herbs to take down his fever."

"Shall I get Ma?" Jeremy asked uneasily.

"I can manage. Just bring me the water and some wood and look after the horses."

As Jeremy picked up the pail and headed for the spring, he acknowledged reluctantly that Lucinda could do most anything. When he returned with the water and stacked some of the wood inside the door, he looked at her curiously.

"How long ya fixin' to stay?" he asked.

"I'm stayin' as long as he's sick! I can't go off and leave a man that's mortal ill and him with no one to do for him, can I? Answer me that, Jeremy Abbot, you're so smart!"

"No, I—I guess ya can't. All the same I don't think Ma and Pa will like your bein' here all alone with him."

"Then let them come after me," she said, hands on hips.

He wanted to slap her but he knew Lucinda was tough. "I'll tell Ma and Pa the Eldridge family is doin' just fine since the new Mrs. Eldridge is lookin' after her man," he said wickedly, running to the door as she grabbed the warming pan.

"Why, ya no-account pole cat," she began, her eyes blazing.

But he was gone.

It was several minutes before she could think clearly. She filled a kettle with water and put it over the fire. Then she tucked the warming pan between the covers of the bed. She'd get his clothes off and wash him and get the herb tea into him. She didn't care what Pa thought about it. George Eldridge needed her.

When Seth Abbot rode over later with Jeremy, he found George feverish and unable to talk, but he could see Lucinda was taking care of him. Seth did not know how to cope with the situation; it didn't seem proper for an unmarried girl to be left alone in the cabin to nurse George. But he knew Lucinda to be capable, and since she had grown up with several brothers, he doubted that she would be exposed to anything very shocking. More important, Lucinda was stubborn, and once she had set her mind to doing something, it was hard to sway her. So he told Jeremy to stay with her and promised to stop over the next day.

Maggie Abbot was upset by her husband's handling of the situation, for she was aware of Lucinda's excessive curiosity. "I know we can trust George Eldridge," she said with asperity. "A man that's sick ain't capable of doin' nothin'. But soon as my baby is born, we must find a husband for her. If there's talk, it's goin' to be mighty hard."

The children stopped their chores to listen.

"Now, Ma, don't fret about it. Lucinda is a right smart girl—we don't need to hunt for a man for her," Seth interposed.

"She should've been a boy," his wife continued.

The children giggled. "She puts me in mind of your sister, Nellie," she said. "She that was so bold and free with herself. Two children out of wedlock she had."

This was going to be a good one, Sarah decided, for Aunt Nellie was the family disgrace and when Ma got going on her, there was sure to be a long, heated argument. Next thing she'd say, "Blood will tell!"

Maggie dabbed at her eyes and sat up straighter. "Blood will tell," she said prophetically.

The third day after Lucinda took over his care, George had a blurred impression of her moving about the cabin, propping him up to drink some tea, wiping his face, and straightening the covers. Jeremy was whittling by the fire. "Ya been takin' care of me?" George asked weakly. "How long I been sick?"

"About three days. How are ya feelin', Mr. Eldridge?" Lucinda asked.

George waved his hand. "Light-headed," he said, closing his eyes.

"Ya was mighty sick. When ya didn't come over to see Thomas, I reckoned somethin' was wrong and came over. Ya was lyin' on the floor with a high fever. Had a time gettin' ya into the bed."

"Then I came lookin' for Cinda and Pa had me stay. I been lookin' after the horses and cuttin' the wood," Jeremy said.

After her father had come and gone, Lucinda noticed her brother looking at the sky. She put on her most winsome expression. "I'll reckon some quail would be just the thing to bring back Mr. Eldridge's appetite," she remarked. "Pity ya ain't brought your gun. I seen some quail over toward the Stotts' when I was comin' over here."

Jeremy's face brightened. "Maybe I could use Mr. Eldridge's gun. He showed me how it works."

"I don't believe he'd mind. Would ya, Mr. Eldridge?"

There was no answer from the bed.

"Ya think Pa'd mind my leavin' for a couple of hours?" Jeremy asked.

"Not now that he's gettin' well."

So Jeremy took up George's gun and went looking for quail. Lucinda watched him until he was out of sight, then slipped out of her dress and drawers and climbed into the bed.

George Eldridge had a momentary impression that Mary Ann had returned, that it was her warmth and softness he felt, her hands that explored his body. Weak though he was, he felt desire stir in him. He opened his eyes to find Lucinda watching him from under her lashes. He was instantly awake, amazed that she should be in bed with him. But when Lucinda kissed him he forgot his scruples. He'd been alone too long.

When Jeremy returned with two partridges several hours

later, George was asleep, a smile about his lips. He looked much better. Lucinda was grinding corn; she exclaimed over the birds and set him the task of plucking them. They would make a fine supper, she said.

When George woke up the cabin was dark, save for a few glowing embers in the fireplace. It was very cold and he shivered as he pulled the quilts more closely about him. He heard a light snoring and saw Jeremy Abbot sleeping by the hearth. Lucinda was stretched out on the floor near her brother, her head resting on one arm while the other held a fur mantle about her. In sleep her face looked relaxed and childish with its full mouth slightly open and her rounded cheeks made rosier by the ruddy glow of the embers. Instantly memory returned. Lord in heaven, he'd lain with her and she'd been a virgin! He had betrayed his beloved wife and the Abbots, who were his friends. What if he'd got her with child? The thought seared his mind and he groaned aloud.

Lucinda turned over and sat up.

George lay with closed eyes, feigning sleep.

"George?" she whispered. "Ya all right?"

He heard her get up and walk to the bed. He was afraid she would get in beside him again, but she only pulled the quilt more closely about him. There was the sound of her stirring the embers and laying another log on the fire.

George did not fall asleep until the first rays of the morning sun shone through the chinks in the walls. He had tossed and turned, trying to find an answer to his problem. He'd have to send Lucinda home and see that she did not return.

George slept late. When he awoke, Jeremy was gone and Lucinda, unaware of his gaze, moved purposefully about. A pot of rabbit stew gave off a tantalizing aroma that made his stomach contract.

George watched her silently, noting the sensuous lines of her body. She had opened several buttons of her bodice and as she turned, he caught a glimpse of her breasts that left him weak.

Summoning his courage, he spoke firmly. "Lucinda, ya can't stay here longer. It ain't right what we done."

She perched on the side of the bed and leaned toward him, smiling. "Ya been real sick, George. It was only neighborly to look after ya."

"Ya know that ain't what I mean."

"You're all alone now and a man needs a woman." She drew back the quilts and touched his thighs.

He pulled her to him, unable to resist her.

The following morning when Lucinda took the leather bucket to the spring for water, George got up for the first time in a week and dressed quickly. Jeremy was seated at the table, eating cornmeal mush. The boy's presence would make it easier to tell Lucinda she must leave.

When she returned to the cabin with the brimming bucket, he was talking to Jeremy.

She smiled. "Ya feelin' better, ain't ya?"

He felt his face grow hot. "Right as rain, thanks to the good care ya and Jeremy been givin' me. I won't be needin' the two of ya now. Tell your pa I'm mighty grateful that he sent ya over." He felt uncomfortable at having to pretend.

"You're sure you can manage by yourself?" she asked.

"Yup. I'll just rest awhile between chores, and since ya brought the water and Jeremy's looked after the horses, I won't need to do much today." He did not know how to thank her; his guilt lay like a stone within him.

"Well then, we'll be goin' home." Lucinda began to collect the few things Seth had brought them. The very naturalness of her remark only added to George's discomfort. As Jeremy darted out the door, Lucinda paused and gave George a lingering look. Was she accusing him of ingratitude? Or telling him she would return?

He started toward her. "Lucinda."

"Well?"

Jeremy was tightening the saddle so he couldn't hear them. "It ain't that I don't appreciate all—all ya done for me. But we hadn't ought to see each other alone again after what happened."

Lucinda did not answer. She looked at him in that provocative way she had, half challenge, half scorn, that left him completely confused. Then she climbed onto the horse behind Jeremy and they were off. George stood in the cabin door watching them until the bitter wind reminded him he'd better close the door.

After George's recovery Ben walked over to ask him about borrowing his wagon for the McCulloughs. As he approached the clearing, he could see Lucinda Abbot in animated conversation with George. The woods hid him from their view, but they were silhouetted against the light, standing just beyond the last of the trees. He paused, not wishing to eavesdrop, and was about to retrace his steps when the girl's raised voice came clearly through the frosty morning air.

"Ain't no use ya waitin' for her, George! She may be dead . . . or livin' as a squaw to one of them savages."

George raised his hand and slapped her on the face. Ben was amazed and his impulse was to interfere, but George's words stopped him. "Ya—ya little slut! It was ya who sneaked into my bed while I was sick!"

Lucinda looked up at him with an expression Ben well remembered. "Ya liked it, didn't you?"

George did not answer but his face flushed.

"You're human. It ain't natural for a man to be without a woman for long. What we did wasn't bad. Ya needed me and I needed ya." Lucinda ran her fingers down his back. At that George turned and caught her to him, bending her head back as he kissed her throat and mouth. The passion with which he took her left Ben aroused.

When he returned home, he picked up his ax and went to the woods where they were beginning to cut a swath through the trees. Jim called to him, but Ben did not answer. When he did not come in for their noon meal, Else sent Robbie to fetch him. "I ain't hungry," Ben said. His face, Robbie thought, looked mad clean through.

When the light faded, Ben started back to the cabin, still struggling with emotions he did not know how to cope with—jealousy, shock that George could so easily succumb to Lucinda when everyone believed Mary Ann to be alive, disgust with himself to be so shaken by their passion, uncertainty about his own attractiveness. She must see him as a poor sort of critter when compared with George, who was older, experienced, and handsome. But George was married.

Some women, he had heard, were drawn to danger, like a child that is excited by fire. Lucinda must be that kind of girl.

At supper conversation was strained. When Robert McCullough asked him about the wagon, Ben did not look up from the rabbit stew he was industriously spooning into his mouth. "I dunno. I ain't had a chance to ask him."

"But that's what ya went over there for," Else said.

There was silence as all looked at him.

Finally he answered in a tone that indicated he would not discuss it further, "I didn't get to talk to him." He got up from the table, put on his deerskin shirt and picked up his gun. As he went out the door, Else caught up her shawl and followed him.

"Ben! I must talk to ya."

He stopped, his stance stiff and unyielding.

"Did ya quarrel with George, son?"

"No, Ma."

"Ya sure about that?"

"Course I'm sure! I ain't a boy, Ma. Ya forget that."

Something in his words made her pause and think. Then she knew. It was something to do with his manhood. "Do ya want to tell me about it?"

"No, Ma, I don't. It's got nothin' to do with us. I can't discuss it. It ain't my business. . . . Now stop frettin' about it."

He strode on ahead of her on the pretext of seeing to the horses. Pulling her shawl about her head, for it was snowing now, Else returned to the cabin. Whatever it was that troubled him, he would have to work it out for himself.

All the next week Ben was preoccupied and grim. The life of the farm flowed around him, full of shared chores, warmth, and sociability, but he stayed apart from it. Finally Robert McCullough offered to see George about the use of the wagon and Ben gladly acquiesced. When Robert returned with the information that George would take the McCulloughs to Carlisle if Mrs. McCullough would look after Thomas, they were surprised. They wondered what had happened that Lucinda was not to continue with the child's care, but assumed it was because Maggie Abbot's time of delivery was near and Lucinda would be busier than usual. Only Ben knew the real reason.

Two weeks later Maggie Abbot began labor, and Jeremy rode to the Enyards' to fetch the women. When they arrived at the Abbots', they found the atmosphere filled with emotion. Lucinda, red-eyed and sullen, barely greeted them. Sarah appeared to be in charge. Seth, usually mild-mannered and sociable, was withdrawn and preoccupied. The younger children had been sent outside.

The women rolled up their sleeves and set to work, realizing it was going to be a long labor. Maggie was in severe pain, tossing and turning in the big bed, her eyes sunken, her skin moist and unnaturally pale. As Maggie's sufferings grew more intense, they gave her something to bite on and provided support as she tried to push the infant from the womb.

Sarah ran to her father and put her tear-streaked face on his shoulder. "Oh, Pa, can't we do somethin'?"

"Ain't nothin' more we can do than we're doin' already."

Hours passed. The woman had fastened quilts to the rafters to screen the bed from the children's view. Lucinda began to prepare their evening meal, her face reflecting none of the concern of the others. The boys trooped in, embarrassed, but full of curiosity about the act of birth. They began to eat, but soon they put down their spoons and pushed their plates away. None could eat in the presence of so much suffering.

Late in the evening the child was born but as the women saw its blue face and the umbilical cord knotted about its neck, they knew it was already dead. Maggie, exhausted from her ordeal, slept.

As Seth looked at the wrinkled form, he turned to Lucinda, who could not take her eyes from the dead babe. "This be your doin', Lucinda Abbot!" he thundered, unmindful of the women. Sarah caught his arm.

"Please, Pa, leave it be. It won't do no good now."

"We done all we could, Seth. It was the Lord's will and none can go against it," Else said.

"Poor little mite. Maybe it's better off so," Annie offered by way of sympathy. "Ain't nothin' but trouble in this life. . . ."

"Is Ma—goin' to be all right?" Jeremy asked.

Else put her arm around him. "She's plumb wore out, Jeremy, but I reckon she'll get her strength back in time. You're all goin' to have to look after her proper and not do nothin' to worry or fret her."

Seth sat down by the fire, his face grim. "She told me and I didn't listen to her," he said, as if to himself. "I was too easy on Cinda and when Ma found out, it near broke her heart. Brought on the babe early. The Lord's punishment, it was. . . ."

The children fidgeted in embarrassment, stealing curious glances at their older sister. Sarah knelt beside her mother, stroking her damp hair. Annie, not knowing what to think, washed the baby and prepared it for burial.

Lucinda stood in the corner, her mouth trembling, her eyes full of tears. "Come, Lucinda," Else said, "fix your Pa some victuals. None of us knows why these things happen and we all do things we're sorry for. There ain't nothin' can't be put to rights if we've a mind to."

The girl said nothing but went silently to the table to get a plate for her father.

Else turned to the man. "It's hard to see it now, Seth, but maybe it's for the best, with things so unsettled in the valley. The important thing now is to help your wife get back her strength."

Seth did not answer.

Annie McCullough went back to the Enyards' farm the following morning, but Else stayed two more days to see her neighbor out of danger. Seth never railed at Lucinda in her presence again, but it was apparent the girl had done something to lose his affection.

When the morning for her departure came, Else spoke of their impending trip to Carlisle. "You'll have your strength by the time we have to leave for Carlisle, Maggie."

Maggie nodded. "I mislike to think of leavin' again. Suppose Felix should come home and find us gone?"

"I reckon he'd find ya some way."

"If I could see him, I do believe I'd feel like I used to. . . ."

"We have to hope. It's what keeps us goin'—George Eldridge and you folks and us," Else said.

There was silence at the mention of George Eldridge's name, and she saw the strain on Maggie's face. Else began to suspect that whatever Lucinda had done was related to him. She thought she knew now why Lucinda was no longer caring for Thomas.

One day in late January Jim McCullough and Ben were chopping trees between the Enyard farm and the Eldridge's when they heard the jingle of horses' bits on harness leather, and a group of militiamen rode up. Ben raised a hand in greeting. "What are ya doin' so far from Fort Lyttleton in the middle of winter?"

The sergeant reined in and looked about uneasily. "Injuns."

"Ya mean . . . ?"

The man nodded. "Family on the other side of Aughwick Crick was massacred yesterday. One of the boys escaped and came to the fort."

"I never heard of no raids in winter," Jim said.

"Well, things is different this year. There's been four or five families killed in the past two weeks," the sergeant told him. "We been searchin' the woods, but ain't caught up with 'em. Only seen what they done to those families."

Ben and Jim exchanged glances.

"Ya been to see the Abbots?"

"Just come from there. They're goin' to Fort Lyttleton today."

"Fort Lyttleton?"

The man nodded.

"And George Eldridge?"

"We're on our way there now."

"Tell him to bring the wagon and horses right away. We're goin' to Carlisle."

"I wish ya luck. It's a long way to go with the woods full of them varmints."

"Thanks," said Ben. "Thanks for warnin' us."

" 'Twas the captain who sent us," the sergeant said as they turned their horses toward the Eldridge farm.

CHAPTER XI

Carlisle

They could take only the necessities with them in the Conestoga wagon, but at the last minute Else Enyard insisted on taking her spinning wheel. Ben was against it, for it was important to travel as light as possible.

Three of the McCulloughs rode with them in the Enyard wagon—Jim, on the high seat beside Ben, Fiona, and Angus, the youngest boy. Jim watched for Indians, and Else had Silas's long gun poking out from the top of the canvas at the rear.

Fiona sat inside the wagon, surrounded by kettles, bullet molds, and household goods. She had a quilt wrapped around her, for it was very cold. Else knew by the way she held herself that she was frightened.

The little boys huddled together, their eyes large with fright. "Will they scalp us, Ma?" asked Peter. "Like they did to Ari?"

Else hesitated. "They don't always scalp people," she said. "Sometimes they take them captive. And sometimes they adopt them."

"Did they adopt Silas?" Angus asked.

"Why, I reckon so. I do believe he's alive somewhere." Her voice carried more conviction than she felt.

"Some man said he saw a boy that the Injuns scalped who was livin' afterward but he didn't have no hair," Angus said.

"Where'd you hear that?" Fiona asked. "You're just makin' that up!"

"I ain't! Over to the fort—a man at the fort said so."

"Well, I don't believe it," Fiona said. "How could a person live with the top of his head gone?"

"Angus is tellin' the truth, Fiona. There's been others who's been scalped that lived," Else said.

Within the wagon Peter spoke. He was four now, a sturdy child with Silas's eyes and a dimple in his chin. "Ma, if—if the Injuns treats them people kind, why can't Silas come home?"

Else spoke carefully. "Well, if he's a captive, they wouldn't want him to leave, now would they? No more than we would." She tried to speak convincingly.

"I want to be an Injun!" said Angus. "I'd never have to wash my neck and ears. Or wear clothes."

"You'd be mighty cold in winter with no clothes," said Else.

Ben had told Else there would be less chance of an attack when they reached the road that ran to Carlisle. Dispatch runners used this route and military supply wagons carried ammunition and pay to Fort Lyttleton on it, he said. They had agreed before starting out that they would stop only to feed and water the horses. They dared not make a fire, for smoke would rise far on a still winter day, so Else passed out fat chunks of smoked venison and johnnycake.

As soon as they had eaten, she picked up the rifle again. Her shoulders ached from propping it against the tailboard and her eyes burned from watching for signs of Indians. When Annibele cried to be fed, she turned to Fiona. "Think ya might hold the gun and keep watch while I feed her?"

"Oh, Miz Enyard, I—I ain't never touched a long gun!" the girl said in dismay.

"Well, you never know when you're going to have to use one. If I was you I'd get Jim or your pa to teach me how to shoot."

Jim shuffled his feet to keep the blood circulating. "Sure is gettin' cold! How far you aimin' to travel before night, Ben?"

"I don't know. Twenty, maybe twenty-five, miles. I'd like to get as far as we can before stoppin'. Closer we get to Carlisle, less chance we have of bein' attacked. I figure we'll find a cabin someplace where they'll take us in for the night."

"Ain't seen no people since we started. I reckon most of the cabins ain't near the road."

"We'll just have to chance it then." As they bumped over the icy ruts, they were so cold and miserable that all conversation ceased. The landscape was devoid of movement save for the Eldridge wagon up ahead. Shadows were lengthening and the chill in the air grew stronger. Ben thought it wasn't just savages they had to worry about. It was the cold and the chance that a horse might go lame or they might break an axle, leaving them stranded.

As the last streaks of sunset subsided, they saw Robert McCullough stand up in the forward wagon and point to the left. In a clearing a short distance from the road stood an abandoned cabin, its shutters flapping in the wind. There was no barn, only a lean-to. Ben signaled for them to stop.

The men took turns guarding the horses while inside the cabin the women dozed fitfully. Only the children slept that night.

They left the cabin before dawn, as the first blue-green light touched the tops of the trees. The horses were nervous and hard to handle and there was a hint of snow in the air.

They had been on their way about four hours when Ben stopped the team, motioning for George to pull alongside of them. He reached for his rifle as he spoke. "Looks like a party of Injuns up ahead, goin' the same way we are. And if I ain't mistook, there's a white man leadin' them."

Robert McCullough rubbed his chin. "Ain't natural for a war party to be marchin' along the road like that in broad daylight."

Annie peered at the moving figures. "It's that Injun interpreter, Conrad Weiser."

When they were within hailing distance, Robert McCullough called out, "Be you Conrad Weiser?"

The white man leading the Indians turned. "That's right. And these are friendly Cherokees. No cause for alarm."

As they approached the party they saw two elderly Indians carrying belts of wampum.

"Where you heading?" Weiser asked.

"Carlisle."

"We're on our way to a parley with the Delaware chiefs at Harris's Ferry."

"Delawares?" Robert McCullough's face paled.

"They raidin' as far east as Harris's Ferry now?" Ben tried to keep his voice calm.

"Oh, they're not raiding in the area," Weiser said. "They're sending a number of their chiefs to sit down with me and our Cherokee friends to discuss ending the war. You planning on staying at Carlisle?"

"Yup, aimin' to join the militia."

"Colonel Armstrong will be glad to have you. He needs every able-bodied man he can get. God go with you!"

"How far are we from Carlisle?" Ben called as the wagons overtook Weiser's party.

"You'll make it before sunset. No need to worry."

When Weiser and the Cherokees were out of sight, the journey seemed lonelier than before.

Occasionally they saw deserted farms, the cabin roofs sagging under the weight of snow, doors gone, windows gaping. There was no sign of life except for a fox that dashed across the road into a thicket and some crows rising above the stubble of a deserted cornfield.

It was well past sunset when the wagons lumbered into Carlisle. They were surprised to find people on the streets and candlelight from unshuttered windows spilling over the snow. On the square was a limestone quarry and a little farther on were stocks and pillory, which gave them a shock. Many houses were two-storyed and built of stone.

They had no difficulty in locating Colonel Armstrong's headquarters. The McCullough men watched the wagons, and Ben and George went to speak with the colonel; the women sat in a small anteroom, holding the sleeping babies, as the children curled up like kittens on the floor.

The women were nodding when Ben and George returned with Colonel Armstrong. "Welcome to Carlisle," he said. "You were wise to come when you did, though I'm sorry you've had a hard journey. Mr. Eldridge and Mr. Enyard have just joined the militia. I'll send an orderly to watch the wagons while the McCulloughs come in. Then we'll find you a place to stay."

Else noted his clear eyes, firm mouth, and round, smooth-shaven chin. He was not a tall man but had a quality that made one think of him as tall. He looked, she decided, like someone you could trust.

They found two small rooms with Mrs. Hetty Graffius, an elderly woman who had a two-story house on the edge of the town. That night they put the children on the beds and slept in their clothes on the floor, too depleted to care that they needed a bath and clean clothing.

The elderly widow whose home they shared was a source of encouragement, as they set about organizing their new life. Hetty Graffius had lost her husband the year before, and a daughter and her family had been killed by the Indians last summer. "They was livin' over near Bigham's," she said. "Didn't have no warnin'—men was out in the fields when the Delawares crept up on them. My daughter and her family wasn't spared. Even the children was scalped." She paused to wipe her eyes. "Wonder how long such things can continue. Must be a purpose behind it. My son wants me to go live with them but I couldn't give up my home. My husband and me spent too many happy years here." Seeing her small black eyes in the crinkled moist face, Else was reminded of raisins in a suet pudding.

The men were completing the fort, which was half a mile beyond the town limits. The work went slowly, for there were few recruits. The anxious settlers coming to Carlisle were eager for the protection of the military but saw no reason why they should join the militia. Beyond the fort some families still lived in their lonely cabins, supplying the town with meat and flour. Colonel Armstrong knew that if the situation became worse, he would have to send militia to protect these people as they planted and harvested.

After some weeks word came that no farms were left standing in the Cove. When they heard the news, Else covered her face with her hands, tears running between her spread fingers. All their hopes, their years of sacrifice and effort—all gone! Ben pulled her to him. "I know what ya feel, Ma. But at least we're alive—and together. And we got a good place to stay. Someday we'll go back to our own land and begin again."

Carlisle was becoming so overcrowded with desperate people that the town was hard pressed to care for them; every house sheltered two or more families. Churches provided shelter, and some slept in barns and lofts. Food was in short supply, especially meat.

"I wonder if they're as short on victuals at Fort Lyttleton as we are? I reckon the Abbots is glad they went there instead of comin' here," Annie remarked one evening when the men had joined them for their meal.

"I heard Mrs. Abbot's determined to stay at Fort Lyttleton in case Felix comes back," Robert said.

At the mention of the Abbots George Eldridge's neck grew florid and he kept his eyes on the stew he was eating. There was a sudden silence and George was aware of Ben watching him. He spoke hastily as if he had not heard the comments on the Abbots. "People can't get outside to go huntin', so the colonel's written to the Assembly for appropriations to buy salt pork and mutton."

The adults stared, puzzled by this abrupt shift in conversation. George glanced about uneasily, then began to eat. His desire for Lucinda was so shameful, he was so guilt-ridden, that he could endure it only by pretending to himself it had not happened. This was possible so long as he was very busy at the fort and there was nothing to remind him of Lucinda. But the mention of the Abbots revived his torment.

In early March a party of rangers from Fort Lyttleton discovered the remains of an Indian campsite, abandoned some time ago, on the other side of the mountain. After studying the arrowheads discovered there, Conrad Weiser told them it had been a Shawnee camp. Tied to several trees near a brook were small strips of calico, much faded by the weather. One piece was sent to Colonel Armstrong, who had it fastened on the wall in his headquarters so those seeking news of missing relatives could attempt to identify it.

That night George Eldridge returned to Hetty Graffius's full of restrained excitement. "It's from Mary Ann's dress!" he told them.

"How can ya tell?" Annie McCullough asked. "I hear it's all faded."

"The pattern is the same as the one she was wearin' the day she disappeared."

"But the women all bought cloth from the same traders," said Robert.

"No, the dress she was wearin' that day was an old one she brought from the Gwynedd Valley."

"If it was Shawnees that took her," Ben said, "she's out in the Ohio country now. Ain't no way of findin' her unless a miracle happens."

But they could not dampen George's hope. For weeks he went about like a new man, confident that his beautiful young wife would be reunited with him and his past would be forgotten. He was briefly his former handsome, assured self.

"I only hope he ain't due for a disappointment," Else said.

Late in March word came from Fort Lyttleton that Felix Abbot had escaped from a Shawnee winter camp in the Ohio country and, after a terrible journey, was reunited with his family.

"Maybe he'll have word of Mary Ann," Else suggested.

"Ya goin' to ask Colonel Armstrong if ya can ride to Lyttleton to talk to Felix?" Robert asked George at supper that night.

George flushed and looked away. "Reckon we're too busy to ask any favors just now."

"Maybe ya could be the courier for a couple days," Jim suggested.

"I'll get the information about Mary Ann in my own time and in my own way. Never ya mind about it!" George snapped. Ben and Else were the only ones who suspected the cause of his anger. They saw the curious glances of the others and changed the subject.

Two days later a deposition of Felix's experience was sent to

Colonel Armstrong. In it, Felix said that he and Mary Ann Eldridge had been made to run the gauntlet, that she had wielded a large German frying pan to protect herself from the blows; the following morning he had been taken with some other male captives to a distant camp, and from there by slow stages to an Indian village near a lake in Ohio. He had never seen Mary Ann again but he remembered one thing: the leader who had captured them was a tall Shawnee called Tawaugoa. He spoke some English and had been much taken with Mary Ann, trying to persuade the other braves not to make her run the gauntlet. In a matter of hours the story had been repeated all over Carlisle, with the usual embellishments and distortions.

One evening as Ben and George were returning to the fort, an ugly fellow with a cast in one eye approached them. "I hear your wife's servin' as a squaw to that Injun that captured her," he said, showing a mouthful of rotted stumps of teeth.

Before Ben could stop him George struck the man in the belly, then the groin. His face was contorted with a murderous rage as he grabbed the fellow by the throat and began to strangle him as Ben struggled to separate them.

"Help me pull him off!" Ben yelled.

A man stepped from the crowd that had gathered to watch. Ben had a glimpse of massive shoulders and a rough black beard. The newcomer enclosed George in a bearlike embrace and lifted him from his victim, setting him on his feet. Without a word he disappeared in the press, but not before Ben saw that he had a clubfoot.

George was shaking, his eyes glittering, his breathing raucous. He picked up his hat and straightened his clothes. Ben had never seen him so angry. "Anybody else got somethin' to say about my wife?" he asked. The onlookers were silent, as they parted to let the two men pass.

"If I was you, I'd not go out alone for a couple days," Ben said. "That fellow is a mean one and likely he's got cronies. No tellin' what could happen."

"Much obliged to ya," George said, his mouth bitter.

After that they noticed a change in him. He became silent and withdrawn and he looked, Annie McCullough said, years older.

Two days later George did not appear for his tour of duty. The officer in charge, suspecting foul play, sent out a patrol to search for him. After an hour's search they found him on a back street, his body a mass of cuts and bruises. He could not tell them the names of his assailants. The patrol took him to the fort to be cared for.

"I'll reckon that Patrick Brady was with them that beat him up!" Jim McCullough said.

"He ain't had nothin' against George," his father reminded him. "Besides, he's still at Fort Lyttleton."

"I think it was the man he beat up that done it. Him and his friends," Ben said.

The McCullough men were on twenty-four-hour duty at the fort, so Else and Annie were not aware of what had happened. When George did not appear for his usual visit to his son, Else was concerned.

"I'm goin' over to the fort to see if George is sick," she announced.

"Take one of the boys along," said Annie. "Take Robbie."

So they set out, picking their way carefully through the milling crowds: farmers in patched clothes; grim-faced women and their hungry, tow-haired progeny; grizzled trappers, squirting tobacco juice and swapping stories; and gangs of bullies, elbowing their way. Else was amazed to see human feces in the street. Then she remembered that many people were living in tents; what could you expect?

Suddenly she saw a face in the crowd that arrested her attention. She stared at the wide-set blue eyes with their thick frame of blond lashes, the deep pink cheeks, and sullen, full-lipped mouth. The girl's hood had fallen back and Else saw her heavy blond hair piled on top of her head in imitation of a lady of fashion. "Lucinda!" she called. "What are ya doin' here?" But the girl turned away. Else caught a glimpse of the big man in frontier clothes who was propelling the girl by the arm. Then the crowd engulfed them.

"Move on, lady. You're blockin' the street," someone said.

She caught Robbie's arm. "Did ya see that girl, Robbie?"

"What girl?"

"The one with the yellow hair—in the blue cloak."

"No. Why?"

"I think," she said, raising her voice to be heard above the din, "I think—it was Lucinda Abbot."

The noise was deafening now. Else regretted her impulse to go to the fort. When she saw someone empty a bucket of slops on the heads of the crowd, she stopped in dismay. "Come on, Robbie! We're goin' home."

The following afternoon Ben came with news of George.

"What's this place comin' to? It ain't safe in daylight for respectable folk to go 'cross town," Else said.

"Ma, I got somethin' to tell ya," Ben said. "Walk with me down to the end of the garden."

"What is it, Ben? Is it somethin' to do with Silas?"

"No, Ma, it ain't about Silas. It's about the new Pennsylvania Regiment Governor Denny's fixin' to start. It'll have three battalions and we'll have to join for three years—that is, if we want to get paid."

"Three years?" Her voice reflected her dismay.

Ben nodded.

"They think the Injun war will last for three more years, Ben?"

"Seems so."

"But what about our land? How can we hold onto our spread that Pa worked so hard to clear if you're away soldierin'?"

"Ma," he said patiently, "with the raids gettin' worse, there won't be any venturin' to the Coves to settle. It won't be safe for any white man on the frontier till the war is over."

"But how will we manage?"

"That's just it, Ma. If I join up, you can stay here in Carlisle, and my pay'll be enough to provide for you. Ain't no way to earn nothin' in this town lessen I join up."

They would have to start over, she thought. In three years the stumps would have put out strong shoots, the cleared ground would revert to partial wilderness. She remembered the soldiers had said there wasn't a cabin left standing in the Coves. It would be a terrible effort with just the two of them, for Peter would be still too young to do much.

"Only other thing is for me to take ya back to New Jersey to your kin in the Passaic Valley when my term is up," he said, knowing she would never agree to this.

"Oh, no, Ben! I couldn't do that! I ain't one for turnin' back. We might have to stay here for a time, and it is crowded, but it's better than askin' relatives for charity." She paused. "You'd best join up, son."

He did not answer.

Then she remembered Lucinda. "Ben, yesterday when Robbie and me was tryin' to get to the fort for news of George, I saw Lucinda Abbot in the crowd."

"She's here, all right. I didn't know if I should tell ya or not. Seems she run off with a soldier over to Fort Lyttleton. Was makin' for Philadelphia when the militia caught up with them. Brought them back here for a court-martial. He was hung."

Else's face went white. "Ben, that's—that's awful!"

"Must've been hard on the Abbots."

"How did ya find out about this?"

"Well, when a soldier deserts his post and runs off with a young girl who's under age, the word gets out."

"What did Lucinda do?"

He blushed. "I don't know if I should tell ya or not, Ma."

"I have a right to know."

"She didn't have no place to go and wouldn't go back to her parents, so she went to work in one of them taverns—the Pot o' Gold, it's called."

"What kind of work is she doin'?"

His face was scarlet now, contrasting strangely with his reddish hair. "She's servin' drinks and—and more."

She looked blank.

"Doggone it, Ma, ya know what I mean. She's sellin' herself to men."

"Oh, Ben, not that!"

"She ain't much good," he said stiffly.

"How could she do such a thing?" She was remembering the stillbirth in the Abbot cabin, and Seth Abbot blaming Lucinda.

"Something happened when Mrs. McCullough and me went over to help with the birthin'," she said. "When the baby was born dead, Seth Abbot blamed it on Lucinda. He didn't mention George but I guessed it was somethin' to do with him—probably happened when he was sick and she was lookin' after him."

"So you knew about that?" he said, amazed.

"I didn't *know,* Ben, I guessed. Oh, Ben, we got to help her! We can't let her stay in that place and ruin her life."

"It's already ruined," he said. "What man would marry her now?"

CHAPTER XII

The Dreamer

In the Shawnee village in the Pennsylvania wilderness Mary Ann Eldridge attempted to keep count of the days of her captivity by placing an acorn in a small hole she had made outside the hut she shared with Melakome. But children found the cache and took the acorns to use in their games.

After that she ceased trying to mark the passage of time. One day flowed into the next with little change. She looked after Ahotah's infant, worked with the other women, and continued to learn Shawnee. At night she dreamed of George and Thomas and occasionally of Tawaugoa. The dreams she had of her captor disturbed her deeply, for in them he reached out to her from a high cliff across a deep chasm, and she tried to go to him but never could.

Mary Ann was shocked by the dream. She loved her husband and had never been attracted to another man. She told herself she was drawn to Tawaugoa because he was the only person in the village with whom she could speak English. She dared not admit that in his presence she forgot about George.

She had seen no more of the two boys who had been captured some weeks earlier. She guessed that they had been taken away to some distant camp. The badly injured woman had simply disappeared, as had the middle-aged German man. His wife was set to work skinning small animals, as she did not appear well enough to grind corn. Mary Ann had smiled at her but the woman turned away, her face bitter. She had seen Mary Ann nursing the Indian baby and assumed the captive was wife to the infant's father.

Mary Ann was determined to find out why the other captives had disappeared but when she asked Melakome, the only reply was a brief statement that they had gone north. Now she tried to find out from Tawaugoa. "That woman, the one who was hurt bad, where is she? I ain't seen her but once since she came," she said in English.

"No here. No more here," he said.

"You mean she's dead?"

"Dead? What dead?"

She resorted to pantomime, giving a slight shudder, then assuming a fixed stare, arms hanging limp and motionless. He stared, then began to laugh, showing strong white teeth.

Mary Ann was shocked. "How can you laugh at that?" she asked, furious. "She was hurt bad, so bad she must of died, and you think to laugh!" His laughter ceased as he saw that she was very angry.

"Not like Maully—woman not strong. No good!" he said.

"You're no better than the others. Savages, all of you."

At first he did not understand the meaning of her words. When he grasped their import, he was deeply insulted. "Go!" he said harshly. "Maully not know Shawanee ways! Go!" he glared at her, arms folded across his chest.

She did not see him for several days.

When at last he sent for her, he looked troubled.

"Maully not happy?" he asked, as if there had been no quarrel between them. She did not answer. His next words surprised her. "When sun come up, we go to Ohio. Far. To winter home. Long walk."

"Tomorrow we leave here?" she asked tremulously. "We go to the winter village of the Shawnees?"

"No village. Camp. Big camp," he said.

The news filled her with despair. Ohio! That was beyond the French fort of Duquesne, many days' journey from here. How could George ever find her? She covered her face with her hands and began to weep.

Tawaugoa sent for Melakome. "What did you say to her?" she asked.

"That we go to our winter camp beyond Logstown tomorrow."

The old woman gave him a sharp look. "You do not understand, nephew. She still grieves for her child and her husband."

As Melakome motioned for the girl to follow her, he looked after them in dismay.

"There is much work to do to prepare for the journey," the old woman said matter-of-factly. "You will not have time for tears, my daughter. They are for the weak. You have a strong spirit."

It was then Mary Ann remembered her plan to tie scraps from her old calico dress to a tree near the brook so the militia would know she was still alive. Later in the day she managed to slip away and head for the brook. She tied a scrap from her old dress to a low-hanging branch, taking care that she was not observed. She was certain the soldiers from Fort Lyttleton would find it and rescue her.

Her spirits lifted as she helped the women break camp, dismantling the bark huts of their simple furnishings, making bundles of hides and household paraphernalia, preparing the foodstuffs for the journey. Mary Ann worked with renewed hope and energy, for the simple act of leaving behind a scrap from her old dress filled her with optimism. She told herself it was foolish to have such a strong certainty that she would be rescued, but the preparations for the journey gave her a sense of purpose.

She wondered where Felix Abbot was. Perhaps he was living in the Shawnee camp in Ohio.

Early the next morning they were off, long lines of men, women, and children, with the two white captives, wending their way west through the tall trees. The woods were brilliant with reds and golds, browns and tawny pinks, the ground crisp underfoot. Long Vs of migratory birds passed overhead. By the brook a bluejay alighted on a branch where a scrap of dark red calico fluttered in the breeze. He turned his neck from side to side, eyeing this strange object; then, deciding that it was not edible, he flew off with a great beating of wings.

As the column traveled slowly westward, autumn advanced. In the early morning when they broke their camp and started on their way, they were wrapped in fog so dense that they could see only four or five feet ahead. No one wandered from the trail, for fear he would not find the group again.

Then the autumn rains began. Mary Ann's moccasins were caked with mud and oozed water at every step. It required energy just to lift one foot after the other. Her blanket was soaked through and afforded no protection against the lashing rain, which left her fine deerskin dress and leggings heavy with the weight of the water. Trudging along the muddy path with the child strapped to her back, she did not know that the morning before they left the village, a messenger from Kittaning had brought a wampum belt telling of the disaster that had befallen the Delaware people there.

They subsisted on pemmican and charred corn pounded into flour and mixed with maple sugar. At night they erected crude shelters of evergreens, but these could not keep out the constant downpour.

Melakome's hand grew knobby from the wetness and her ankles swelled. Mary Ann was certain she was in pain, but she never complained. Many of the Indians developed coughs and several had fever. The children were particularly miserable. The older ones were stoical but some of the smaller ones kept up a fretful obbligato that Mary Ann would hear in memory whenever she recalled that autumn journey.

When Mary Ann's milk dried up the cradleboard was given to another young woman, but Mary Ann felt too light-headed to care. She developed a pain in her chest and her breathing was labored.

Melakome observed the change in her and spoke to Tawaugoa. "Maully is sick. Very bad. She says nothing but I do not think she can continue much longer."

"What kind of sickness?"

"Here," she said touching her chest.

"Is it a sickness of the spirit?" he asked.

"No, it is not that. She cannot take in air as one does who is strong."

"We are not far from Fort Duquesne now. It is only a day's journey by river to our camp. The sweat bath will make her well." He spoke confidently.

"Perhaps. I am not sure, Tawaugoa."

Alarmed by her words, he pushed his way through the line to Mary Ann. She did not respond to his greeting but continued to look down at the trail. "Melakome tells me Maully sick," he said.

She raised her head and he saw her flushed face and cracked lips, the unnatural brilliance of the eyes, and heard her labored breathing. "We not far from river at French fort. We go by canoe to Shawanee camp. . . . You understand?"

She tried to smile, but she felt very ill. He touched her hand, felt how cold it was. Calling to Wa-we-tah to help her, he went forward to lead the column.

At length the trail widened and they saw between the trees a massive fort, its flag bearing the white-and-gold fleur-de-lis of France, and smoke curling from its chimneys. *Couriers de bois* in knitted caps and tight leather breeches mingled with Indians in front of the stockade. A broad muddy river, the Ohio, flowed near the walls and was joined by the Allegheny and the Monongahela to form a rough Y.

The huge stockade gate opened to emit an officer in a fine uniform with several soldiers at his heels. There was a low-pitched conversation between the officer and Tawaugoa. Then the officer strode toward the two white captives. He was a short man with lively dark eyes and a disdainful manner. As his eyes swept the middle-aged German woman from head to feet, he said something that made his men laugh and wink. Then he came to Mary Ann, lifting her chin and peering at her as if she were a slave to be auctioned. "C'est une très belle femme! Qu'est-ce qui ne va pas? Elle est malade?" he said.

Mary Ann did not know what this meant but the sound of the strange language filled her with fear, for it was the French who had stirred up the Indians to attack the English settlements. It was they who offered bounties for English scalps. The officer put his hand on her breast. As she shrank from his touch, Tawaugoa came to her side and roughly pushed the Frenchman's hand away. "Elle n'est pas à vendre!"

She was surprised to hear Tawaugoa speaking French. His tone was harsh, and sick as she was, she saw that he was very angry. The officer shrugged and turned his back on them. The soldiers who accompanied him looked at her with frank curiosity, their eyes undressing her as she waited, her cheeks glowing with fever.

As the Frenchmen returned to the fort, there was a hurried conversation among the Shawnee leaders. They determined not to tarry at the fort but to leave at once for Logstown, the trading post on the Ohio that was near their camp.

They were descending to the river when a soldier came running after them. "Un moment, mes amis! Attendez, s'il vous plaît!"

They recognized him as a member of the group that had accompanied the officer. "My captain sends you a message, my friends," he said, trying to catch his breath.

The Shawnee leaders waited in silence.

"He says to you zat we put zis woman in ze fort hôpital. To take care of her. When she ees strong, we send her to you."

Tawaugoa looked at him with contempt. "Tell him that is not possible."

The soldier approached Mary Ann and lightly touched her hand. "Et vous, mam'selle? Voulez-vous rester ici? Ils sont sauvages, vous savez."

She did not know what he was talking about, but she sensed he was not trying to rescue her. She looked at Tawaugoa and the imperceptible turning of his head gave her the information she needed. Summoning all her strength, she lifted her chin and told him no.

As they descended the muddy bank, Mary Ann slipped and fell. Tawaugoa heard Melakome cry out and turned to see Mary Ann lying among the rushes, her eyes closed, her breathing so shallow that it was barely perceptible. He knelt beside her, calling her name, but she did not answer. Gently he lifted her in his arms and bore her to the foremost canoe, where Melakome waited. The old woman looked at him questioningly as he laid Mary Ann on the floor of the slim craft and then took his place at the stern. His face was bitter with shock and grief as he thrust the paddle vigorously into the water and the canoe glided swiftly up the Ohio, moving northward and west, toward Logstown.

CHAPTER XIII

Lucinda

Catching a glimpse of Mrs. Enyard's face in the crowd made Lucinda Abbot confront things she wished to forget. She linked her arm with that of her companion and said with a note of urgency, "Hurry, Rufe! Let's git back to the tavern."

"Thought you wanted to buy goods for a fancy dress," the man said, his eyes narrowing as he regarded her. He was tall and large muscled, and had a rough, dark beard and a crooked nose. His eyes, set far apart under heavy brows, were piercingly blue and seemed at odds with the rest of him.

"Well, I changed my mind."

"What's goin' on? You seen somebody you knows?" His big spatulate fingers dug into her arm.

"That hurts, Rufe! I don't feel so good."

He noticed that her cheeks were pale and she seemed anxious. He looked her over critically. It always took time with such girls. Her family had probably protected her, but she was healthy and strong and in a month or so would be bringing in a pretty piece of business. She couldn't go on wearing that drab homespun dress, though. Made a man feel guilty to be treating her like a fancy woman—like making sport with your own sister.

"Listen here," he said. "I'll take you back to the tavern but you got to understand one thing: You *ain't* Lucinda Abbot now! Do you hear?"

She looked up at him. "What do you mean?"

"I don't want no trouble—that's what. I don't fancy your pa comin' to look fer ya and gettin' me in trouble with the law.

You're goin' to forget where you come from, who your folks is. From now on you're"—he paused, trying to find a suitable name—"Sally Bridges."

She tested the name to get the feel of it. "Sally Bridges. . . . Where'd ya get that name, Rufe?"

"Never ya mind." He'd been patient with her at first; now it was time she learned what he expected of her. She knew a trick or two. . . . He thought of the soldier Lucinda had run off with. He was hanged right over by the new fort. It wasn't a pretty sight, a good-looking young fellow with curly hair, turning slowly from the end of the rope.

She had come to the tavern, asking for work, saying she couldn't go back to her folks for the disgrace of it, for her folks were respectable. He had laughed. She'd gotten mad and started to go, but when he told her, "If you're lookin' for a 'respectable' place to work ya come to the wrong tavern," he had seen from the look in her eyes that she wasn't so innocent. So she'd stayed and pleasured him first and often.

"Look here," Rufe said, "there's another thing. When ya want to go out, you'll go with me or one of the girls. Mollie can buy the goods for that dress. You'd best get it sewed soon, for I'm sick of seein' ya in that homespun."

"But I want to pick out what I'm goin' to be wearin'."

"Mollie knows what's wanted." He squeezed her arm, hard.

Lucinda stared at herself in the cracked mirror, unable to tear her eyes away from the elegant girl in the low-cut crimson gown. Never had she dreamed of looking so grand. Mollie had arranged her hair, crimping it with a hot poker to form little curly tendrils about her eyes and piling the rest on top of her head. She had showed Lucinda how to cut the dress so that it seemed to be slipping off her white shoulders, exposing the top of her breasts, and had sewed a ruffle of lace to the sleeves just below the elbow. The waist was so tight Lucinda could scarcely breathe, and the crimson folds of the skirt revealed her ankles. Mollie got her some purple hose—and blue garters with rosettes of ribbon. Lucinda wished George Eldridge could see her now. He would forget Mary Ann.

Ma and Pa would never understand the excitement of having men want her, their hands tearing at her clothes and their look of stunned admiration when they saw her white breasts and long smooth legs. If she had a customer she didn't like, she'd learned how to fake her response so they thought she was pleasured as much as they. If a man stank or was too rough, she took heart, knowing it would be over in a few minutes.

She would never go home to her parents! Never would she be treated as a child again, forced to listen to Ma's complaints and wear those ugly old homespuns, her hair in braids, her charms hidden.

A memory interrupted her thoughts: a slender young man, hands tied behind his back, his neck bound with a rope as he sat upon a horse beneath the gallows tree. One of the soldiers switched the horse and it took off, leaving the boy twisting and jerking as the rope tightened. She saw his face turning red, then purple, his soft curly hair tossing in the wind, finally his eyes bulging, tongue protruding. She heard the slow intake of breath from the spectators, the shrill frightened cries of the women.

Lucinda was trembling now; the eyes in the mirror were dark with the horror of it. "It wasn't my fault," she said. "I didn't mean him no harm!" He'd been so crazy about her he'd do anything to get her, promising to take her to Philadelphia, where he had an aunt who would take them in until he found work. How was she to know what would happen to him? She hadn't believed they would really hang him.

Oh, Lord, would she ever be able to put it out of her mind? It was worse at night, and she was glad when the customers wore her out. When she was too spent and aching to lift a finger, sleep would come.

Rufus Pincus opened the door downstairs in the public room and hollered up, "Get on down here, Sally! There's customers!"

"I'm comin'."

As she entered the low-ceilinged room in which a bright fire crackled, she saw the men look up. Most were soldiers from the fort, with a few trappers and traders.

"Well, look what we got here!"

"Got to hand it to you, Rufe! You sure can pick 'em."

Lucinda walked on, swinging her hips, head high, her crimson skirt swishing.

"My, ain't we grand!"

Someone gave her a pinch. An older man, somewhat tipsy, lifted her skirt and let out a whoop at the sight of her legs in the purple hose. She let him have a look, then moved over to the group playing cards at a battered oak table near the fire.

Only one of the four men playing euchre did not look up when she entered the room, a gentleman, by the look of him, with his fine tiered cape thrown back over his shoulders as he dealt the cards. His hands were white and slender, with long tapering fingers, on one of which a gold signet ring shone in the firelight. He wore a canary velvet weskit and a snuff-brown frock coat, but his stock was soiled and his lace cuffs needed mending.

Conscious of her gaze, he looked up, giving her an appraising glance. He had a high forehead and fine eyes; his arched nose gave him a high-born look. His mouth twisted at one side as if about to laugh. Even before he spoke she knew he was English.

"My apologies, my dear. Won't you join us? Pray sit beside me. Perchance you may bring me luck." He rose with a little bow and offered her his seat, pulling a stool from another table.

Lucinda felt shy. She saw Rufe watching her with approval as she sat down and crossed her legs, hoping the gentleman would see the purple hose.

The man picked up his cards. She knew this was a serious business, this game of theirs, for the other three, after giving her a bold stare, turned their attention to the hands they had been dealt. One of them had a stack of gold coins, and the gentleman had a silk purse from which he extracted a sovereign from time to time.

Ordinarily Lucinda would have become bored with the game when no one paid her any attention, but there was something about the man in the cape that drew her. She wondered where he came from and what he was doing here. He was superior to the others and knew it; he took it for granted, but he showed no contempt for them. When the three threw down their cards, and he showed his, some of their gold coins were added to his. They looked annoyed. "Shall we continue, gentlemen?" he asked.

By the end of the third game several men had come over to the table to watch. When the gentleman again gathered in the coins, the other players looked at him with undisguised resentment. Rufe Pincus had joined them, sensing that trouble might be brewing. He wanted no knifing in the Pot of Gold. Abruptly the man with the cape stood up, sweeping the gold coins into his silk purse.

"Ya ain't quittin' without givin' us a chance to win back the money?" one man asked. His clothes smelled of horse manure, and tobacco juice trickled from one side of his mouth onto his matted beard.

"Another time," the man answered, placing his arm about Lucinda. "Sorry to keep you waiting, my dear. So fair a creature should not have to suffer the indignity of waiting. . . ."

She didn't know what to do. She looked at Rufe. He nodded so slightly that the three men never noticed. As she rose, the stranger bent and kissed the back of her neck, whispering, "Courage!"

There was a growl of anger as she led him to the stairs. She heard them push back their stools. "Why, ya dirty yellow-livered horse thief," one yelled.

"Can I get ya a hot noggin of rum, gents? There'll be plenty of time to get your money back later," Rufe said.

The gentleman shut the door of the public room tightly behind them and drew out a large linen handkerchief to wipe his brow. "A bit of a close shave, that!" he said with a laugh. "If you hadn't come to my assistance, I really think there might have been a bit of trouble."

"They're mean, and that fat one that smells so bad don't like to lose. Rufe says he cheats. . . ." She stopped in dismay. He might say something to Rufe, and then she'd be in trouble.

He patted her shoulder. "I shall not repeat your remark."

They emerged from the steep stairway into the small room where she took her customers. Lucinda's old homespun dress was thrown in a corner, the washbasin filled with dirty water was still standing on the chest, and powder had spilled on the table. But he seemed not to notice, as he tossed his cape onto a chair, and threw himself onto the bed. "God, but I'm weary!" he said.

Lucinda stood awkwardly, looking down at him, her hands clasped loosely. "Can I get ya somethin'?" she said.

He waved his hand languidly and gazed at the ceiling. She removed his shoes with the silver buckles, still unable to decipher him.

"Do you know," he said finally, "I've only just arrived from Philadelphia, the quaint city of Quakers and brotherly love."

"Ya come from Philadelphia to Carlisle?" She was amazed. "Why would ya come here? The settlers are pourin' in to escape the Injuns—they ain't got no place to stay. Some's sleepin' in their wagons, them that's got wagons."

He turned to look at her. "It was my misfortune to be discovered cheating at cards . . . a weakness of mine, my dear. Men do not take kindly to card cheats, you know. When it is a question of life and death one cannot be too particular." His eyes lighted. "Demme, but you're a fine gal! What is your name?"

"Luc—I mean Sally. Sally Bridges."

"Sally! Good old name. Sound as Yorkshire pudding. Allow me to introduce myself, my dear. Geoffrey Moncrief, third son of Lord Cecil Moncrief of Hadley Hall, Stokes Harrow, Kent." He got up and bent his leg in a courtly bow.

Lucinda blushed with pleasure. "How do ya come to be in the provinces?"

"I do not know if you are acquainted with our custom in England in regard to inheritance, Sally."

She shook her head.

"By law, the eldest son is the principal heir to his father's estate. The remaining sons are expected to go into the army or the church. My second brother did as he was expected to do, but I had neither the taste for military life nor the vocation to go into the church. I went to Oxford, where I had hopes of becoming a tutor. All would have been well, had I not discovered a talent for cheating at cards. Now cards are an accepted thing in English society, but no gentleman cheats. I was sent down from Oxford, and my father shipped me off to the colonies with just enough of an allowance to keep me in food and pocket money."

What was this Oxford, she wondered. Was a tutor the same as a schoolmaster?

As if reading her thoughts, he went on. "Oxford is England's greatest seat of learning, Mistress Sally, where men study the classics and dissect the soul. Oh, I wasn't a very devout Catholic, in spite of a pious upbringing. The family is actually Scottish. My grandsire was involved in the Jacobean wars and had to flee Scotland, so he found an estate in Kent and settled down to the life of a squire. The family became English and stayed out of politics." He laughed lightly. "They are still Catholic but not so open about it. It was a bit of a blow to my father when I refused to go to mass or confession."

Lucinda was aware of a door opening onto a larger and more splendid world. She listened, her lips slightly parted.

"About the tutoring . . . I had the talent for it, they said, but lacked the character. One who instructs and molds the minds of England's future leaders must be above reproach. My mother wept over me and my father spent hours in the family chapel, praying for my soul." Here he flashed her an amused smile. "So—here I am, unrepentant and unreformed!"

Geoffrey Moncrief sat up and looked at her with interest. "I say, Sally Bridges, I'm dashed hungry! Think you could bring me supper? A bit of Madeira and some roast capon, perchance?"

His request was so unexpected that she stood there speechless, wondering how she could tell him Rufe charged extra for having food brought to the girls' rooms. But he anticipated her, pulling out the silk purse and extracting two gold coins. "I should think that would do it—for the food and the wine and the pleasure of your company," he said.

Lucinda gasped. "It's a lot more than you'll need, Mr. Mon—"

"Moncrief. Just think of the verse 'With Geoff Moncrief, she came to grief.' "

She laughed and picked up the coins. "It has a funny sound. I never heard that name before."

"Probably not," he said dryly. "When you return you shall tell me what a young lady like you is doing in such a place as this."

When Lucinda returned, he was stretched out on the bed asleep. She set the tray on the table and swept off the specks of powder before she woke him. "Mr. Moncrief, here's some victuals for ya."

He sat up, stretching and yawning.

"I brought you some cider and a piece of cold mutton and a roasted apple. There wasn't nothin' like ya asked fer."

He sat down at the table, raising her hand to his lips. "Served by such as you, my dear, 'tis fit for the gods." Then he attacked the mutton, eating as if he had not had a meal in days. Finally he paused. "Any sign of my erstwhile companions?"

She shook her head. "I reckon they got tired of waitin'. Mostly the customers don't take long. . . ." She blushed furiously.

"I suppose not," he said, glancing up at her.

"If I was you, Mr. Moncrief," she said, "I'd be careful tonight. They just might be waitin' when ya leave the tavern. They don't forget if they thinks somebody's got the better of 'em."

"I suppose you're right," he said, wiping his hands on his linen handkerchief. "What do you suggest I do, Sally?"

"I think you'd be safer to stay here until just before the sun comes up. They'll think you're makin' a night of it and get tired of waitin'. Then when it's still dark ya can slip out. . . . Won't be no trouble from Rufe, with all that money ya give for the victuals."

He regarded her with a mixture of surprise and amusement. "By Jove, I believe you are right! And now you shall tell me your story."

She intended to make up a fine tale, but his charm and the novelty of talking to a man who was truly interested in her made her trust him. "My folks is respectable, Mr. Moncrief."

Geoffrey nodded. "I believe you, my dear."

"We was stayin' at Fort Lyttleton after the raids started and there was a young soldier who took a shine to me. Ma and Pa was always hollerin' at me, and with Ma expectin' every year, I had to do her work 'cause she was poorly. I just couldn't stand it no more, so when Johnny was so partial to me I—I asked if he'd ever thought of goin' back to Philadelphia."

"Your parents were very strict with you?"

She nodded. She couldn't tell him about George Eldridge. It

was too shameful. "So Johnny borrowed a horse belongin' to the army and I rode behind him. We got just beyond Carlisle when the militia caught up with us. Said he was a deserter and a horse thief. They hanged him in Carlisle." Her eyes reflected her horror. "He was goin' to send money to Captain McWhirter to pay for the horse after he found work."

When Geoffrey made no comment, Lucinda continued. "I couldn't go back to my folks at the fort with everybody knowin' about it. They'd of disowned me!"

Geoffrey's voice was low, almost as if he were talking to himself. "We are both the black sheep in our family flock. . . . They condemn us and then wonder why we don't reform."

It sounded as if the things she had done were no worse than cheating at cards.

"The life you have chosen isn't easy," he said. "There are certain risks, you know . . . the pox. Or unwanted pregnancy."

"Mollie told me how to get rid of it if I was to git with child."

"Have you tried?"

"No, I ain't needed to."

"But you may," he said, swinging his legs over the side of the bed. "You aren't afraid to try if you should conceive?"

Lucinda turned her face away. She thought of her mother and the stillborn babe, and heard again the screams torn from her in the agony of birth. She paled.

He sensed that her distress stemmed from fear of childbirth. And something more.

She was crying silently. "I won't go home! No matter what happens, I won't go back!"

Geoffrey Moncrief put his arms around her. "You seem to have got yourself into a bit of a muddle, Sally Bridges. Would I could extricate you but, alas, I'm not in a very favorable position myself. Come, dry your tears, my dear." He pulled her onto his knee and patted her shoulder as if she were a child.

She put her head on his shoulder and looped an arm around his neck. An unfamiliar feeling of peace came to her.

He was reciting something now, his voice unlike any she had ever heard.

"Weep not, my wanton, smile upon my knee;
*When though art old, there's grief enough for thee."**

When Lucinda awoke some hours later the room was dark and quite cold. Geoffrey Moncrief slept in exhaustion next to her, his soft fair hair splayed across his forehead, his mouth with a suggestion of a smile.

His love-making was different from anything she had experienced. She could not have described it, but it was romantic, gentle, and, at the same time, daring. She thought of George Eldridge. There had been little tenderness in George's desperate taking of her; it had been hurried, furtive, always with a sense of shame. Geoffrey kissed the hollow of her throat. "You are so young, Sally, so fresh and sweet. Like a May morning in Kent with the meadows bright with cowslips. . . ."

She got out of bed and reached for his cloak to spread over him. Then she wrapped hers around her to ward off the chill as she fumbled in the dark for the tinderbox and the candle. In the small glow she picked up his shirt and began to sew the tears in the lace cuffs. He could not stay here, and since he did not know Carlisle, he would not know where to go.

Outside the garret window she heard a cock announcing that day was at hand. Geoffrey would have to go now. She shook his shoulder lightly. "It's time ya was goin'."

He rolled over on his side and opened his eyes, looking about him as if surprised. "Good morning, Mistress Sally. And how is the world treating you this fine morning?"

"Fine, thankee," she said blushing. "It's gettin' light out and it's best ya leave before anybody sees ya."

He ruffled his hair. "I could do with a good bath."

"Mr. Moncrief," Lucinda said anxiously, "you'd best be off. Them men'll be back lookin' for ya."

Geoffrey listened. "Your argument is well taken, my dear. . . . And where shall I find accommodations in this—er—town that is now full of those fleeing the Indians?"

* Song from *Menaphon* by Robert Greene, *Century Readings in English Literature,* 3rd ed. (New York: The Century Company, 1929), p. 187.

She thought a moment. "There's an inn over on Juniper and Fourth, the White Horse Inn. It's respectable and clean, though I reckon it's full, like every place in Carlisle."

"I see. Well," he said, beginning to dress, "I shall make do, somehow."

She hesitated. She wanted more than anything in the world to see him again, but she couldn't ask. Things she would have done with her own kind, she could not do with him. "I sewed the lace on your shirt." It was a small offering.

"Why, so you did!"

"I would of washed your stock, but it wouldn't of dried in time."

He gave her a kiss on the cheek. "Thank you, my dear. I fear your talents are wasted in an establishment like this." He extracted two gold coins from his silk purse and put them on the table.

"For you, Sally. For offering refuge and comfort and soul's delight to a stranger." He took her face in his hands, all traces of mockery gone. "You must believe this is not payment for an ordinary romp, though God knows I've had my share of them. This is no place for you, Sally. Keep the coins. When you decide to leave you'll have need of them!"

She tried to smile.

"Hide them so Rufe doesn't know. He's already been amply paid."

"Where will ya go?"

"I shall send you a note of my whereabouts."

"But I . . . can't read!"

He flashed her a crooked smile. "Someday I shall have to remedy that. But for now, au revoir!"

"Wait," she called. "You'd best get ya some other clothes, so's ya won't stand out from the rest. And let your beard grow."

"I shall take your advice this very day. And now farewell, Sally, until we meet again." He went lightly down the stairs and closed the door at the bottom, and she threw herself on the bed and wept that she might never see him again.

* *

Rufe noticed a change in Lucinda after that. She lost interest in the work and refused to go to bed with the men who had played cards with Geoffrey Moncrief. "I ain't takin' on that fat one," she said firmly. "He smells like slops!"

"Kind of fancyin' yourself, ain't ya?" Rufe asked. "Forgettin' your place?"

Some tag end of spirit and independence asserted itself. "You can call it what you will, but I ain't doin' it. End up gettin' the pox, most likely."

Rufe had been in the business long enough to know it didn't pay to beat up the girls—might spoil their looks, and there was always the chance one of the customers might have a special interest in one. His only recourse was to hold on to their pay.

"Ya been talkin' of wantin' to git a green cloak. Ain't no way ya goin' to git it effen you ain't servin' the trade! Any gal that don't work don't eat." His eyes were watchful.

"I don't care about no cloak!" she said scornfully. "What's it matter with that riffraff?"

He hit her across the mouth with the back of his big hand, drawing blood. Instantly she raised her knee and jerked it hard against his groin, catching him off guard. He cried out in pain and attempted to hit her again, but she bit the fleshy part of his hand. "Ya bitch!" He lunged for her, but she darted out the door and was gone, leaving behind her old cloak and the crimson dress.

She would return. With no money and no friends, where could she go? Rufe didn't know about the two gold coins Geoffrey Moncrief had given her.

As Lucinda pushed her way through the choked streets, she was too excited to feel the cold. The crowds were so dense that they gave off an odoriferous body heat. She had no plan; she was just determined to get away from Rufe Pincus. The people were too absorbed in their own misery to notice another desperate young girl. Men urinated in the gutters while children defecated in plain sight. The stench was unbearable. Sitting on the seat of a buckboard wagon, a woman nursed a sickly-looking baby. When a spasm of coughing shook her, she leaned over the wagon rail to spit. Lucinda saw blood in her spittle.

At the corner a traveling preacher was haranguing a curious crowd; he stood on a broken chair, shaking his fist and describing the terrors of the fiery pit. "You think life in Carlisle is hell. Well, I tell you, my brethren and sisters, this is but a foretaste—a *foretaste*—of the real hell to come!"

Lucinda shuddered; she could not escape from the thundering voice.

"Repent, for the battle of Armageddon is at hand, when the Forces of Darkness shall do battle with the Forces of Light! When those with unclean bodies shall be cast into the fiery furnace to be roasted alive. Those that have followed the pleasures of the flesh, that have lusted after another's wife or husband, shall know the everlasting torment of eternal damnation! They will cry aloud in their agony, 'Just one more chance, Lord! One more chance!' But it will be too late! Too late to repair the damage they have done to the innocent, too late to change the lives they have corrupted by their lust!"

Lucinda's heart constricted in fear. She thought of George, who, she had learned from gossip at the tavern, now lay in the fort's small hospital, and wondered if his guilt had caused him anguish, even though he was not to blame. She had done a terrible thing, taking someone else's husband, playing upon his need when he lay helpless. She would go to beg his forgiveness.

"Only through atonement," the voice began, then was lost as a horse neighed and a man swore loudly.

"I got to tell him I'm sorry," she said to herself.

When she reached the fort she asked to see George Eldridge. "He's laid up in the hospital, ma'am," the soldier on duty told her.

"But I got to see him!"

"Be you kin to him?"

Lucinda tried to find a means of convincing him of the urgency of her request. "It's important! I got to tell him somethin' that's a matter of life and death." It was not a lie, she told herself; her salvation depended on telling him she had done a great wrong, and begging his forgiveness.

"Can't let you see him lessen you're kin, miss. He's been real poorly."

At that moment Ben Enyard came through the door from the fort's headquarters. He stopped in amazement when he saw Lucinda.

"What are ya doin' here?" he asked.

"I come to see George. Oh, Ben, I got to see him—to tell him somethin'," she said. He saw that she had been crying and had lost much of her bloom. The boldness was gone and the self-confidence.

The guard looked from one to the other, trying to discover what was going on.

"I ain't tryin' to—to make up to him, Ben!"

"Well, whatever it is, it ain't goin' to bring him no peace of mind to see ya. There's things he'd like to forget. You'd best do the same."

She turned away, and he saw her shoulders slump as if she had given up all hope. She was changed—more than he would ever have believed possible. Ben's conscience troubled him that he had sent her away so abruptly. He turned to the guard. "Tell the colonel I'll be back in a little while."

When Ben called her name, Lucinda stopped without turning around. Long strands of her hair had come loose and fell about her shoulders.

"Lucinda," Ben said, "I didn't mean ya no harm. Ma's livin' here now with the two little ones. They're stayin' with Mrs. Graffius—them and the McCulloughs—over on Elm Street on the edge of town. Why don't ya go over to see her? I know she'd be right pleased to see ya."

He saw the despair in her eyes and noticed the ugly cut on her lower lip. Her voice was so low he had to strain to catch her words. "I do thank ya. Your ma's a real fine woman. I will go to see her."

He felt embarrassed and was ashamed that he had spoken so rudely to her. "Well," he said awkwardly, "well, take care of yourself, Lucinda."

She tried to smile but her lips trembled as she turned away.

Ben watched her until the crowd shut her from view. His mind and emotions were in turmoil but the predominant feeling this time was pity.

Mrs. Graffius answered a knock on the door and smiled brightly at the girl in the homespun dress whose blond hair was piled on her head. She had no wrap and the day was chilly. She looked very upset.

"Come in, dear. Mrs. Enyard's upstairs with Annibele. I'll just go tell her you're here. What's your name?"

"Lucinda."

"Well, now, ya jist come right in and make yourself to home. I'll go fetch her."

As Lucinda entered the snug room she saw Fiona McCullough helping a handsome little boy to walk. She held out her arms to him, her face lit with pleasure. "Thomas! Well, ain't ya got big! Walkin' already!"

The child, who was now a year old, glanced uncertainly from her to Fiona, then took a few wobbly steps, lost his balance, and sat down abruptly. Lucinda laughed, her cares momentarily forgotten.

Fiona helped him up. "He does better if you git hold of his dress," she said shyly.

"How are ya, Fiona?" Lucinda said, recovering her poise. "Ya growed up some since we was at Fort Lyttleton."

"I'm fourteen now," Fiona said, with a touch of resentment. "Won't ya have a seat?"

"Ya really got a good place here. Almost like home." She stopped and glanced down at her hands. "Thomas's growed so I'd hardly know him."

At that moment Else Enyard entered the room. "This is a surprise, Lucinda. Come and sit down and tell me how you've been." She kissed her cheek.

"Yes, ma'am." Lucinda did not meet her eyes.

"Take Thomas out in the yard, Fiona. The sun'll do him good," Else said.

Lucinda turned to Else. "I didn't know where to go and then I heard ya was livin' in Carlisle now. I ran away from the—the place I was workin'. When they hung Johnny, I hadn't any place to go." She stopped at the look on Else's face. "We was plannin' to get married in Philadelphia," she added.

"I see. And now you're expectin'?" Else made her tone matter-of-fact.

Lucinda's eyes opened wide. "Oh, no, ma'am. Nothin' like that! I wouldn't let him do nothin' till we was married. . . . I didn't know they'd hang him fer leavin' the fort."

"Desertin' the fort is a mighty serious thing. Dozens of people depends on the soldiers to protect their lives, ya know." Else tried to remember if she'd been so thoughtless at that age. Maybe it was just part of being halfway between a child and a woman.

Lucinda sat silent, twisting her fingers.

"What did ya do after that?" Else asked, her voice warm.

"I didn't know where to go. I—I couldn't go home to Ma and Pa. They'd of died of shame."

Else nodded.

"So this Rufe Pincus at the Pot o' Gold give me room and board and promised me somethin' extra if I'd—entertain the customers." It was out now. Lucinda felt a vague relief at having confessed. She expected Else Enyard to be shocked, but the older woman's expression did not change. "I just couldn't go on with that life, Miz Enyard."

"You want to go home now, I expect?"

Lucinda shook her head. "I'll never go back, never in a million years! I—I ain't proud of what I done. I don't want Ma and Pa to know how I been livin'."

"Well, if it was my daughter I'd be so glad to have her back that . . ." Else didn't finish, afraid of her emotions.

"Ma and Pa ain't like you."

"No, I suppose we're all different. But how are ya goin' to manage? Where'll you live?"

"I ain't tryin' to have ya take me in," the girl said with dignity. "I come to ask if ya knows where I can get work."

"Let me talk to Mrs. Graffius about it. She's lived here a long time, so she knows the townspeople well." Else patted her arm. "Ya must share our room till we can find somethin' for ya."

Lucinda's lower lip trembled.

"Where's your things?" Else asked.

"I ain't got any. . . . I left them at the tavern when I run away."

"Well, we'll manage."

Lucinda remembered the gold pieces. "Rufe wouldn't give me what I earned, but an Englishman who was real kind give me two gold sovereigns, so I can pay."

Mrs. Graffius suggested Else might go to see a couple named Pratt about work for Lucinda; they owned the Forge Inn and might need some help. Yes, Dorcas Pratt said, she would give the girl room and board and four shillings a week in return for scrubbing, cleaning, emptying the slops, and washing up after meals. Else was afraid Lucinda would refuse such an offer. "I know it's a lot of work, Lucinda, but they seem real kind. It would be protection for ya in case that Mr. Pincus comes lookin' for ya."

"I ain't afraid of work," Lucinda said firmly. "I ain't never tried to stint on that."

"Ya won't have much time to yourself."

"I ain't worried about that."

The Forge Inn stood next to a blacksmith's place, and was made of stone from the quarry on the square. It boasted six fireplaces, so that it was the warmest place in town. There was a large cheerful public room, a dining room, a spacious sunny kitchen filled with the pungent scents of herbs, and ten bedrooms. The inn had a welcoming atmosphere and was very clean.

Mrs. Pratt pointed out what Lucinda would be expected to do. She was a middle-aged woman with a florid complexion and a mouth pursed like a tightly drawn reticule. As they climbed the steep stairs to the second floor, the girl noticed that her ankles were swollen and that she panted from the exertion.

"I can't do as much as I used to. My health ain't so good," Mrs. Pratt said. "We're full up all the time now. Only last week my husband turned away some folks. I suppose we could put up extra beds in each of the sleepin' rooms, but what's the use? In the beginnin' of the troubles, the families was able to bring some of their household goods and we give them room and board fer trade. But now most of the people comin' in jist managed to get out with the clothes they was wearin'. Ain't got no money and nothin' to barter." Mrs. Pratt paused for breath, then continued. "Think you can keep up with the work?"

"Oh, yes, ma'am! I'm used to workin' hard."

"Another thing, Lucinda. I won't have ya goin' out nights like that Clara did. Mrs. Enyard told me ya was from a good family. Well, I aim to protect ya like I'd look after my own child."

"Yes, ma'am," Lucinda said meekly. "Ma always tried to bring us up proper-like." That much was true.

"I'm glad to hear that. Ya can't be too careful today, with so many evil men just waitin' to lead a young girl astray." Mrs. Pratt sighed deeply.

Later Lucinda thought about that remark. Why did people always speak of men as the guilty parties? It was she who had seduced George Eldridge, and talked Johnny into leaving Fort Lyttleton. Now he was dead, fit only for worms, and she was still alive. She thought of the men she'd served at the Pot of Gold. She had a lot of atoning to do, but she was going to live differently now so she need not be ashamed. . . .

She remembered Geoffrey Moncrief, with his faintly mocking voice and long white fingers. He had treated her with respect and tenderness, and if it hadn't been for the two gold coins, which she still kept in her shoe, she might not have had the courage to run away. Oh, Lord, she thought, it would be wonderful to see him again.

Suddenly she sat up in bed, all the peaceful contented feeling she got when she thought of him shattered now. *She had forgotten to tell him her real name!* If he was trying to find her, he'd be asking for Sally Bridges.

CHAPTER XIV

Susannah

As the canvas-topped buckboard wagon with its freight of pelts rumbled along the dusty road to Carlisle, its two passengers looked about with keen interest. The driver was a grizzled wiry fellow in his fifties who handled the team expertly so that they avoided the deep holes made by the spring rains. He shifted his quid of tobacco and spat over the side of the wagon, then raised his head to scan the skies.

It was a fine day with brilliant sun making a patchwork of light and shade through the foliage. Tree trunks in the distance appeared red from the newly flowing sap. Across the sky floated fat cumulus clouds, violet on their undersides, luminous white on top. Here and there an apple tree dropped pink petals on the newly turned earth.

"A mighty fine day!" observed the driver. "Never thought we'd make it by the middle of May."

The slender small-boned youth seated beside him did not answer. His dark hair was tied back tightly with a leather thong and looked as if it had not been washed in months. His complexion resembled an Indian's, but his features were uncommonly delicate. He was wearing a buckskin hunting shirt, fringed trousers turned up several inches at the bottom, and moccasins, all of which had seen hard wear.

"How ya goin' ta git word ta yer husband that yer back?" the man asked.

His passenger's face clouded with anxiety. "I don't know, Mr. Snodgrass. Fort Shirley is the nearest fort to our farm. I suppose he might have gone there after the massacre at Bigham's." Susannah Graves, disguised as a boy, her fair complexion stained with walnut juice, regarded the driver anxiously. "I've got to tell him about Rachel."

She sat up straighter as she sniffed the fragrant air. "You can't imagine what it's like to be free after all those months of captivity! It's been almost a year!"

"That's quite a spell to be livin' amongst savages."

"I feel as if I'd been reborn! It's as if the countryside were reborn too!"

"I got ta admit, Miz Graves, yer a mighty plucky woman. I had some misgivin's 'bout helpin' ya escape out there in Ohio, but ya sure kin talk a man inta doin' what his common sense tells him is jist plain crazy. I could 'a lost my scalp if they'd ketched me. . . ."

"But our plan succeeded, Mr. Snodgrass. I told you we could do it. You brought me out of the wilderness just like Moses leading the Israelites into Canaan." She realized the example was not very apt, but Snodgrass was pleased.

"Well now, I never thought o' that," he said, flattered.

"Think what a story you'll have to tell your grandchildren some day."

He flicked the whip lightly. "Ya'll have a story ta tell yourn."

A look of pain crossed her face. "Maybe I should have stayed with the Mingoes. Even if I was separated from Rachel I could still see her."

"Now don't ya go ta thinkin' that way. Them Injuns will be tryin' ta ransom them children one o' these days, sure's my name's Sam Snodgrass. Ya'll be reunited with her this side o' the pearly gates."

"Oh, I hope so! But you were right; even if we had somehow managed to get her away from the Mingoes, she might have died on the journey."

"That child would never 'a lived through all them floods and that turrible weather. Only way to git her back is ransom. I bin tradin' with them Injuns five, mebbe six, years. Come ta know their way o' thinkin'."

"I was always opposed to traders selling or giving them spirits.

Yet if you hadn't given them rum, I'd still be a captive."

"They sure goes wild when they gits the spirits in 'em," he said. "Can't seem ta put the keg down till they drunk every last drop. And then when they gits ta quarrelin' among themselves, look out! Out comes the long knives and pretty soon someun's been killed."

She shuddered. "The women who adopted Rachel never touched it. They always kept the children out of the way and hid the captives."

"Ya know," mused Snodgrass, anxious to change the subject, "I cain't git over how ya larnt their speech. Ya didn't live with 'em fer years like some whites I know of, yet ya kin speak the Mingo tongue. It beats all how ya done it."

"When it's a matter of staying alive, a human being can learn many things," she said.

He flicked his whip again, to hasten the horses' pace. As soon as their journey was over, he would give them special treatment as a reward for bringing them from beyond Logstown in the Ohio wilderness. There were two or three times in the past six weeks when he'd been afraid they wouldn't make it, but the team had struggled on.

His passenger had never complained. She was a mighty pretty little woman. He was glad he had thought of the walnut juice to disguise her fair complexion. That and the buckskin trousers and shirt she was wearing had made possible their escape, for the Indians would be searching for a young white woman, not a boy in buckskins. The spring rains had helped, for the streams were too flooded for a search party to go far from their permanent village.

As they entered Carlisle, they were surprised to find the streets choked with wagons, furniture, tents, horses, and pushing, shouting people. Women were cooking over open fires, while others nursed their infants on the seats of the wagons. Children scampered about, whining for a scrap of meat or a bit of bread. Men, looking as if they had not washed in weeks, tended the horses, or fought their way through the crowds with buckets of water.

Susannah was shocked. "What's happened?"

Snodgrass pushed his hat on the back of his head and

scratched his chin. "Derned if I know. Must 'a been some emergency took place to bring all them folk into Carlisle." He leaned over the side of the wagon and asked a man standing near, "What's a'goin' on here?"

The man's eyes were hard as flints. "Where ya been, mister? Ya jist come from Philadelphy?"

"We jist escaped from the Injuns—back in Ohio."

The fellow gave him an appraising look, then studied Susannah. "That true?"

She nodded.

"Then ya ain't heard how bad it's been?"

"We ain't seen a white man fer six months!" Snodgrass answered.

Convinced that he was not being lied to, the man became expansive. "Then ya ain't heard of what them savages been doin' to this part of the province? Got so bad this spring Fort Lyttleton couldn't hold all the people so we come here. Give up everythin', just after the spring plantin'. Don't know what we'll do when winter comes."

Mr. Snodgrass clucked his few teeth in sympathy. Susannah wondered how she'd find John in this bitter, suffering mass of people.

"Colonel Armstrong's been writin' the Assembly in Philadelphy for help, but them danged merchants won't do a thing!"

"How long has it been like this?" asked Susannah.

"We come nigh onto three weeks ago. And there was already lots of folk here when we arrived." He would have continued, but Mr. Snodgrass interrupted him.

"Colonel Armstrong in charge here?"

"Ya been away a long time, mister. Lieutenant colonel, he is, since last May a year, in charge of all the forts of the Second Battalion on the west side of the Susquehanna." He paused, then added on a note of bitterness, "What's left of them. Ain't but two now."

Susannah leaned forward. "What of Fort Shirley?"

"You mean Aughwick? Oh, they give it up last fall—shortly after the raid at Kittaning. Wasn't no way they could defend it with no water inside the fort."

Susannah's face registered shock. "Kittaning? When was the raid?"

"In September. Colonel Armstrong took three hundred militia to rescue the captives. Burnt the village to the ground. Didn't git all of the captives though. You heard about Granville, ain't ya?"

"I was tradin' in the Ohio country then and she was took over ta Bigham's last June, so it's all news ta us," Mr. Snodgrass said.

The stranger stared at Susannah. "Ya a gal?"

She nodded, too stunned by the news to answer.

"Well, I'll be jiggered! Ya sure do look like a boy."

"We got to see the colonel to find out where her husband be. But we cain't git the wagon through the streets," said Snodgrass.

"I'll come with ya to show ya where to go," said the man. He started off in the direction from which they had come.

"There ain't room ta turn the wagon," Snodgrass called.

The man turned and bellowed to the crowd, "Let these folk through. They just escaped from the Injuns out in Ohio country and they got to see Colonel Armstrong." Slowly the crowd moved back so that the big wagon could turn around.

Colonel Armstrong was reading the latest dispatches from Fort George and Fort Lyttleton when Susannah and the trader entered. He rose and came around the desk to greet them. "So you have just returned from Ohio territory! Welcome back. It's extraordinary that you were able to get through unharmed," he said, offering them chairs.

"If it hadn't been my good fortune to meet a gentleman like Mr. Snodgrass, I'd still be captive."

The trader shifted his plug of tobacco. "There was a couple times I wan't certain we'd make it."

Armstrong seated himself behind the desk. "Before we go on to other matters, would you be good enough to tell me about your capture and your escape, Mrs. Graves? I need as much information as I can get to present our situation to the Provincial Assembly in order to obtain some financial relief for the people who fled here."

"First, I would like to find my husband, Colonel Armstrong.

We had to leave my little girl behind with the Indian women who adopted her. I must see Mr. Graves so we can ransom her," Susannah said.

"Sometimes even a ransom doesn't help," observed the colonel. "The Indians are partial to children, and they consider them blood kin once they've adopted them."

"I shall never give up," Susannah said firmly. "There must be some way—"

"Forgive me," interrupted Colonel Armstrong. "I sympathize with you, ma'am, about your daughter. But I must get details of your capture. It could be very helpful to us to know how and when it happened. Which tribe captured you?"

"It was Delawares," Susannah said. "I didn't know it at the time, for I'd never seen Indians in war paint before."

The colonel nodded, watching her.

"I shall be glad to write it all down, sir, as soon as I've seen my husband."

Colonel Armstrong hesitated. He picked up the quill pen and studied it. "You had better tell me how it happened first."

He heard her sigh.

"It was in June," Susannah began. Both men leaned forward to catch her words. She spoke without emotion, Armstrong thought, as if holding in the terror and anguish of the experience.

"When Francis Wilson rode up alone, shortly before the Indians attacked, I thought that John—Mr. Graves—had been killed. Later Mr. Wilson told me John had stayed behind to water his horses. The savages seized Mr. Wilson, who had not dismounted, when they came out of the woods. As soon as they'd scalped those lying on the ground, they led us off into the woods."

"Which direction were you heading?"

"West."

"How many captives were there?"

"Francis and Maria Wilson and their two little boys, a man named Cletus Wolf, a boy of about fifteen named Morton. . . . Then there was James Duffield and a McCahan boy, the brother of the girl who was killed. And the two of us." She began to cry, the tears making clean runnels on her dusty face.

Snodgrass started toward her but Armstrong waved him back.

"You have been through a terrible ordeal, ma'am, but I must ask a few more questions. I regret the pain this must cause you."

"It's all right, if it will help to bring back Rachel."

"Where did they take you?"

"To their village of Kittaning. Oh, we didn't go that far the first night. It was midafternoon when we left the blockhouse—what remained of it. We had to go single file because the route was very rough. I carried Rachel at first but it was hard to keep up with them and they indicated I should put her down. She—she held on to the back of my skirt." Susannah broke down and it was several minutes before she could continue.

The colonel waited for her to gain control. Snodgrass was acutely distressed by her tears.

Susannah wiped her wet cheeks. "I had to leave her behind with the two women who adopted her."

"If you'll just tell us the events in order," suggested the colonel.

"Yes, of course. As we went on the boys began to ask for a drink of water and finally Mr. Wilson asked the braves for some. One of them knew some English. He told him they should drink their—their own water." She stopped in embarrassment.

"I'd like ta git my hands on 'em," muttered the trader.

"We know their ways are not like ours, Mrs. Graves. Where did you spend the first night?"

"I—I'm not sure where it was," she said. "It was somewhere in the woods. We stopped at dusk and they gave us some parched corn and some dried venison—they call it pemmican. We spent the night surrounded by the savages. . . . The next day it was the same. When we lagged, they shoved us with the butts of their rifles.

"Rachel never whined or cried. I told her in the beginning to do as they said and to show she was a brave girl. Sometimes they would point to her and shake their heads and smile. At first I was afraid this meant they had some sinister intent, but as time went on I realized they liked her. They would give her choice morsels of food when we ate.

"When we reached Kittaning, we found the Indians living in

houses surrounded by cornfields. There were a number of other captives there from the English settlements. The men and older boys were separated from the women and children. Mrs. Wilson and her little boys were placed in the same house with Rachel and me and three other women."

The colonel, who had been writing steadily, put down his quill. "How long did you stay at Kittaning, Mrs. Graves?"

"Three days."

"Where did they take you then?"

"To Fort Duquesne. The trail was rough in places and we saw no sign of cabins, for we were too far north and west. When we reached the fort and saw the French flag flying from the ramparts, the braves gave a great shout. It was blood-curdling!" She glanced out the window before continuing. "You might think we'd be pleased to reach a fort where there were white men, but I wasn't at all relieved. I had learned the French were the instigators of the Indian massacres and that they were offering bounties for scalps. They had scalps hanging from the stockade fence." She closed her eyes as if to shut out the memory.

"They ain't no better'n the Injuns, an' they calls theirselves Christians! Real heathens, they be, effen ya wants my opinion," said Snodgrass.

"What happened when you reached Fort Duquesne?" Armstrong asked.

"They let us bathe and treated us civilly. Then I learned why. The officers expected I would stay there and . . ." She stopped, not knowing how to phrase the rest of her sentence.

"And?" prompted the colonel.

"And be a fancy woman to them."

"Danged bastards!" said Snodgrass, going to the fireplace, where he blew his nose, then wiped his sleeve across his face.

Colonel Armstrong's florid face was a shade redder than usual. "What—er—what happened after they told you that?"

Susannah lifted her chin, and her voice was full of contempt. "I told them—in French—that I would never be so degraded. They could kill me if they wished, but I would never willingly suffer one of them to lay a hand on me. I said I had been brought up a Christian, as their wives and sisters had, and asked them how they would like to have their womenfolk humiliated."

"Ya sure had a lot o' guts—er—fortitude," said Snodgrass.

"Did your remarks have any softening effect on them?" asked Armstrong.

Susannah's eyes flashed. "One of them, bolder than the others, attempted to put my words to the test. He—he put his hand on my shoulder. I struck him across the face with the flat of my hand. He tried to draw his sword but the others restrained him. After that they did not touch me. They offered me inducements—even promised I could keep my child with me. I told them I preferred to take my chances with the Indians. Apparently that was a grave insult, for they released us with a statement that I did not have blood in my veins but ice!"

"You were very fortunate," said Armstrong. "According to some accounts we've had, they don't scruple to have their way with women captives."

"I think they were ashamed," Susannah said. "I told them I had learned their language and their history because the French are considered among the most civilized people in the world, but that their manners belied France's reputation. The simple savages who had captured us had not insulted me as they had done."

"Ain't that sumpin'?" Snodgrass slapped his thigh in delight. "I ain't never seen a woman like her. Ain't afeared ta speak up ta nobody."

"It might not have turned out so well," observed the colonel.

"The commander of the fort, a man named Vaudreuil," Susannah continued, "said something about the effrontery of a provincial trying to remind French officers of their manners; then he bent a leg to me and left. But two of his officers came later, to apologize and assure me of their good offices."

"You have had more than your share of trials. What did you do then?"

"There was a great feast at the fort with the Indians providing venison and wild turkeys. We were invited to share in it. I—I never saw Rachel enjoy food as she did then, after the poor rations we had with the Delaware."

"What was the occasion for the feast?"

"I don't know," she said. "Perhaps to celebrate the Delaware bringing in prisoners and scalps. The third day we saw a number of canoes coming downriver. The French told us they were Mingoes from the Ohio country beyond Logstown.

"Two of the women looked over all of us captives and we were told the Delaware had sold Rachel and me to them, so we got into canoes with them and started upstream. After that things improved. The women took a fancy to Rachel and decided to adopt her to take the place of a brother who had been killed in the raids earlier. They were kind to her and she came to trust them. Only they wouldn't let us be together. It was a terrible thing not to be able to speak to my own child, to see savages caring for her. Since she was now considered their child, they didn't want her speaking English or being near me."

"How did you meet Mr. Snodgrass?" the colonel asked.

"I come ta trade," said the trader. "Plenty o' game in the Ohio territory an' them Mingoes is good hunters. I bin goin' out there ta git their peltries fer five, mebbe six, years."

"They saved their best pelts to trade with him," Susannah said. "They liked him and trusted him. I heard the women say Mr. Snodgrass was honest in his dealings."

Snodgrass straightened his shoulders, pleased that Colonel Armstrong should hear of his good points.

"Go on, Mrs. Graves."

"Well, it's the custom among traders to bring kegs of rum among their goods—the Indians refuse to trade with anyone who comes without it—so when their trading was over, Mr. Snodgrass brought out the rum. He was preparing to leave and we'd spoken briefly several times. I said something about his giving them rum, and he explained that it was necessary to get them to trade their peltries. It was then I had the idea of escaping. I thought if I could find my husband, we could ransom Rachel, so I persuaded Mr. Snodgrass to hide me in his wagon when the Indians were drunk. He objected at first, but finally he agreed, cautioning me that we ran the risk of being drowned in streams flooded by melted snow."

The colonel turned to the trader. "When did you leave?"

"As near as I kin recollect 'twas about six weeks ago. I couldn't risk goin' near the other Mingo er Shawnee villages an' so I come by a roundabout way ta avoid them that's hostile. Took longer but we come through with our hair."

"You still had Delaware territory to cross," said Colonel Armstrong.

"Yup. We was jist lucky there. Had a couple o' times when I thought fer sure we'd be captured."

"You are very fortunate."

"I wanted to go to Fort Shirley to find John but Mr. Snodgrass suggested it was better to come to Carlisle," Susannah said.

Colonel Armstrong played with the quill pen. "A lot has happened in the past few months. We had to abandon Fort Shirley in the late autumn. Granville had already been destroyed, with considerable loss of life." His listeners looked shocked. "The picture is not at all hopeful. We thought the raids would stop when cold weather came but they didn't."

"I must get word to my husband," Susannah said.

Colonel Armstrong rose and walked to the window, looking out at the street as he spoke. "I'm afraid I have sad news for you, Mrs. Graves. I'm sorry to have to tell you John Graves died in March."

For a few moments no one spoke. Snodgrass could hear the ticking of the colonel's big pocket watch, people on the street shouting to each other, the clop of horses' hoofs. He cleared his throat and looked at Susannah, who sat very still, looking small and frightened. Finally she spoke. "How did he die?"

"Pneumonia. He had joined the militia at Fort Shirley last summer and was determined to find you and your daughter. He took part in the raid on Kittaning and was an excellent soldier. Later, when Fort Shirley was abandoned, he came here and helped with the building of the new fort. I knew him well, Mrs. Graves, and respected him as a responsible soldier and a fine man."

Susannah tried to smile. "Thank you."

"He spoke of you many times and asked if he could send a letter to your uncle in Philadelphia to tell him of your capture and to send him his will. He asked him to post a reward for information about you and Rachel."

Susannah's eyes had an inward look; her lovely mouth was tightly drawn.

"One time in the summer he had been out on a search party and found himself in the vicinity of your cabin. It was still intact and he brought back a cloak of yours and a quilt, and he asked me to keep them in case you returned. After his death we found a couple of books—a Shakespeare and a book about ancient Greece."

"The *Iliad.*"

"Yes, that's what it was. He had also saved something from his military pay for you. He left that in my care as well. I'll get that for you directly. And there's a locket that was found in the woods."

"My locket?" Her face looked haunted. "He found my locket! The ways of the Lord are strange beyond belief."

"I am glad you are a religious woman, ma'am. It will be a comfort to you now," said Armstrong.

"Did you say you had our books?"

"Yes, I have them and the locket. The cloak and the quilt he left in the keeping of Mrs. Graffius."

Snodgrass spoke. "I'll stay here until I see yer well sityated, Miz Graves. I ain't a-leavin' ya all by yerself till I knows ya found a place ta stay."

"Oh, no, Mr. Snodgrass," Susannah replied. "I can't hold you up any longer. You must take your peltries to Philadelphia and claim your reward."

Armstrong left the room and returned with a small leather pouch, the gold locket, the *Iliad,* and a tattered volume of Shakespeare. Susannah still had not grasped the significance of her husband's death. It happened frequently, Armstrong knew. When too many catastrophes happened in quick succession, one was not able to accept so much tragedy.

As he handed her the things her husband had left, she asked, "Who cared for John when he had pneumonia?"

"He was lodging at a place called the Forge Inn, run by the Pratts."

"Do you think he received proper care?"

"I'm sure of it. I sent the physician from the fort to attend him and he reported the Pratts were concerned and conscientious. John seemed to have lost hope of finding you and Rachel after the raid on Kittaning. When the Wilsons were rescued, they said you had been taken away, they didn't know where. After that I noticed a change in him."

"A change?"

"Yes. He gradually lost hope. Never said much, but the despair was there."

She put her hands over her face.

Snodgrass went to her and patted her shoulder. "It don't do no good ta give in ta yer feelin's, ma'am," he said. "Life's a mighty strange thing. Sometimes seems like it sends one blow after another. We gotta show we ain't goin' ta let circumstances git the best o' us. . . ."

Susannah caught his hand and held it. "I—I don't know what to do. . . ."

Colonel Armstrong regarded her in silence for a moment, then said, "You have an uncle in Philadelphia, a lawyer, I believe, a Mr. Josiah Norris."

She nodded.

"You could go there after you've had a chance to rest for a few days, but I must advise you the trip has its dangers. There have been raids to the east."

"I don't think I can face another long journey. Not now." She suddenly felt drained.

"Perhaps you should go to the Forge Inn and speak with Mrs. Pratt."

But she didn't hear him. They saw her droop, then very quietly she slipped off the chair and fell to the floor in a small heap.

Susannah had a blurred impression of being carried to the wagon by a stranger in buckskins, of trying to smile her thanks to the big man who was protecting the horses and the wagon. She had wanted to speak to the colonel again but was too exhausted to remember what it was she intended to tell him. She was taken to an inn, then upstairs to a large room, where a bustling middle-aged woman and a girl with yellow hair undressed her, placed towels under her, and scrubbed her. Then they put a nightdress on her and lifted her into a clean, sweet-smelling bed.

Susannah knew something terrible had happened, that her life would never be the same again. The knowledge hovered just beyond the fringe of consciousness, but her head ached too much to try to remember.

Hours later she awoke in a sun-filled room and found herself lying in a maple four-poster. On the floor was a braided rag rug and on the small table a washbowl and pitcher with a design of blue forget-me-nots.

The window, which had a pane of real glass, was open, and from the world outside came the fresh scent of grass, lilacs, and apple blossoms. She heard horses stomping in a stall, the honking of geese, a flapping of wings, and voices raised in argument. She closed her eyes. It was so wonderful to lie in a bed after all those months.

She was awakened by the sound of someone bustling about. Susannah opened her eyes to see the blond girl dusting everything in the room. The girl, unaware that she was being watched, paused by the open window, drinking in the scene outside. She was quite young and her faded calico dress did not hide the voluptuousness of her breasts and hips. She had a rosy complexion and a full mouth that looked determined in spite of its sensuousness.

"Good morning," Susannah said, trying to smile. Her body ached in every muscle.

The girl seemed preoccupied, as if Susannah had interrupted her private thoughts. "It ain't mornin', ma'am. It's most time to start fixin' supper. Ya sure slept like it was your last sleep. . . ."

"I seem to remember being carried up the stairs by a soldier from the colonel's headquarters. It was you who bathed me, wasn't it?"

"Yes'm. Me and Miz Pratt." A fresh, vital quality emanated from her that reminded Susannah of newly plowed earth.

"I'm very grateful. I must have been a sorry sight. Six weeks without a bath! It's beyond belief. I apologize for having offended your sensibilities."

The girl looked puzzled.

"I mean I'm sorry to have put you to so much trouble. For my being so dirty and offensive."

"Ya couldn't help it, ma'am."

"How long have I been here?"

"They brought ya here yesterday just before supper. Colonel Armstrong sent word to Miz Pratt, askin' if we had room for ya. Then he sent a soldier and a trader."

"Mr. Snodgrass," said Susannah, wondering where he was.

The girl nodded. "Miz Pratt and her husband own this here inn. The Forge Inn, it's called. They took care of Mr. Graves when he was stayin' here."

"Did you know my husband?" The realization that John was dead was coming back.

"No," the girl said. "I wasn't in Carlisle then. I'm Lucinda. Lucinda Abbot."

"This isn't your home, then?"

"No, I work for the Pratts. It's too much work for them takin' care of this place by theirselves."

From below stairs a woman's voice called, "Lucinda! It's time to start supper."

"I'm comin'." The girl hurried off, closing the door behind her.

Susannah tried to put her legs over the side of the bed, but the effort was too much. She was wearing a larger woman's nightdress, which smelled of soap and sun. What bliss it was to be clean and among civilized people! Tomorrow she would wash her hair. Resolutely she determined not to remember the details of their trip.

But John. She couldn't believe he was dead. John wouldn't leave her when she needed him to help her recover Rachel. She shifted to find a more comfortable position, and slept.

* *

An hour later Mrs. Pratt opened the door.

Mrs. Pratt was at her best in an emergency. Narrow, quick to judge and to condemn, obsessively clean and neat, she took a rather grim view of humanity most of the time, but let trouble occur and all her latent sympathies were awakened. At such times she spent her energies freely on behalf of the distressed. So she had been during John Graves's fatal illness, and so she was with Susannah.

When Susannah awakened the afternoon of the second day, she found Mrs. Pratt checking on Lucinda's dusting. "Good morning . . . or is it afternoon?"

"Well, now, it's nice to see ya awake. It's afternoon. I was beginnin' to wonder if you'd survive after all them things you went through."

"And I am not so strong as I thought. . . . It is heavenly to sleep in a bed between sheets with a clean nightdress! I understand it was you and Lucinda who bathed me."

"Well, I tried to make ya as comfortable as I knew how." Mrs. Pratt tactfully decided not to mention her aversion to letting Susannah sleep in her sheets in the filthy condition in which she had arrived.

"Bless you, Mrs. Pratt! I'm afraid I shall be indebted to you for the rest of my life. Colonel Armstrong told me you looked after Mr. Graves when he was so ill."

"Yes, he was stayin' here. Wasn't ill but four or five days before he passed." Mrs. Pratt sat down on the rocker, fanning herself with her apron. Outside bees droned among the blossoms and bright-winged butterflies swooped low, then fluttered up into the blue air.

Susannah felt a swift stab of pain, which moved upward from the pit of her stomach to her throat. "I must know how he died. Tell me, please."

"We was right fond of Mr. Graves," Mrs. Pratt began, determined not to be hurried. "He come here just after they abandoned Fort Aughwick, with Colonel Armstrong and some others. Your husband was our favorite. He never used no bad language, wouldn't touch spirits. He was quiet-like, but ya could see somethin' was troublin' him. He was here four or five weeks before he told us about ya and the little girl. He couldn't seem to stop blamin' himself fer leaving ya at Bigham's. Mr. Pratt and me tried to encourage him, sayin' you'd probably be ransomed."

"Did you—did you notice a change in him shortly before he died?"

"Yes, we did. At first he was countin' on findin' ya soon. Wasn't till February he began goin' downhill. Stopped eatin', didn't talk to nobody, got so thin his clothes just hung on him. One day he told me he guessed he wasn't meant to have so much happiness, that he'd had more than mortal man was due." Mrs. Pratt stopped, for the tears were flowing on Susannah's cheeks. She made a move to rise, but Susannah waved a hand to her to continue.

"One evenin' he come in after ridin' out with some of the others, searchin' for traces of them red varmints. He couldn't get his breath. The physician bled him and tried poultices but it wasn't no use." Mrs. Pratt paused and wiped her eyes with her apron.

Susannah spoke by an effort of will. "Did—did he say anything toward the end?"

"He wasn't in his right mind, ramblin' about takin' ya back east for protection. . . . Toward the end he was callin' to ya to wait for him. 'Susannah, wait, I'm comin',' he'd say."

Susannah buried her face in the pillow, her body shaken with sobs.

Mrs. Pratt patted her on the shoulder. "There, there, Miz Graves, ya have the comfort of knowin' ya made him happy. I guess we ain't meant to be too happy in this life." She thought a moment. "Ya know they always says the good die young."

She could not understand the complexity of Susannah's grief. Susannah had not loved as deeply as she had been loved. There had been contentment, but the kind of emotion she had read about—the quickening of the heart or racing of the blood that foretold the approach of the beloved—had been missing. She wept for herself, that she had failed to love deeply and for him, that such a good man should have had less than he deserved.

* *

Snodgrass, assured that Susannah was in good hands, departed after the fourth day for Philadelphia, promising to see Josiah Norris, not only to collect the reward but to tell him of Susannah's present circumstances and John Graves's death.

Lucinda was surprised to find Susannah in tears after his departure. "I reckon your uncle will be mighty glad to hear you're safe. Will ya be goin' to Philadelphia to live?" she asked.

Susannah wiped her eyes. "I don't know what I shall do, Lucinda. I think Uncle Josiah found it difficult to share his privacy with me after my parents died. We were never close."

"Was that where ya was livin' when ya met Mr. Graves?"

Susannah nodded.

"It's wonderful how ya rode off to the wilderness with him. Ya must have knowed right away that he was the one for ya. I'd have done the same thing. If I found my man, I'd go with him anywhere."

Susannah gave her a startled look. She wondered what it would be like to be Lucinda, direct, uncomplicated, capable of passion. Lucinda was not pretty but she had a certain earthy charm. She looked as if she would give herself to whoever appealed to her, with no backward look of regret. She was warm, open, unpretentious. And, Susannah was sure, ardent.

Susannah thought perhaps this was what had been missing in her marriage to John Graves. He had been shy of asserting himself in love. He was tender and solicitous, but never had he swept her away on the strength of his own passion. She had gone through four years of marriage like an unawakened young girl. Their relationship would have been richer and deeper if she had been able to respond to him as Lucinda would have, but she could not pretend to something she did not feel. She feared she lacked the capacity to love deeply, to give herself freely without restraint. Sighing, she began to read.

The following day Susannah spoke with Mrs. Pratt. "I can't go on sitting in my room while you and Lucinda are working. I'm well now and healthy. I'd like to help with the work, to be useful."

"Why, I never heard of no payin' folks helpin'," said Mrs. Pratt, her sense of propriety deeply shaken.

"That's the problem. I have only the money my husband managed to save from his pay. It won't last long, and I don't want to accept your hospitality without some payment."

Mrs. Pratt's practicality struggled with her latent generosity. "Well, if ya really think you're ready for it, I could use some help in the kitchen."

"Fine," Susannah said. "I'm a good cook. Perhaps I could also keep the records of the guests' payments and figure out how much they owe."

"Records?"

"Yes. If you keep a ledger showing how much you receive for rooms and for meals, you can tell how much profit you've made. It's sound practice for any business."

It had never occurred to Mrs. Pratt that such skills as reading, writing, and ciphering could be useful in running the hostelry. But with increasing prices, it would be a smart thing to do. "I reckon we might just work out somethin' between us. Course ya know I can't pay ya."

Susannah smiled. "Suppose we agree that my doing all the cooking will pay for my room and board. Do you think my handling the accounts would be worth five shillings a week? The militia at the fort get three shillings a day, you know."

Mrs. Pratt knew she had met her match. "Well, now, I wasn't thinkin' of it that way. I'll speak to Mr. Pratt and if he's willin', we'll do that."

When Colonel Armstrong asked Ben to deliver Susannah Graves's cloak and quilt to her at the Forge Inn, Ben's initial response was dismay. He had avoided Lucinda Abbot and did not want to see her again, yet many nights her image kept him from sleep. He would tell himself she was a fallen woman, only to be aroused by vivid mental images of her disporting herself at the Pot of Gold. He would imagine himself as one of her lovers, taking her ever more daringly, until, spent and ashamed, he would finally fall into a deep sleep. She was like an inflammation of the blood from which he could not recover.

His feeling for her swung between lust and pity. When he was dominated by the first, he told himself he despised her for her wantonness. Then, after he had taken her violently in imagination, he would remember how thin and pale she looked, how hopeless. He would feel remorse for his savage desire and pity for her forlorn state. He feared the physical hold she had over him might lead to action for which he would pay dearly.

Now as Ben entered the inn he saw Lucinda scrubbing the floor of the public room with her back to him. She had not heard him approach, so intent was she on her task. He stood for a moment looking at her taut waist and rounded hips. Her hair had loosened from its knot and damp tendrils snaked across her shoulders. He felt a wave of desire and immediately sought to hide it by assuming a distant manner. "Where can I find the Widow Graves?" he asked without greeting her.

Lucinda turned and gave him an appraising look. Resuming her scrubbing, she said offhandedly, "She's not seein' no visitors."

"I ain't a visitor. Colonel Armstrong asked me to bring her things from over to Mrs. Graffius's."

"What things? She don't know Miz Graffius." Two bright spots glowed in her cheeks.

"Mr. Graves took some of her things to Mrs. Graffius for safekeepin'."

"Why didn't ya say so? I'll see if she's willin' to see ya."

Lucinda went into Susannah's room, her mouth tight with repressed anger. "Miz Graves, Ben Enyard's come to bring your things."

"My things? Who is Ben Enyard?"

"He's workin' with the militia buildin' the fort. Lives over to Miz Graffius's with his mother and little brother and sister."

Susannah tried to recall where she had heard the name Graffius. "Oh, yes, I remember. Colonel Armstrong said my husband left my cloak and a quilt with Mrs. Graffius. Please send him up."

She was sitting in the rocker going over the accounts when

Ben walked in. He saw a small, very pretty woman in a calico dress that was much too large. Her face and hands were as dark as an Indian's, but on her forearms the flesh was white and fine as an infant's. He couldn't see her features, for the light was behind her, touching the thick dark hair with red and gold.

"Please come in, Mr. Enyard," she said.

"Mrs. Graves, I'm Ben Enyard, with the Second Battalion of the Provincial Militia," he said.

Susannah looked up at him for a long moment. She saw the clear gray eyes with their rusty brows, the clean lines of his mouth, the reddish hair, the strong, square-fingered hands with their light dusting of freckles. He looked, she thought, fiercely independent.

"Yes, Mr. Enyard, won't you sit down?"

"Thank ya. Colonel Armstrong asked me to fetch you some things that your husband left with Mrs. Graffius. . . . I'm real sorry about Corporal Graves, ma'am."

"Thank you," she said. "Did you know John?"

"I seen him first at the raid on Kittaning last fall. He was a brave man, Mrs. Graves. Ya can be proud of him."

"Please tell me about him, if you have the time."

Ben carried the chair from the corner and placed it near the rocker. He forgot about Lucinda as he talked with John Graves's widow. She was different from any woman that he had ever met, finer, more delicate, yet at the same time he sensed a strength beneath the soft manner of speech. She reminded him of pink arbutus. "Er, what was ya sayin', ma'am?"

"I was saying I wish I could thank Mrs. Graffius in person for taking care of these things."

Ben's heart beat faster. "Why, I'd be pleased to come and walk ya over to Mrs. Graffius's when I'm off from the fort. My family are livin' there now."

"I wouldn't put you to any trouble."

"No trouble at all. I go to see my mother and the little ones every time I'm off duty. Ma'd be right pleased to make your acquaintance."

So it was arranged. As Ben left, he did not notice Lucinda. His mind was on the young widow he had just met.

Susannah laid aside the account book. She gazed at the sun-dappled landscape beyond the window but her thoughts were elsewhere: she was thinking of the slender, gray-eyed man who had just left her, of his hands, which looked so capable and yet so gentle.

CHAPTER XV

The Forge Inn

Lucinda Abbot was learning that it was not easy to please Mrs. Pratt. She demanded perfection. If she saw Lucinda pause in her work to glance out the window, she immediately reminded her of chores not yet done. It was difficult not to speak out. But Lucinda was determined to do her best and to stay.

Mr. Pratt was a thin, balding man with a habit of squinting. He supplied the garden produce to feed the guests, took care of the cows, pigs, and chickens, and kept the fireplaces stocked with wood. Rarely did he express an opinion; he had learned early in his marriage to keep his thoughts to himself.

Lucinda did not know what he thought of her, for although he was never unkind, he had not addressed more than a few words to her since her arrival. She suspected that Mrs. Pratt was secretly jealous of any female within his orbit who was younger and more attractive than she, so he had learned to show indifference.

Lucinda had no awareness of why she subjected herself to this hard life, any more than she understood what had made her debase herself at the Pot of Gold. She was not introspective. She only knew she was not as troubled now by what she had done to George Eldridge and to Johnny. When she lay down in her small room at the end of a long day, Lucinda was so weary she could not keep her eyes open. She would remember a fair-haired Englishman with a crooked smile. The next moment she would be asleep.

She wondered what was happening to her family at Fort Lyttleton. From conversations overheard at the inn's dinner table she knew that all the cabins in the valley had been destroyed. Did her parents miss her? Or was their shame so great that they only wanted to forget her? She had heard that Felix had escaped and come home.

Else Enyard had come to see Lucinda four days after she'd started work, but Mrs. Pratt had let her know Lucinda was too busy to spend her time visiting. As Else rose to go, she had patted Lucinda's hand, noting the broken nails and coarse, reddened skin. "I'm sorry, Lucinda. I didn't know it would be like this." Lucinda had not answered. Her face was inscrutable, but as Else walked away, she stood in the doorway watching her with eyes full of a dull misery.

It was a comment of Susannah's that provided the opportunity Lucinda needed to leave the inn for a few hours.

"I wish I had enough energy to walk through town to a store to purchase some yard goods for some dresses," Susannah had said. "I can't go on taking advantage of Mrs. Pratt's generosity in letting me wear one of hers."

"I could go fer ya," Lucinda offered, "if ya speak to Mrs. Pratt about it."

Mrs. Pratt agreed, and as Lucinda started off, she was in high spirits. It was wonderful to be free from Mrs. Pratt's surveillance for a few hours. The day was warm and she opened the two top buttons of her new pink dress that Else had made. Lucinda decided to purchase a length of material for herself with one of the gold coins Geoffrey had give to her. At the thought of him, she felt the excitement his memory always evoked. Meeting him had changed her. Never again would she go to bed with a man she did not love. Geoffrey Moncrief had given her self-respect.

He would be surprised to find she had learned to write her name and was beginning to read and cipher. Lucinda had Susannah Graves to thank for that. Shortly after Susannah had taken over the cooking and had devised a way of keeping track of the money taken in, Lucinda made a remark that started a new train of events.

Watching Susannah at work in a corner of the big fragrant kitchen, Lucinda said, "I wish I could write my name. . . ."

Susannah put down the basting spoon and turned to her, her eyes thoughtful. "You can't read and write, Lucinda?"

"No. There wasn't no school in the valley. Pa knew how but he was too busy with all the chores to learn us."

"That's unfortunate. Everyone should be taught to read and write and cipher."

"Even girls?"

"Of course. Someday this province will have need of educated men *and* women."

At that moment Mrs. Pratt bustled in, chins quivering, a smile lighting her round face. "Miz Graves, the boarders is all talkin' 'bout that suet puddin' of yours. Said it was the best they ever et."

"Thank you," Susannah said. Then, summoning all her charm, she added, "I've been thinking it's high time Lucinda learn to read and write. Now that I'm helping in the kitchen she's not needed as much. There would be time in the evening for me to teach her, either here or in my room."

Mrs. Pratt's mouth set in a thin line with tiny puckers of disapproval radiating from it. "With the Indian troubles we cain't waste candles on such like."

"But it stays light almost until nine o'clock on summer evenings, Mrs. Pratt. We won't need candles until late August, and then you can take them out of my five shillings a week."

"I don't see what's the good of it," Mrs. Pratt began, sensing the winds of defeat. Susannah had a way of putting things that made it hard to hold out against her.

"Her father is an educated man. I'm certain he will be very grateful to you for looking after Lucinda's welfare as you do. And to allow her to learn to read, write, and cipher will put him eternally in your debt. He was never able to teach her himself because of the hardships of frontiering."

While Lucinda listened silently, marveling at the way Susannah made her father sound so—so grand, Mrs. Pratt vainly sought arguments to counter those she'd put forth. "Some folks fergits their station when they kin read and write," she said lamely.

"My uncle, Josiah Norris, who is a lawyer in Philadelphia,

considered it sufficiently important to send me to dame school when I was growing up," Susannah answered. She had gauged Mrs. Pratt correctly. The mistress of the Forge Inn was one of those individuals who are always impressed by those they consider their betters. If Josiah Norris, Esquire, thought an education was important for his niece, she had no further argument. Though it did sound dangerously modern.

The crowds were even greater than Lucinda had remembered and she was glad she'd put the money in her shoe. Drinking in the sights and sounds, she made her way to the shop that Mrs. Pratt said sold cloth. Lucinda had never had money of her own before, so choosing the material was an event. After much deliberation, she selected a soft green muslin with a tiny floral pattern for herself. Choosing for Susannah was more difficult. There was no black fabric, and for a recent widow, the reds and bright blues were not suitable. She finally settled on a buff nankeen and a lavender muslin with black stripes. She was certain Mrs. Pratt would object on the ground they were not proper, but after all it *was* Susannah's money.

The man behind the counter looked at her with curiosity. Few people in Carlisle had money for cloth; most wanted to barter. "Thread? Buttons?" he asked.

"I'm glad ya reminded me."

He noted her clean, scrubbed look, and decided it was best to speak up. "Beggin' your pardon, miss, but it ain't safe for a young lady to be out by herself. There's some mighty rough men in Carlisle now." Lucinda was tempted to tell him she could take care of herself, but thought it might not sound ladylike. "Thank ya, sir. I'll be real careful." Picking up the bundle of cloth, she left the shop.

Now the pressure of the crowd was denser. Suddenly she was stopped by two young men who were weaving tipsily among the crowd.

"Look what we got here!" said one, sweeping her with an appraising glance. "Pretty—ain't she, Jediah?"

The second man caught her chin and peered at her closely.

"She's the gal from that place, what's it called? The Pot o' Gold."

"Let me go!" Lucinda cried. "Keep your hands off me!" She shoved the man's hand away, but the first man caught her arm.

"Rufe Pincus been lookin' for ya. He'll be glad to hear we found ya, Sally Bridges." He gave her a pinch on the buttocks.

She kicked him hard in the shins.

"Why, you dirty little bitch!" he cried.

She could deal with one but she wasn't confident she could ward off two, and the crowd was no help.

As the men grabbed Lucinda and attempted to lift her skirt, a voice came clearly above the din—a cultivated English voice she had feared she would never hear again. "What are you doing to my cousin? Let her go!"

The crowd parted as a stranger with a light brown beard pushed his way to Lucinda and her assailants. The reactions of the men who had accosted her were considerably slowed by the quantity of rum they had consumed.

Lucinda had a feeling she was dreaming. "Geoffrey! Where'd ya come from?"

"Just a moment, my dear. Let her go! Or by gad, you'll have reason to regret it."

The more clearheaded of the two relaxed his grip on her arm. "Who are ya?" He peered drunkenly at Moncrief.

"I've a mind to teach you two a lesson, by Jove! Accosting a young lady, treating her as a common tart!" Geoffrey lunged, grabbed the pair by their necks, and cracked their heads together. The crowd roared in appreciation. He was a wonder, this soft-talking stranger from the mother country.

Geoffrey took Lucinda's arm. "Where have you been, Sally? I've searched the town for you."

"Oh, Geoffrey," she said, her face radiant, "I'm that glad to see ya!"

"So you ran away. Where did you go?"

"After you left I—I couldn't put up with that life. Rufe was real angry with me for refusin' to serve them that was waitin' to get even with ya. He hit me, so I ran away. I went to see Mrs.

Enyard, who was neighbor to us. She's livin' here now."

"You are staying with Mrs. Enyard?"

"No, she found work for me at the Forge Inn. I do the cleanin' and washin' and the dishes."

"I'm glad to hear you left the Pot of Gold. It was no place for you, my dear." Noting how thin and pale she was, he asked, "Are you all right, Sally?"

"I ain't Sally Bridges. My real name's Lucinda Abbot."

"You never told me your proper name, you know."

"There wasn't time. Ya had to get away in a hurry that mornin'."

"Quite true. And now, tell me, are you well—and happy?"

No one had ever asked her if she was happy. "Mrs. Pratt is real particular, but she and Mr. Pratt are good folks. And the customers treat me"—she hesitated—"like a lady."

"Well, that's an improvement," he said dryly.

"But Geoffrey, what about you?"

"Oh, I manage. I found a room in a small inn and wrote to my agent in Philadelphia to inform him of my whereabouts. After I grew a beard, I purchased some frontier clothes and presented myself to Colonel Armstrong."

"Ya joined the militia?"

"I am a journalist of sorts."

"What's that?"

"A writer for newspapers. I supply two of the London papers with firsthand accounts of what is happening on the frontier."

"That's grand!" Just to be with him brought her a feeling of happiness such as she had never known.

"It's a small beginning." He paused. "What of your family, Lucinda?"

He noted that she caught her lower lip between her teeth to hide its trembling.

"I—ain't heard nothin'. I guess they're still at Fort Lyttleton. All the cabins in the Coves has been burnt."

"I wondered if you knew that."

"Some of the men that works for the Provincial Assembly stays at the inn when they come here. . . . I wish I'd hear of Felix."

"Felix?"

"My oldest brother, who was captured by the Injuns in August. . . . He's home now."

"Why are you out alone?" Geoffrey asked. "You could have had a nasty time with those ruffians."

"I guess it was risky. Ya come just in time."

"But why did you go? Was it something important?"

"Mrs. Pratt give me leave to go get some yard goods." To change the subject she asked, "Do you have friends in Philadelphia?"

He laughed. "My family hoped I would marry a young lady there who is a cousin of friends in England, but my gambling put a stop to all romantic interests. My mother thought perhaps Mistress Ashley could reform me. Though she tried, it was not to be."

"Does she know you're here?"

"No, it would only have added to her conviction that I am unredeemable. You know, the third son of an English lord who is a Catholic of Scottish ancestry is not considered an outstanding catch."

"You ain't got a sweetheart?"

"Who would have me? A twenty-eight-year-old man whose only talents are translating Latin and Greek and writing articles. And a certain skill with cards." He grinned.

They were almost at the Forge Inn. "I have to go now, Geoffrey. Mrs. Pratt will be wonderin' why it took so long. Will I ever see ya again?"

"I'm coming with you to see if I can find lodging there. My present room is dark as a bat's cave."

"Oh, no, she'd suspicion you knowed me!"

"Bring me to your Mrs. Pratt, my dear. Trust me."

Lucinda was amazed at how smoothly he handled Mrs. Pratt.

"Mrs. Pratt? Allow me to introduce myself, Geoffrey Moncrief, late of Kent, England. I chanced to be in the shop when this young lady came in. When she mentioned your inn to the clerk, I recalled that I had heard excellent reports of the Forge Inn from Colonel Armstrong."

"From Colonel Armstrong? Ya got business at the fort?"

"I've been engaged in taking care of his correspondence with the Provincial Assembly."

"I see."

"I've heard many good things about your establishment and made inquiries shortly after I arrived, but there were no rooms available at that time."

Lucinda could see Mrs. Pratt beginning to unbend.

"How did ya say ya met Lucinda?" she asked.

"At the draper's, madam. When she mentioned the Forge Inn I asked if I could accompany her so that I might inquire about a room. Also, I thought to offer her my protection, for there is a rough element in the streets now."

He had won her over. "There's no room free now, but if ya come back in four or five days, I'll have one fer ya," Mrs. Pratt said.

"Thank you kindly. Your servant, madam." With a slight bow he was gone. Lucinda gazed at his dwindling figure as he pushed his way through the crowds. Her heart was racing and her legs felt weak. He was coming to live at the Forge Inn! It was the most amazing thing that had ever happened to her.

Mrs. Pratt's voice aroused her from her reverie: "What's got into ya, Lucinda Abbot? There's work waitin'."

Susannah found that doing the cooking and accounts took her mind from the pain of John's death and the loss of Rachel. She had to continue to live, she told herself, for she hoped that her daughter would be returned to her someday. Now teaching Lucinda Abbot kept her from dwelling on her loss. As she got to know her better, she sensed Lucinda had been through some shattering experience that would have destroyed a weaker person.

Lucinda was eager to learn and had an agile, if undeveloped, mind. She was determined to compensate for her lack of education now that she would be seeing Geoffrey Moncrief. At times she felt a pricking of anxiety. How could a farm girl from the Coves whose reputation was destroyed by the life she had lived possibly capture his affections? When such doubts arose, she would be moody, easily distracted.

Susannah, aware that something bothered her, was patient. "You're doing fine, Lucinda. Just try it once more."

She wondered why the girl was in such a hurry to finish the sprigged muslin dress. "It's better to take smaller stitches, Lucinda. They won't pull out as quickly so you won't have to repair them as soon." Lucinda did not answer, but her face reflected a suppressed excitement.

"You look as though you have a happy secret," Susannah ventured.

Lucinda blushed. "I just wish some folks would know that I'm learnin' to read," she said.

Susannah tried another approach. "Who is the man who is moving into the front room tomorrow? Mrs. Pratt said you met him at the shop when you went to buy the yard goods."

"He's gentry, an English gentleman. He writes things fer newspapers in London."

"Really? I wonder why a man like that would come to Carlisle . . . to the Pennsylvania frontier."

"Maybe he's tryin' to forget somethin'."

Susannah gave her a sharp look. It seemed a penetrating remark for Lucinda. "I can't see why anyone would come here unless he was on the Crown's business or fleeing the Indians."

"Folks has all kind of reasons for doin' things. I guess ya can't understand them less you be in their shoes," Lucinda said.

When Geoffrey Moncrief moved in two days later, Susannah was sure she had the answer to Lucinda's new bloom. Moncrief's breeding was at once apparent. Though not a handsome man, he had an air of distinction that, coupled with his good manners and his humor, made him a person of great charm. There was nothing to indicate that he had ever met Lucinda before their alleged encounter in the shop.

He spent most mornings in his room, writing. During the afternoons he went to see if Colonel Armstrong had any correspondence to be copied. After dinner he was usually found in the public room, talking with the other guests.

One evening Susannah saw him reading *The Pennsylvania Gazette* and asked how he had been able to procure a copy. Moncrief rose. "Please be seated, Mrs. Graves. It's a month-old copy but it's better than doing without news of the world. My agent in Philadelphia sends it to me. Would you like to read it?"

Susannah smiled. "I should be delighted—that is, when you have finished with it."

"Please take it. I've read the things that interest me. The advertisements of sales and nostrums are of little importance. By the way, there is one chap, who writes under the pseudonym 'Friend of Plato,' whose articles I believe you will enjoy. He is said to be a lawyer in Philadelphia, a man named Josiah Norris—"

He didn't finish what he had to say, for Susannah leaned forward. "Not Josiah *W.* Norris?"

"I can't say. Do you know him?"

"Josiah W. Norris," she said, "is my uncle. He raised me after my parents' death."

"Was he a writer?"

"He wrote scholarly papers for the Philosophical Society, but he never discussed politics with me."

"Fighting the Assembly requires courage," Geoffrey said. "And discretion. A certain classicist who calls himself Plato's friend has brought down their wrath on various occasions by pointing out the need for military support for the frontier."

"It's high time," Susannah answered. "I hope it is Uncle Josiah who is Plato's friend. I never found him especially sympathetic, though he *was* interested in my education."

"Does that not suggest to you," began Moncrief with a twinkle in his eyes, "a certain advanced approach? Most men believe that women should be relegated to the drawing room—or the kitchen and the nursery, depending on their social position."

They continued their conversation, unaware that Lucinda had peered through the doorway several times. Seeing them thus, she felt the stirrings of jealousy.

That night when Susannah excused herself and went upstairs to find Lucinda for their lesson, the younger girl was tempted to send her away, but curiosity overcame her jealousy. "What was you and Mr. Moncrief talkin' about? Ya was at it long enough."

Susannah was still in a state of euphoria at having found someone with whom to discuss ideas. "We were discussing a man who writes for *The Pennsylvania Gazette,* who calls himself 'Friend of Plato.' "

"Did he tell you about goin' to that big university in England?"

Susannah was surprised at her question. "We did not discuss personal matters. After all, we've only just met." When and where would Moncrief have confided such information to Lucinda? She began to suspect that their chance encounter in the draper's shop was not their first meeting.

There are many reasons for wanting to learn, Susannah thought; the desire to appeal to a learned man is one that is usually overlooked. In the following weeks she was amazed at Lucinda's progress in reading and ciphering. The girl was also trying to imitate Susannah's speech and behavior. All of this was not wasted on Geoffrey Moncrief. He made it a point to chat with Lucinda, commenting on the spotlessness of his room and offering to help her with writing. Gradually he began to take over Susannah's role as teacher.

Because of Mrs. Pratt's vigilance, Lucinda was never alone with him. Susannah arranged that their lesson was held in the kitchen after the evening dishes were done. To satisfy Mrs. Pratt, she would sit by the chimney, reading from the books John Graves had left her.

She was so engrossed in her book that she was unaware of Geoffrey's frequent glances. Moncrief had never met anyone like Susannah Graves. He had been able to learn the outline of her story from Lucinda. It was her total lack of coyness and her interest in ideas that appealed most to him. One evening he interrupted his instruction. "I say, you've done a good job with Mistress Abbot. She'll soon be ready to write a letter."

Susannah smiled. "You might want to write your parents at Fort Lyttleton, Lucinda. To let them know how you are and to find out about your brother."

Lucinda did not answer but bent her head over the word she was writing so that they could not see her eyes.

The following morning Moncrief heard a timid knock shortly after he started writing in his journal. "Come in," he called.

The knock came again. He opened the door and saw Lucinda standing there.

"Come in, my dear. What is it?" He pulled up a chair and motioned for her to sit down.

She began to pleat the corner of her apron. "Geoffrey, I'm that sorry to bother ya, but I can't write to my folks."

"That's your privilege. Mrs. Graves thought they would want to know where you are, that you are safe."

"She don't understand. They *disowned* me! I told ya about runnin' away with Johnny Appleton, the soldier who was hung."

He nodded. She was as provocative as Eve, he thought. Not exactly pretty, but blessed with the kind of looks to stir a man. In that green sprigged dress with that white kerchief folded across her shoulders and her thick, pale blond hair neatly braided and coiled about her head, she looked demure and sweet. He had noted how thin she had become and how her former rosy color appeared only when she was excited, as she was now. That infernal Mrs. Pratt worked her too hard; he wished he could do something about it.

Lucinda took a deep breath, "I—I ain't told ya all of it," she was saying. "George Eldridge and his wife was our nearest neighbors back in the Cove. Last summer his wife was captured by the Injuns with my brother Felix. She wasn't never found. George brought the baby over to us and the next day we all went to the fort. I took care of Thomas for him. Well, when we returned to our farm after the raids was over, George left Thomas at our place and he'd come over every other day to see him. One day when he didn't come, I went over and found him real sick. I got him into the bed and was nursin' him when Pa come. He didn't like my takin' care of him alone so he sent one of the boys to stay. . . ."

Moncrief smiled. "You're saying you found a way to outwit your father?"

He noticed that she really was upset; this was not just a ploy to get into his room.

"I ain't proud of what I done, Geoffrey. When George was mendin' I crept into bed with him. I couldn't help it. . . ."

"Did this—er—arrangement occur again?"

"As often as it was possible. George was real tore apart over it. He really loved Mary Ann. I was the one started it."

"You're feeling regrets. Is that it, Lucinda? Is that why you punished yourself by letting men use you at the Pot of Gold?"

Tears brimmed over and fell on her clasped hands. "Pa said I was no good."

Moncrief knelt beside her. "Come, child, it's no use weeping. None of us is in a position to judge another. You've punished yourself enough."

"But it ruined George's life. He ain't been the same since."

He was silent.

"You know what I'm tryin' to say?" she asked.

"I think you've come to realize that the ultimate evil is what we do to hurt others. I do understand your anguish."

"Did you ever do anythin' like that?" she asked naively.

His eyes were troubled. "I killed a man in a duel once over a game of cards. As long as I live it will be with me."

"I shouldn't of asked ya."

"It's all right, Lucinda. We are both flawed. But you're going in the right direction now."

Before she could answer they heard Mrs. Pratt's heavy tread on the stairs. "Compose yourself!" He tiptoed to the door and noiselessly opened it.

As Mrs. Pratt's round face appeared at the top of the stairs, he raised his voice. "If you will bring my dinner to my room, Mistress Abbot. Explain to Mrs. Pratt that I have a great deal of work to finish."

"Yes, sir," said Lucinda.

"Ah, there you are, Mrs. Pratt," he said. "I was just asking Mistress Abbot to bring my dinner to my room today."

"I heard ya, Mr. Moncrief, but we're too busy for such services."

"Well, in that case I shall forgo dinner today."

Mrs. Pratt softened. "I reckon Lucinda might bring ya some

cold mutton and some bread after the others is served."

"That will do nicely, thank you. And now I must get on with my work."

As she followed Mrs. Pratt downstairs, Lucinda hoped her employer could not hear the thunderous beating of her heart.

A week after their first meeting, Ben appeared at the inn to take Susannah to Mrs. Graffius's home.

They began to talk of the general dissatisfaction with the Provincial Assembly. "It don't seem reasonable that men in Philadelphia who don't know nothin' about the frontier should be makin' policy for people livin' hundreds of miles away," he said. "How can they decide what's best when they never lived here?"

"When the Indian troubles are over, this province is going to need people like you to determine its future," Susannah said.

"The Assembly represents the Crown and decides policy. We ain't got nothin' to say about it."

"It won't always be so, Mr. Enyard." Ben thought about her remark. Did she mean that men like himself, with no education save that acquired through experience, would someday have a role in determining the future here?

"You are an intelligent man, Mr. Enyard. The people will not always be willing to accept the present state of affairs. This province needs men like you."

"I never had schoolin'," he said in embarrassment.

"That can be remedied. There is an Englishman staying at the Forge Inn who has a fine education. He might tutor you."

"I always wanted to learn to read and write but there wasn't no opportunity. What's this man's name?"

"Geoffrey Moncrief. Would you like me to speak to him for you?"

"No, thank you, I'll ask him myself."

Susannah saw that her suggestion had stirred him. He was different, she thought, from other men she had met, far more perceptive, a serious man with an ability to look deeper into circumstances than most. And he had an inner strength.

* *

Fiona McCullough answered the door when Ben and Susannah arrived at Mrs. Graffius's home. Fiona's deep blush when she saw Ben revealed much to Susannah, but he seemed unaware of it.

"This is Fiona McCullough. Her family was neighbor to us in the Cove."

Susannah smiled. "I'm Susannah Graves, Fiona."

"Please come in," Fiona murmured shyly.

The cheery room bustled with life. An old lady and a woman with auburn hair streaked with gray sat on a settle, carding wool, while a handsome little boy and a plump little toddler with red curls played on the floor. A gaunt woman was mending. As they entered, the woman with reddish hair came toward them with outstretched hands. Her resemblance to Ben was striking.

"I'm so pleased to meet ya, Mrs. Graves," Else said. "Mrs. Graffius told us about your husband, and Ben's spoken of how brave he was. It must make ya proud." Before Susannah could reply the other women came to greet her and she was touched by their warmth and friendliness. They talked about conditions in Carlisle, the shortage of meat and flour, and wondered when the Assembly would send supplies. They were interested to hear what Philadelphia was like, for they had heard Susannah came from there.

When there was a pause in the conversation, Else asked, "How is Lucinda gettin' on at the inn?"

"She's learning to read and write and cipher."

"Ya don't say!"

"You're a-learning her?" Annie McCullough asked.

"A guest at the inn is helping her. They study in the kitchen when her work is finished."

"I'm real glad to hear that," Else said.

Annibele stood quietly at her mother's knee during this exchange. She took her finger from her mouth and pointed to the gold locket Susannah wore. "Pretty!" she said.

They laughed.

"Would you like to see, Annibele?" Susannah asked. "Come to me and I'll show you."

The chubby baby wobbled over to Susannah, who put her on her lap. She played with the locket.

Susannah hugged her. The child's softness and innocence brought back memories of Rachel, and Susannah began to tell them about her. "I keep wondering if I did the right thing in leaving her in the Mingo camp. I thought if I could find John, he would discover a means of ransoming her. . . ."

"I'm sure ya did what ya thought best at the time," Else said. "Ya couldn't know things would turn out as they did."

"You'll find her, ma'am. It's just a matter of time," Ben said.

Their words released a torrent of emotion in Susannah. She began to sob, crying out her loss and grief. She felt Else Enyard's arms about her and was dimly aware that Else knelt beside her and was smoothing the hair from her forehead. There was silence except for the murmur of Else's voice, warm with sympathy: "Do ya good to let go at times, dear. We can't always be strong. When we feel things deep down inside, it ain't natural to keep them locked up."

Susannah felt comforted by Else's words. When she lifted her face, she saw that Mrs. Graffius, Annie McCullough, and Fiona had taken the children from the room and there was only Ben waiting beside his mother. She sat up and wiped her eyes. "I'm so ashamed, Mrs. Enyard, for making such a spectacle of myself."

Else caught her hands and held them. "I'm goin' to call you Susannah, is that all right? I lost my little girl, Ari, and my husband in a raid, so I know how you feel. Honest grief ain't somethin' to be ashamed of. I couldn't get over my sorrow until I started tryin' to help them that was worse off than I was. . . ."

Susannah tried to smile. "You—you are wonderful, Mrs. Enyard. Please apologize for me to the others."

"No need for that, dear. We all understand. It's our common sufferin' that binds us together."

As Ben escorted Susannah back to the inn, he was aware of a new and powerful emotion: he was in love. Susannah's grief had shaken him; he wanted to take her in his arms and tell her she could depend on him. But it was too soon for that.

Ben would not admit to his mother that Susannah Graves influenced his decision to get an education. He had been mulling it over in his mind for some time, he told her. He needed to read and write and cipher to find out what was going on in the world beyond Carlisle and to have some means of directing his life so that he need not be at the mercy of people in authority.

Several days later Ben visited Geoffrey Moncrief at the inn.

"Come in, sir. To what do I owe the honor of a visit?"

"I'm Ben Enyard of the militia, Mr. Moncrief. Mrs. Graves said ya might be willin' to tutor me."

"I see. Have you had any schooling, Mr. Enyard?"

"No, sir."

"My reason for asking you this is a personal one, as you will see. I'm writing a series of articles on the frontier for two London papers, and your experiences as a frontiersman could be invaluable to me."

"I was at Kittaning," Ben said.

"Tell me about it. And about how you came to Carlisle."

Ben forgot the time as he talked. Geoffrey watched him, noted the tension mount as Ben told of his father's and Ari's deaths. Suddenly Ben saw that the sun was declining and he rose. "It's gettin' late. Mr. Moncrief, I almost forgot what I come for. Will ya teach me?"

"With pleasure. God, what an experience you've had!"

"How much will I owe ya?"

Geoffrey laughed and waved a hand. "Let's say I will teach you in return for your telling me of your experiences. Is that agreeable?"

Ben looked amazed. "Ya mean it?"

"Yes, indeed. You have something of value to offer me."

Ben ran down the stairs, bumping into Lucinda at the bottom.

"Why don't you look where you're goin'?" she asked.

"I'm sorry, Lucinda. Mr. Moncrief's goin' to tutor me," Ben told her, bounding out the door.

Lucinda was aware that Geoffrey spent more and more time talking with Susannah. One evening he asked Susannah to go for a walk. As they sauntered down the tree-lined street Lucinda watched them, her emotions in turmoil.

* *

Geoffrey did not know how long he had been asleep when he heard a slight sound at his door. Picking up his pistol, he threw open the door to find Lucinda standing in a patch of moonlight in her nightgown.

"What are you doing here at this hour, Lucinda?" he whispered.

She put her finger to her lips. "Shush! Let me in, Geoffrey. I need to talk to you."

He drew her into the room and quietly closed the door. "It's a good thing I'm a cautious man with a pistol. I thought you were an intruder."

He saw that she was trembling, though the night was warm. A breeze fluttered the leaves in the tree outside the window and a shaft of moonlight outlined her figure beneath the thin stuff of her gown. God, she was desirable, he thought, but he must use his head.

"Why did you come? You know you risk everything in coming here."

"It don't matter. I can't sleep when you're in the same house just a few doors from my room."

"But, my dear, you must understand. You've made a fresh start. Someday you'll want to marry. I can't offer you that, Lucinda."

"Nothin' matters but bein' close to you." She pulled the drawstring of her gown and stood before him naked.

"God, Lucinda! Why do you do this? I don't want to take advantage of you."

"But you do like me, don't you, Geoffrey?"

"You know I do."

"Then don't be afraid for me, Geoffrey." She took a step toward him and lifted her face to receive his kiss.

No woman had ever excited him as she did. Sweeping her up in his arms, he carried her to the bed.

CHAPTER XVI

Growing

The dispatch rider who carried mail from Philadelphia to Colonel Armstrong brought Susannah the following letter in late June.

Philadelphia, June 8th, 1757

My dear Niece,

When your letter arrived late in May, I was confined to my bed with a painful attack of gout. My delay in answering was the result of my infirmity and should not be misconstrued as lack of sympathy for you. The sad news of John Graves's untimely death was distressing. The province has need of his kind, particularly in these parlous times.

I can appreciate how grievous it must be for you to have had to leave Rachel with the Mingoes. Mr. Snodgrass brought me word of the rigors of your life among them and explained the impossibility of taking her with you when you escaped. He could not find suitable words to express his respect and admiration for your courage and tenacity. I am offering a reward of fifty pounds for Rachel's return. Mr. Snodgrass will be leaving in the near future to trade with the tribes of the Iroquois League, who have contacts with the Mingoes, Shawnees, and Delawares. He assures me that news of the reward will reach them in this manner.

I am entrusting ten pounds to Mr. Snodgrass to deliver in person to you. This sum should enable you to meet your needs and be sufficient for you to journey to Philadelphia, where you will be welcome to make your home with me.

I have been contributing articles to Mr. Franklin's *Pennsylvania Gazette* concerning the province's lack of preparedness for the present war, and am particularly disturbed about the Provincial Assembly's dilatory response to requests for help. If their diverse commercial interests were threatened, the pious Quakers would have to face the fact that attempting to purchase the Indians' loyalty is absurd. When I think of what is happening, I become so incensed that my cardinal humors are disturbed. My physician has warned me to exert control or suffer the consequences.

Now that I am growing old—I will be fifty soon—I find myself regretting my lack of sensibility toward you as you were growing up. Never having married, I had little understanding of children. It has troubled me that I permitted you to journey to the western frontier at the tender age of sixteen. Should you decide to share my home, you will be most welcome. Since the journey is not without danger, I do not presume to counsel you in this; do as you see fit. I shall send you money from time to time, as it would add to my distress were you in want.

With affectionate greetings, Your Uncle,
Josiah W. Norris

Susannah slipped the letter into the pocket of her apron. It was incredible! She never would have believed anything could touch the heart of Josiah Norris. She wondered what had brought about the change. Was it ill health, with a growing awareness of the shadow of the grave? Or had Mr. Snodgrass's eloquence prompted this new sensitivity? She took up her pen and wrote to her uncle.

Carlisle, June 22, 1757

My dear Uncle,

Your letter has just arrived. It was most generous of you to offer me a home until the Indian troubles are over and to send ten pounds with Mr. Snodgrass. The ransom you have offered for Rachel is a Godsend!

I am sorry to hear of your being ill and pray for your rapid recovery. It came as a surprise to learn you are the "Friend of Plato" whose articles in the *Gazette* reflect the desperate plight of hundreds of settlers. There is an Englishman staying at the Forge Inn, Geoffrey Moncrief, who lends me his month-old copies of the *Gazette.* He admires your work and brought it to my attention. Heaven knows we need someone to plead our cause.

Your offer of hospitality touched me. However, I shall stay here in case the captives are returned. I have not given up hope that Rachel will be restored to me.

I am busy cooking for the inn's customers and taking care of the accounts. It is good to be fully occupied as it leaves less time to grieve about Rachel and John. It is amazing to discover how many fine people there are; people who would never be considered brave under ordinary circumstances now show a valiant spirit, a resourcefulness, that never fails to impress me. Of course, there are some who do nothing but complain, but fortunately, they seem to be in the minority.

Do take care of yourself.
With affectionate greetings,
Susannah

Her letter finished, Susannah opened the door to the hall. She heard Geoffrey Moncrief's laugh, although the door to his room was closed, and she wondered what he could be reading to provoke such pure mirth; there wasn't much to laugh about these days. Then his door opened and Lucinda Abbot emerged. The girl did not see her, for she appeared preoccupied. Susannah hastily closed her door.

Surely Lucinda was not so foolish as to believe Moncrief would seriously consider marrying her. An Englishman from an old, titled family would not allow himself to become interested in a frontier girl with a questionable past. If marriage was what Lucinda wanted, she was focusing her attentions on the wrong man.

Susannah had learned something of Moncrief's background during their occasional evening walks. He had spoken often of his ancestral home, Hadley Hall, in Kent, of his family, Catholics, originally Scottish, who had moved to England during the Jacobean wars.

"Do you still embrace your family's religion?" she had asked.

"Let us say I respect it. I happen to have incurred my father's displeasure—no, that is too mild a term: wrath would be more apt—over my gambling. They shipped me off to the colonies with a small allowance, hoping life in Philadelphia would reform me." He gave her a twisted grin, half shame and half amusement. She saw in him the boy who had gotten into scrapes and charmed his way out of being punished.

"You plan to stay in the colonies, then?"

"Yes, I shall stay. Although I did not come by choice, I have learned to appreciate what America has to offer. Men are more free here to follow their inclinations."

"What do you plan to do when the war is over?"

"I should like to continue my writing, to record what is happening, to raise certain questions that must be raised if America's riches are not to be despoiled by those interested only in profits."

"It is a noble aim."

"To pursue it I shall first have to establish myself. And what of you, dear lady? You cannot return alone to your plantation when peace comes."

"I could go live with my uncle and perhaps start a school. But the challenge lies in continuing the work my husband started. I can't abandon John's dream."

"You will undoubtedly marry again."

She flushed. "It is so exasperating that what I want to do is considered impossible unless I have a husband. I could employ some Negroes to do the heavy labor."

"It sounds like a lonely life for a beautiful woman."

Susannah ignored the compliment. "I am determined to provide a good life for Rachel."

"Rachel?"

"My daughter. She is still in captivity." To her surprise, she began to tell Geoffrey of their capture and her escape.

He was grateful that she shared this with him. "I'm sorry I

cannot offer you the comfort of religion, for I am an agnostic. I believe in a rational universe."

She thought about that. "I haven't the courage to be so. I cannot accept the dogma with which I was raised, but I do believe in God and His purpose."

As if reading her thoughts, he said, "You must not blame yourself for leaving Rachel. You did what seemed best under the circumstances."

She had been comforted by his words.

Remembering this conversation, Susannah wondered what Geoffrey could find in Lucinda to attract him. Apparently, he was susceptible to the girl's obvious physical charms and did not scruple to take advantage of the situation. She was certain that Lucinda loved him but was equally sure Geoffrey did not reciprocate. Susannah felt a twinge of jealousy. She had not felt his physical appeal, but she knew that he fancied himself in love with her. It was a new and stimulating experience to have met a man whose education surpassed hers.

On a recent walk they had been discussing Shakespeare's sonnets, and Moncrief had quoted one that she especially liked:

"When, in disgrace with Fortune and men's eyes,
I all alone beweep my outcast state,
And trouble deaf heaven with my bootless cries,
And look upon myself and curse my fate,
Wishing me like to one more rich in hope,
Featured like him, like him with friends possessed,
Desiring this man's art and that man's scope,
With what I most enjoy contented least;
Yet in these thoughts myself almost despising,
Haply I think on thee, and then my state,
Like to the lark at break of day arising
From sullen earth, sings hymns at heaven's gate;
For thy sweet love rememb'red such wealth brings
*That then I scorn to change my state with kings."**

*Sonnet XXIX

She was silent when he had finished, sharing his mood as they walked through the scented dusk of early evening. "It speaks across the years," she said.

"That is some men's immortality—to touch others in future times with the freshness and power of their words. . . . It is all the immortality I should want."

"And I," she said. "But I do not have the poet's gift."

"You have the gift of living, Susannah." He turned to her. "May I call you that?"

She nodded, too surprised for speech.

"You have meant much to me, how much you cannot imagine. . . ."

"Please," she said. "This is not the time to speak of such things."

"Forgive me, Susannah. I meant only to assure you of my devotion."

"I have appreciated your friendship," she said, choosing to misinterpret him.

"I do not refer to friendship."

"Please, Mr. Moncrief, it is not appropriate to speak so."

"If I might hope that in the future—"

"I cannot listen to such things."

He gave her a long look. "You are so lovely," he said.

He did not mention this conversation in the days that followed, but seeing Lucinda come out of his room made Susannah remember. She noticed how much happier Lucinda looked lately; her mouth had a new softness, her eyes greater depth and expression. Susannah had heard her humming as she worked. It troubled her that Geoffrey would take advantage of Lucinda's devotion while telling Susannah that he loved her.

Snodgrass stopped to see Susannah two weeks after she received her uncle's letter. He had much to say about Josiah Norris, since he had been asked to take supper with him.

"He were real consarned 'bout ya, Miz Graves." Snodgrass reached into his boot, pulled out a grimy envelope. "Here's the ten pounds he sent ya."

"Thank you, Mr. Snodgrass. You've done me a great service. Come and sit down." Susannah led him to the place in the kitchen where Lucinda had her lessons. "I don't have to start dinner for an hour or more."

"Ya doin' the cookin', eh?"

"Yes. And keeping the accounts. I had to do something."

"Wall, ya won't have ta now. Yer uncle is real anxious ta have ya return."

"I think it's better to wait here for Rachel to return, Mr. Snodgrass. Did you hear any news about an exchange of captives?"

"Nary a word. Seems there's a fella by the name of Washington who's tryin' ta start an offensive war agin them red varmints an' the French. Mr. Norris said there's some talk of the eastern band of the Delaware makin' a separate peace."

"That's good news, Mr. Snodgrass! If they are willing to stop the war, the others may be also."

"I dunno," he said. "Yer uncle said they ain't heerd."

It was now midsummer and the war continued unabated, with sporadic raids as far east as Lancaster. The settlers living near Carlisle had to take refuge in the town, and were organized into groups to harvest their fields under the protection of the militia. Food was more scarce.

Ben was among the militiamen sent to protect the harvesters. The men were posted forty feet apart, surrounding the fields where the farmers worked. As soon as the wagons were filled, they were driven back to Carlisle with two outriders for protection. The wagons were unloaded and sent back for more produce.

One day when Ben and Jim McCullough were assigned to protect the wagons, Ben felt apprehensive as they started back to town. It began with an uneasy feeling in his stomach, and he could not shake off a foreboding that something terrible was about to happen. All went well until they returned to the farm. Mutilated bodies were scattered over the field, and carrion crows feasted on the remains.

With mounting terror Ben and Jim searched for living among

the dead while the men driving the wagons watched the woods for Indians. They had collected three wounded and were about to leave when they heard a rustling in the bushes that edged the fields and saw two militiamen running toward them, one bleeding from a wound in the shoulder, the other white-faced and shaken.

"Thank the Lord!" one gasped.

"What happened?"

"A Delaware war party. Happened soon after ya left."

"We lay down and pretended to be dead. Thought they'd scalp us."

Ben took charge. "We can't take time to bury the dead. We'd best get back to Carlisle." When they reached the fort and reported to the colonel, Ben felt that he had aged ten years.

Susannah, when she heard of it, felt faint; it was not the nearness of the raid nor the tragedy itself that appalled her, she realized, but the knowledge that Ben might have been killed. She was startled at the depth of her feelings for him.

In mid-August Geoffrey Moncrief received a letter from his agent, informing him of the death of his paternal aunt, Mistress Judith Moncrief, a well-to-do spinster who had lived at Hadley Hall. He had always been his aunt's favorite and she had made him her sole beneficiary. Some eight thousand pounds, dispatched as a letter of credit, awaited him in Philadelphia. His aunt wanted him to live in circumstances appropriate to his upbringing, his agent wrote.

Moncrief was filled with remorse. He had not written to his aunt since his arrival in the colonies nearly two years before. That she should care for him in spite of his disgrace affected him deeply. He was ashamed that he had not communicated with her. After much soul-searching, he decided to journey to Philadelphia to claim the inheritance and start life anew. If he could establish himself as a scholar and a gentleman, perhaps he could blot out his past indiscretions and win the hand of Susannah Graves.

When he thought of Lucinda, his conscience troubled him. He was fond of her and knew that she loved him, and he had tried not to take advantage of her simple devotion. But propinquity and nature, plus her generous offering of herself, had weakened his resolve. It had been an enriching experience. Lucinda's spontaneity and naturalness had delighted him. She had brought a freshness to their love-making that surprised him. But she was not suitable to be his wife.

Moncrief tried to ease his conscience by remembering that from the beginning he had not deceived her with talk of love. Yet I did take her, night after night—and enjoyed every moment of it, part of him whispered. It wasn't as if she had been a virgin. She sought me out just as she sought out the first man—what was his name?—George Eldridge. And the deserter, Johnny Appleton. She's an aggressive and charming minx. But she would never be acceptable to the Moncriefs.

That night when Lucinda stole to his room, he said, "I'm sorry, my dear, I've had some beastly news from home."

"Is it about your family?"

"My aunt—my favorite aunt. She died in June. Now I must go to Philadelphia to settle some matters relating to her death."

"To—Philadelphia?"

"Yes, my dear."

"But it's so dangerous. People been killed goin' from here to Lancaster! Oh, Geoffrey, must you go?"

"I'm afraid so, Lucinda."

"When will you be comin' back?" She looked utterly defenseless, stricken.

He couldn't tell her the truth. "I'm not certain. I may have to return to England." He had never felt so despicable in his life, not even when he had killed the man over a game of cards. That had been a duel with two well-matched antagonists; in this he had all the advantages.

Lucinda stood looking out the window, saying nothing.

"I'm sorry, Lucinda. I shall never forget you," he said quietly.

She turned and gave him a half smile. Walking to the door, she said so softly that he scarcely heard, "I hope you'll be happy, Geoffrey." With that she was gone.

* *

Three days later Susannah awoke to find a letter slipped under her door. Picking it up, she saw it was addressed in a bold masculine hand and was amazed to discover it was from Moncrief.

The letter was brief and direct:

August 17, 1757

My dear Susannah,

Recently I received word from my agent, Timothy Pickering of 10 Locust Street, Philadelphia, of the death of my father's sister at Hadley Hall. It seems I was Aunt Judith's favorite, though why she should have felt this way I can only guess. At any rate, I am her sole beneficiary.

I am leaving tomorrow for Philadelphia to collect the inheritance and to establish myself. Mr. Pickering will know my whereabouts. I comfort myself with the hope that you will answer this brief letter. I cannot—nor would I want to—forget you. The moments we were together were some of the most meaningful I have ever spent.

May I continue to hope that when your mourning is passed I may tell you what is in my heart?

Faithfully,
Geoffrey Moncrief

Susannah's first reaction was surprise, then disgust that he should write to her in this vein after disporting himself with Lucinda. She was outraged that he would attempt to deceive her, as well as Lucinda.

But she would miss him.

As she went downstairs to prepare breakfast, it was as if some energizing force in her environment was being removed. She saw that Lucinda and Mrs. Pratt had been told of his departure. "Now do be careful, Mr. Moncrief," Mrs. Pratt admonished. "Them Injuns has been gettin' bolder every week. I hope ya got plenty of protection."

He laughed. "I'm traveling with some drovers who brought supplies to the fort. They'll be with me as far as Lancaster, and I am armed, Mrs. Pratt."

She shook her head. "You'll be lucky to get through safe.

Why only last week that dispatch rider was scalped about twenty miles east of here."

Susannah saw Lucinda pale, then slip out of the kitchen. As she deftly slipped the eggs and corn bread onto his plate, she saw Moncrief watching her. "I trust you'll have a good journey," she said.

He smiled. "That sentiment will help to lighten it."

"Will you be returnin'?" Mrs. Pratt asked.

"I can't say. It will depend on several matters, but it won't be before spring." He gave Susannah a long look and she felt herself flush.

"We'll miss ya, Mr. Moncrief. We don't see many real gentlemen," Mrs. Pratt said.

"Thank you. I shall miss my friends here."

He bent over Susannah's hand when the saddlebags had been packed. He spoke softly since the Pratts were standing close by. "Please give my thanks to Mistress Abbot for all that she did to contribute to my comfort, Mrs. Graves."

Susannah's temper flared. "I presume you've told her yourself."

He looked startled, his poise shaken. After adjusting the saddle girth, he mounted the horse. "Adieu," he said. "I had hoped it would be au revoir."

Lucinda was subdued and preoccupied that day. She picked at her food until Mrs. Pratt remarked, "What's got into you, Lucinda? I don't recollect you ever eatin' so little."

"I jist ain't hungry."

That evening when it was time for her lesson, she did not go to Susannah's room. After waiting half an hour, Susannah knocked on her door. There was no answer, but she could hear the sound of muffled sobbing.

Summoning her courage, Susannah opened the door. Lucinda lay on the bed, her body shaking with sobs, her clothes in disarray. Susannah knelt beside her. "What is it? What's wrong?"

Lucinda did not answer.

"Is it because of Geoffrey's leaving?"

The storm continued unabated.

"Please, Lucinda, you'll make yourself ill."

Susannah waited. Finally Lucinda raised her head. "I'm goin' to have a child."

Susannah was speechless. She felt a wild anger at Geoffrey Moncrief for taking his pleasure and then, when his fortune improved, leaving Lucinda to face the future alone. When she had control of her emotions, she asked, "Does he know?"

"No. I didn't want to win him that way. I wanted him to love me—to come of his own free will." Her mouth trembled. "He told me he didn't love me before we started, but it didn't matter."

"But Lucinda, it's his responsibility as much as yours! What will you do?"

"I don't know." She bit her lip to stop its trembling.

"But Lucinda, you must plan. How long have you missed your monthly flow?"

"This is the third month," the girl said tonelessly.

Susannah sat down on the bed and took the girl's hands. "Well, then, in six months you will be bringing a child into the world—with no one to do for you but yourself. Can't you return to your family at Fort Lyttleton?"

"They don't want nothin' to do with me!"

"But why? Surely now they'll take you in."

The girl shook her head.

"It can't be that bad."

Lucinda took a deep breath, then began to tell her story. Susannah felt that she was seeing the girl's soul laid bare. When she had finished, Lucinda put her head on Susannah's shoulder. "What can I do?"

Summoning a spurious optimism, Susannah stroked the blond braids. "Try not to worry. I'll think of something."

She wondered what Uncle Josiah would think if she were to arrive on his doorstep with a pregnant young woman. Then she remembered the ten pounds. "I have some money my uncle sent me. He said he would send more, but I suppose with the raids it's not been possible. But no matter, what I have is yours."

The tears began to flow again. "Do you think he'll be all right?" Lucinda asked.

"Geoffrey? Well, if you want my opinion, Geoffrey Moncrief has nine lives. He will survive." If Susannah sounded bitter, Lucinda was too miserable to notice. "You had better get some rest. Do you think you can sleep?"

"All I can think of is I won't never see him again!" Lucinda lay back on the pillow and sobbed.

"Now stop that, Lucinda! You can't afford to give way to your feelings." Sympathy only increased Lucinda's tears, so Susannah would have to be firm. "I'm going down to the kitchen to make you some tea. You will have to be calm if we are to plan for your confinement."

Geoffrey Moncrief's journey to Philadelphia was not without its dangers. Several hours after the convoy left Carlisle the outriders saw Indians moving in the trees to their left. Geoffrey felt his scalp prickle with fear as the quiet was shattered by rifle fire. It was difficult to pick off the Indians, for the dense underbrush provided cover for them.

For a brief time the firing was heavy and the Indians' guns made several holes in the canvas tops of the two wagons. One of the drivers suffered flesh wounds, but within fifteen minutes the Indians had fled and all was quiet. Geoffrey was bathed in sweat and he could not relax until they arrived at Lancaster. The remainder of the journey was without incident.

Shortly after his arrival in Philadelphia Geoffrey went to see his agent, Timothy Pickering. It was a golden mid-September day; an errant breeze tossed the late asters and marigolds in the gardens behind the white picket fences and ruffled the yellow and gold leaves. Sunlight spilled onto the cobbles and was reflected off the brass door knockers. The hand-blown glass windowpanes gleamed with the brilliant light.

He wondered how he would adjust to living in this stronghold of pacifism after being exposed to the rigors and deprivations of life in Carlisle. People he passed looked prosperous, well-fed, content with their lot. There was an atmosphere of peace and plenty. After his months in Carlisle he would never again be able to take these for granted.

He decided to stop at the London Coffee Shop on the corner

of Front and Market. The place was crowded. Its rack of English and American newspapers carried special advices, both foreign and domestic, on the days the post arrived. Merchants met here to receive reports of ships, commodity prices, and other news important to their commercial interests.

He found a small table, ordered a coffee, and selected an English newspaper from the rack. He was engrossed in an account of recent Parliamentary acts when someone addressed him and he looked up to see a well-dressed middle-aged gentleman smiling down at him.

"Do you object, sir, to my sharing your table? The others seem to be taken."

"Not at all." Geoffrey smiled.

"Thank you. This place has become so popular one can hardly find a seat." The man was wearing a claret-colored velvet suit with an embroidered waistcoat of gray satin. His black tricorne hat was trimmed with silver braid, and the effect was of quiet elegance.

He ordered a pot of tea and made no further attempt at conversation. Geoffrey, sipping his coffee, put down his cup. "Could you perhaps tell me where an attorney named Josiah Norris lives?"

The man stared. "I am Josiah Norris."

"This *is* a bit of luck! I haven't been in the city long enough to inquire where I might find you. I am acquainted with your niece, Mrs. Susannah Graves, sir. Allow me to introduce myself. I am Geoffrey Moncrief."

"Ah, yes, Susannah mentioned you in her letter. You are English."

"Yes. I stayed at the Forge Inn." Geoffrey explained how he had met Susannah. "She is an extraordinary young woman."

"So I am told," said Norris. "I haven't seen her since she married and went off to the wilderness. It was a shock to hear she and Rachel had been captured and that John died before her escape. How recently have you seen her?"

"I left Carlisle twelve days ago and saw her as I was leaving."

"She was well? And in good spirits?"

"Yes, she is a woman of great strength and courage."

"That's reassuring. Tell me, Mr. Moncrief, are conditions in Carlisle as bad as reports would have us believe?"

"The town is so overcrowded that many live in the streets; some sleep in churches, some in improvised tents. It's a wonder there hasn't been an epidemic."

Josiah's bushy eyebrows drew together. "The Assembly is dominated by Quakers, as you probably know. They have many admirable qualities—they have built almshouses and charity wards, encourage education for girls as well as boys, and are fair and honest in their business ventures, all of which springs from their religious beliefs. Yet they deny any kind of protection to the settlers who have gone to the Pennsylvania wilderness to homestead. They are 'persuaded'—their word for it—that to bear arms for self-defense is contrary to God's will."

"It is a pity religion tends to blur issues. If there were only some means of enabling men to work together for the common good without believing their convictions are the only ones worth having," Geoffrey said. "The unfortunate thing is that time is running out for the people living on the frontier. Something will have to be done to assist them."

"I'm afraid not much will be done until conditions pose an economic threat," Josiah said. "The assemblymen respond to pressures from the purse. They are not good administrators. At this moment, some of our worthy Friends are courting the Indians in the artless hope that their goodwill can bring peace. I fear their convictions are not always practical."

"Yet the city is prospering."

"Quite so. We Philadelphians are a mercantile people. Our merchants will not be dictated to by members of Parliament, who have little understanding of our situation. The British navigation acts limit our trade to British ports, yet there is demand for American wheat, flour, and hides all over Europe. So we ignore Parliament."

"Distance from the mother country has bred a certain independence of mind and character, then?"

"Quite true. Only the Anglicans are inclined to honor the laws made by Parliament."

"It's a bit difficult to attempt to enact laws for people living under conditions so different from those in the mother country."

"Precisely, sir."

"I wish the canny citizens took more interest in land-bound commerce," Geoffrey said. "On my recent ride from Carlisle I found the roads were little more than cart tracks. Hardly conducive to farmers' sending produce here."

"It all stems from a lack of imagination, a certain insular point of view," Josiah said. "They are eager to encourage immigrants to go west to the Pennsylvania wilderness but take no responsibility for them. Without a proper road, how are we to transport cannon and supplies should the war worsen?"

Geoffrey changed the subject. "May I inquire if you are the anonymous 'Friend of Plato' whose articles in *The Pennsylvania Gazette* have so delighted some of us?"

Josiah gave a semblance of a smile. "So you have read them?"

"Yes, indeed. It's time someone pointed out to the Assembly how their wretched piety is affecting the frontier. . . ."

"Speaking of Quaker piety," Josiah said, "in spite of the emphasis on religion, Philadelphia has more than its share of quacks and peddlers of dubious nostrums. Take a walk to the High Street market sometime and you will be surprised at what you discover."

Geoffrey remembered the block-long covered passageway of the old market with its displays of fresh produce, flowers, toys, penny almanacs, fish, poultry, herbs and spices, knives, scissors, buttons.

"Not only do they sell the usual preparations to remove warts and unwanted hair but such things as prevent—or induce—conception, cure venereal disease, or stimulate one's sexual appetite. Oh, they are careful to give their potions deceptively innocuous names—Hannay's Preventive, Keyser's Pills, Kennedy's Elixir of Life, The Ladies' Secret—lest the religious be offended and expel them from the stalls."

"A city of contrasts," Geoffrey said. "That holds true of Carlisle as well. The war has thrown together a remarkable assortment of individuals, some of the most despicable, others of real quality. I've been impressed by the courage and resourcefulness of persons who are quite undistinguished by ordinary standards."

Norris looked skeptical. "I was under the impression it was mainly people who had neither the talent nor means to live in the cities, or those escaping from the law, who pioneered."

Geoffrey thought of the circumstances that had led him to flee Philadelphia, and smiled. "There are many reasons why men choose to leave settled places for the unknown of the wilderness. Land and room to grow is the principal one. Our system of the oldest son inheriting the entire estate puts a burden on the younger sons."

"You have a point there, Mr. Moncrief. Many things need changing. One must adapt one's laws and customs to the new world. By the way, you have heard of our American Philosophical Society, have you not?"

Geoffrey nodded.

"Our discussions are quite stimulating. We have dealt with the newest methods of draining swamps, of raising and conveying water, of propagating and classifying plants, herbs, roots, and trees, of preventing and curing disease, and so on. We are determined to improve life in the colonies."

"I read in the *Gazette* that physicians have been inoculating against smallpox in Philadelphia, with remarkable success," Geoffrey said.

"I would advise you to have it done, sir. My servants and I have been inoculated, with no ill effects. Will you be staying here?"

"I'm in the process of finding a suitable house."

"Splendid! Then perhaps you will go as my guest to one of the meetings of the Philosophical Society. I assure you, you will find it interesting."

"I accept with pleasure, but I'm afraid I will not be free for a time."

"But you are interested?"

"Assuredly. I do a bit of writing—mainly articles for London papers—on what is happening in America, so I'm eager for information."

"A writer, eh?" Norris's shrewd eyes lighted. "Then you'll find many members to interest you. The best minds of this province. Where shall I find you, Mr. Moncrief?"

"At present I'm staying at the King's Grenadier. Perhaps it would be best to write my agent, Timothy Pickering, on Locust Street near Third."

Norris extracted a small notebook from an outsized pocket of his coat, called for a quill and ink, and carefully wrote down the information. "You will be hearing from me, Mr. Moncrief. I'm pleased to have met you."

Geoffrey felt fortunate to have made the acquaintance of Josiah Norris. An invitation to the Philosophical Society would enable him to meet the most influential men in the city, and it might help his suit with Susannah to become a friend of her uncle.

His inheritance from Aunt Judith would provide him with income enough to devote himself to writing. In his journal he was attempting to distill his views on primogeniture, his Oxford years, and his experience on the Pennsylvania frontier. He hoped it would shatter the complacency of some readers, but he knew that those responsible for the sorry state of affairs were not inclined to read unless they had to. First he must establish a reputation as a responsible man, one who could be trusted.

The crisp September air carried a hint of the sea as he hurried off to see Timothy Pickering.

Mr. Pickering, a rotund gentleman in an ill-fitting bag wig, watched him approach. There was a great change in Moncrief's appearance, Pickering observed. Moncrief was wearing fine new clothes in keeping with his present circumstances: an elegant tricorne hat, a bottle-green coat with handsome silver buttons, a lace cravat, and a striped vest above buff breeches and clocked hose. His shoes were in the latest fashion, with square toes and large silver buckles. He looked like a man of taste and affluence.

"Good day to you, Mr. Moncrief," he said.

"Good day, Mr. Pickering. How are you this fine day?"

"Oh, middling, sir, just middling. Have you found a house to your liking?"

"I think so." Geoffrey crossed his legs and looked at ease.

"Snuff, Mr. Moncrief?"

"No, thank you."

Mr. Pickering helped himself to a generous pinch from the silver box bearing his entwined initials on the top. "Clears the head. A bit of catarrh."

"Yes, of course."

Mr. Pickering emitted several robust sneezes and mopped his nose. "Where was this property you fancied, Mr. Moncrief?"

"At Fourth and Pine. A gracious house with a lovely walled-in garden in the rear."

Mr. Pickering held first one nostril, then the other. "There, that's better," he said. "That's the Hawkins property. But isn't it a bit small for you, Mr. Moncrief?" Most men who had inherited money wanted something to show for it.

"I think not. It has three bedrooms, a large drawing room, a small ladies' parlor, which I shall use as a study, and an adequate dining room and kitchen, in addition to the servants' quarters on the third floor."

"But if you should marry, sir, three bedrooms are hardly sufficient for a family."

Geoffrey gave him a crooked smile. "That is not a consideration at the moment. Should I marry in time and have a family, there is space enough. But I shall want the mantel in the drawing room changed. And I have made a list of other alterations."

Mr. Pickering adjusted the small square spectacles on the bridge of his nose and took up his quill pen. "There's Richard Wainwright, who was apprenticed to Mr. Adams in England. He makes fine copies of Mr. Adams's mantels, corner cupboards, what you will."

There was a discreet knock on the door, and a clerk entered carrying the mail. Removing his hat, he handed the letters to Mr. Pickering. "These just come, sir."

"Thank you, Jenkins." Glancing through the small packet of letters, Mr. Pickering peered more closely at one. "Here's one for you, Mr. Moncrief."

Geoffrey recognized Susannah's handwriting. Had she had a change of heart toward him? "Your pardon, sir, but this appears to be of some importance," he said, as he tore open the seal.

"Not at all, not at all." Mr. Pickering picked up the list and reread it to be certain he'd noted all the details. His client was silent for so long that he peered over the top of his spectacles. "Nothing wrong, I trust?"

Geoffrey did not answer.

"I trust it's not bad news, Mr. Moncrief?"

"I shall have to ask your indulgence, Mr. Pickering," Geoffrey said at last. "I must attend to something before we go further. I will return tomorrow—or the following day."

Moncrief was stunned by the news in Susannah's letter. "I am taking the liberty of writing you about Lucinda's coming child, for I believe you to be a man of honor. I know you would not want her to suffer more, nor would you willingly abandon your child. The creation of a baby is a joint responsibility," she had written with her usual forthrightness.

His thoughts were in turmoil now, as he headed for the quay. A little breeze had sprung up on the river and set the ships' rigging to groaning. It ruffled the water that lapped the pilings, distorting the reflections of the tall ships that swayed against the dockside. There was an odor of dead fish and tar in spite of the fresh breeze.

Several fishermen seated on the pilings looked at Moncrief with curiosity, wondering what such a fine gentleman would be doing in this area. Geoffrey was unaware of them. He was astounded that Lucinda had not told him of the coming child. He pulled out Susannah's letter. "I didn't want to win him that way," Lucinda had said. "I wanted him to love me—to come of his own free will." She had admitted that he told her he did not love her, but it did not matter, she had told Susannah.

Now, just when his life was beginning to prosper and he had something to offer Susannah Graves, he was trapped for having lain with a generous, impulsive girl who acted on instinct and did not count the consequences. She had followed the promptings of her heart. But he did not have even that excuse, he told himself. He had found her desirable and ripe for it. He had not thought where it might lead.

He thought of the child growing within Lucinda, a child in whose veins would flow the blood of the Moncriefs. There had been bastards in the family before—love children born of passionate secret meetings, and others conceived in haste, without affection. But his coming-together with Lucinda had been like neither of these.

As he left the waterfront he passed the Copper Kettle, the most attractive coffeehouse in Philadelphia. The memory of its cheerful atmosphere made him retrace his steps to peer in. The sun poured through the many small panes and was reflected on the shining plates and cups in the huge pine cupboard. The comely owner, Mrs. Beddows, was knitting in a wing chair near the light. There appeared to be no customers at the moment.

As Geoffrey entered, Kate Beddows laid aside her knitting and came toward him, the dimples in her rosy cheeks deepening, a light in her green eyes assuring him of a special welcome. Geoffrey assumed she was in her early thirties. She was an attractive woman with a manner both tactful and provocative. She was wearing a handsome dress of flowered chintz with a rose silk stomacher. The whiteness of her arms was accentuated by pleated lawn ruffles and her low décolletage, outlined with ruching, revealed plump white breasts.

"Why, Mr. Moncrief, it's nice to see you." Her glance took in his disturbed state.

"I've been looking for a house to purchase," he said.

"I see. Well, come and sit down. It's a tiring business, searching for a place to live." She let her hand linger on his shoulder as he sat down. "What can I get for you?"

"Tea, please."

"I will join you."

When the tea arrived, she poured two cups and handed one to him. His eyes lingered on the cleft between her breasts. She laid a hand on one of his hands. "You look tired. I have some brandy upstairs. It would be just the thing to restore your spirits."

Geoffrey smiled. Well, why not forget his problems for a while? Kate Beddows looked as though she could satisfy a man. God knows he needed something to restore him.

She was expert in the art of seduction, and as Geoffrey removed her garments, he felt a mounting desire that swept away thoughts of his problem with Lucinda. Even the fine lines he discerned about her laughing mouth, the slight sag of the beautiful breasts failed to dampen his ardor.

She was a woman of strong appetites and he found himself passionately involved. When it was over he was filled with a rich languor. It was almost as good as being with Lucinda, he thought absently, just before falling asleep. When he awoke, Kate was gone. The light coming through the narrow windows was beginning to fade, and he realized he must have slept for hours.

He felt better and resolved not to think about the situation with Lucinda. He found a sheet of paper, a quill pen, and some ink and wrote a brief note: "Gracious lady, how can I thank you? You are most generous. I shall send you a token of my gratitude shortly. G. Moncrief." He propped it on the pillows and left quietly by the side door. He would send her some lace.

Back at the King's Grenadier, his head began to ache. He remembered Lucinda's freshness, her guilelessness, her love for him. He regarded himself in the mirror: his fair hair was beginning to thin at the temples; the lines in his forehead and about the eyes were deeper than usual.

What makes you think you are so superior to Lucinda? he asked himself. You were brought up to believe you were finer than others, yet you took advantage of her simplicity. You have always relied on charm and a good mind to escape the consequences of your acts.

The man in the mirror looked back, his lean aristocratic face haunted now by a new self-awareness. God, I've made an unconscionable mess of things! he told himself.

CHAPTER XVII

The Challenge

"Lucinda, what's keepin' ya? I want them upstairs rooms scrubbed by dinner time!" Mrs. Pratt called.

"Yes, ma'am. I'm takin' the pail up now."

Susannah, making salt-rising bread, heard the bucket overturn and bump down the stairs, then a gasp. She dropped the dough and ran into the dark hall, where Lucinda leaned against the wall halfway up the stairs, one hand pressed to her back.

"What is it? Are you all right?"

"I—I reckon so. I felt kind of dizzy and tripped. I couldn't—"

She was interrupted by Mrs. Pratt, her mouth set in lines in disapproval, both chins quivering. "What's got into ya? You're gettin' clumsier every day."

"I tripped."

"You just come into the common room, Lucinda Abbot, where I can take a look at ya."

"It's just an accident, Mrs. Pratt," said Susannah. "Nothing to be upset about. I'll clean it up."

"You keep out of this, Miz Graves!"

In the bright sunlight streaming through the narrow windows of the common room, Mrs. Pratt looked Lucinda over. "Now then, I want to know what's got into ya these last weeks. Takes ya twice as long to do your work."

"I ain't feelin' so good."

A thoughtful look appeared on Mrs. Pratt's face. Lucinda had not had much appetite lately. Several mornings she had left the table to run to the garden and returned looking pale and shaken.

Now she saw that the girl's breasts were fuller and there was a slight thickening of her waist. Of course, that was what ailed her! "So you got yourself with child, have you, miss?" Mrs. Pratt was outraged that this chit of a girl, whom she had taken in "out of the kindness of her heart," had abused her trust.

Lucinda's cheeks flamed and she opened her mouth to protest. "I ain't done nothin' to ya. Ya leave me be!"

Mrs. Pratt slapped her sharply across the face leaving red marks on the white-and-rose skin. "Don't ya sass me, Lucinda Abbot!"

Lucinda gasped, rubbed her stinging cheeks. "Ya got no call to slap me!"

Mrs. Pratt's face reddened. "I thought ya was a decent girl when I took ya in! Treated ya like my own daughter! All the time ya was fornicatin' with the guests under my own roof! I suppose you'd have tried your wiles on my poor husband if he'd paid ya any attention!"

Lucinda's eyes filled with fury. "That ain't true! I ain't been with nobody but Geoffrey Moncrief! Ya don't have to worry about Mr. Pratt—I wouldn't have him if he was the last man alive!"

Mrs. Pratt gasped, turned pale, and her breathing became labored.

Susannah caught her arm as she raised it to hit Lucinda. "Control yourself! There's no reason to get this angry!"

"I'll not have her livin' under my roof another day!"

The kitchen door banged and Mr. Pratt stood in the doorway, his Adam's apple working, his eyes wide with alarm. "What's goin' on here? I heard ya all the way out to the barn."

As she opened her mouth to denounce Lucinda, Mrs. Pratt clutched her chest, her face distorted with pain. She turned blue-gray and her skin grew moist. She reached out for support and, finding none, slid to the floor.

"She's havin' a spell!" Mr. Pratt turned to Susannah. "Let's put her on the settle."

They lifted her carefully while Lucinda ran for a mug of water.

* *

The physician they sent for bled her and ordered her to bed.

The kitchen was strangely quiet. Mr. Pratt sat near the big chimney, holding a bowl of bread and milk. Drops of milk clung to his scanty beard and the lines in his face were deeper.

"Ya ain't hungry?" Lucinda asked.

He shook his head. "Got too much on my mind to eat."

"But ya got to eat."

He did not hear her. "It's happened before, when Clara run off with that married fellow. Mrs. P. gets so upset she can't control her feelin's. Doctor's warned her. She's got a weak heart."

"I didn't mean to upset her. Truly I didn't!"

"I know ya didn't." He felt some sympathy for Lucinda. She worked hard and was clean and mannerly, and he had never seen her behave improperly. Yet he was not shocked that she had gotten herself with child by Moncrief. The fellow had a certain trait—he didn't have a name for it—that appealed to women. Even Miz Graves had gone for walks with him, and his wife thought the man could do no wrong, which was probably why she was so angry.

He wondered how they would manage if Lucinda left. The physician insisted Mrs. Pratt stay in bed for several weeks, and Susannah could not do all the work. If Lucinda would stay until Dorcas was better, it would help.

"I'd take it kindly if ya was to stay on until she's better," he ventured. "Miz Pratt won't know. Miz Graves and I'll tend to her."

Lucinda flushed with embarrassment. "I'd like to, Mr. Pratt, but your wife don't want me here now."

He was silent for so long she thought he had not been listening. Finally he said mildly, "I reckon ya ain't the first nor the last to be havin' a child without bein' wed. Don't see that it'll make much difference—till she's up and around again. If ya find totin' them buckets is too much for ya, just let me know. I can help."

Relief flooded Lucinda. She felt ashamed that she had ridiculed him to Mrs. Pratt. "I'll try to do my best to keep things the way she wants them," she told him.

He got up stiffly. "Seems like there's always somethin' to worry a body." He walked slowly to the door, an air of defeat upon him. He was forty-three years old but moved and thought and felt like an old man. Lucinda, watching him, was moved to pity.

"Do you know," Susannah said to Lucinda one evening, "we've not seen Ben for a while. I hope he's all right. Dear Lord, will we ever be rid of this war and live a normal life again?"

"I don't like him."

"Why not?"

Lucinda would not explain.

"He's made splendid progress in his studies. Most people never try to improve themselves. They cling to old habits, ways of looking at things, refuse to change."

"You sound partial to him," Lucinda said.

Susannah laughed. "Of course not! Why do you say so?"

"Because whenever he comes, I seen the way you look at him."

"Nonsense, Lucinda! You are in love and you think everyone else must be, too." But Lucinda's words stayed with her. That night as Susannah tossed and turned on the straw mattress, she wondered what it would be like to have Ben's arms about her, his body pressed close, his mouth on hers. She wanted to run her hands over the hard muscles in his arms, to touch his thick, dark red hair. Sometimes when he looked at her she felt breathless. She knew that much of her desire to stay in Carlisle was due to Ben's presence.

Mrs. Pratt was up and about after two weeks. The day before she left her bed, Lucinda went to stay with Else Enyard. A pinched-face spinster, Jennie Staples, had been hired to do the laundering, and Mrs. Holland, who lived in an improvised tent while her husband served in the militia, was to do the cleaning. When they had gone for the night, Mrs. Pratt, looking gaunt and unwell, sat down at the kitchen table. She began a lengthy litany of complaints.

Susannah listened for a time, then lost patience. "If you had not sent Lucinda away, things wouldn't be in this state. I know Jennie Staples is a gossip and Mrs. Holland's standards of cleanliness are not up to yours, but you won't find anyone to take Lucinda's place."

Mrs. Pratt opened her mouth to tell her this was not her business, but remembered that Susannah was her mainstay. It was better not to offend her. She sent Jennie Staples off but Mrs. Holland stayed.

Susannah was busy with the cooking when Mrs. Holland came into the kitchen, wiping her large red hands on her apron. "Someone askin' fer ya, Miz Graves."

"Who is it?" Susannah pushed back a curly tendril as she stirred the stew.

"I dunno. He didn't say."

"Well, I'm busy now, Mrs. Holland."

"He said it was important, ma'am."

"Oh, dear! Can you keep an eye on this for me? I won't be long." Susannah rolled down her sleeves, slipped off the big cooking apron, and tucked a curl into her knot.

Geoffrey Moncrief, weary and travel-stained, was waiting in the common room. A stubble of light brown beard covered his chin and his clothes smelled of sweat and horses. He smiled and kissed her hand. "I came as soon as I could find some drovers who were coming to Carlisle. It's too dangerous to travel alone." Susannah felt the blood mount to her face.

"It took courage for you to write that letter, Susannah. You must have thought me totally irresponsible."

"Lucinda told me you did not know. Have you returned to stay?"

"No, to accept my responsibility."

"You mean . . . ?"

"To marry her, Susannah. Your letter made me face certain things about myself I did not want to recognize. It's not particularly encouraging to discover what a fool one has been."

"But you came back!" Her eyes were warm. "Forgive me for doubting you, Geoffrey. I wasn't certain you would respond to the letter. Many men would have ignored it. I was afraid you'd think me a meddlesome woman."

"I would never think that, Susannah!"

"You can't imagine what a relief it is to know you've come."

"What would you have done had I not come?"

"I planned to take her to Philadelphia to my uncle's. It would have been presumptuous, but I couldn't just abandon her."

The admiration in his eyes deepened. "You constantly amaze me," he said. "I must talk with you in private. Perhaps a walk?"

"Yes," she said recklessly.

When Susannah returned twenty minutes later, Geoffrey was on his way to see Lucinda. Mrs. Pratt was fanning herself with her apron and looked angry. An odor of burned corn bread filled the air.

"Where was ya?" Mrs. Pratt demanded. "Ya went off and left the corn bread in the oven and now it's burnt."

"I had some important matters to attend to—more important than corn bread."

"Well, of all the impudence!"

When Mrs. Holland left, Mrs. Pratt began to criticize her. "She don't get the corners clean the way Lu—the way they ought to be. It's a lick and a promise."

"It's not easy to find someone. Most of the women driven here by the raids have small children, and the older ones can't do such heavy work."

Mrs. Pratt's eyes narrowed. "Then we'll just have to get Lucinda back."

Susannah could not conceal her pleasure. "I don't think that will be possible."

"And why not? That girl ought to be grateful to work in a respectable place now that she's expectin'."

"She's going to live in Philadelphia."

"Philadelphy? Why in the world—"

"She's marrying Mr. Moncrief. He didn't know about the baby until I wrote to him. He came back as quickly as he could."

"You wrote him about it?" Mrs. Pratt's small mouth stayed open in dismay. One hand flew to her heart to protect it from further shock.

* *

The wedding took place the following day at Mrs. Graffius's home. Mr. McCullough, scrubbed and self-conscious, had been prevailed upon to give the bride away. A Moravian missionary passing through the town performed the ceremony.

Lucinda's happiness gave her an ephemeral beauty. Wrapped in a creamy cashmere shawl that Geoffrey had brought, which concealed the slight thickening of her waist, she stood with downcast eyes, clutching a nosegay of fall flowers. Susannah marveled at the transformation wrought by love.

Geoffrey stood beside Lucinda. It was impossible to gauge his emotions, for his manner was gracious and courtly, particularly to his bride. He thought of his parents in Kent: his father, who insisted on facing up to one's mistakes, and his mother, who set the greatest emphasis on breeding and class. His father would grieve about this marriage but would think it proper he had gone through with it. His mother would be humiliated, her sense of decorum outraged.

The minister was asking Geoffrey if he would cleave to his wife till death parted them. "I do so promise," he said. It was his solemn word; there was no escape now. He heard Lucinda repeat the vows, her voice tremulous. It was amazing how innocent she looked.

"I now pronounce you man and wife," the minister said.

Lucinda looked up at him, waiting for his kiss, and as he bent to her, he caught a whiff of lavender. She looked scrubbed and wholesome, a handsome farm girl with a superb figure. His eyes sought Susannah's as he raised his head. Feeling the intensity of his look, she glanced at him, then quickly looked away.

Geoffrey was anxious to return to Philadelphia before Lucinda's pregnancy made such a journey infeasible. It would be far more difficult if they were to await the child's birth and make the journey with an infant.

They would start out as soon as there was a convoy of militia leaving for Lancaster. Geoffrey spoke to Colonel Armstrong and learned that a detail with two covered wagons would leave in three days to bring back flour, beeves, and other foodstuffs.

Geoffrey and his bride could travel as far as Lancaster with them.

The next problem was to find two men who were expert shots and had horses to accompany them to Philadelphia. This was not easily solved, for most of the farmers had joined the militia, the nonresisters would not bear arms, and the others available might rob them once they left the convoy.

Finally Geoffrey found a powerful-looking man with a club-foot, Mathew Tarnes, who was willing to accompany them for a generous fee. His family had been killed on Raystown Creek, he said.

As Geoffrey was talking with Tarnes, a sturdy lad of about fifteen ran up and begged to be allowed to go with them. He had a horse and had known how to shoot since he was ten, he said. He wanted to take his grandfather to the home of his married sister near Lancaster and then to join the militia. Geoffrey reluctantly agreed the old man could ride in one of the wagons with Lucinda, and the boy could join Tarnes as outrider.

As they said their good-byes, Susannah gave Lucinda her red cloak.

"But won't you be needin' it?"

"There'll be time before winter sets in to make one. Besides, red is not suitable for a widow."

Lucinda was engulfed in embraces from friends, and Geoffrey turned to Susannah, whose face had spurred him on during his journey from Philadelphia. "We are in your debt," he said so none could overhear, holding both her hands. "Without that letter I would not have known about the child."

"Be good to her, Geoffrey. She needs your understanding and . . . loyalty."

"You have my solemn promise of that." He noted she had not said "love" but "loyalty." She knew at what cost he was trying to fulfill her expectations. "If ever you should need assistance of any kind . . . " He stopped, knowing he'd touched her pride. "When Rachel is restored to you, you must consider that my home—*our* home—is yours. It would be a privilege to be of service to you."

She looked away, embarrassed by the directness of his gaze.

"Thank you." She released her hands. "I wish you both every happiness."

"You will write to us? To let us know how you fare and about Rachel? My agent, Mr. Pickering, will know where we are lodging until the house is ready."

She nodded. As she moved away, she knew that although Lucinda now bore his name and carried his child, it was she who held his heart.

They set out from Carlisle at dawn with Corporal Stennis and two privates leading the little cavalcade. The wagons followed, with Lucinda and the old man riding in the first. Geoffrey Moncrief, Matthew Tarnes, and the boy rode beside them, and two militiamen brought up the rear.

They had been on their way about two hours when they first saw the Indians. It was still early enough so that ribbons of fog engulfed them, making it difficult to see clearly.

It was the old man who first cried, "Savages!" His voice quavered with excitement. "Over to the right in them woods."

The drivers flicked their whips and they began to pick up speed. The outriders rode closer to the wagons, their long rifles primed and ready.

"Better lie down inside the wagon, ma'am," the driver told Lucinda.

"I can shoot," she retorted. "You got any extra rifles?"

"Under them blankets, ma'am, if you're sure ya know how to handle them. They're heavy and they got a powerful kickback."

"I used to go shootin' for game with my brothers. I can handle a gun as good as a man."

The old man, seeing her lift a rifle from the pile of blankets, chuckled. "That's the spirit, Miz Moncrief! I'm goin' to pick me off some of them red devils before this day is over."

Geoffrey cantered near the wagon. "Are you all right, Lucinda?"

"I'm fine. Mr. Boyle and me, we're loadin' the guns. We can cover the trail from the back."

He turned his horse, swinging round to the rear of the wagon until he could see her face. "Should you be doing that?"

"I've been shootin' with a Pennsylvania rifle since I was twelve, Geoffrey Moncrief." This was an exaggeration, but she was determined to show him she could cope with things.

Lucinda and the old man felt their arms grow numb from the tension of holding the rifles propped against the tailboard. Their eyes burned from trying to watch the distant woods for a sudden movement or puffs of smoke. The vapors lifted as a pale sun filled the countryside with tremulous light. Always, as the party moved eastward, they saw the Indians following them. Though they were too far away to count, it did not appear to be a large war party.

Corporal Stennis decided on a strategy in case they were attacked. "Ain't no way we can make a run fer it with the wagons and the trail as it is. If they attack and they're a large party, we cut loose the two teams and leave the wagons. Everybody will have a horse then."

"What if it's a small war party?"

"Then we make a stand, close in to the wagons."

Geoffrey brought the information to Lucinda.

"Are you certain you are all right? Would you rather ride with me on my mare if we abandon the wagons?" She nodded, pleased that he should think of it. If the worst came, she would be with him.

The attack came at ten o'clock. It began with war whoops and bursts of rifle fire, followed by dense smoke. They heard the thud of the Indians' horses as they sped over the space between them and the cavalcade. The drivers lashed their teams and the wagons lurched forward, throwing Lucinda and the old man from side to side. She felt a dull pain in her back and thought of the child. She braced her feet against one side of the wagon while holding on to the other side, to keep from being thrown back and forth. The trail was hardly more than a cart track in places and the wagon swayed perilously. "Dear Lord, don't let it overturn!" she whispered.

The old man had been dozing with his rifle propped in the rear opening of the canvas. "What's goin' on?" he cried.

"It's startin'!" Lucinda motioned with her head to the distant trees.

The outriders fired and the corporal shouted to his men to pick a target and not waste their powder. The wagon swayed too much for Lucinda to use the rifle. The pain that had started in her back was now creeping around to her lower belly. Sweet Jesus, don't let anything happen to the baby, she prayed.

The old man was trying to brace himself to take aim. "You can't hit 'em when the wagon's movin' like this," Lucinda said to him, but the din was so intense she could not make him hear. Biting her lower lip to keep from crying out, she motioned to him to give up trying to shoot. She heard their driver scream as a blast from one of the Indians' guns shattered his arm. He dropped the reins, toppling sidewise onto the seat.

She heard Geoffrey yell, "The driver's been hit! Get those horses!" and then the wagon tilted as the terrified team dashed off. She let go of the rifle and clung with both hands to the side board. The old man cried out as his head hit the floor.

Matthew Tarnes raced after the runaway team, leaned far out from his saddle to grab the reins, and exerted all the force in his powerful shoulders to bring the horses to a stop. The boy rode up, jumped into the driver's seat, and took the reins firmly. "Can ya help the driver? He's been hurt bad!" he called to Lucinda.

She turned to the old man and motioned for him to help. Gingerly he moved to the front of the wagon, rubbing his head, and he and Tarnes lowered the driver onto the floor.

Lucinda tore her petticoat into strips and tried to staunch the flow of blood, which had soaked the driver's pants and coat and was making the floor slippery. The smell of the blood made her sick. She lurched to the back of the wagon, where the old man was now busy shooting, pushed him aside, and leaned out the opening to vomit. Abruptly the old man jerked her down as a blast from one of the Delawares' guns tore a small ragged hole in the canvas two inches from her shoulder. She lay on the floor, white and shaken, too filled with pain to move.

The old man cautiously took aim. She heard the blast of his long gun, then his jubilant, "By Tophet, I got one!"

She was dimly aware that the firing had ceased and she heard Corporal Stennis say it was over. "They'll wait till we're gone, then come back to collect their dead. It's their custom."

She propped herself on her elbows, her nose wrinkling in distaste from the odor of blood and vomit. On the floor behind the high seat the injured driver moaned. His blood was soaking through the bandages she'd made from her petticoat.

The old man was jubilant, saying something about getting one to make up for his son.

Geoffrey climbed into the back of the wagon. His face was drawn as he knelt beside her. "Are you all right?" Then he saw the blood on her hands and cloak. "Good God!"

She shook her head.

"You didn't miscarry?"

"No. It's from the driver. I couldn't get him to stop bleedin'."

Geoffrey carefully cut back the driver's sleeve and examined the shattered bones. "It wants a tourniquet." Geoffrey and Matthew Tarnes pieced together the broken bones, bound them tightly with strips from her petticoat and applied a tourniquet.

Lucinda watched them, feeling better now. "Where'd you learn how to do that, Geoffrey?"

"I studied anatomy—the parts of the body—at Oxford, though I'm not trained to set bones."

"Think ya can look after him till we reach Lancaster?" the corporal asked.

She nodded. "How many others was hurt?"

"The driver's the only one hurt bad. Two of the outriders got grazed—nothin' serious, thank the Lord."

"How far is it to Lancaster?"

"We can't make it today, ma'am."

"Then we'll have to sleep in the wagons?"

He nodded.

They saw no cabins that day. It was frightening to discover how far east the raids had come. When the sun began to decline, they found a protected spot to camp for the night. Lucinda stretched out on the floor, but sleep would not come. Geoffrey was serving as lookout, so he would not be free for four hours. It was not a very good beginning for their marriage, she thought, with no chance to be alone, her clothes smelling of vomit, her hands and face grubby and no way to wash. At least the pain was less.

When Geoffrey finally lay down beside her, she pretended to be asleep. She couldn't let him kiss her when she smelled so bad. He eased his body into a comfortable position for sleep and flung his arm across her shoulders. Tears ran down her cheeks as she fought to keep from making any sound.

The following day they made good time and saw no more of the enemy. At Lancaster they found a physician to care for the wounded driver, then bade good-bye to the militiamen.

In the small inn that Geoffrey located he and Lucinda took turns bathing in the tin tub provided by the landlord. When they finally lay in the creaking bed with its clean sheets and lumpy mattress, he took her gently in his arms.

"You were very brave, Lucinda."

"I was scared of liftin' the gun because of the baby."

"Women should not have to do the shooting. That's man's work."

"On the frontier everybody has to know how to handle a gun."

"We shouldn't have any trouble from here to Philadelphia," he said to reassure her.

"I was so scared for the baby."

"Well, the worst is behind us. Try to get some sleep." He kissed her cheek and rolled over.

"Geoffrey? Do you think we could start out for Philadelphia tomorrow instead of restin' here for two days?"

"If you think it's not too hard for you. It's a lot of riding in your condition."

She wished he would make love to her. There would be time for that later when they were settled in Philadelphia, she told herself as she listened to his regular breathing.

The remainder of their journey was in marked contrast to the beginning. The countryside now had a settled look, with large stone farmhouses, huge two-story barns, and herds of cows and sheep grazing in lush pastures. There were stands of trees, but none of the dark somber woods she was accustomed to.

"I never seen a barn with two floors," Lucinda remarked.

"They are built like those in Switzerland and Germany," Geoffrey said. "These people are German-speaking, from the Palatinate. They are some of the nonresisters you have heard of."

"I'd like to git my hands on 'em," muttered Matthew Tarnes.

"They are very decent folk, honest and industrious. They are convinced that it is against God's will to bear arms."

"I'd like to see 'em go through what some of us went through."

"But that's just the point, Mr. Tarnes. These people have no idea what the frontier is like. It's difficult to change a cherished belief if one cannot imagine the alternatives."

In Philadelphia they found accommodations at the King's Grenadier on a tree-lined street near the city market. Lucinda had been having back pains and a recurrence of the cramps since they left Lancaster and felt light-headed. "You go downstairs and get some dinner. I'll just lay down for a while," she told Geoffrey.

"Can I send you something? Some tea, or a noggin of hot buttered rum?"

"No, you go alone." She did not want him to know that she had discovered blood spots in her drawers.

"I think I'll go over to see Pickering after I've eaten. That is, if you are all right. I want to find out how they are getting on with the repairs to the house."

"You go on Geoffrey. I'll be fine soon as I've rested."

After he left she tossed and turned, sweat beading her brow as the cramps worsened. She had felt strangely tired ever since the first day of their journey, but had thought that the tension and terror of the Indian attack were responsible. The bleeding was new and frightening, a sign that something was wrong.

Sunlight streamed in through the hand-blown panes, leaving greenish patterns on the quilted coverlet. The room was fresh and bright, with polished brass at the fireplace and pewter candle sconces, but she was too ill to appreciate this. She bit her lip as a harder pain seized her. She knew now she was losing the child—his reason for marrying her.

When Geoffrey returned several hours later, she was lying in the bloodied bed, unconscious. The fetus lay on the floor, its blood staining the scrubbed white wood. Lucinda was so ashen, he feared she might be dead, until he felt her pulse.

He ran down the stairs to ask the innkeeper to summon a physician. "Tell him to hurry! My wife is very ill!"

When he reentered the bedroom, he glanced about, uncertain what to do. He looked down at Lucinda and pity overcame him. She had been very valiant. He was on his knees beside the bed, his head in his hands, when the physician entered.

Dr. Tomlinson completed the examination and removed his small square spectacles. He had just come from the Pennsylvania Hospital; a faint odor of putrefaction clung to his clothes in spite of a sprinkling of oil of cinnamon. He was an austere man, and Geoffrey decided he would not have him again.

Tomlinson put his hands behind his back and walked to the window, looking down at the street. "She has lost a great deal of blood and will require at least two weeks in bed. Then she may sit up for two hours in the morning and in the late afternoon. I would suggest a glass of port twice daily with a raw egg beaten into it, and a diet with plenty of red meat."

"You don't think this will seriously affect her health?"

"No, she is young and strong."

"Will she be able to have other children?"

"Most assuredly! But I must caution you against resuming marital relations too quickly."

Geoffrey's mouth tightened in anger. What sort of fool did the man think him?

"You will need a dependable woman to care for her until she is able to be up. She must not overtax her strength when you move into your home."

"Have you someone to suggest?"

"There is a widow, Mrs. Agnes Stinchcomb, who earns her living by taking care of the sick. If you like, I'll drop by her lodgings and see if she is free. She is very reliable."

Geoffrey reversed his opinion of the man. "That's good of you, sir."

When Lucinda regained consciousness, she saw a wide-hipped woman putting things in order. Her dark hair was tucked inside a white mob cap, her black nankeen dress covered by a large apron. She had rolled back her sleeves, for she had been scrubbing blood stains from the floor. On her chin was a pea-sized wart.

The room smelled fresh. The windows had been propped open and autumn sunlight filtered in between the branches of the trees that lined the street. A smell of burning leaves came from outside, where a boy's voice cried, "Hot cross buns! Two for a penny!" On the hearth a small fire glowed, sending its warmth through the low-ceilinged room.

Lucinda had been bathed and put into a fresh nightdress and the bed linen had been changed. She felt weak but relaxed.

The woman smiled. "Your husband was quite wore out. He went below stairs for a pot of tea. Just rest easy, ma'am. Doctor said you'll be well in a few weeks."

"The child?"

"I took care of it. Some folks thinks it's bad luck to get rid of the afterbirth, but I won't be havin' children, being widowed and all." Lucinda started to cry, so the woman put down the bucket and reached for her hand. She was surprised to find the skin coarse and rough and the nails broken off—not the kind of hand you'd expect a lady to have. "There, there, don't cry. Doctor said you'll be fine in time. There will be other children, you mark my words!"

A sob broke from the girl on the bed.

"You don't want your husband to find you cryin'. I'll just comb your hair and make you look pretty for him."

The sobbing increased. Mrs. Stinchcomb patted Lucinda's shoulder, but the girl was unaware of her presence. "Ain't no use tryin' to calm her. She's been carryin' a load of trouble for a long time. It ain't good for her to hold it in," Agnes Stinchcomb told herself.

When Geoffrey returned, the storm was over and Lucinda lay against a fresh pillow, her face blotched and swollen. She saw by his expression that he was shocked at her appearance.

"The physician assures me you can have other children when you are fully recovered," he said after Mrs. Stinchcomb had left.

Her face crumpled. He took her hand. "It may be just as well that it happened as it did, Lucinda. It will be easier on you settling in when you are not expecting."

"But you wouldn't of married me except for the baby."

He looked down at their clasped hands and sighed. She noticed new lines in his forehead. "What's done is done." He tried to keep the despair from his voice.

She glanced at him, eyes frightened. "Are you fixin' to leave me, Geoffrey, now that there won't be a child?"

He looked at her in amazement. "Of course not! When a Moncrief gives his promise, you may count on it."

To divert her he resumed their lessons, pleased that she wanted to learn. Her aptitude for figures amazed him. She wanted to know how to handle the accounts, to weigh prices, to do the marketing herself, for Agnes Stinchcomb had described the city's High Street market.

He explained that ladies did not go to markets, they sent their servants. She was adamant. Finally they temporized: when she was well, she could go if accompanied by Mrs. Stinchcomb, who agreed to stay as housekeeper when the house was ready.

He sought to inform her taste. "I'm having a new mantel built by Richard Wainwright, who was apprenticed to Mr. Adams in England."

"One fireplace is as good as another, so long as it draws proper and you can bake in the oven."

"It is not for cooking, Lucinda; this is for the drawing room. It should be aesthetically pleasing as well as practical." He spread out fine scale drawings of the proposed changes, but she ignored them. Disappointed, he replaced them in the portfolio.

Another evening he came back enthusiastic about a new project. "I've ordered some china from England's finest new potter, Josiah Wedgwood."

"Wedgwood?"

"A dinner service in fine china."

"Will we be needin' that?"

"Of course. The carpenter is painting the inside of the china cupboard to match, and I found some hand-painted fabric from China to cover the upper part of the walls."

"I ain't used to all that, Geoffrey. I don't know how the gentry lives."

"You will, Lucinda. I shall see to it."

He was determined to make a success of his marriage, to prove to himself that he could assume responsibility. He felt a growing affection for her; she satisfied him physically and was showing a surprising adaptability. She could be shaped, her character given direction, for she was intelligent. He reminded himself that life was a process, a becoming; there was always the potential for growth.

But at times her simplicity annoyed him. "Lucinda, you do not treat Mrs. Stinchcomb as a friend. She is a servant. I know you are fond of her, but one doesn't fraternize with one's servants."

"What did I do?"

"You were telling her about your work at the Forge Inn."

"What's wrong with that?"

"It's a private matter. Servants should not be privy to one's personal life."

She gave him a searching look. He was ashamed that she had been a whore and gotten involved with a married man and enticed a young soldier to his death. This was the Lord's punishment for all the evil she had done.

"I'm only trying to protect you, Lucinda. We are going to build a new life in Philadelphia. The past is dead. We must learn from it, but not carry it about with us. You are Mrs. Geoffrey Moncrief now. No one will hurt you but yourself." As he spoke, a dream formed within him. "When you are quite recovered, we will have a dancing master come to the house to give you lessons. And we must find a good seamstress to make you some new clothes."

Her eyes began to shine. "Oh, Geoffrey, it sounds grand!"

"Perhaps," he continued, musing aloud, "we might find a lady of good connections to show you how ladies conduct themselves."

Her temper flared. "No, I ain't havin' somebody tellin' me how to act! I'm me, Geoffrey Moncrief, and you liked me good enough to go to bed with. I want to learn to read and write and cipher. And I'd like to learn to dance those fancy steps you told me about, but I ain't copyin' someone else's ways."

He looked at her as if seeing her for the first time, then laughed.

Her eyes were blazing. "Are you makin' fun of me?"

"Not at all, my dear. I thought I was teaching you, yet you show me what is true. You must be yourself!"

She looked perplexed. When he lifted her from the bed and put her on his knee, she knew a rush of joy.

"We'll set our own fashion and men will think me the luckiest chap in town."

The day arrived for him to take her to the house. Mrs. Stinchcomb had polished the fine mahogany furniture until it shone; the brasses gleamed, the china cupboard was resplendent with its display of Wedgwood and other porcelain. Late-blooming asters from the garden brightened the drawing room.

When they entered the gracious hall, Lucinda stood speechless before the perfectly proportioned staircase. She rubbed a hand over its smooth balustrade, looked down at the shining floor with its Turkey carpet, then flew to his arms. "It's better than a dream! I can't believe it's really ours."

He kissed the top of her head. "Welcome, Lucinda, to our home."

For a reluctant bridegroom, he told himself, you are beginning to act like a devoted husband.

Among the members of the Philosophical Society was a Quaker, Samuel Woolcott, a soft-spoken man of middle years whose gentle manner masked a keen mind. He was equally at ease in the world of business and in intellectual matters. Woolcott invited Geoffrey to lunch at Philadelphia's finest tavern, and two weeks later asked him to dine at his home with him and his wife. He was not aware that Moncrief had married.

Geoffrey accepted. Before introducing Lucinda to Philadelphia society, he needed to find a cultured woman who could guide her through its treacherous shoals. Lucinda would need an ally.

Hannah Woolcott was just the woman. Warm and unpretentious, she was in her early thirties, a fine-boned woman with humorous brown eyes and beautiful teeth. Her loveliness sprang from a deep spiritual harmony and she was known for her tact and kindness.

Toward the end of the dinner he spoke of Lucinda.

"Oh, friend, we were not aware that thee was married! We would have invited thy wife," Hannah said.

"That is understandable. Lucinda hasn't been here long, and we've just gotten settled in our house."

"I shall call on her to welcome her to Philadelphia. Perhaps I can be of some assistance in helping her get acquainted."

Lucinda had been nervous at the prospect of meeting the Quakeress, but Hannah Woolcott put her at ease.

"She's the nicest person, Geoffrey," Lucinda told him after Hannah's visit. "She puts me in mind of Susannah, so ladylike and yet she don't put on airs."

Geoffrey winced at her mention of Susannah. Perhaps it would be possible in time to remember her without a sense of loss.

"It's odd, how she and Mr. Woolcott are invited everywhere, when they're Quakers and don't play cards or dance."

"There are many of their faith in Philadelphia. They observe their own practices but do not impose them on others."

"She wants me to go callin'—I mean calling—with her next week."

Geoffrey nodded, pleased.

When he saw Samuel Woolcott a week later, the Quaker smiled and took his arm. "I must confide in thee, Geoffrey. Thy young wife has quite won over my Hannah. I haven't seen her take such pleasure since our little girl died."

CHAPTER XVIII

Changes

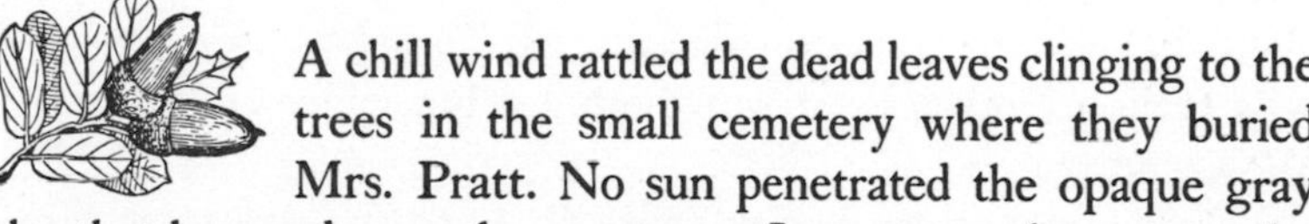

A chill wind rattled the dead leaves clinging to the trees in the small cemetery where they buried Mrs. Pratt. No sun penetrated the opaque gray sky that hovered over the mourners. It was a somber scene, the houses huddled against the force of the wind, the dead grass oozing water from the morning's rain, the trees bending. Those gathered about the grave shivered and pulled their cloaks or shawls more tightly about them, rubbing their hands to get the blood circulating.

The minister wiped his dripping nose with a large pocket handkerchief. He was suffering from a head cold and looked miserable. Susannah hoped he would make his eulogy brief, but he continued on in his phlegmy voice about the virtues of the departed. It was apparent that he had had no firsthand acquaintance with Mrs. Pratt, for the qualities he was extolling—meekness, gentleness, and humility—were not associated with her. Perhaps there was to be another burial today, and he had confused the two, Susannah thought.

When it was finally over Mr. Pratt said, "I'd take it kindly if ya was to come back to the inn fer some victuals. There's apples to roast and Susannah can make cornmeal puddin' and sassafras tea."

The mourners' faces brightened. It would lift their spirits to be together in the cheerful atmosphere of the inn.

"It's just like they used to do in the settlements after a funeral," whispered Annie McCullough.

"He's lonely," Else said. "He's dreadin' the time when everybody leaves but Susannah and the guests."

When they removed their wraps in the big firelit kitchen, the snugness of the room shut out their memories of the bleak graveside. There was a friendly hum of conversation as Susannah prepared supper.

"She was always so particular," sighed Mrs. Graffius, who had visited the inn only twice before.

"Clean as a pin. You could eat off the floor the way she kept it." Annie raised her voice. "Susannah, did she scrub every day?"

Susannah was amused by the conversation. "Why no, Mrs. McCullough, we scrubbed twice a week."

"I reckon Dorcas Pratt was the finest housekeeper in town," Annie said.

They nodded; then having paid tribute to the deceased, they turned to livelier topics. Susannah told them about a letter from Geoffrey Moncrief in which he described their hazardous journey and Lucinda's losing the child. They were shocked.

"It's a pity," Else said. "Geoffrey Moncrief may have wed Lucinda from duty but it's plain she loved him."

"That puts me in mind of somethin' happened yesterday when George come to see Thomas," said Annie. "That child has growed so tall and he's smart as can be. I told George if Mary Ann was to come back she wouldn't know Thomas. George gives me a look, his eyes glitterin' and full of spite. 'Miz McCullough,' he says, 'I'd thank you not to mention her again. I ain't in a hurry fer Thomas to find out about his mother.' 'But what'd she do, George?' I asked him. 'She couldn't help it if she was captured!' He gits a mean look. 'I don't want to talk about it,' he says, and walks out."

"That's odd," said Else. "I wonder what in the world he meant. . . ."

The arrival of the men cut short this conversation.

"Come in and join us," Mr. Pratt said. "There's plenty of provender fer ya."

They hung up their damp coats and stretched their legs to the fire gratefully.

"Sure is snug here," remarked Robert. "Bad night outside."

Mr. Pratt's hospitality was boundless. "I got some cider put away. Made it before all this Injun trouble started."

"Put a hot poker in it," Ben suggested. "Here, I can help."

"When I was a lad in New Jersey," Mr. Pratt said, "our house was always full of friends droppin' in to visit. Seems to make things easier."

"What'll ya do now to keep the inn goin'?" Annie asked.

"I been givin' it some thought. There's too much work for jist one woman. I was wondering if Miz Enyard might consider movin' in and helpin' Susannah—for pay, of course. It would be real nice to have the children."

Else hesitated. "It is crowded at Miz Graffius's, though she's been so good to take us in. I wonder if ya realize all the things Peter and Annibele can get into. It wouldn't be as tidy and quiet as it is now."

"It'd liven things up."

"Go on, Ma, you'd enjoy it."

She smiled. "Well, I would like havin' all this room, if ya wouldn't mind the children."

With the coming of the Enyards the atmosphere of the Forge Inn changed. There were children's sticky fingerprints on the scrubbed tables and chairs, but the women wiped them up. The inn had a new warmth and friendliness. The change in Mr. Pratt was astonishing. He was learning to assert himself. The children adored him and Annibele would climb onto his lap and fall asleep, secure in his arms. In spite of the war and its privations, they were happy.

Susannah had taken on the responsibility of tutoring Ben after Geoffrey's departure, and Fiona had joined them. As winter wore on, they resumed their lessons. Ben would stop at Mrs. Graffius's to escort Fiona to the inn and afterward see her home.

Fiona looked, Susannah thought, like some tragic heroine, with her fine pale skin and wistful expression. Whenever Ben appeared, Susannah noticed Fiona's sudden color, which she assumed was due to romantic fantasies common to adolescence. It amused her that Ben was unaware of it. He must still think of Fiona as a child.

One evening in January, when the streets were covered with ice and a cold wind drove all to take shelter, Fiona insisted on going for their lesson. When they arrived, Susannah looked at them in astonishment. "Why, Fiona, I didn't expect you on a night like this! You must be frozen. Let me have your cloak, and come sit by the fire." She rubbed the girl's hands and feet while Else wrapped a quilt around her.

"Ya want to stay here tonight, Fiona? Ya can share my bed," Else said. "Ben can tell your ma, so she won't worry."

Fiona did not answer. She had seen the warmth of the looks Ben and Susannah had given each other and remembered his teasing remarks on their way to the inn: "You're gettin' to be a young lady, Fiona. Pretty soon the boys will be comin' round. When ya find the right one, can I be the first to know? You're my little sister, remember." She struggled to keep from bursting into tears.

Else decided she had taken cold. "Ben, you'd better go tell Fiona's ma she's stayin' here tonight. Don't say nothin' to worry her, just that it's so cold I think it's best she stay."

Susannah went to the door with Ben. "Do be careful, Ben. The storm has grown worse."

His glance swept over Susannah's face as if he wanted to memorize each feature. "Don't worry," he said.

"I believe camomile tea'd be good for her," Else said, reaching up to the beams, where bunches of dried herbs hung.

"It's mighty strange," said Mr. Pratt, "how some of them herbs is medicines if ya know how to use 'em, but can kill ya if ya take too much. Like that foxglove Dorcas used for her spells. She'd make a potion of it and pretty soon her heart'd be beatin' normal. But it can kill ya if you take too much."

"Horseradish can be dangerous, too," Else said. "You got to dry it before you use it or it's poisonous."

Fiona looked up at the neat bundles of herbs: some were for flavoring, others for dyes, and some were used as medicines. She had helped her mother prepare brown dye from hemlock and poultices from deadly nightshade, and had seen the one Mr. Pratt mentioned—foxglove.

As she tried to swallow the hot tea, she felt the pain in her chest worsen. It throbbed in her temples, formed a great lump in her throat, knotted her stomach. She wanted to cry out her anguish that Ben could be so indifferent. She had feared that he was in love with Susannah; now she was certain of it.

When Ben returned he stamped the snow off his boots and shook the dry flakes from his hat and greatcoat. "It's gettin' worse. The wind is pilin' it up in drifts. I had a hard time keepin' my footin'."

Susannah, taking his wraps from him, touched his hand accidentally.

Fiona saw her rosy color, which the faded walnut stain could not conceal. Whenever their glances met, Susannah's expression revealed the same longing as Ben's. Fiona could think of nothing but their love for each other.

"Will you try this page, Fiona? You still aren't feeling well, are you?" Susannah asked.

Fiona avoided Susannah's eyes. "I guess I was thinkin' of somethin' else."

"Are you all right?"

She nodded. Something perverse made her continue to sit with the two of them long after the others had retired. She began to exaggerate trivial remarks or incidents, bending them to the dictates of her heightened imagination.

"Why don't you forget about reading tonight?" Susannah suggested. "You can catch up next time."

"Are you and Ben goin' on with the lesson?"

"Why, yes. We planned to cover one chapter tonight."

They want to get rid of me to do the things lovers do when they're alone, Fiona told herself. She'd punish them, she thought. If she were to die, Ben would never forget her, would carry her memory with him wherever he went. And Susannah, whose husband wasn't dead a year, would pay for her flirty ways.

Fiona looked up at the bundle of foxglove that Mrs. Pratt had used for her palpitations. She knew which bunch it was, for she'd seen Susannah take it down and prepare the potion when Mrs.

Pratt was sick. If she were to make it extra strong, she'd be free of this pain; she'd be with Jesus, beyond suffering.

"I'm goin' to bed," she announced. "But if I can't sleep, can I come down and make more tea?"

"Of course. You know where everything is. The fire will die down, but there's plenty of kindling."

"Sleep well," Ben said.

Fiona started up the steep stairs to Mrs. Enyard's room.

"Wait! You'll need a candle!" Susannah ran after her with a lighted taper.

They called good night and Susannah added, "Call me if you need anything, dear."

Fiona did not answer.

It was later than usual when Ben and Susannah said good night. Wrapped in two quilts, Ben stretched out on the hearth in the common room, feeling a peaceful drowsiness. In two months Susannah's year of mourning would be over. . . . He turned over and fell into a deep sleep.

Ben was awakened by something bumping against furniture. He got up quietly and tiptoed to the kitchen, from which the sound had come.

"Fiona! What's wrong?" He caught her arm. "What is it?"

She would have fallen had he not held her up. Ben carried her to the settle and threw some kindling on the fire. In the sudden glow he saw an empty mug on the table with broken pieces of herbs lying beside it. Remembering the foxglove, he looked up at the bunches of herbs tied to the beams, then caught her shoulders.

"Fiona, did you make a potion of foxglove? Answer me!"

Fiona opened her eyes and smiled faintly.

"Ma! Susannah! Come quick, Fiona's sick!"

Else ran downstairs and stared in disbelief at the girl, then saw the mug and the bits of foxglove. "Oh no, Ben, not that!" She searched for the burdock to prepare an emetic.

"What happened?" Susannah asked as she came into the kitchen.

Else nodded toward the broken herbs.

"You mean Fiona—"

"She took it all right," Else said grimly.

When Fiona had vomited, Else settled her near the fire and put her arm around her, and Susannah wrapped a quilt about them.

Else stroked the girl's hair. "Now then, child, what was ya tryin' to do?"

Fiona did not answer.

"Ya know that foxglove can kill ya."

"I didn't want to go on livin'." Fiona's voice was so low they could barely hear her.

"Ya know, Fiona, that takin' your own life's a terrible thing. Why would ya want to do such a thing?"

Fiona shook her head. "Now can I sleep?"

"It's too soon," Susannah said. "We must keep her awake until we are sure she has none of it left in her. You go on to bed, Mrs. Enyard. I'll look after her."

"I'll help you," Ben said.

Early the next morning Ben waded through snowdrifts to see Annie McCullough.

"Why, Ben, what are ya doin' out this early?" Annie asked.

"It's about Fiona." He did not want the children and Mrs. Graffius to hear. "She—took a chill last night. She's all right now but we thought you ought to know."

"Mercy sakes! I'll go right over."

On the way to the inn, Ben told her what had happened.

"Dear Lord!" she said, her homely face crumpling. "Whatever made her do such a thing?"

"We couldn't get nothin' out of her. She's sleepin' now; she's goin' to be all right."

Annie looked at him sadly. "I seen she was moonin' about ya ever since we was at Fort Lyttleton."

Ben stopped. "Are you tellin' me she fancies me? Me?"

She nodded, swallowing hard before answering. "I thought maybe ya seen it."

"Good Lord, Mrs. McCullough, I never gave her any encouragement."

"Young girls don't need no encouragement. They spend most of the time daydreamin'. Did she say anythin' peculiar last night?"

Ben tried to recall their conversation. "I was teasin' her about growin' up and said she'd have to tell me first when she picked a suitor because she was like a sister to me."

"That was it!"

"But—why?"

"She's been livin' in a dream that you'd care for her."

"Marry her? I never gave her such an idea!"

"It appears like she just couldn't face up to knowin' how ya feel about Susannah."

"Does it show that much?"

"Well, your face gives you away when ya sees her."

Three days after Fiona went home Mr. Pratt took a message to her: Susannah would like her to come to the inn.

When the girl arrived, Susannah took her to her room. "I have missed you, Fiona. It's been four days since your last lesson. You were doing so well that it's a shame for you to give it up."

A faint flush stained Fiona's cheeks.

Susannah took her hand. "You don't need to be embarrassed. I understand. I want to be your friend. We all make mistakes as we are growing up. Sometimes it's easier to live in an imaginary world than in the real one."

Susannah had her attention. "It's easy to mistake admiration and gratitude for love, especially when someone has come to your aid. But real love is a mutual thing. When you've lived longer, you'll find it is true."

Fiona looked away.

"During the time I was a captive there was no one for me to talk to. They wouldn't let me near Rachel. I had time to think about things I had never considered before—such as what life is about and what love means; and friendship and human frailty."

The girl was listening, now.

"You are cheating yourself by living in a dream. You can either let yourself pine away, which is foolish and wasteful, or begin to live, to grow. We could use you here at the inn. There wouldn't be much pay, but you could go on with your lessons."

She saw the pain in Fiona's eyes. "I know you are thinking of Ben. You will have to accept the fact that this is his home now, so you will see him. But why should you avoid each other? He still cares about you as if you were his sister. Be grateful for that, Fiona. No one will ever know about the other night." When Fiona began to sob, Susannah put her arms around her. She wondered if there would be someone to comfort Rachel when she needed it.

Two days later Fiona came to tell Susannah she would accept her offer. She was subdued and shy the first week, but Else's presence helped. Gradually she began to enjoy the lively atmosphere of the inn, though she still had difficulty with her feelings for Ben and would disappear when he came.

One day Susannah found her weeping. "Have you ever transplanted a seedling that was growing in the wrong place—moved it to get the sun?" Susannah asked.

Fiona did not answer.

"If you had, you would know that it takes time to change and grow strong." With that Susannah closed the door and went back to work.

In a few moments Fiona appeared in the kitchen, her eyes puffy from crying. She continued with her chores, and Susannah knew her words had taken root.

The Indian attacks began again in February and the homeless were now sleeping in churches. Food was portioned even more carefully.

Susannah was on her knees scrubbing the floor of the common room one afternoon when Ben dashed in. She looked up in surprise at his glowing face.

"Do you know what day this is?" he cried.

"Be careful! I haven't rinsed that part yet."

"It's the first of March!" He sounded so exuberant that she looked puzzled.

"The first of March?" She pushed a curly tendril from her forehead.

"It means your year of mournin' is over. I want to marry you as soon as—" Ben didn't finish, for he slipped and fell on the soapy floor.

Susannah began to laugh. "Oh, Ben, if you could see how you look!"

"This ain't the way I planned it," he said, trying to rise, but instead sliding toward her.

"I thought you would never ask me!"

Ben pulled her to him and kissed her as if he would never let her go. They were sitting on the soapy floor when a surprised guest walked in.

CHAPTER XIX

The Forbes Road

Brigadier General John Forbes, a Scot, was appointed by the new Prime Minister, William Pitt, in the spring of 1758 to command an expedition against Fort Duquesne. Forbes had started out to study medicine, but circumstances had changed the course of his life. Now he held one of the keys to the future of British expansion on the North American continent. He was forty-eight, an excellent commander whose simple tastes and lack of ceremony contrasted sharply with his breeding. He dealt with the colonists frankly and directly and had succeeded in winning their confidence. The sorely tried frontiersmen took heart; at last the government in England was alert to the danger that they could lose the province of Pennsylvania unless they did something to support the settlers.

The army Forbes assembled consisted of almost six thousand men: Royal Americans, for the most part German Americans, led by officers who were professional soldiers of diverse European nationalities; Scottish regiments, referred to as Highlanders; Provincials from Pennsylvania, Maryland, Virginia, Delaware, and North Carolina.

By the middle of June most of the army was on the march westward. It consisted of four battalions with men drawn from various British regiments, in addition to the Provincials. One of the battalions was commanded by a professional soldier of Swiss birth, Colonel Henry Bouquet. He and his men were now camped at Raystown on the eastern heights of the Alleghenies, twenty-eight miles west of Fort Lyttleton, where they were building a supply depot and a stockade.

Bouquet sat at mess in his tent reviewing the situation. Before he left Philadelphia he had had a long talk with General Forbes about the route to be taken in building a road to the French fort of Duquesne. He could hear the general's voice with its heavy Scottish burr: "I'm concerned, Henry, about the problems of supply. You can't have an army strung out like ninepins along Braddock's bloody road. You know the Indian way of fightin'—hidin' in the trees, pickin' the soldiers off one by one. We didn't have experience of it before the general was killed, but I hope we've learned our lesson. It's necessary we have forts along the way for supply depots and to protect the advance columns."

"You plan to advance by slow stages?" Bouquet asked.

"It's the only way, my friend. When they approach Duquesne, they can't be hampered by supply wagons and packhorses. The men must be able to maneuver. . . . There's also the question of morale. Every last man in this army will be rememberin' Braddock's defeat three years ago if we use the old road."

Sitting at the opening of his tent in the refreshing breeze of early evening, Colonel Bouquet believed Forbes's plan made sense. The Scot had a way of putting a problem in perspective, claiming that soldiers fought better when adequately rested and fed and when there were supplies and reinforcements near at hand. He had little patience with the idea that the traditional European method of fighting could be used in such settings as the wilderness. He advocated emulating the Indians, whose means of making war were admirably adapted to the terrain.

Bouquet had brought with him several bottles of fine wine, and his leather traveling case containing six glass goblets. He could never bear to drink wine from a pewter cup. Now, as he sipped his Canary, he thought about a dispatch that had just arrived from the general. Forbes was unable to leave Philadelphia for Carlisle, as he had suffered an attack of bloody flux that affected his stomach and vital organs. He would set out as soon as he was able to ride.

Bouquet felt some anxiety. Forbes's handwriting was usually precise and legible, without flourishes; this barely legible scrawl was an indication that he must be in pain. Bouquet wondered how long Forbes's departure would be delayed; his absence would place additional responsibility on Bouquet as battalion commander of the western area.

The following morning was hot and sun-splashed in the new army encampment at Raystown. Although it was barely nine o'clock, the soldiers had been at work for several hours. The Pennsylvanians were complaining.

"Dunno why we always git the dirty work! Diggin' trenches in this here heat is enough to fry a man's privates," said Jeb Hawkins.

"Why ya worryin', Jeb? Ain't no use for them nohow in this wilderness. Nary a woman within forty mile of here."

The men guffawed. "Ya sure as hell hit the bull's eye on that," said one.

"I'd rather be puttin' up palisades or splittin' logs for the stockade fence," said Hawkins, annoyed at their hilarity at his expense.

George Eldridge, who was in charge of the detail, put down his shovel. He was exasperated by their boorishness and complaints. At times he was sullen and withdrawn, but he managed not to show this before his superiors. He had won their respect for his hard work and willingness to do what was required of him. "I'd like to see ya try liftin' them twenty-foot logs, Jeb Hawkins. You'd find it takes a man's strength and will to lift them. The Highlanders were given that duty because they ain't afraid of hard work."

George heard a whispered remark about soldiers in petticoats. "The next time I hear anyone say somethin' about kilts," he bellowed, "I'm goin' to ask Colonel Armstrong to have a wrestling match between the Highlanders and the men in this detail. We'll soon see who're the real men here!"

There was silence. The men in the ditch knew this was no idle threat. Corporal Eldridge was tough. He had broken the jaws of several who hinted that his wife was serving as a squaw to her captor. He'd been reprimanded for his conduct, but not punished, because the officers thought a man had a right to defend his wife's honor.

Ben Enyard thought that it was just bad luck that George had been put in charge of the most troublesome detail in the Pennsylvania Regiment. The men under Ben's command were better disciplined.

To the right of Ben's men the Scots, working in four-man teams, puffed and groaned as they lifted the stout poles into place for the stockade. Most were tall and well-muscled, with big chests and strong hairy legs below their moleskin breeks. On hearing that they wore skirts in Scotland, Ben had wanted to laugh, but acquaintance with the Scots' courage and self-control had taught him to respect them. They were manly and tough and made fine soldiers.

When it was time to eat Ben put down his shovel as Jim McCullough joined him. Jim had filled out, lost some of his bony awkwardness. The grim look, so like Annie's, was gone.

"How is it over in your trench?"

"Slow work," Jim answered, wiping his brow with his forearm. "Them big black flies near to drive ya crazy with their bitin'."

"How did you like workin' next to the Virginians?"

"They're good workers, but right opinionated. Talked all morning about which road the army should take to get to Duquesne. Their colonel—fellow by the name of Washington—was with Braddock, and he says the only way to go is Braddock's road."

"I heard that General Forbes is plannin' to cut a new road through the mountains and build magazines to hold supplies. That way the army wouldn't be strung out like they was in fifty-five."

"The Virginians says it's goin' to take too long to build. Winter will be here before we could get very far. It's a mighty hard thing to build a road in these mountains when the woods is full of Injuns."

"They persuadin' you to their way of thinkin'?"

"Course not, Ben! I'm just tellin' ya what they said. I heard the Virginians started a land company in Ohio and just want to protect their interests there by usin' Braddock's road."

"What do you mean?"

"They're afraid if we get the new road, folks'll go into Ohio and grab those lands for theirselves. They'd be followin' a shorter route."

"So that's what the argument is about! I couldn't figure out why everybody was so riled up over it."

"Do you think that's the reason the Virginians is so set on usin' the old road? Would Colonel Washington be arguin' for Braddock's route just to protect their land company?"

"I reckon there's a number of arguments for it, Jim. I hear Washington is honest and right smart. He must have good reasons for it."

Jim changed the subject. "Guess who I seen this mornin' when I was fillin' my canteen."

"Who?"

"Felix Abbot."

"You don't say! When did he come?"

"Yesterday. You heard how he was taken out to Ohio by the Shawnees and escaped and made his way to Fort Lyttleton, didn't you? Had a terrible time gettin' through the woods, near died of starvation. After he joined his family, they went to Shippensburg to live."

"It must be a real comfort to Mrs. Abbot to have him back."

"She died this past winter. They took it hard."

Ben was saddened by the news. When the war ended there would be many familiar faces missing. "Did he ask after Lucinda?" he asked.

"Never spoke of her."

It was dusk before Ben was free to look for Felix. When a man in Felix's company pointed him out, Ben was surprised to see how mature he looked. They thumped each other on the back, then stood apart, looking for changes.

"You're a sight for sore eyes, Ben Enyard!"

"I don't believe I'd of knowed you, Felix."

"Guess I ain't changed that much."

"Just the amount it takes for a boy to grow to be a man."

"Well, how about yourself? Jim McCullough tells me you got yourself a real pretty wife."

"Susannah Graves, she was. I met her in Carlisle just after she escaped from the Mingoes. Her husband died during her captivity."

"Must've been hard for her."

"I was sorry to hear about your ma," Ben said. "She was a real fine woman."

Felix swallowed before he could trust himself to answer. "I can't get used to her bein' gone."

"I know what you mean. Ma found it hard to go back to the farm after Pa and Ari was killed."

"I heard ya took your family to Carlisle."

"We got there before it was so crowded." Ben paused. "When you're ready to talk about it, Felix, I'd like to hear what you been through."

"Some other time."

"You know Lucinda's married and livin' in Philadelphia. She's got a fine husband, an Englishman by the name of Geoffrey Moncrief. His father's a lord or some such."

Felix stared, his grief forgotten. "She's married? Did you say married?"

"I didn't know if you knew or not."

Felix took Ben's arm. "Let's go over by the crick. I got to ask ya somethin'."

They sat on the bank where oaks threw long shadows. "What happened to her, Ben? Pa won't let any of us speak of her."

Ben was silent, trying to find an answer without betraying Lucinda or George. "Didn't Sarah or the boys tell you?"

"Nothin' much. Somethin' about her goin' over to the Eldridges' and nursin' George when he took sick. Knowin' her, I guessed she was up to somethin'."

"She suffered for what she did."

"I figgered that was what it was. Pa wouldn't let any of us even speak of George Eldridge."

"He never mentions what happened between them," Ben said. "It's changed him. George started to believe those rumors about Mary Ann servin' as a squaw to the Injun that captured her."

"Where'd such rumors start?"

"It was after you returned and gave Captain McWhirter your

statement about your capture."

"I never said nothin' like that!"

"You said the Injun who captured you seemed sweet on her."

"But that's the truth, Ben."

"You know how evil some folks are. They started gossipin' about Mary Ann."

"Oh, Lordy, Ben, I didn't mean that!"

"I know you didn't, Felix. Nobody who knew her thought that. George started to believe them. He never mentions Mary Ann now."

Felix looked shocked.

"For a long time he talked about her comin' back, but then he changed. When he's in one of his moods he talks of wipin' out Indian villages, murderin' the babies and women and old people."

Felix's voice was so low Ben could barely catch his words. "We didn't know how lucky we was before this war started. Seems like everythin's bein' destroyed."

Later Felix came upon George sitting alone, cleaning his gun. He stared in disbelief. The handsome young man he had envied two years ago was now a thin, almost haggard, middle-aged man, his face covered with a black beard, the mouth misshapen from missing teeth. He did not look up until Felix had spoken several times. Then his scowl deepened, and his eyes were full of resentment.

"What do ya want of me?"

Felix was at a loss for words.

"Speak up! State your business. I've work to do!"

"I just wanted to talk to ya. We was neighbors." Felix knew he sounded like a boy.

"I got nothin' to say to any of the Abbots."

"I thought maybe you'd like to catch up on news. Our family's livin' over to Shippensburg now. Ma . . ."

George Eldridge laid down his gun and rose. His face in the deepening twilight looked menacing. "I don't want to hear nothin' ya got to say. Keep out of my way, boy!"

Shocked and depressed, Felix moved away.

* *

Colonel Bouquet, Colonel John Armstrong, and some of the troops remained at Raystown to complete the stockade and supply depot while the Virginians and a detachment of Pennsylvanians worked on the road to Fort Duquesne.

By August they had not made much progress, for they were under constant threat of Indian attacks, and the work of blasting and laying fascines and gabions was dangerous and difficult.

In the advance camp on the Loyalhanna Creek Sir John Sinclair, the army's quartermaster-general, was in charge.

Ben Enyard and Jim McCullough were among those assigned to work with the Virginians on the road. One hot noon they took their tin plates to the steep bank of the stream, where tall trees shielded them from the sun.

"I wish I could hear from Susannah," Ben said.

At that moment they overheard Lieutenant Colonel Stephens speaking with indignation of an incident that happened that morning. Sinclair had ordered them to lay dynamite to blast a clearing in the mountainside. The men he chose at random had protested that they had never used dynamite.

The quartermaster-general had grown livid at this. Brandishing his sword, he had ordered them to lay the charge at once. Twenty minutes later one of the men ran back to camp, a bloody stump where his hand had been. His companions were dead, their bodies splattered over the crater.

Lieutenant Colonel Stephens's soft Virginia voice was harsh with indignation. "You can't ask a man to lay dynamite who's never handled it unless you show him how to place it properly!"

At that moment the corpulent figure of the quartermaster-general approached them, his pendulous chins shaking. "What's this, Stephens?" Sinclair roared. "You have the goddamned insolence to criticize my orders? I'll break you for this, you and your sniveling Virginians!" He brandished his broadsword at Stephens. The men around the two officers closed in, their faces full of hatred for the Englishman. Sinclair hesitated, aware that the odds were against him. These Colonials weren't disciplined like the soldiers in England.

Stephens stood his ground. "You have it in your power to kill me, sir. But there will be many witnesses."

There was a low rumble from his men.

The quartermaster-general lowered his sword. "What can one expect from a crowd of goddamned whores' sons? How in the hell can you make soldiers of such scum?" There was a gasp at his words. The Virginians were known to be the best disciplined men in Forbes's army.

Stephens clenched his sword hilt. "If I were not under military orders, sir, I'd call you out for your remarks!" His voice trembled. "I would rather break my sword than serve under you!"

"Why you damned bastard . . ." The quartermaster-general's voice was lost in a cheer from Stephens's men. His face purpling, Sinclair stomped away.

By four o'clock Stephens had been arrested on charges of insubordination and Major Lewis had been appointed to take his place. Lewis knew how to deal with the Virginians, since he was one of them. "I want to congratulate you for the fine spirit you have shown in buildin' this road. It's been hard, dangerous work, and yet you have not complained. We are only fifty miles from the French fort. We must not lose heart but press on until we capture Duquesne," he told them.

The western base of Laurel Hill, with the Loyalhanna Creek flowing past its banks, had been designated as the point at which Forbes's army would assemble before making its final march against Duquesne. No one knew when this would happen; it depended on the state of Forbes's health, the weather, and how quickly they could complete their supply depots and finish the road.

Late in August, twenty-five hundred of Bouquet's troops were at the Loyalhannon camp. Colonel James Burd, a Pennsylvanian, was in charge of the men who were erecting a stockade and entrenchments while work on the road continued. One day Colonel Burd dispatched a party of five scouts to bring back the cows, which were allowed to wander in the forest. When the men had been gone for several hours, he began to worry and asked for volunteers to search for the missing scouts.

Ben Enyard heard Jim McCullough call out, "I'll go, sir!" Ben, watching him, was troubled.

An hour later one of the scouts ran into the stockade, his eyes dilated with fear. "Where's the colonel?"

"What is it, Schofield?" Burd's voice was calm.

"They killed some of the cows and shot the men!"

"All of them?"

"I ain't sure. They was scalpin' one when I run out. When they saw me, they took off into the deep woods."

"Was the man alive?"

"I ain't certain. There wasn't no one but me, and I thought I'd best come back for help."

"And our other men? What happened to them?"

"I didn't see them. We went in different directions, sir."

"Then they may be still alive?"

"Yes, sir."

"We have to find them. Can you lead a search party?"

The man hesitated. "Yes, sir."

Ben put down the ax. He knew he would never be able to live with himself if he did not try to find Jim. When the stockade gate closed behind them, Ben felt totally vulnerable. As they moved deeper into the woods, he glanced back at the stockade and saw men patrolling the catwalk, heard the ring of axes on wood, voices raised. The normality of the scene added to his fear.

A sudden movement in the bushes made him drop to one knee and raise his rifle. He felt the rush of air as a tomahawk flew past his shoulder and lodged in a tree trunk. He fired and saw a naked, brown arm drop, heard the soft thud of a body falling. Running forward in a crouching position, he saw a slim brown youth lying on the ground. Ben's fear vanished and was replaced by wonder. The brave's mouth and chin were boyish and the muscles of his legs and arms had not the girth of a man's. Something akin to pity awoke in him for the young boy, whose life had been but a promise.

He moved on and came upon two volunteers carrying a badly wounded man. Three scouts had been killed, they said, and there were more wounded.

With a racing pulse, Ben ran on. The body of a Jersey cow lay near a dead horse whose neck had been pierced by an arrow.

Flies swarmed over their carcasses and a stench filled the air, for it was very hot, even in the depths of the forest.

Suddenly Ben noticed a man's boot protruding from a thicket. Pushing aside the bushes with his rifle, he cautiously moved toward it. Jim McCullough lay beneath a tall oak, his face half hidden by forest debris, one hand still clutching his long gun. An arrow protruded from his back below his left shoulder. He moaned and appeared only partly conscious. Ben bent over him, noting the shallow breathing. "Jim, Jim, can you hear me? It's Ben. I'm goin' to take you back to the fort."

Jim's eyelids fluttered, then opened. There was a flicker of recognition, then his eyes glazed with pain. Ben lifted him carefully, and staggered back to the stockade, leaving their guns behind. When he lowered Jim to the ground in front of the camp physician's tent, Ben rubbed an arm across his sweaty face, aware that he had been crying. The doctor looked at him curiously. "Pull yourself together, Ensign. I'll need someone with steady nerves to hold him down while I get that arrow out." Ben noticed the physician's bloody apron. An odor of putrefaction emanated from the tent. He felt nauseated and moved away, spent and heartsore. Then he heard a familiar voice say, "I'll give ya a hand, Doc." He turned and saw Patrick Brady take hold of Jim's ankles and arms.

"You'll have to hold on to him, for it's buried deep. I'm going to have to cut it out." The doctor's voice sounded matter-of-fact.

Ben went over to the little stream and lowered himself to the steep, mossy bank. He bowed his head in his hands. There was a scream as the doctor cut deep, then Brady's voice, "Steady now, McCullough!" Then the doctor exclaimed, "There! A good job, if I do say so. I'll just cauterize the wound and give him a few drops of laudanum so he'll sleep."

"He gonna be fit, Doc?" he heard Brady ask.

"Oh, yes. It didn't puncture the lungs. After a few weeks' rest, he'll be fit for soldiering. Unless the wound mortifies. Never can tell about that."

Jim's cries subsided to a long-drawn-out moan as the laudanum began to take effect. Ben was thankful that they had such medicine, now that General Forbes was in command.

Patrick Brady was examining the arrow when Ben approached.

"I want to thank you, Brady."

Brady scratched his whiskered chin, then spat a dark stream of tobacco juice. "Wasn't much."

"I won't forget it."

CHAPTER XX

Autumn 1758

Colonel Bouquet anxiously awaited General Forbes's arrival. Soon the autumn rains would begin and the newly built road through the mountains would be a sea of mud. To add to Bouquet's worries, the woods were full of hostile Indians, who continued to kill their cattle, steal their horses, and kill or capture their scouts. He wondered if they could complete the fort before winter set in. With the continual loss of men, it was doubtful.

Forbes had ordered Bouquet to erect breastworks along the proposed route to Fort Duquesne, and to garrison them with sufficient troops to protect the army on its march. They would also serve as supply bases. It was a masterly plan, and Bouquet thanked Providence he and his men had made some progress.

Within the Loyalhannon camp tension mounted. The French had not made an attack, but depended on their Indian allies to harass the British. The men grumbled and quarreled, wondering when the French would come. Some of the more superstitious were uneasy because, in extending the ditch, they had uncovered an Indian burial ground. Scouts said it was bad luck to disturb the bones.

It was Jim McCullough, now able to lift a light shovel, who found the Indian woman's remains. George Eldridge was working nearby, breaking the ground, when Jim's shovel uncovered the woman's skeleton with bits of long black hair and fragments of a deerskin dress.

"Good Lord! Look at this, George! Ain't that somethin'?" He felt a shiver of horror as he stared at the shallow grave.

"Nothing to get shook up about, Jim. She's just a squaw, no better 'n an animal. Toss it to one side."

"It don't seem right to do that."

"What ya worryin' about? Them crazy notions about the Delawares puttin' a curse on disturbin' their graves? She's dead." George put his shovel under the skeleton and began to lift it. As he straightened, the vertebrae snapped in two, and he tossed half of the bones beyond the ditch.

"Maybe we ought to bury her decent like," Jim said.

"Bury a squaw? Injuns ain't humans!"

"It don't seem right to just throw away her bones like she was a dumb critter."

"I ain't wastin' any sympathy on savages. I had a bellyful of their tricks."

Jim began to shovel the remaining bones and bits of deerskin, but he could not shake off the feeling that it was wrong.

Under Colonel Bouquet's command at Loyalhannon was a portly, red-faced Scotsman named Major James Grant. He had seen service at Fontenoy, Culloden, and in Flanders and Ireland before being sent to America to command a company of Highlanders assigned to Forbes's army. When Bouquet ordered two companies of one hundred men each to protect the soldiers sent to bring back horses and cattle, Major Grant drew him aside.

"Colonel, I'm surprised at your sendin' only two hundred on such a mission. Such small parties never accomplish anythin' but to lose their men. If you will give me five hundred of your best men, I will lead them on foot to Duquesne to reconnoiter the enemy's forces. From the latest reports there are only six hundred French and Indians left there. By erectin' an ambuscade I can take prisoners."

Bouquet chewed his lip. "That is a large number for reconnaissance, Major."

"It's necessary if we are to stop those savages from ambushin' our troops. A show of strength is what's wanted. We need more information as to the numbers of French and their Indian allies at the fort. We can't rely on a few escaped captives or our scouts for it."

A faint flush brightened Bouquet's sallow face. "That is true." Turning to an aide he spoke crisply. "Send Colonel Burd and Major Lewis to me."

When Burd and Lewis appeared, Bouquet explained Major Grant's proposition. "I have discussed a plan with the major to make a night attack on the Indians whose huts surround Fort Duquesne. Our losses in men killed or captured are discouraging; many of our militia have become so fearful that when they are attacked they throw down their arms to flee faster. We must put a stop to these attacks! My disposition would be for Major Grant to take three hundred Highlanders, a hundred and fifty Virginians, one hundred Marylanders, one hundred Pennsylvanians, and all the Tuscaroras and Nottaways who have come over to our side. They should regulate their march to be five miles from Duquesne by evening. If Major Grant believes the French and their allies are not aware of their presence, he should advance on the hill half a mile from the French fort to reconnoiter, and plan accordingly. If he sees the enemy sitting about their fires, he should send parties to attack them soon after midnight, using bayonets so as to proceed as quietly as possible. He should then retreat to the height and, as soon as his troops are gathered there, retire from Duquesne before daybreak to form an ambuscade, in case the enemy should follow. If they do, he should overcome them at the ambuscade and then return to Loyalhannon. If he is discovered, he should retire at once. What think you of this proposition, gentlemen?"

There were no objections.

The expedition was within eleven miles of Duquesne when Major Grant called a halt. "Captain Bullitt," he said, "I'm leavin' you responsible for the baggage. Keep two subalterns and fifty privates with you and remain here until I send for you."

The boyish captain straightened his shoulders. "Very well, sir."

At two in the morning on September 14 Grant's expedition reached the summit of a hill two miles east of the French fort, having encountered none of the enemy en route. Grant concluded that only a small force held Duquesne; otherwise the commandant would have posted sentries.

He turned to Major Lewis. "Take half of your detachment, major, and descend to the plain in front of the stockade. Set fire to the wigwams and the storage sheds. If you meet any resistance, kill them!"

"That will rouse the French, sir. Colonel Bouquet—"

"Are you presumin' to question my orders?"

"No, sir."

"Then carry them out! Deploy half of your men in the area where the savages are camped outside the stockade. When you've fired their wigwams and killed them, retreat to the top of the hill, where the rest of the troops will ambush your pursuers."

Lewis swallowed, his eyes troubled.

Grant's close-set eyes glittered. "Well?"

"Yes, sir."

Shortly before dawn, fog blanketed the woods, making it impossible to see more than a few yards. Major Lewis approached Grant, who stood on the brow of the hill, his hands clasping the hilt of his broadsword.

"Why haven't you followed my orders?" Grant demanded.

"It appears my men lost their way in this fog, sir."

"Damn the fog! Find them!"

"We have been tryin' to for the past hour, sir."

Grant swore softly. Lewis waited, standing formally at attention. "Well then, Major, since your men aren't eager to fight"—Grant saw Lewis's mouth whiten—"and you can't keep them together, I'll send my Highlanders down. Take your men to the rear. You can help Bullitt with the baggage train."

He is dividing his forces in the belief that the fort contains few men, thought Lewis. But there was no assurance of that. He hoped Grant's brashness would not cost the lives of the Highlanders. There was no reasoning with the man. He was like one possessed.

To the right, toward the Allegheny River, Ben Enyard and George Eldridge were among the Provincials detailed to guard the right flank. From where they waited in the trees they could see on the left Captain Mackenzie's detachment of Highlanders.

They also had a clear view of the plain below, where Fort Duquesne lay wrapped in fog, its white-and-gold fleur-de-lis flags barely visible above the low-lying mists. From time to time they saw through the shifting vapors details of wigwams scattered about the space in front of the fort's tall gates. There were also suttlers' wagons, what appeared to be a granary, various sheds, and a smithy. Framed by trees whose autumn colors were muted now in the predawn light, the scene was deceptively tranquil, like an old engraving whose colors had been dulled by time.

"Quite a place they got there," George said, checking his rifle again to be certain the priming was in place.

Ben, feeling the familiar tightening of his stomach before the prospect of reconnoitering the enemy's stronghold, suddenly pointed. "Look what's happenin'! Over there."

The fog had lifted now and the sun was spilling tremulous shafts of dawn light over the plain. Every building stood out in bold relief. The trees were brilliant in their autumn colors; the French flag fluttered serenely in the crisp early morning breeze.

"Good Lord!"

On the hilltop facing the fort Grant had posted Captain McDonald's company of Highlanders and now, as Ben and George watched, they heard with disbelief the high skirl and whine of the bagpipes and the ominous counterpoint of drums.

"They'll wake the dead! What's the matter with them?" Ben asked.

"It's that ass Grant. He's disobeyin' Colonel's orders, the connivin' bastard!" George spat in contempt.

"He must be drunk! Nobody in his right mind would send men on reconnaissance with pipers and drummers!"

The Highlanders were marching down the hill in battle array. They were a brave sight, disciplined and well trained.

"Now there's sojers fer ya!" George said in admiration.

Ben did not answer for at that moment pandemonium erupted. A trumpet sounded within the fort. The stockade gate opened to emit dozens of Frenchmen in nightshirts, brandishing swords and rifles. Close behind them ran their Indian allies. They dashed across the plain, firing at the approaching Highlanders, stopping only to reload.

The Scots began to fall before the devastating fire. Ben and George watched in horror as the French bullets hit their targets. Men crouched behind their dead comrades and took aim. The smell of blood, urine, and excrement was overwhelming. The screams of the dying mingled with war whoops and imprecations. McDonald, in command of the left flank, fell from a tomahawk blow, which split his head in two, his brains obscenely spilling onto the forest floor. It was difficult to see clearly in the continual smoke from the guns. After three quarters of an hour the Highlanders began a disorderly retreat.

Two miles to the rear Major Lewis and his men heard the sounds of battle. Leaving Captain Bullitt with a small detachment to guard the horses and equipment, they set off in the direction of the firing. Major Grant, retreating on the path he had taken the night before, did not encounter them, for they were following a more direct route. When he reached the baggage wagons, Grant was panting from exertion, his heavy face dripping with perspiration. "Where the devil is Lewis?" he asked Bullitt.

"He went to your aid, sir."

Grant had lost his sword and his hat, and his protuberant belly, clad in an undershirt, showed in the gaps in his uniform where buttons had been torn off. "God in heaven," he gasped, "I'm ruined!"

Bullitt did not reply. He had rallied some of the retreating men and posted them behind the baggage wagons to form a barricade. "Sergeant Cullinane, put the most valuable baggage on that roan and take it back to the camp at Loyalhannon as fast as you can." He turned to the men waiting behind the wagons. "Here's what we're goin' to do." Briefly he outlined his strategy.

As the men checked their rifles, they were startled to hear a heavily accented voice cry in loud tones, "Do you surrendair?" In his despair Major Grant had wandered off and been captured. He had offered no resistance.

Bullitt and his men, waiting in the clearing with the baggage train, saw Indians advancing through the trees three hundred yards away. They had not had time to apply their war paint. To the waiting Provincials it came as a shock to see them without it.

"Hold your fire till I give the word! It's our only chance," Bullitt cried. As the Indians advanced in greater numbers, the soldiers could smell the rancid odor of bear's grease, which would always remind them of this encounter.

The Provincials had impaled a scrap of white cloth on a bayonet. A corporal stepped out from behind the wagons, his trembling hands holding the symbol of surrender. As the Delawares and Shawnees and Mingoes began to confer, Bullitt's men followed the corporal, advancing slowly with every appearance of preparing to lay down their arms. The Indians waited, their faces austere and proud. There would be many captives, and later, ransoms. When the Provincials were within eight yards of the foremost group of the enemy, Bullitt called "Aim!" There was a pause. "Fire!"

The attack was so well timed that it caught the Indians completely by surprise. Before they could charge, the first line of Provincials fired, then ran to the rear of the barricade of wagons, as those who had been behind them knelt and fired. They were followed by soldiers with bayonets. The Indians were completely confused. Many fell from the first two volleys; others died from the bayonets. The rest turned, stumbling over the bodies of the fallen, and ran toward the fort as marksmen picked them off.

Bullitt, seeing several of his men about to scalp the dead, for the English paid well for scalps, called sternly, "None of that! We've no time for scalps. Collect our wounded and put 'em on the wagons. We leave for Loyalhannon at once!"

Reluctantly most of the men set to work loading the wagons with the wounded. One man, ignoring Bullitt's order, continued hacking off an Indian's hair.

"Stop that, I told ya! The first man I see stoppin' to collect scalps I'll shoot!"

The man dropped the bloody object and hurried to help with the wounded. He knew Bullitt meant what he said.

Their return to Loyalhannon was a horrifying journey none would ever forget, for the trail was strewn with the dead and dying. The sufferings of the wounded were intensified as the wheels jolted over ruts and rocks. At times the able-bodied carried the wounded in order that the wagons could negotiate a precipitous stretch of trail.

The small detachment of Pennsylvanians had been cut off from the rest of the company. They attempted to maintain a heavy return fire on the right flank of the hill but were outnumbered by the French and Indians. Their only means of survival was to cross the Allegheny.

"Come on! The only chance we got is the river," Ben yelled to George. "Take off your boots."

"But I'll need them," George protested.

"It's better than drownin', ain't it?" Holding his rifle aloft with one hand, Ben plunged into the water.

George, unable to swim, hesitated. He had no idea of the depth of the river but decided to chance it. Dropping his rifle and powder horn, he followed Ben, but he had not gone more than a few yards when the river suddenly deepened and he realized he could not maintain his footing.

"Ben! I cain't swim!" A strong current caught him, knocking him off his feet, and he went under, swallowing water. When he surfaced, he had just enough breath to yell again before he went down a second time.

Ben heard the frantic cry. He turned, deliberately letting go of his rifle, and swam with powerful strokes to where George had been standing. As he kicked, he felt a heavy object obstructing his foot. He dove under water, grasped George by the hair, and pulled him up. George was semiconscious and had swallowed a lot of water.

"Don't fight it! Let go and I'll tow you!"

Ben began to swim across the broad expanse, one hand clutching George. It was punishing work. When he saw how far off the shore was, he knew that he couldn't make it. Then he realized that he was swimming against the river's powerful current. If he swam with the current, he could save his strength and come out far above the French fort. He changed course and felt the water bearing them along. It was cold in places. The arm that held George felt numb. With every stroke the shore seemed more distant. He wondered how long he could keep up this grueling swim.

Susannah's face appeared before him and he thought of the coming child. Lord, he couldn't die now. He began to pray.

Some time later, spent and gulping air with lungs that felt about to burst, Ben pulled George's inert body from the river. They were on a beach miles above Duquesne, under a rock overhang above which oaks and chestnuts towered. Ben shivered in the bright sunlight and began to rub his arms briskly to get the blood circulating. There were no signs of the French or Indians here, only a long stretch of sand and trees.

He went to George and looked down at him anxiously. His face was a strange grayish-blue. Pulling and straining, Ben dragged George to a large rock and then pulled him, face down, over the boulder, in order to get rid of the water George had swallowed. He began to push in the small of George's back, push, pause, finding that if he maintained a rhythm he did not feel so exhausted. After several minutes his efforts were rewarded. Water and mucus streamed from George's mouth and nose. Suddenly he began to vomit. Finally he fell back on the sand, his chest heaving, eyelids fluttering.

"We made it, George!" Ben cried. "I don't know where we are except that the current carried us north of the fort," Ben continued. "As soon as you're fit to travel we'll find our way back to camp."

When the remnants of Grant's expedition began returning to the camp at Loyalhannon with accounts of the defeat, Colonel Bouquet and his aides were appalled. The loss was incredible: two hundred and seventy known dead, forty-two wounded, and scores missing.

To Jim McCullough it was the most shattering, painful experience of his life, for his friends Ben Enyard and George Eldridge had not returned. He wandered about, plying the survivors with questions, his long bony face etched with grief. He could not eat. When he stretched out in his blanket on the hard ground to sleep, the tightness in his chest kept him wakeful through the long nights. He recalled all of the experiences he had shared with Ben and George. He thought of Mrs. Enyard, left alone now with two small children to provide for. And Susannah, whose child was due in December. Both were strong women, but they needed a man to protect them on the frontier.

Three days later Ben Enyard and George Eldridge staggered through the stockade gate, half naked, weak from exhaustion, their faces covered with stubble and grime, their eyes haunted.

There was a great cheer from their fellow Pennsylvanians. Men dropped their rifles and shovels and came running to thump them on the back or grasp their hands. Instinctively each man knew his own chances for survival were strengthened by the return of two of their regiment; they were all less vulnerable to the menace that was part of their daily lives because these two had endured.

Jim pushed his way through the crowd. When he caught a glimpse of the survivors, he stared in astonishment, then ran to throw his arms around them, too moved to speak.

Ben smiled, his eyes revealing the depth of his misery. Then he fainted.

For ten days survivors of the rout came stumbling into the camp. Some had festering wounds; all suffered from near-starvation and exhaustion. Their stories of the defeat were similar—orders ignored by Major Grant, needless exposure to the enemy, then slaughter and retreat. The threat of an attack hung heavy over the camp. Colonel Bouquet instituted daily drills so that each man would know what to do when the enemy came.

The Indians at Fort Duquesne—Delawares, Shawnees and Mingoes—began to return to their villages, laden with the spoils of Grant's defeat. It was their custom to return home after a battle, successful or not. Futhermore, they were growing dissatisfied with their French allies since the Moravian missionary Christian Frederick Post had visited the western Delawares along the Ohio on a peace mission for the English.

The French commandant, Captain DeLigneris, sanguine after Grant's defeat, decided on a bold move. He did not have precise intelligence as to the number of men at Loyalhannon but he decided to send a thousand Frenchmen, with the two hundred Indians who remained at Duquesne, to attack the camp. The English would be taken by surprise, for the French had made no forays against them other than their defense of Duquesne.

Colonel James Burd was in charge of the camp that day, as Colonel Bouquet had left that morning with a detachment of artillery and militia to bring back supplies from Stoney Creek. At a quarter to eleven in the morning a corporal posted as lookout stared at the woodland trail in disbelief. A long line of Frenchmen was trotting briskly through the woods, shafts of sunlight striking a rifle or a blunderbuss.

"Sound the alarm! The French is comin'!"

Bouquet's drills were rewarded; there was no panic. Cannon were rolled into place opposite the gates. Men were sent to bring in the horses and cattle. Sharpshooters on the platform aimed the barrels of their muskets through the loopholes. A bucket brigade carried water from the creek and filled the wooden barrels placed at strategic spots within the compound. Kegs of gunpowder were being rolled into place when the first shots rang out.

"Secure the gates!" yelled Colonel Burd.

"But we ain't got all the horses and cattle in," protested a recent recruit.

"Too late for that!" thundered the colonel. "Fasten those gates!"

Ben, kneeling on the platform of the stockade, saw the French and their Indian allies swarming through the woods like a vast wave. A burst of gunpowder momentarily obscured them. He heard the thud of bodies falling and saw the sun glance off bayonets as tomahawks whirled through the air and lodged in the stockade wall. There was the sound of timber splintering. "Over here! Concentrate your fire on the left!" Burd cried.

Ben heard the terrified whinny of horses, the sharp tattoo of their hoofs, the cries of the wounded and dying mingled with the boom of the cannon, bursts of rifle fire, war whoops, commands shouted in French. He had barely time to reload when a face loomed over the top of the stockade wall. He gazed in astonishment into the eyes of a young Frenchman and saw a similar surprise reflected there just before he pulled the trigger. The face disintegrated before his eyes. A second man was trying to pull himself over the palisade. There was no time to reload. Ben turned his heavy rifle and brought the butt down on the man's head.

Suddenly a cry of "Fire! Bring the buckets!" rose above the din. There was a sound of dry wood bursting into flames, as billows of smoke rolled upward. Ben felt the heat sweep over him and he ran in the opposite direction, coughing and rubbing his eyes. The fire crackled briskly as it reached one of the ladders and began to consume the wood. There were screams as men jumped or fell.

The assault continued. Gradually the spit and crackle of burning wood died away.

Someone yelled, "Got it under control, Colonel!"

"Good work!" Burd cried.

A moment later a new blaze broke out in another part of the stockade. Ben smelled the stench of burning flesh and cloth as a militiaman enveloped in flames ran toward him. He pulled off his deerskin hunting jacket and threw it around the man, but there was no room on the narrow catwalk to roll him about to smother the flames. George joined him in trying to beat out the fire. When at last it was extinguished, they realized it was too late. They gazed in horror at the man's blackened face and seared body. "God in heaven, what a way to die!" George wiped a grimy hand over his face.

Ben looked at his blistered hands. It would be impossible to handle a rifle now. He felt a savage anger that he could do nothing to repulse the enemy. But the sounds of battle were fading.

George peered over the stockade fence. "They're retreatin'!" The French were leaping over their fallen comrades and running into the woods, but their Indians allies were collecting their dead. Ben was too exhausted to move. He slumped down against the wall of the stockade, holding his hands palms up. He closed his eyes to shut out the sight of the dead and dying, then heard George's voice: "I've got a score to settle with them bastards." He stared in amazement as George jumped from the platform and moved among the wounded Indians lying within the compound, plunging his bayonet into each man again and again. He seemed possessed, his lips moving soundlessly, his face contorted. Ben was shocked. This was not the George he knew.

Carrion crows circled over the stockade. The air was heavy with the odor of gunpowder and charred wood. The dead lay staring at the sky with its drift of creamy clouds. The pain inched up Ben's arms until he bit his lips to keep from crying out. It was then he remembered Jim McCullough. He'd been too busy to think of him during the battle. Wearily Ben started down the ladder. Halfway down he fell and lay on the parade ground, too exhausted to rise. Nearby men carried the wounded on litters.

Ben sat up gingerly, knowing he had something important to attend to, but he couldn't remember what it was. Someone helped him to his feet. It was Brady.

"Better get them hands tended ta."

Ben remembered then. "I have to find Jim . . . and Felix."

"I seen Felix waitin' ta be treated over by one of the surgeons' tents. Looks like he ain't hurt bad."

"Where's Jim?"

"I ain't seen him."

"I got to find him!"

"You go sit with Felix while I look fer him. That suit you? Git some grease and lint on them hands."

Reluctantly Ben went to find Felix. He knew it would be a long wait before he could see a physician. The wounded limped in or lay on their stretchers, sometimes groaning, sometimes cursing or praying. He felt ridiculous to be seeking help, when all he had was burned palms.

Felix was cheerful as usual. "You think this wound will make me popular with the girls? I can tell them I got wounded by the French. When they asks to see the wound, I'll just pull down my britches, eh?" He chuckled.

Ben smiled wanly.

The sun began to decline and still they brought in the wounded. By this time even Felix had exhausted his conversational stores. Ben wondered what was keeping Jim. He remembered that men had gone for the horses and had not all returned when the attack began. A sudden sensation of fear clutched him and he could not shake it off.

The surgeons were now operating by candlelight, and darkness mercifully hid the broken bodies, the arms and legs that were piled to one side. Ben raised his head and saw that there were stars in the distant sky. He heard the homely chirp of crickets and felt the night breeze that was sweeping away the odors of putrefying flesh and offal.

He heard footsteps approach, hesitate, and then draw near.

"Ben Enyard!" It was Brady.

"Here I am. Did you find him?" Ben knew by the silence that followed that the news was not good.

"Where's Jim?"

"He's dead."

Ben had a feeling that this was all a nightmare, that he would wake to find Jim cleaning his long gun. "The surgeon can see you now," an orderly said, touching Ben's shoulder. Ben was still in a daze as he stumbled to his feet and went into the physician's tent.

When Ben came out of the tent with bandaged hands, he was surprised to find Patrick Brady waiting.

"Told me to get some sleep," Ben said "Gave me some medicine for it."

"Sorry about Jim," Brady said. Ben did not hear him. He was still in shock.

They stretched out in the shadows of the unfinished blockhouse. As Ben closed his eyes, he knew there was some terrible thing he would have to face . . . tomorrow.

When Ben woke it was late in the morning. He looked for George and Jim and Felix. Some distance away a crowd gathered about fresh graves in the fort burial ground. Ben could hear the chaplain speaking: " . . . Then shall the dust return to the earth as it was: and the spirit shall return unto God who gave it."

Remembrance smote him. Jim McCullough, whom he loved as a brother, was dead. The pain, so long dulled by shock and laudanum, overwhelmed him. He struggled to his feet, unmindful of his burning palms, and ran to the group about the graves. "Where's Jim?" he demanded. Then, seeing the surprised looks on their faces, he added, "Jim McCullough." Someone pointed to one of the fresh graves. Ben threw himself down beside it, aware only of the intolerable ache in his chest, of the loss of his friend.

Colonel Burd nodded to Felix Abbot. Quietly he went to Ben. "Come on, you're interrupting the preacher. Ya want Jim to have a good burying, don't ya?"

Early in November General Forbes and his troops reached the camp at Loyalhannon. The fort was still not completed, owing to the loss of men and the winter storms. The general was forced to sleep in a tent in spite of his illness and the severe weather. Seeing the man who was in charge of the expedition against the French put heart into the troops. The dogged, ailing Scot who had crossed the mountains in a litter won their respect and loyalty.

They were still harassed by roving bands of Indians, and toward the middle of the month Colonel Washington took a small scouting party into the forest to seek them out. It was a crisp autumn day: the leaves had fallen from the trees and now lay in deep drifts, lightly touched with snow. Overhead wild geese were silhouetted against the sky.

The scouts were about to return to camp when Washington motioned them to silence. They hid as best they could before a hunting party of five Delawares glided noiselessly along the path, carrying a large buck lashed to a branch. The foremost brave held up his hand for the others to be still and looked about for signs of an enemy.

At a signal from Washington, the Virginians surrounded them. As the Indians struggled to free themselves, one spoke to Washington calmly. "I'm a white man, been a captive of the Delawares since August of fifty-six. I was captured at the Great Cove."

The Virginians noticed his blue eyes and blond scalplock.

"You have been away a long time, sir!" Washington said. "Welcome back to your own kind."

There were angry murmurs from the braves. The white man said something in Delaware.

"What did they say?" Washington asked.

"That they ain't a war party, as ya can see for yourself, sir. We ain't wearing war paint. I told them you'd not harm them."

"Oh, you did, did you?" Washington was half annoyed, half amused by the fellow's assurance that all would be well.

"Ya see, they're my blood brothers. They ain't in the pay of the French at Duquesne."

"They adopted you and now you feel a certain loyalty?"

"That's right. They ain't spies. Ya can hold me as hostage if any of them causes ya trouble."

"What is your name?"

"I'm Silas Enyard. My family has a farm in the Great Cove near Fort Lyttleton."

"Tell your 'brothers' they will not be harmed, but they are our prisoners. We're taking you to the camp at Loyalhannon."

Silas looked at him in surprise. "That was where their village was before we moved north."

Felix saw Silas as Washington led the captives to General Forbes and Colonel Bouquet. "Well, I'll be jiggered! It can't be . . . " he said aloud. Then he hollered, "Silas! Silas Enyard! Is that you?"

The big fair-haired man in Indian clothes stopped and grinned as Felix ran toward him. "Felix! How are ya?"

They looked at each other, amazed and delighted, thumping each other on the shoulders.

"I'd have known ya anywhere in spite of them Injun trappin's." Felix said. Then he turned to the colonel. "Can I have a private word with ya, sir?" Washington nodded. Felix spoke quietly; Washington nodded again.

As Felix dashed off, Silas gazed after him with curiosity.

A moment later Ben ran toward Silas, his face glowing. They hugged each other, both talking at once, their laughter close to tears.

The Indians watched with suspicion.

Washington's aloof manner softened. "I'm sorry, Ensign, but I shall have to take your brother to the general. As soon as he's questioned him, you can continue with your reunion."

As Silas went off to see General Forbes, Ben looked after him, his eyes shining. He had lost Jim, but Silas had returned.

Ben wrote his mother about Silas's release, sending the letter to Susannah. A dispatch rider would carry it, along with news of their advance, to the fort in Carlisle.

CHAPTER XXI

Fort Duquesne

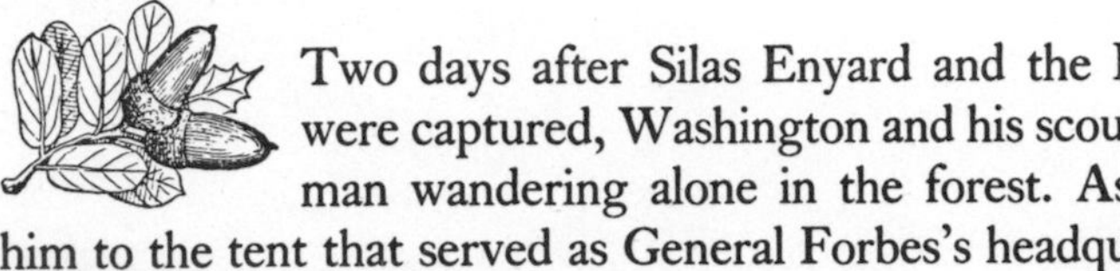

Two days after Silas Enyard and the Delawares were captured, Washington and his scouts found a man wandering alone in the forest. As they led him to the tent that served as General Forbes's headquarters, he had to reach out a hand to steady himself.

"Get him a stool, Fergusson," the general told his aide-de-camp.

The man sat and hugged himself; his teeth chattered.

"Bring a blanket. He's chilled to the bone."

Forbes studied the figure hunched before him. "How long has it been since you had a meal, sir?"

"I can't recollect, General. It was the evenin' of my escape—about two days."

"You escaped from the French or the Indians?"

"The French. I was a prisoner at Fort Duquesne for seven months."

Forbes's eyebrows shot up. He turned to his aide. "Go after my orderly and have him bring this man some hot food. And send for Colonel Bouquet. Tell him we need some of his Canary."

Some time later Johnson heaved a sigh of relief and belched in contentment. He looked at the two men sitting opposite him: the pallid general with the penetrating eyes and the debonair Swiss colonel.

"Now then, sir, we will get on with your information. Your name?"

"Algernon Johnson."

"Your age?"

"Thirty-two."

"Where did you live before you were taken prisoner?"

"About ten miles west of Carlisle. A place called Turkey Hollow."

The general put a hand to his stomach. "Damned nuisance this malady I've got." He poured a few drops of oil of peppermint into a mug and added water before drinking it. "What can you tell us of conditions at the French fort?"

"Well, sir, after the French captured Major James Grant and some of the other men that was with him, they thought they'd licked your army. So the Canadians that was with M'soor Ventri's troops went back to Canada. And the Ohio Injuns—the Shawnees and the Mingoes—went back to their villages. It appeared they wasn't too pleased with the French."

"How did you come to that conclusion?"

"I heard some of the French complainin' about the Injuns desertin' them."

"When they attacked this camp there was a sizeable part of Indians with them."

"They was the only Injuns that stayed. Before that there was hundreds. Now there ain't more 'n fifty or sixty."

"You could understand the French?" Bouquet asked.

"I don't speak it, but I been around them enough so's to understand some of it."

Bouquet made a statement in French. "Will you be so kind as to translate what I said, sir?"

"You said somethin' about wine bein' the way to unlock a man's speech."

Bouquet smiled. "For that you shall have a second cup of Canary."

"What effect did the French defeat at Loyalhannon have on their morale?" Forbes asked.

"They'd been certain of victory and when you drove 'em off and they lost so many of their men, they got discouraged. I heard some of their officers sayin' that supplies intended for Duquesne was destroyed or captured at Fort Frontenay."

"Fort Frontenac in the city of Quebec."

"That's it! Officer by the name of Bradstreet was responsible."

"Colonel Bradstreet."

"That's right. The commander at Duquesne was so worried about how to feed his men that he started dismissin' whole companies. I'll tell you, the rations we ate in the last ten days wouldn't keep a dog alive. That's when the French troops from Illinois and Louisiana left."

"So they are really in bad straits, are they?" Forbes paced the hard-packed dirt floor, one hand on his stomach.

"It would be easy to lick 'em now."

The general appeared to hold himself upright by willpower alone. "We owe you a great deal, Mr. Johnson. I shall send my orderly to see that you get warm clothing and a place to sleep. . . . You belong with the Pennsylvania Regiment?"

"I used to be in the militia over to Fort Carlisle."

"As soon as you have given us details of your capture, you can go on over to where the Pennsylvanians are bivouacked and report to Colonel Armstrong."

Fifteen hundred men under Washington were extending Forbes's road westward to Fort Duquesne in early November. Colonel Armstrong, second in command to Bouquet, was ordered on November 13 to advance with a thousand men.

General Forbes's health was so uncertain that he was unable to depart until the seventeenth. He left only a small garrison, the wagons, and the heavy equipment behind at Loyalhannon.

Silas Enyard felt no qualms about marching in Armstrong's advance column, for his blood brothers had made peace with the British. Only a few of the western Delawares were still loyal to the French. A smith at Loyalhannon had removed his nose ring and ear hoops and a coonskin cap hid his scalplock.

On the twenty-fourth, when Forbes's men met up with Armstrong's advance column, the entire army camped on Turtle Creek, twelve miles from Duquesne. The Pennsylvanians had been warned not to light fires. They sat on the hard ground, eating hardtack, sharing reminiscences.

When Felix joined his friends to hear about Silas's captivity, George got up.

"I ain't partial to spendin' my time in the company of liars and troublemakers," he said.

Silas looked at him in amazement. Felix started to rise. "Leave it be, Felix," Ben said.

As George moved out of range of their voices, Felix stared into space.

"What'd I do to him that he's so set against me? All's I ever done was speak the truth about the Injun that captured us."

"What did the Injun do to her?" Silas asked, trying to sound calm.

"Nothin'. When we got to their villages there were some braves lined up to make us run the gauntlet. They motioned for me to go first, so I made a dash for it. Got through with nary a scratch!"

Ben remembered Silas's feelings about George Eldridge's wife. Why, he still loves her! he thought.

Felix continued. "There was a big argument about makin' Mary Ann run the gauntlet; the leader didn't want her to. The others made her do it, but she held on to a long-handled iron frypan, swingin' it right and left! It was somethin' to see!"

Silas felt some of the fear drain from him. "What happened then?"

"The leader brought an old woman over and then she led her away. They took me to the Ohio country and I never seen Mary Ann again."

"So you don't know where she is?"

"Nope. I escaped the following spring."

"Why did your report turn George against ya?" he asked.

"I opined that the leader was sweet on her," Felix answered. "But that don't mean a thing." He spat into the fire. "Some men in Carlisle started rumors that she was livin' as this Injun's squaw. I never said that, and I never thought it!"

Silas was stunned. Surely George did not believe this.

During the day Silas found it easier to dismiss his anxiety for Mary Ann but at night he was tortured with memories of her: her mouth when she smiled, her eyes full of laughter, her high cheekbones, her hair catching the sun. He thought of her generosity, her humor, her devotion to those she loved. Somewhere overhead an owl hooted. In the distant sky a full moon rose, serene and pure. A feeling of calm, of peace swept over him. It was a majestic night: the light falling through the bare branches left a glow that transformed everything with magic. The wind sighed in the trees, and the hush that followed was so alive that Silas felt all nature breathing. Finally he slept.

When, on November 24, Forbes's entire army was twelve miles from their goal, the general consulted with Bouquet as to the best means of obtaining information about conditions within Duquesne. The Swiss thought of Silas Enyard.

Silas removed his coonskin cap out of respect for the general.

Forbes sized him up. "Colonel Bouquet tells me those Delawares captured with you can be trusted to bring us information of the French fort."

"Yes, sir. They left off fightin' on the French side months ago."

"Why was that?"

"It was a combination of things. They was tired of losin' so many of their braves. And they felt the French was takin' advantage of 'em."

"Can they be relied upon?"

"I believe they'd be glad to show us some sign of friendship."

Forbes noted his use of the word "us." His loyalties were not in question at any rate. "Very well, then. Go with them to Colonel Bouquet. You can serve as interpreter."

In his headquarters at Fort Duquesne the French commandant paced the floor, unable to shake off his depression. He had given the order for his men to evacuate Duquesne within twenty-four hours and to blow up the fort, a decision that cost him dearly. He felt old, tired, drained. He could not have foreseen the Indians' desertion or the capture of supplies by the English general Bradstreet, he told himself. The rout at Loyalhannon in October was another matter: he was accountable, for he had relied for his intelligence on some western Delawares who were anxious to return to Ohio. Their reports had proved entirely erroneous. He wondered what this would do to his career. Mon Dieu, he was sick of this wilderness, the big trees encroaching on all sides, the lack of stimulating conversation, good wine, proper food, the company of elegant women. . . .

When the Delawares sent to reconnoiter the French position returned, there was disbelief at their news. The French were leaving. They had seen long lines of them going north. As they left, a soldier had followed, pouring gunpowder on the trail. This was confirmed later, when other scouts returned with news that the fort was in flames.

The army's elation was unrestrained: men hugged each other, cheered, the Colonials demanding a ration of rum to celebrate. General Forbes viewed their behavior with some distaste; his professional soldiers were more disciplined. Bouquet urged him to issue half a noggin of rum to each, warning them he would tolerate no drunkenness.

Early the next morning the army advanced toward the French fort. As they approached they could smell burned powder and smoldering wood. Quickening their steps, they ran lightly along Forbes's road, and when they caught sight of the crumbling walls, the men gave a cheer that rang through the forest. It was a moment that they would remember as long as they lived.

The Provincials first saw the stakes, driven in the ground near the destroyed palisades, on which the heads of the Highlanders killed during Grant's defeat were impaled. When the Highlanders saw the mutilated bodies of their comrades and the heads on spikes, there was a buzz as of thousands of swarming bees. They ran toward the smoldering ruins, swords drawn, their faces distorted with rage, pushing the Provincials aside, swearing vengeance on the French "pigs" who had committed these barbarities. But the enemy had fled.

Detachments were sent to collect and bury the remains that were scattered over the area. They found some of those killed during Braddock's defeat more than three years before. Colonel Bouquet delivered a brief eulogy. "As we commit our comrades to the earth, let us remember that they fought and died for the right of men of many nationalities to live here: Dutch, English, Scots, Irish, French, Swedes, Germans, as well as the Indians.

There is room for all. The men we lay to rest had many reasons for coming. Some were English who crossed the sea so that British laws, values, and traditions might continue here. Others were Scots, called Highlanders, though many were from the Lowlands as well. Their bravery and boldness are legendary. There were Royal Americans of German ancestry, who are famed for their discipline and devotion to duty. There were men from many European countries who came to fight because they saw the beginnings of a new epoch of expansionism in America. There were the Provincials, who uprooted themselves and their families to conquer the forests and create a prosperous society here. Let those of us who survive these years of war live in such a way that, wherever fortune takes us, we may serve king and country with the same honor, and courage, and devotion."

Ben felt proud to be part of this. Their goal assumed greater importance now. If only he could educate himself so that he could represent the people of the frontier in the Provincial Assembly.

He saw that Silas, too, was moved by Bouquet's remarks.

Colonel John Armstrong raised the British flag over the smoking ruins of Fort Duquesne on November 25. The men cheered, threw their caps in the air, shouting their defiance of the French. A few were silent in memory of those who had died. Ben Enyard remembered his friend Jim McCullough with a profound sadness.

CHAPTER XXII

The Seekers

News of the advance of General Forbes's army was received with mixed feelings in the Mingo camp from which Susannah Graves had escaped. Most of the Mingoes no longer cared about a French victory. It had become clear to them that they were being used: French trappers had encroached on their hunting grounds and French traders gave inferior goods for their prime pelts.

To those who had adopted child captives the news of the British advance brought anxiety, for they would be expected to relinquish these children when peace came.

In the camp near Logstown Rachel Graves played happily as two Indian women discussed the situation. "We cannot give her up! She is like our own flesh and blood," one said. "We must hide her in the woods when they come."

Her sister looked thoughtful. "I do not know what is best to do. I care about her happiness."

"But Summer Skies *is* a happy child," the first woman said. They had given that name to the tall, fair-skinned child because her eyes were serene and lovely as the summer sky at dawn. She wondered how much the child remembered.

Leaving her sister, she went to Rachel. "Come, Summer Skies, let us go into the forest. I must talk with you." The little girl, who was not yet six years old, looked up at her expectantly.

"What is your first memory, child?"

Rachel was silent for so long that the woman spoke again.

"I'm thinking," Rachel answered. She did not want to speak of her memories. Some were too terrifying; others left her confused about who she was or where she belonged. Most of all she shied away from memories of her mother, who had gone away with a funny old paleface trapper. Sometimes she heard her aunts talk about it when they thought she was asleep. It was a shameful thing.

She remembered her mother whispering, "Be brave, dear, never show them you are afraid. Do as they say. . . ." She didn't seem bad.

After a long pause, she began. "I remember a big clearing on a riverbank. There were lots of trees and a high fence around a big house, and paleface men running around. My mother was scared of them. She held my hand. Then you and Aunt Twila took us away in a canoe."

"Is that as far back as you can remember?"

Rachel hesitated. "Sometimes I remember a man—a paleface—who used to put me on his knee and pretend I was riding a horse. He sang something. He was the very nicest man I ever saw. He loved me more than anybody, I think." She caught her lip between her small white teeth to stop it trembling. "But he went away."

"Who was this paleface man?"

"I don't know. Maybe my father."

"Are you happy here with us, child?" The woman studied her with eyes warm with love.

Rachel did not answer. She put her head on her aunt's shoulder. She knew Aunt Twila and Aunt Sosoka would never leave her, as her mother had done. "I don't want to be a paleface. I don't like them."

"You are a Mingo now. You belong to us. Since we are at peace, the English are sending men to take back our captives. They will want you to go with them."

"Do I have to?"

"No, you don't have to if you do as I tell you. You understand?"

Rachel nodded.

"Then listen carefully. When the paleface men come to take the captives back to their families, this is what you must do."

* *

It was spring when a representative of the English king came with an interpreter named George Croghan. They spoke with the chief about the peace that was being concluded and asked about captives. Six of the settlers' children hid in the woods, protected and fed by the women.

The man in uniform spoke slowly, conscious that he represented authority. Croghan translated. "A man in Philadelphia has offered a reward for the return of his niece's daughter, Rachel Graves. She would be six years old now. She and her mother were captured three years ago. The reward is fifty pounds sterling. It will buy many blankets, kettles, cloth, beads." He was careful to omit guns and powder now that peace was at hand.

"Why does the representative of the Great White Father think we know this paleface?" the Mingo chief asked.

"Because the child and her mother were taken to the forks of the Ohio by the Delawares. They were sold to some Mingo women, who took them to the Ohio country. They adopted the child."

"Where is the child's birth mother?"

"She escaped in the moon of maple sugar. She prays to the great Manitou to restore her child."

The chief's deeply recessed eyes betrayed nothing. "We do not know this child." He folded his arms across his chest.

The officer began to protest and Croghan tried to quiet him. "He asks you if—" he started to say but the chief turned and went into his hut.

After the unsuccessful attack on the camp at Loyalhannon, many of the Shawnees had left the French to return to their winter camp in the Ohio wilderness. Only the western Delawares were still at war when wampum belts telling of the destruction of Fort Duquesne reached Tawaugoa. He was now the sachem of his Shawnee band and called their tribal council to discuss this news. The men gathered around the council fire wondered what changes this would bring. They had tired of the war and its privations.

Tawaugoa wished Melakome were here, but she had gone to join her ancestors shortly after the attack on Loyalhannon. He missed her. There was only one thing in which her judgment had been lacking: she had urged his marriage to his brother's widow, as was the custom. It had proved disastrous. His wife had tried to usurp his authority and had borne him only one puny girl, an ugly child of whom he was ashamed.

Because he was a sachem, Tawaugoa could not get away from her by going to war, so they had lived together as strangers. When she began to spread lies about Mary Ann, Tawaugoa moved out of her wigwam. He lived alone, with an old woman to cook his food. He was careful to avoid Mary Ann, for he did not want to add to the difficulty of her position.

There had been a time when Tawaugoa feared she would marry Ahotah, who had been attracted to her from the first. Mary Ann had refused. Tawaugoa remembered what she said to the brave: "I cannot be your wife. I have a husband back in Pennsylvania. Before Manitou I was promised to him." Since Melakome's death she had shared a hut with two old women, and he saw her only by accident.

Now he spoke to the elders. "The French are leaving Fort Duquesne and returning to Canada or to their forts in Illinois and Louisiana. We can no longer rely on them. The English are here to stay. The time will come when we will need their friendship."

"The palefaces are all feathers from the same vulture," said an old man. "They cannot be trusted."

"It is only a matter of time before they push us from our hunting grounds," said another.

"Would you let them take from us the graves of our ancestors, our sacred lands? You speak as sniveling boys, not as proud Shawanees!" said a former warrior.

"The belts say the army of General Forbes is like the sands by the lake—too many to count. They have cannon and powder, and new guns. We have no cannon. Our guns do not speak with the same thunder as theirs, for we have little powder left," Tawaugoa reminded them.

They were silent, confused and uncertain about their future.

At length one spoke. "The English gave us better trade goods for our furs."

"They despise us. They treat us as inferiors—we who are Shawanees!" The old warrior's voice shook with indignation.

"You think the French are our friends? Because they sleep with our women, and slap us on the back and call us 'frères'?" the speaker asked scornfully.

One who had remained silent spoke. "It is good that we go to our old summer camp near Duquesne. We can keep our eyes on the British."

Tawaugoa decided to resume his lessons with Mary Ann. It would be important for him to speak English in order to protect the Shawnees' interests. As she sat opposite him on a bearskin rug, he studied her. It was the first time he had spoken to her since Melakome's death. He was startled to see how thin she was. Melakome's passing had left a void in her life.

"You are well, Maully?"

She nodded, refusing to meet his eyes.

"I have missed our lessons," he said. He was aware that she understood why he had avoided her.

"And now you wish to learn English again?" she asked in Shawnee.

"Belts of wampum came some days ago. They told of the French blowing up their fort at the forks of the Ohio."

"Duquesne?"

He nodded. "They have fled to their forts in the north and in Canada."

Her eyes began to glow. "And the English?"

"They marched there in a great army, so vast they could not be counted, and raised the English flag over the fort. Your people and mine are no longer enemies."

She looked radiant. The beauty that first attracted him was now more marked because it had been shadowed by her despondency. "Then I can go home to my child and my husband?"

It hurt him to see the eagerness in her face. "Do you want so much to return to them?"

She put her hands over her face and began to sob. He watched her, troubled that he had caused this terrible unhappiness. "I shall miss you. I thought that we were friends."

"We—we are! But they're my family."

"When the birds fly north, I will take you to the English at Pittsburgh."

She leaned forward to kiss his cheek. "Thank you, thank you!"

He was both moved and shocked by her action. It was not the Shawnee way to show emotion, especially for a woman to touch a sachem.

"If you will behave properly as Shawanee women do, I would like to go on with the lesson," he said stiffly.

"I meant no disrespect, Tawaugoa. I am so happy! That was all."

"Let us begin." He realized that soon she would be gone, that he would never see her again. Never to see her . . . The pain began. He knew it would be with him for the remainder of his days.

In the middle of February 1759 the troops at Pittsburgh, which was growing up around the ruins of Fort Duquesne, received their first mail in two months. Ben received a letter from Susannah, brought by the military dispatch rider.

December 28, 1759

My dearest—

We have a son, born December 15, whom I have named James in accordance with your wishes, and Benjamin to please myself. *James Benjamin Enyard.* It's a proud name.

Oh, Ben, he is such a fine baby! I'm so eager for you to see him. He is strong and healthy and a greedy little creature. Mama says his hair will turn darker in time, that yours was just this color.

You could not have given the McCulloughs a better gift than to call him after Jim. Mrs. McCullough had a hard time not crying when she first held him. Mr. McCullough says it is an honor to have an Enyard named for his son.

Your mother looked after me and knew just what to do. When I had Rachel the delivery took much longer.

I've rambled on without mentioning Silas. The news that he was safe brought your mother such joy! She spoke of nothing else for days.

Do you know when the captives will be brought back? If it were not for you I don't know how I could endure life without Rachel. I miss her dreadfully. It was folly to leave her with the Mingoes. I will never forgive myself for this. What must she think, Ben? *That I deserted her?* Your mother tries to comfort me, telling me Rachel will be restored to me in time. But *it's been three years!*

Later: Forgive me for burdening you with my grief. I realize that I would not have met you if I had stayed in the Mingo village. You have given me so much happiness that I have no right to grieve. If at times I feel torn apart, it is because Rachel is a part of me, even as Jimmy and you are.

Now for some news, Geoffrey Moncrief writes Lucinda is expecting a child in June and they are very pleased about it. She has been in excellent health.

More news: Captain McWhirter has come courting Fiona. They seem a strange pair, but to everyone's surprise, she has accepted him. They will be married in June and live in Philadelphia.

Mama can hardly wait until you and Silas return. She talks of us building a cabin near the site of their old one and having a covered passage between them. It sounds like a good idea but it will be up to you to decide. The place where John and I lived will always remind me of the massacre at Bigham's. I should like to sell it, and then we would have more than enough for a team of oxen. I want us to stay near your family, for I love your mother and the children.

Peter and Annibele have grown so that you will hardly know them. They are delighted with the baby. Peter is learning to read from a hornbook Geoffrey sent.

Tell Silas we are counting the days until the two of you are with us.

Your loving wife,
Susannah

The letter brought Ben such delight that he read it over and over, quoting parts of it to Silas, and George.

"Sounds like ya got yourself a fine wife," Silas said. "I hope ya do decide to build next to us. What're your plans, George?"

"Same as yours. McCulloughs are goin' to settle where they was, so Mrs. McCullough can look after Thomas for me."

"But Mary Ann'll be comin' back."

"Maybe she will and maybe she won't. Guess I'll manage if she don't."

Silas and Ben exchanged looks.

"You know that unless she's dead she'll return," Ben said.

George did not answer. He spat expertly beyond Silas's boots, then walked away.

Silas left Pittsburgh in late February, since he could ride in one of the supply wagons going to Carlisle. Ben, George, and Felix still had time to serve with the militia.

"You'll bring Susannah here when they bring back the captives, Silas? She'll want to come to get Rachel, and I don't want her to come alone. I mightn't be discharged then," Ben said.

"Course I will. I won't let no harm come to her." Silas climbed into the wagon and the driver switched the reins for the team to move off.

Ben watched as the Conestoga rumbled down the forest road between patches of sunlight and shadow. The snow lay deep in places and his breath hung in the frosty air. "I'd give a lot to see Ma's face when she sees Silas," he said.

"She sure set store by him. Hope she won't be disappointed," George said.

"Why would she be disappointed?"

"He lived with them stinkin' savages, even bedded one of 'em. It rubs off on a man."

Ben's first impulse was to grab George by the throat and make him take back those words. He forced himself to go on with his work. "You'd best mind your tongue, George. I ain't standin' for insinuations about Silas, and I'm right sick of hearin' your remarks about Mary Ann, too. We been friends a long time and I always thought a lot of you. But I ain't listenin' to more of that talk. Get hold of yourself! You ain't the only one suffered, you know."

George clenched his fists. His eyes narrowed and glittered with resentment.

"Come on," Ben said, "let's get on with our work. You got a lot to look forward to—a fine boy, and a good wife comin' home soon."

"Everythin's gone—burnt or stole by them rotten savages," George muttered. "Ain't nothin' left."

"We all have to start over. It won't be easy, but we'll help each other. It ain't as if you'd be startin' out alone."

George continued as if he had not heard him. "She was a girl when we married. Nobody'd touched her—not even me."

"I told you what Susannah said about her captivity with the Mingoes. They don't force women. Silas told you the same thing."

George gave him a crafty look. "Can't trust women. Never know what they'll get it in their heads to do."

Susannah was dusting the furniture when a stranger entered, removing his coonskin cap. She noticed that his hair had been plucked and was beginning to grow again: it stood up in short blond tufts all over his head.

"Is this where Mrs. Enyard lives?"

"Why, you must be Silas!"

He smiled, and there was no mistaking his resemblance to Peter. "That I am. And you're Susannah?"

Before she could answer, he had put his arms around her and was giving her a hug; then he held her at arm's length. "Ben told me ya was prettier than a mornin' in June. He didn't exaggerate."

"You can't imagine how eager we have been to see you, Silas. Your mother talks of nothing else. Welcome back."

At that moment a black kitten scampered into the room, followed by Annibcle.

"Are you Annibele?"

She looked from him to Susannah, her eyes round with curiosity.

"It's Silas, dear. Go to him while I find your mother. Where's Peter?"

"He's helpin' Mr. Pratt." Annibele made no attempt to get closer to this big man with the funny hair.

"You was just a baby when I was captured so you won't remember me at all," Silas said.

"Did they scalp you?" Annibele asked, her eyes on his hair.

Silas laughed. "No, they pulled it out so's I'd be bald except for one long piece."

Else came running and the next moment was caught in his arms. "Silas! The Lord be praised! It's like a dream to have ya back."

Susannah saw the tears on his face and felt the familiar ache for Rachel. "Annibele, please fetch Peter," she said, her voice unsteady.

When Peter saw his brother, he remembered that day when his mother had carried him and Annibele into the woods to escape the Indians who had killed Ari and his father. Silas lifted him, pretending to groan with the effort. "Peter Enyard, you've grown so's I'd hardly know you. Last time I seen ya, ya was no bigger than a tadpole and Annibele was just a baby."

Peter laughed and put his arms around his brother. Silas had always talked to him as if they were equals. "I'm glad you're back," he said.

"So am I," Annibele whispered as she gave Silas a shy kiss.

In the days that followed Else Enyard noticed subtle changes in Silas. He spoke of his long captivity reluctantly and did not want to talk about his Indian wife. He told them only that she had been given to him after his adoption, and that she had died of lung trouble when he returned from a bear hunt.

"Did ya love her, son?"

"I don't want to talk about it, Ma. She was real good to me. Let's just leave it at that."

Susannah understood his reluctance. She saw that he had loyalty and affection for his captors, yet he did not expect his mother to understand this.

"He's changed some," Else said.

"We all have changed. You can't expect him to be the same after what he's been through. Give him time, Mama. He just needs time."

The British were erecting palisades and temporary quarters on the ruins of Fort Duquesne, now named Pittsburgh. Colonel Hugh Mercer was in command of the greatly reduced garrison, for Colonel Bouquet had gone to Fort Ligonier (formerly the encampment at Loyalhannon) and General Forbes, whose health had worsened, was in Philadelphia.

Ben, George, and Felix were among the militia still at Pittsburgh. Now that the danger had passed, they were eager for discharge. Ben was impatient to see Susannah and his son, and to return to the farm and start to rebuild. With Silas back, it should not be too difficult. Felix itched to be with his family and to find a suitable girl to marry.

When word came that the Crown's deputy Indian agent, Sir William Johnson, was sending George Croghan with a deputation to the western Delawares, Shawnees, and Mingoes to arrange for the return of captives, the garrison celebrated. They built a great fire on the parade ground and kept it burning throughout the night, dancing about, Indian fashion. Colonel Mercer issued a noggin of rum to all who were not on guard duty.

Ben, who did not care for rum, sat with George that night, listening to the sounds of revelry. He wondered what would happen when Rachel was restored to Susannah. He felt a presentiment that this reunion might not be as joyous as Susannah hoped. Thank the Lord there was Jimmy to occupy her time and her heart.

In Carlisle word came that the captives were to be brought to Pittsburgh in June. Susannah was ecstatic, for she could see Ben when she went there to meet Rachel.

"Oh, Mama, I'm so excited I can't sleep. *It's been three years!* You don't think she won't recognize me, do you?"

"I reckon she's just as eager to see ya as ya are to see her, dear."

"I feel as if I'd been carrying a heavy burden and now it's lifted." Susannah began to weep.

"There, there, it'll do ya good to cry, child." Else stroked Susannah's curls.

"I don't know what I'd do without you," Susannah said. "I'll take Jimmy to Pittsburgh when I go to get Rachel. That way Ben can see him."

"Take the baby?" Else forgot that she had taken three children through the wilderness seven years before. "Ya don't know what's ahead, dear. It might be weeks before the Injuns bring in the captives."

"I will manage somehow."

"I could take care of him for ya. With Mr. Pratt's cows, there'd be no trouble feedin' him."

"But I don't want to wean him! And I want Ben to see him. Can you imagine how it must be for him, never having seen his son? We don't know when he'll be discharged—it might be a year."

Else spoke privately to Silas about it but he agreed with Susannah. "She's right, Ma. Ben would be real disappointed if she went to Pittsburgh without takin' the baby."

"Ya don't think it's dangerous? That the Injuns might take to the warpath again?"

"No, Ma. Worst thing that could happen would be to have the wagon break an axle. There'll be lots of folks travelin' to Pittsburgh to find their kin. And I'm goin' with her."

Else put her hand on his arm. "I don't think I could stand it if anythin' was to happen to ya or Ben or Jimmy and Susannah. Be careful, Silas."

"I promise ya, Ma." He kissed her cheek. "Ben got himself a real pretty little woman but nobody can hold a candle to you!"

"It's time ya was marryin' and sayin' such things to a girl of your own." She looked thoughtful for a moment. Then she spoke quietly. "I reckon I got to do a lot more prayin'. I'm right concerned about Susannah. She's settin' such store on findin' Rachel, but suppose she don't come back?"

"You're just borrowin' trouble, Ma. When we return you'll

most likely have a new granddaughter. The one I'm worried about is Mary Ann. George has changed so's you wouldn't believe he was the same man."

She gave him a long look. "Ya love her, Silas."

"Ya ain't shocked?"

"I lived too long to be shocked by things. Lovin' someone is the finest thing on this earth, but I don't want to see you hurt."

"I suppose it ain't right, accordin' to what the preachers say."

She surprised him by her answer. "They don't know what's in the Lord's mind. If love was evil, why did He give us lovin' hearts?"

Twelve wagons filled with settlers set out from Carlisle on a June morning in 1759.

It was a day to remember, with iridescent dew clinging like diamonds to every blade and leaf, and sunlight highlighting the sheen of birds' wings. Bees droned in the wildflowers, and butterflies swayed among clumps of mountain laurel, whose clusters of delicate pink-and-white blossoms contrasted sharply with the cool dark greens of the woods.

Susannah felt her spirits lift that the settlers and the Indians were at peace, and most of all that soon she would be with Ben and Rachel. She sat beside Silas on the high seat and looked at the healthy baby in her arms. The child had her eyes and fine features and a cap of curling red-gold hair. He was a handsome baby.

The settlers in the caravan stayed together so that if a wagon broke an axle, there would always be men to help. At night over a campfire the men swapped stories and soon everyone joined in singing folk songs and hymns. They were rough-mannered, quick to take offense, but equally quick to help a neighbor.

Silas was accepted by them from the beginning. It was only when they asked questions about his captivity that they saw his open manner change. He would mumble some excuse and go see to the horses. When the men discussed Indian atrocities, he took no part in the conversation. They let him be.

At first the women kept a distance from Susannah, feeling

awkward and ill-favored in contrast to her dainty beauty and her educated way of speaking. But as the story of her missing child was passed from one to the other, their sympathies were aroused. By the time they arrived at Pittsburgh they wished her well.

CHAPTER XXIII

The Captives

The arrival of the wagons at Pittsburgh was greeted with jubilation, for it meant news of home, and reunions with loved ones and friends.

Ben Enyard, waiting tensely for Susannah and Silas, could hardly contain his impatience. As soon as Silas brought the team to a halt, Ben caught Susannah in his arms, holding her as if he would never let her go. Finally, breathless and torn between laughter and tears, she pulled away and looked him over.

"Oh, Ben, I've missed you so!"

"You're a sight to gladden my eyes, Susannah! How's the baby?" He turned to Silas and hugged him. "Ain't no one else I'd trust to bring them but you. How's Ma? And the children?"

"They're fine, Ben. Here's the newest Enyard waitin' to see you." Silas lifted a cradle from the wagon and Ben gazed at his sleeping son. Susannah laid him in Ben's arms, her face glowing. Jimmy awoke, yawned mightily, and looked up at his father, then caught the finger Ben held out to him. "He's some boy," Ben said.

Felix Abbot pressed forward to see the child. "He's sure better-looking than his pa. Lucky for Jimmy all he's got of yours is that red hair—that and certain unmentionables."

Ben laughed. "This is our neighbor, Felix Abbot, Susannah."

"I'm mighty pleased to meet ya, ma'am."

Her smile was radiant. "Ben's told me of you, Felix. Won't you call me Susannah?"

"Seems friendlier for neighbors."

George Eldridge had come to meet them.

"This is George Eldridge, another good friend."

Susannah knew the story of George and Mary Ann. She smiled to hide her shock at his appearance.

George's words carried no warmth. "How do, Miz Enyard. I hear ya come to find your little girl."

"Why, yes."

"Well, I hope ya git her back. Some of the settlers' children never come back, and them that does will be so changed their folks will be sorry to see 'em."

Susannah paled.

Ben's eyes were hard. "It don't do to borrow trouble. We'll find her."

To ease the tension Silas turned to George. "Ma said to tell ya Mary Ann can stay with her at the inn till you're discharged."

"We're so eager to see her. We'll do all we can to help her," Susannah said.

George stared at the stockade wall as if he had forgotten their presence. "Could be she won't be comin' back," he said laconically.

"We have to hope," Susannah said.

"Hope?" George snorted in derision. "Hope's for folks that can't face the truth." He turned and walked away.

"Whatever is the matter with him? He didn't even ask about Thomas!" Susannah exclaimed.

The settlers in search of missing kin had come prepared to camp out, since no one was certain when the tribes would bring in their captives. They sat in the shade of the big trees, the women fanning themselves with their aprons and chatting, while the men swapped yarns and engaged in wrestling matches and footraces.

The Delawares were the first to arrive, with twenty-two captives. Some of the children had run off in the forest and delayed their arrival. Several had to be tied to prevent them from returning to the Indian villages. There was a strained silence. The Indians' faces were impassive, their manner proud. Their colorful feathers, silver bands, and body paint contrasted strangely with the drab grays and browns of the frontier folk. George Croghan stood in the middle of the parade ground, trying to maintain order. "Just a minute, folks! I know you're anxious to be with your kin, but we have to do this in an orderly way. As I call out a captive's name, step forward if you know that one. Then we can cross the name off the list."

Those who were not claimed would be taken to Lancaster and then assisted in returning to their kin. The children who had lost their parents were the saddest lot. They stood looking about, lost and afraid. Susannah, watching them, could not hold back the tears. She turned to Ben, burying her face in his shoulder.

Silas went to speak with the Delawares about Katoochquay and the others he had known. When the settlers saw his friendly manner toward the Indians, there were whispers of "Injun lover" and "turncoat."

Ben, grown testy with the heat and the ordeal, confronted the most vocal critic. "You better watch your words—that happens to be my brother you're slanderin'. He's no more disloyal than you are. He's lived as a captive for three years, but he ain't lettin' hate and vengeance rule him!"

The man shook his fist in Ben's face. "What do ya know about it? Them savages killed my wife and oldest boy and stole my three youngest!"

"They killed our father and sister," Ben said, some of his belligerence leaving him. "But we're never going to have peace unless we put aside the past."

Susannah tugged at his sleeve. "Please, Ben. Come away!"

The man continued to shout. Several others sided with him, and it wasn't until two soldiers came that the group finally quieted.

Shortly after that three children, all of them tied to keep them from running off into the forest, were led to the middle of the parade ground. They did not look up as the man who had called Silas a turncoat approached. He showed no sign of affection as he pushed them toward a wagon at the rear of the enclosure.

The oldest, a girl of about thirteen, cried out, "Ya ain't never goin' to do them things to me agin, Pa! I'll kill myself before I let ya!"

The man struck her sharply across the face, drawing blood.

The girl cried out and put a hand to her cheek, and the two younger ones cowered in fright as he led them away from the crowd.

"Oh, Ben, can't we do something?" Susannah cried.

"What can we do? They're his children. Nobody can tell him how to treat them."

"But that's terrible! You heard what the girl said."

He shook his head. "It's evil but there's nothin' we can do."

They had been waiting eleven days when a small party of Mingoes arrived. Susannah did not recognize any of them, nor their captives. Before Ben could stop her she ran across the parade ground to the officer with George Croghan. "Please, gentlemen, can you tell me where my daughter is? Rachel Graves. She was sold to two Mingo women three years ago."

"There's no one by that name in this list of captives, ma'am."

"That name sounds familiar," Croghan said. "Wasn't there a ransom offered for her, a sizeable sum if I recollect?"

"Yes, my uncle, Josiah Norris, offered a reward of fifty pounds for her return."

"I visited the Mingo villages and asked about her, but none of them knew anything," Croghan said. "It don't mean that she's dead, ma'am. Indians don't like to give up those they've adopted."

"The chief of the village was Susquepena," Susannah said. "He was a tall man with a small scar on his left cheek. He was very fond of Rachel—and he spoke a little English."

"I remember him," Croghan said, stroking his chin reflectively. "He said he didn't know of Rachel Graves. I'm sorry."

Susannah looked as though she was about to faint. Ben put his arm around her. "Come on, honey. Jimmy needs you. Silas ain't experienced with babies."

Susannah turned back to Croghan. "Will there be any more Mingoes bringing in captives?"

"No, that's all. Tomorrow or the next day we're expecting the Shawnees, according to our scouts."

"Oh, Ben, I wish your mother were here."

"I know what Ma would say: Prayer is the answer. There does seem to be a power in it."

Five days later, the Shawnees arrived. The delegation was led by a handsome young chief accompanied by twelve braves and six captives. One was Mary Ann Eldridge.

"There she is, George!" cried Felix Abbot, waving his hat to attract her attention.

When Silas saw her, he was oblivious of all else. He could not have expressed in words the overwhelming gratitude he felt that Mary Ann had returned.

Susannah looked at Mary Ann with more than ordinary interest, noting the eager expression on her lovely face, the shining hair, the glowing color of her skin. There was a grace and beauty about her that made the onlookers stare. "She's so beautiful!" Susannah murmured. "I've never seen a lovelier woman. . . ."

Mary Ann hesitated, searching the faces of the crowd, as Tawaugoa spoke to George Croghan, then beckoned to the first of the captives.

"What an impressive-looking man he is!" Susannah said, referring to Tawaugoa. "Where is George?"

"I'll go look for him." Silas moved off toward the edge of the crowd.

"Listen, honey, if Silas can't find George, I'm going to tell her Ma wants her to stay with you at the inn," Ben said.

Silas found George sitting with his back against the palisade, cleaning his long rifle. "Come on, man, she's here and waitin' for ya!"

George looked up, his face expressionless, then rose and walked unhurriedly toward the parade ground.

"She looks fine, George, just as she did before her capture."

As the crowd parted, Mary Ann caught sight of her husband. She stared in disbelief at the bearded man with the long matted hair and the disfigured mouth. "George?" It was barely a whisper. Silas, watching her, felt her anguish.

She took a step toward him, still not able to believe this was her beloved. "Is that you, George?"

His mouth twisted in a sneer. "Forget what I look like?"

The crowd grew quiet, watching as she moved toward him.

Tawaugoa called to her in English, "Good-bye, Maully! Good-bye!"

She turned to wave to him, as a blast of powder shattered the silence. George Eldridge lowered his smoking rifle.

Mary Ann turned and ran toward the body of Tawaugoa that was sprawled grotesquely near George Croghan, blood from a great hole in his chest spreading over the dusty grass. Before anyone could reach her she fainted.

For a few moments the peace was threatened as the crowd surged forward and the Shawnees gathered round their fallen leader. One woman cried, "Got what was comin' to him!" Colonel Mercer ordered the crowd to stand back and stationed soldiers with bayonets between the Indians and the settlers, shouting to make himself heard. "Seize the man that fired! Bring him here at once." There was a brief scuffle as several militiamen seized George and wrestled his rifle from him.

Susannah turned to Ben. "Oh, do something, Ben!"

Silas pushed through the crowd to speak to the officer, and then the soldiers made way for him and he knelt by Mary Ann. "It's all right, lass! Everythin' will be all right!" he whispered.

"You know this woman?" Croghan asked.

Silas looked up. "She and George was neighbors to us in the Cove."

"What's her name?"

He answered mechanically, his attention centered on Mary Ann.

"Will you be responsible for her, then? See that she has a way to return to her home?"

Silas nodded.

"Well, then take her away."

Silas carried her through the press of people to Ben and Susannah and laid her on the ground. "I told him we'd be responsible for her."

"Yes, of course," Susannah said. "Here, Ben, take the baby, and Silas, bring some water."

Colonel Mercer's voice boomed over the shocked murmurs of

the crowd: "George Eldridge, for killing a man in cold blood and endangering the peace, I order you to be hanged by the neck until dead."

"Oh, God!" Susannah closed her eyes.

There was a hush as of many indrawn breaths. Then they heard George's voice: "Whore of Babylon! Strumpet! Consortin' with savages, ruinin' my good name!" Mercifully, Mary Ann did not hear him.

Spittle formed around George's mouth as the soldiers looped the noose around his neck. He continued to scream and wrestle with the soldiers.

"He's gone mad," Ben said.

Mary Ann opened her eyes and looked from Ben to Silas and then at Susannah. "Silas, Ben, what are ya doin' here? What's happened?"

"You're goin' home with us to Carlisle to stay with Ma," Ben said.

"Carlisle?"

Before they could explain they heard the ominous rattle of drums. Instinctively they moved to shield her. There was the crack of a whip and then the sound of hoofbeats as the horse bearing the condemned man galloped off. The crowd sighed.

It was over.

Silas carried Mary Ann to the wagon, with Susannah and Ben following closely so that she could not see the limp body twisting on its rope from the gallows tree.

"Where is George?" Mary Ann asked. "What happened to him, Silas?"

Silas did not answer. He laid her inside the wagon and Susannah climbed in and took her hand.

Mary Ann sat up. "All I remember was he looked so—different. And then someone shot Tawaugoa." Her eyes grew dark as the suspicion took shape. *"Did George kill him?"*

He nodded, his eyes tender.

"Why would he do such a thing?"

"He'd gone mad, Mary Ann."

She lay back on the floor of the wagon, trying to fit it all together. There was a terrible emptiness inside her. "It don't seem real. Tawaugoa was my friend. But George . . ." She did not finish.

Just before sunset the wagon rumbled into Carlisle. As they drew up to the Forge Inn, Silas turned to the others. "I'm askin' ya to stay in the wagon until I go in and talk with Ma."

Inside the big fragrant kitchen Silas explained to his mother that Rachel had not been returned.

"It must be a terrible blow to Susannah," Else said, wiping her eyes. "What about Mary Ann, son?"

He did not look at her as he told her what had happened.

Else touched his cheek. "When she's found Thomas she'll begin to live again. . . . And it'll help Susannah to have Mary Ann here; she's got a givin' nature and it'll take her mind off Rachel."

A flicker of hope began to dawn in him.

"I'll ask Mr. Pratt to fetch Thomas before I welcome them home."

"Ya always know what to do to comfort a body," Silas said.

Silas laid Jimmy in Else's arms before lifting Susannah down. Else gazed at the sleeping child. "I missed you so. Jimmy looks fine. How is Ben?" She did not mention Rachel, and Susannah was glad of this. They had to think of Mary Ann first. Later she would pour out her grief to Ben's mother.

Then Silas lifted Mary Ann from the wagon. "Here's Ma."

"Welcome back, child! The Lord be praised that you've come home!"

"It's good to see ya, Mrs. Enyard," Mary Ann said, trying to smile.

"We want ya to feel that this is your home, that you're part of the family." Else embraced her, feeling a tremor go through Mary Ann. "Come in and I'll fix ya somethin' to eat."

They had gathered in the kitchen when Mr. Pratt entered, holding a bewildered Thomas by the hand. The little boy bore a striking resemblance to his father.

Mary Ann caught her breath. "Thomas? Is that you?" She

knelt and caught him to her, tears streaming down her face. "I'm your mother, Thomas. I'm home again, son."

"Did the Injuns let ya go?"

She held him off at arm's length and nodded, then put her arms around him, rocking him as if he were a baby.

Else saw the love and concern on Silas's face. "It'll take time, Silas, but she'll heal." She looked at Susannah, whose eyes were bright with tears. "We still have hope, Susannah; we must always have hope."